THE MAGE OF MOURNING

THE MAGE OF MOURNING

OTHERWORLDLY ANARCHIST

BOOK TWO

Dreamer's Riot

Podium

Podium

THE MAGE OF MOURNING

CHAPTER ONE

The Burning One

Sarafyna

I have never been happier than I am today. Yeah, I'm not rich or powerful, and I never will be, but none of that matters. Today, my family has bought my future. Not the future of a housewife or handmaid, but a proper life I can be proud of. This is what I have always wanted, the life I used to tell my mom about for hours on end. In front of me is a run-down storefront with a cracked display window and a door hanging askew on its hinges.

"I know it's not the nicest, Sara, but I can help you fix it up. In a few months it'll look good as new, I promise!" my dad stammers, a nervous look on his face. I beam at him. He actually bought us a store. He has always known I wanted to run a hat shop. I have been obsessed with hats since I was a little girl, ever since the first time I saw a noble lady on a summer day.

It's always been no more than a wish, but a wish I treasured deep in my heart which I then wore on my sleeve. When I was a child, my parents thought it was a passing obsession. After a few years, they accepted it wasn't going anywhere but didn't treat it as an actual option. I never wavered, however, and here I was reaping the benefits of that determination. "I love it, Dad. It couldn't be more perfect!" I practically squeal, pulling him into a hug.

I feel the tension leave his body as he returns my hug. The poor man has always done his best for me, and he has always been worried he wasn't doing well enough. My mother passed to the first plane when I was only nine, and he has been trying to raise me alone since then. It hasn't been easy on him being a single father and working full-time at the east gate's stables. Even so, he has never once neglected me and has always pulled enough money together to get me everything I need.

He has only been this tense a few times, however. The first time was when I had my first monthly. The silly man rushed me to the clinic in a panic as if he hadn't been married to a woman for years. The knowledge just fled from his addled mind the moment he found me sleeping in a bloody bed. It wasn't his fault he panicked, and I never blamed him, but he still gets adorably embarrassed if I tease him about it.

The second time was when he was first approached by a potential suitor for me. I am, to put it simply, remarkably beautiful. Not just among commoners but even when compared to many noblewomen. Collector knows I'm not trying to be prideful here; it's just the truth that I have grown prettier with every passing year. As a result of this, my father has been approached by either suitors or their parents for the past couple of years. It's only gotten worse as I've started to develop.

The first time this happened, my dad was at a complete loss. He didn't want to upset me, he didn't want to upset the boy who lived down the street, and he certainly wasn't ready to see me married. We are all the other has, however, and he knew he had to ask me about it. I've heard a lot of women get very little choice in their marriage, but my father would have none of that. He always asks my opinion on everything, and my future husband certainly wasn't going to be an exception.

So he approached me, nervous and toying with his own hat, to tell me about the interested boy. The amount of relief that washed over him when I said I wasn't interested makes me laugh to this day. Years later, after rejecting dozens of proposals, he is much less nervous. It has become clear that I'm not going to accept any of them. Romance has never interested me, and neither has marriage. I don't hate the concept, it's just . . . not interesting to think about.

I only have eyes for my hats. I have been consumed by learning how they are made and keeping up with the latest fashions in both common and noble circles. I even convinced a hatter's wife to show me a few things. I never really believed I'd have the chance to work in a hat shop, much less run one. I should have known something was up when my dad started picking up extra shifts and covering for other stable hands. He has been working himself to the bone for years, and this is why.

It makes me want to cry. He sacrificed so much to give me this, and he's nervous I will be disappointed? Never. Of course, I won't be the actual owner of the shop—that's illegal—but it will be mine nonetheless. Lots of women run shops owned by their husbands or fathers. I even know one whose brother owns her shop. I don't have to worry about that, however. Dad will support me and it will feel like mine.

"You really like it?" he asks, a hint of nervousness lingering in his voice.

I pull away and wipe a happy tear from my eye with the base of my hand. I brush my auburn hair behind my ear and answer, "More than anything, Dad. This must have taken years to save for. Thank you. Thank you so much."

He scratches the back of his head shyly. "I'm glad you like it, Sara. It wasn't much—" he starts, but I don't allow him to sell himself short.

"None of that now! Nothing much indeed; you've been working yourself into an early grave. If I'd known it was for me, I'd never have let you. This is everything, Dad. It means the world to me," I reprimand and praise in equal measure.

He gives me a sheepish grin, clearly pleased at how pleased I am. "It's good to see you so happy," he says. "I wish your mother could be here to see it." Every happy event has had that melancholy caveat for the past five years. I understand exactly how he feels. I miss her every day, and nothing is quite as joyful as it would have been if she could share it with us. At the same time, it breaks my heart even more to see the family I have left wearing grief like a chain, tethering him to his wife's grave. I want him to be happy again, instead of pouring all his energy into making up for my mom's absence.

"She probably would have smacked you across the back of your head for overworking yourself," I laugh, trying to lift the mood.

"You're probably right," he agrees with a melancholic smile.

More than anything, I hate feeling helpless to comfort him. The inability to relieve the pain of the people you love is like blocks of ice around your feet. Even worse, it seems like the occasions where he doesn't seem burdened perfectly coincide with the waves of grief that still incapacitate me without warning. It's like we have a steel ball we drag around with us, and if one of us stops, we feel so guilty the other immediately takes over.

Of course, feeling that way also makes me feel guilty, which makes me feel sick, which causes the sorrow to well up all over again. This cycle goes on and on, and he and I can only lean on each other. There is no solution to it. There is no bucking up and feeling better. We just have to let our regrets wax and wane like the moon while the gaping wound in our family slowly scars over.

Today, however, is a day for joy. I want my father to feel the joy he worked so hard to bring me, and I want to honor my mother at the same time. "We'll name it after her," I announce after a moment. He perks up a little and smiles gently at me.

"She'd like that," he agrees. "She'd like that a lot." I feel warmer as his smile grows more honest.

"It'll be like she is here with us. A part of the shop and still a part of the family. Evalina's Heart: Hat Emporium," I say, and Dad actually laughs. "What? What's wrong with that?"

"Nothing, Sara, nothing at all. It's wonderful," he chuckles. I can tell he doesn't really like it, but what matters is his smile is real. I can workshop the name.

I take another look at the building my father bought for us and my heart wells up again. "So, what's next?" I ask, wanting to draw out the happy moment.

"Well," Dad responds, "we'll need to fix it up. But first, I have to register the business. It's not official until we are registered."

"Okay, no problem, where do we do that?" I ask excitedly. I don't want to lose this momentum, and truth be told, I am insanely excited about this.

"Oh, uh, I think it may be better to go on my own . . ." he starts, but I am shaking my head three words in.

"Not a chance, Dad! We are doing this together! We are going to be partners, the whole way through, got it?" I challenge, and he gives me a wry smile.

"Even with the repairs?" he asks, and I pause. Well, it's not my area of expertise, but why not?

"You know what? Yeah, I'll help with the repairs! It'll go twice as fast! Or, well, a little faster at least, probably!" I respond proudly, and Dad laughs again.

"Well, the help will be welcome!" he assures me. "And what about the hats? You want my help with those?" I scrunch my nose. "Not a chance! You keep your hands off!" I demand, and he laughs harder. It's good when he is this happy, and my day grows even better.

"Well, if we are going together, I suppose we had better head out," he says, making a slight bow and gesturing to indicate I should go first.

"Quite right," I say, and begin walking back up the road. I don't actually know the way, but he'll step in before I go too far astray. It feels like we're taking the literal first step toward a new life. Away from the backbreaking labor that defined his life and into what feels like the first hopeful day since we lost my mom.

"Oh, one more thing," my father says as we pass the shops that will be our neighbors, and I look toward him inquisitively. "You are fourteen now. Before we get too distracted by everything that needs to be done for the shop, we need to stop by the temple of the Collector."

I understand what he is getting at, and he's right. Mom was always the most devout of us, and she would be furious if we got so caught up in this that we neglected our souls. "Right," I agree, "I nearly forgot about the rite of confession."

CHAPTER TWO

The Old and the New

There will be two others traveling with you. Take care of each other on the road, and maybe you'll have a couple of friends when you get there," Emeric says, continuing his lecture as we walk to the west gate. There we'll meet a carriage Godfrey has hired to take me to Visenar, the capital city of the Kingdom of Potestia and the home of Facinley University.

After everything that happened with Baldwin and . . . everything I knew would happen, Godfrey took the rest of my family to Visenar ahead of me. It was the safest option to avoid any possible reprisal. Reprisal targeting either Baldwin's killer or his fiancée. For my part, I have been living quietly with Emeric acting as my guardian. Well, a certain definition of "quietly." The half year since has been, to say the least, difficult. Since Godfrey, thankfully, had more important things to return to, the nobles of Satusmor spent months without anyone to rally them. This was a boon for several reasons but challenging for others. On the one hand, I was able to spread magic far beyond my initial Mages of Penance. Around the area, farmers, sex workers, and other groups—even bakers and cobblers—have begun to learn magic.

This went unnoticed by the nobility far longer than it would have if a new city lord had been assigned sooner, but it couldn't last forever. A couple of months after Godfrey left, a new lord arrived to take stewardship of Satusmor. As new commanders often do, Lord William wanted to establish his authority as soon as he got here. He organized the guards and nobility with frightening efficiency and immediately found signs of what I had been up to.

Food had become more readily available, of a higher quality, and cheaper. All while the city was in crisis. Street kids could be found stealing less frequently, and fewer people were going to confession. On the other hand, some more public-facing people had failed to suppress their mana around actual nobles, and with a little organization, reports of this had popped up all over the city.

A very few citizens, usually docile but victims of divine magic, had managed to break free from their brainwashing with endoaspected mana, and a couple of residents of penance houses had managed to return to their families. Then there were the incidents of violence and the guards. Learning useful spells takes a fair amount of education and practice, and at first, none of my mages could cast anything. More educated commoners, however, were able to figure out simple spells and aspects rather quickly.

Like how farmers were able to improve their craft with magic in a short amount of time, or butchers could keep their product fresh for longer. No one could do anything too dangerous yet, but several commoner mages could create short bursts of fire or mold the earth a little if they focused all their training on one spell. Of these, a few had gotten into violent altercations. Most of them with guards, finally fighting back, but a few with each other. Some even targeted commoners who had no magic or who had magic but no spells. These I or other groups had to deal with.

One predictable problem with spreading magic en masse is that I can't keep it contained forever. Some guards, after altercations with a commoner mage, tracked down the source of their magic and tried to learn it themselves. These and a thousand other things revealed a drastically changed city once William took over as City Lord of Satusmor. Had he gotten here a little faster, he might have been able to stop it entirely, but it was too late.

Enough people the city needed in order to run had already become mages and learned to handle mana. Like with the Mages of Penance, learning to suppress mana and hide from the authorities was the priority for most commoners. This made it difficult for authorities to identify them, much less the source of their knowledge. And magic continued to spread. Had William thought ahead, he might have allowed the guards their magic, but if the nobility wanted magic guardsmen, they would already have them. Any guard discovered with magic was treated the same way as anyone else.

As of now, Satusmor is showing the early signs of something akin to a modern-day drug war. Well, except the "drug" in question is the basic education and ability necessary to improve lives and exist free of brainwashing. The nobility is actually more concerned with the falling value and increasing availability of food and other goods than the mages who attempted violence. A mage with a half-baked combat spell is a far smaller threat to their power than the loss of control over the economy and food distribution. As with soap, goods like food, medicine, and tools that should always be widely available have been controlled for decades. Even knowledge of how to create some simple things had been jealously guarded. Now, they are increasingly available. Merchants are losing profits and noble houses are losing incentives. As a result, arrests are on the rise and violent altercations between factions are rising.

Guards, street kids, gangs, the temple, and the nobility are all growing hostile to each other at different levels. I have had to deal with newly empowered guards, angry nobles, indignant priests, and even misguided slaves and beggars directing their pent-up rage at innocent targets. It has been . . . ugly. Not uglier than it was before, but certainly less clean and a lot scarier for people who had grown used to being comfortable.

That is just the tip of the iceberg, however. All of that was more or less expected; taking down a monarchy isn't going to be pretty. Things had gotten . . . a lot more personal, however. After what had happened with . . . well, I have a hard time talking about them. What matters now is it has grown beyond me. I am no longer at the center of the changes in this city and it's time for me to move on. If I want to change things in this entire kingdom, and more importantly spread knowledge, I need to be in a better position.

There is an item I need to know how to enchant. I can only do so much more here, but I can help this and other cities more once I know more about enchantment. That and I see reminders everywhere I go of . . . yeah. I had promised Godfrey I would attend the academy, and that is where I am headed now.

"Lillith, are you still with me?" Emeric asks, and I snap out of my introspection.

"Yes, sorry, I was a little lost in thought," I say, and he laughs.

"A little nervous, huh?" he asks, amused. It's rare I show anything like the child-ishness he expects from me, and he always chuckles when he perceives it. "You'll be fine, nothing to worry about. If anyone should be worried, it's the academy," he teases, and I crack a smile. I can't exactly refute him.

"Nah, just reflecting," I answer, and he gives me a placating nod as if he will agree to pretend that's true. I just laugh at the light teasing as we approach the gate.

"Ah, here we are," Emeric announces jovially. A sturdy, covered wagon waits with a single coachman. "Looks like your traveling companions haven't arrived yet, but we are early. They should be here soon!"

I appraise the wagon approvingly. It's not ornate or fancy in any way but prac-tical and roomy. Plenty of supplies have been loaded up and it looks like there is plenty of room left for people. "Where are the guards?" I ask a little apprehensively, but Emeric just looks at me, confused.

"Why would the guards be here?" he inquires, and I realize I've made a silly assumption. Three noble kids traveling with a coachman in medieval Europe would definitely have an escort, but this isn't Europe. The ratio of nobility to commoners is completely different, social structures don't look the same, and, oh yeah, all the nobles have powerful magic. Mages don't really need guards; they typically only fear each other. The social conventions and politics that keep them from directly attack-ing each other are far more effective than a few dudes with spears. Moving around with guards is, funnily enough, seen as a sign of weakness.

The number of nobles pretty much excludes the possibility of every low-ranking child having an escort as well, and my nobility rank is definitely low. I knew all this—Hugh never had an escort when he came to hit on me and it was clear enough why. Despite all that, traveling on the open road, the knowledge of monsters, and memories from my past life all had me expecting an escort on this trip.

This is a completely different world and society from Earth, but my precon-ceived notions still color my view. There are probably a million different ways a society like this will differ drastically from medieval Earth for a million different reasons, and I didn't even try to think about them. I am always a little internally embarrassed at my lack of imagination when I make these assumptions.

"N-nothing, never mind," I answer, blushing a little. I should really try a little critical thinking before I ask dumb questions like that. From the first day I woke up in this world, my expectations have been challenged. Something as easy to make as soap was presented to me as a luxury. Twenty-seven years of common sense aren't so easily dismissed though. Oh well, Emeric will probably shrug it off. I'll have to keep track of this sort of thinking when interacting with nobles at the academy, however, or I will embarrass myself again.

Speaking of the devil, a pair of nobles about my age approach Emeric and me. Both are blond and look remarkably similar, the boy in a sensible blue tunic and the girl in a short, red traveler's dress. It annoyed me to no end when I learned women don't even wear pants while traveling, but gender norms like that have never been sensible in any setting, so I shrugged it off.

"Hello, a pleasure to meet you!" the boy says with a wide smile on his face. "Are you coming to the school with us?"

"Don't be rude, Augie," the girl says. "You haven't even introduced yourself yet! Don't mind my brother, he's just a little overexcited."

"I'm not worried about it," I answer. "I've never been one for etiquette anyway. Always made Sybillia furious."

"Oh, Sybillia was your tutor as well?" the girl asks, while the boy responds, "I like you already—all that nonsense is a waste of time!" They speak at the same time and I hesitate before answering either.

First, I listen to the girl in red. "She was, although our lessons were cut short fairly abruptly." I then give the boy a conspiratorial nod to indicate I agree with him as his sister smacks the back of his head.

"Ah, the Forrester twins have arrived at last," Emeric says cheerfully. I suppose these are my traveling companions. "Lillith, allow me to introduce August Forrester and Autumn Forrester. August and Autumn, allow me to introduce Lillith of Endings!"

Autumn and August look at me with wide eyes and Autumn bursts out, "Lillith of Endings, as in *the* Lillith of Endings?" she asks. I sigh a little. Thanks to Godfrey wanting to share the credit with me, I haven't stopped turning heads since Baldwin's death.

"No, I'm the other one," I answer flippantly, and she laughs.

"You have got to tell us everything!" August insists, and I resign myself to retelling the story Godfrey and I made up about the night I killed Baldwin. At least neither of these nobles seems too bad yet, although as always, I can't help but feel my hackles rise around them.

"Allow me to say my goodbyes to Emeric, and I'll tell you on the wagon," I agree, and the twins nod excitedly. This trip is supposed to take three months, so I suppose it's best to start off on good terms. I bid farewell to Emeric, who has grown on me over the months, and climb into the back of the wagon. As the coachman begins the drive, I regale the twins with an entirely fictional story of my fight with Baldwin.

CHAPTER THREE

The Calm Before the Storm

Oh, quit your complaining and set up the other tent!" Autumn reprimands her sulking brother as I work on setting up a tent myself.

"Come on, it's not like we haven't shared a tent before; I won't have anything to talk about with the coachman!" August protests.

"So you want a lady to share a tent with a strange man? How does that make sense? Collector, you are such an idiot!" Autumn replies.

"Oh, Lillith will be fine, won't you, Lillith? Besides, if he does anything stupid, she'll probably push him all the way to the capital with that weird mana of hers!" he retorts.

"And then one of us will have to drive the carriage. Do you know the way to the capital?" she quips, voice dripping with sarcasm.

I drive a tent peg into the ground with a fist and sigh. This argument has been going on for the last hour of the trip. There's only room for two tents in the wagon with all the supplies for the trip, and it's pretty much sitting room only.

August and Autumn are used to sharing a tent while traveling, and the twins have different ideas about this trip. As we approached the end of the day's journey, August mentioned playing a card game with his sister and the argument started. I couldn't tell if the two just had that twin energy, if August really just didn't want to share a tent with the coachman, or if Autumn was excited about sharing a tent with another woman.

Whichever it is, I'm not enthusiastic about sharing a tent with anyone. Not because I feel I'm in danger; the twins don't suppress their mana and I far outclass them put together. August was right as well: I don't have much to fear from the coachman. The problem is . . . I don't sleep much. With the growth of my mana over the last year, I am down to about three hours of sleep a night. Sharing a tent likely means either sitting in the quiet for hours or answering some awkward questions about my sleeping habits.

"No, but that's not the point!" August protests. "The point is it's perfectly safe!"

"Not for you," Autumn groans. "Besides, it'll be nice to not have to trade places just to change clothes." That comment actually startles me a bit. I'm not shy, but . . . I do have a dangerous magic circle tattooed onto my body. This whole idea is growing less and less attractive as the argument goes on in the background.

I finish setting up the tent while the debate rages on. After a while, I realize

August has no intention of winning. A noble kid like him wouldn't dream of asking me to share a tent with a man I hadn't met; it would be a scandal. It becomes more and more clear he is riling his sister up, and I chuckle to myself. It reminds me a bit of my own brother—Annie's brother—before he died. A warm but melancholy cloud passes through me and I shake it off.

I decide to introduce myself to the coachman. Might as well get to know my last traveling companion. "Hi," I say as I approach the man while he feeds the horses. "I'm Lillith, a pleasure to meet you." The man jumps at the interruption and the nearest horse snorts in offense. "Oops, sorry, didn't mean to startle you," I apologize.

"It's no matter, my lady," he says meekly, looking down. Oh, gross, being treated like this doesn't feel amazing. I stand awkwardly to see if he will say more, but he doesn't speak again.

"Uh, you can just call me Lillith if you like," I say, breaking the silence. "I prefer it, really."

He tenses up at that.

"I . . . I can't do that, my lady," he answers, turning around but not meeting my eyes.

"Wh—" I start before it hits me. Fucking customs and courtesies. I can give him permission not to use my title as much as I want, but I'm not the only person who will punish him for being too casual. I don't think the twins would either, but promises of kindness from people with power over you can never really be trusted. "Okay, I understand. Do you mind telling me your name?" I ask instead.

"W-Wallace, my lady," the frightened man responds. "Um, m-may I go now?" I really don't like commoners being afraid of my title. I'm going to need to figure out a way to handle that when I get to the capital. I examine him for a moment, trying to evaluate his emotional state, but I give up. He's too afraid of me.

"Sure, Wallace, go ahead. I'm sorry for bothering you," I say, and he hurriedly returns to his work.

I sigh. He is suspect number one. When we first left Satusmor, my mana started to gradually grow weaker, a little at a time. Once we were far enough away, however, it had started growing in power again. Just a little at a time. I didn't understand at first, but then I realized one of my companions must be grieving something.

Perhaps the twins missed their parents or the coachman was leaving a family behind. This was a long trip, and he might not have had the option of turning the trip down. Idiot that I am, I hadn't even thought about needing someone to actually take me to the capital. I want to help whoever it is, but I don't want to push and pry too much. I have time, however. There is a long road ahead.

I see August setting up a tent and Autumn is huffing as she storms in my direction. "I am sorry about that moron," she apologizes. "He is just . . . impossible!"

I actually laugh at that.

"You know he was just messing with you, right?" I ask, and she glares, not in anger at me but with residual frustration.

"Yes!" she answers. "That's what's so frustrating about it! He knows I can't help but argue with him about it! It's like an itch in the middle of my back, that's why he does it!"

I put my hand over my mouth to cover my laugh this time. I have to admit the pair is growing on me. This makes me want to avoid learning more about them, as it would suck to learn they are actually horrible. As a pair of nobles, it's not unlikely, and I have actually started to enjoy their company.

I probably should anyway, and perhaps I will be pleasantly surprised. "That's brothers for you. I get it," I sympathize.

She blows a loose curl out of her flushed face. "Oh, you were cursed by the Collector too, were you?" she asks insincerely. I smile as I use earth mana to build a firepit and a couple of makeshift benches. "Wow, you already have quite the handle on earth mana! And what did you call it, force mana too? Are you sure you even need the academy?"

I put my hand to the side of my head and crack my neck while I answer her. "I just practice a lot, that's all." Really I just have a much more thorough understanding of what *earth* is than anyone else and was able to aspect it much more quickly, but that answer is just going to inspire more questions. "And yes, I have brothers too."

"*Brothers* as in multiple?" she asks. "My condolences." She pats me on the shoulder and I chuckle. She jokes, but it's obvious she wouldn't know what to do with herself without August. It makes me miss Henry, seeing the two of them together, and I feel the urge to distract myself. I laugh it off and retrieve firewood from the wagon. "Let me get that," she offers as I place the wood in the firepit.

I stand back and see her collecting fire mana to light the wood. I quickly toss in the kindling I prepared to ease the process for her. Her spell is . . . incredibly inefficient. She pours buckets of pure fire mana into the spell until a burst of flame envelops the pit and all the kindling lights at once. It's a good thing I added it because the logs themselves would not have lit. A piece of flint would probably have been easier, but I suppose she wanted to show off her magic.

"Impressive," I applaud, wondering if I could light it faster just using heat mana. She presents herself proudly and puts her fists on her hips.

"That's right, you aren't the only one who prepared for the academy ahead of time!" she boasts.

"Well, of course," I answer. "I would expect no less." It's a little strange how quickly I clicked with this pair of noble siblings. It kind of hurts, actually. I don't know to what extent they participated in the atrocities of the nobility, but they have obviously lived a comfortable life. They were born into it, but it doesn't necessarily mean they are anything more than oblivious kids. Either way, they will probably hate me someday, when I help take it all away.

Who knows, maybe they will recognize the necessity for it . . . Well, probably not. It's hard to just . . . give up wealth and power. They are young, however. They have a lifetime to learn why I have to do this.

"Good job!" August says as he approaches the fire, his tent constructed not far from mine. He then examines the stone benches and neat firepit. "Lillith, did you set this up?"

"What do you mean? This was here when we stopped, did you seriously not notice?" I answer, and Autumn gives me a confused look.

"Seriously?" he asks. "No way, I was just over here like five minutes ago—this wasn't here!"

"Sure it was," I answer, straight-faced. "Did you really miss it? I could have sworn you sat down right there." Autumn seems to pick up that I am helping her get revenge and smiles. It's a pretty childish joke, truth be told, but they are children after all.

"No, she's right, Augie. You were brushing off your boots, remember?" Autumn chimes in.

"Wait, really? I don't think—" he starts, and I cut him off.

"Stop teasing her, I know you aren't that oblivious!" I insist, and he looks between us, confused. After a moment of indecision, he breaks out into a grin.

"All right, you got me, Lillith. Sorry, Autumn, I just couldn't help myself," he says, and Autumn and I start laughing.

"Of course Lillith made it, you idiot," Autumn teases. "We were literally standing ten paces away when we were arguing."

He blushes and gives me the side-eye. "You traitor," he accuses, and I chuckle.

"You kind of deserved it," I reply. It's that moment, as we settle around the fire, that I realize why I have been getting along with them so easily. They have been respectful to me from the moment we met, sure, and August hasn't said a single sexist thing to me, despite the society he grew up in. I figure that might have something to do with his twin. They are also extremely friendly and have an amiable charm about them. That's not really why, however.

I have, for what feels like forever, been putting out fires. From the moment Hugh grabbed my wrist, I haven't had a chance to rest. I have been on the move, fighting, learning, and stressing. Channeling the grief of a city into the weapon it needed. Today, I sat in a wagon and started a fucking road trip. I sat in a wagon and told stories, joked, and laughed. I am finally, finally, taking a fucking break.

I should remind myself to be wary. I need to remember not to trust so quickly. It's no use though. I'd probably shoot the shit with Cthulhu at this point, if he sat down and told me a funny anecdote about his twin sister as a kid. I am so, so tired of moving. Of fighting. Of raising my hackles whenever a noble says my name. Maybe, just for a little, I can enjoy myself.

"Is it true we have to pass near the Radiant Woods to get to the capital?" August asks Wallace, and I tune back in.

Wallace, who is standing nearby but not sitting with us, startles again and responds, "Y-yes, my lord," he answers, and an ominous feeling pushes down on my shoulders.

"Really? Do you think we'll see any monsters?" Autumn asks, more interested than scared.

"Oh, definitely," August answers. "Dozens of them. We'll probably be swarmed!"

"N-no, my lady," Wallace answers nervously. "The monsters never leave the woods, and we won't be entering, just passing by."

Autumn crinkles her nose and sticks her tongue out at her brother. I don't know why, but I feel a sense of dread at the conversation. Perfect.

After a while, we retire to our tents. Wallace tries to sleep cooped up in the wagon, but August won't hear of it, insisting he joins him in the tent. Autumn and I enter our own tent, and I awkwardly try to change into my nightgown without facing her. I cast a bad illusion on my tattoo just in case. It won't stand up to inspection, but it looks the right color at least.

Fortunately, she is too preoccupied to look so closely. "So, tell me, what do you think of August?" she asks, and I groan inwardly at the tone in her voice.

"I think he could make a great friend," I answer cautiously.

"Message received! Sorry, I had to ask," she responds with a laugh. I relax as she easily and respectfully drops the topic. "I suppose you aren't looking for romance after your last . . . arrangement."

"Yeah, not really," I answer, appreciating her understanding. "I barely twisted my way out of that engagement; I'd rather be married to my work for a while."

"No joke. Some of the rumors I've heard about Lord Baldwin . . . Well, I'm glad I wasn't in your shoes!" she responds. "If you ever want to talk about . . . anything, I'm happy to. You can trust me, I promise."

I smile. "Thanks, Autumn. I'll keep it in mind," I answer. We speak for a while longer and I actually feel comfortable in my bedroll for once. "Actually," I say after a while, "I wanted to ask, is there anything wrong? For you or August?"

"Not at all," she responds. "Why do you ask?"

"I just . . . have a bad feeling," I answer. My mana is still responding to some source of grief, and it's not normal. It's like . . . oil flowing through my body. It's tainted somehow, and it makes my stomach churn. "A really bad feeling."

CHAPTER FOUR

This Way Madness Lies

Still feeling sick, huh?" August asks me, concerned. I answer by puking out the back of the wagon as we travel. We have been on the road for about four weeks now, and the feeling of oily grief in my mana has only intensified. I no longer believe it is being caused by one of my traveling companions. It has grown far too intense, and it specifically grows as we travel. My power remains steady overnight and intensifies as the wagon moves.

I already feel far more powerful than I was when I killed Baldwin, and I had a group of people supporting me then. I have had to use less magic recently. Whoever we are approaching has a strong enough effect on my mana to make it entirely invisible. I'm still unsure why my grief mana does this, but I know it's not common and would like to avoid questions about it. Controlling an endoaspect at my age is uncommon enough on its own, but such an identifiable side-effect will make me easy to track down if too many people are aware of it. Is it the capital? Could the conditions there be so bad I can feel this much power from months away? It has a larger population, but surely it can't be miserable enough for that? Whoever we are headed toward, they are in a state of intense and constant sorrow.

And it feels wrong. So, so wrong. Like poison. Allowing it to affect my mana feels like wading through sewage. No, it feels like sewage is permeating my skin and slowly crawling through me like a slug. I have been growing increasingly sick as my abilities increase. Today, however, felt like all the changes of the past week combined, and I have been emptying my stomach for several minutes.

"I think she's getting worse," Autumn says, concern in her voice. She leans forward and puts her hand on my back but quickly topples onto me as the wagon jolts and falls to the ground on one side. I crumple over the back of the wagon with Autumn piled onto my back. I groan, and she quickly recovers, pulling herself to the seat next to August.

"What in the third plane?" August says as I clumsily climb out of the wagon. The horses are loudly complaining, and Wallace is examining the problem: a wheel has fallen off in the back. I take a look at it with him for a moment while the twins climb out after me. "Ah, man, why does it seem like this happens every time we go anywhere?" August asks when he sees the problem.

"Well, it fell off on your side; maybe you should go on a diet," Autumn quips.

"You're right," he agrees. "My muscles have grown far too dense."

I roll my eyes at both of them and walk over to the wagon.

"Help me lift this," I instruct the twins while crouching to get a grip on it.

"Right, sorry," August agrees, and takes his position on the other side of the corner. "Maybe Wallace should help me lift this?"

"Wallace has the best chance of fixing the wheel," I answer. "Besides, we are mages. I guarantee this will be easier. You ready, Wallace? Autumn, can you help him?"

"Sure, no problem," Autumn agrees while Wallace stammers, "N-no p-problem, my lady!"

Both get closer, Wallace picking up the wheel.

"On three," I say. "One, two, three!" I grunt and pick up the wagon, holding it level. Wallace and Autumn do not move to fix the wheel. They just . . . stare at me. "What? What are you waiting for? August, are you do—" I start to ask, until I look at August. He is not holding the other side. I lifted it too quickly, right out of his hands, and am now holding it up alone. Shit.

"How . . . " August and Autumn say in unison. "Lillith, how are you doing that?" Autumn asks, wide-eyed. Come to think of it, there is no way we should have been able to lift it without magic anyway. What was I thinking? I should have at least cast a spell at the same time. I'm not thinking clearly with my twisted stomach and headache.

"I'm using force mana?" I say in an unconvincing attempt to explain myself. All three of them look skeptical, including Wallace. I find that interesting since he should have no reason to doubt me . . . unless he is a mage. I am no longer familiar with every commoner mage from Satusmor; it is perfectly possible.

"And we just . . . can't see your mana?" August asks, clearly not believing me.

"Lillith, we have seen the color of your force mana before. You aren't using any mana at all!" Autumn chimes in, equally skeptical.

I sigh; I'm not sure how to explain why I am as strong as I am. I don't want to reveal my circle yet, and I'm pretty sure the changes it made to my body are technically blasphemy. That's when it occurs to me: I do actually have invisible mana, and I can explain it to them. It isn't always, but right now, my magic is in fact invisible. I don't want to reveal more than I have to, but at least endoaspected mana is a known and accepted phenomenon in the world, unlike my physical strength. "Oh, my mana is sort of . . . invisible . . . sometimes," I say.

The twins raise their right eyebrows in unison.

"And how is that?" Autumn asks while August and Wallace get started on repairing the wheel.

"It's a quirk of my endoaspected mana," I explain. "It changes the opacity of my mana, even to me."

The twins both widen their eyes at this.

"You already have an internal aspect?" they clamor together. I suspected they would respond that way; very few people are able to aspect internal mana, and most who do certainly aren't fourteen. It's hard enough that I can't help but wonder how bards manage to use multiple aspects.

"I do," I confirm. Oh well, there are worse secrets they could have learned.

"What aspect?" August asks, his words tripping over Autumn's: "So why are you still holding the wagon with your hands?"

Autumn then gently backhands August's arms. "Augie, that is such a rude question!"

They start bickering again while Wallace, now working alone, fixes the wheel. I suppose Autumn makes a good point; I can't claim I am using mana while I am clearly holding the wagon up with my hands. I cast a force spell to hold up the wagon, which jerks a bit as I adjust the force. "Sorry!" I apologize as the wheel nearly jerks out of Wallace's hands.

My hands now free, I brush them off, and Wallace finishes his work. I roll my eyes at the twins again. The pair don't mind chipping in, but they get distracted by each other extremely easily and often leave the bulk of the work to Wallace and me. It's not arrogance or laziness that leads to this, however, so I don't hold it against them too much. I can usually cover for what they forget easily enough.

My musings are cut short as I finally turn and look past the wagon. When I got out, I had been facing the other direction, and when I puked, I had only looked down, afraid watching the countryside would make me sicker. I get my first look at the Radiant Woods. We are far closer than I realized, close enough I could walk into it right now. They have been hidden by the mountainous terrain we've been navigating, but at some point today we must have rounded the mountain. I feel . . . confused.

These woods . . . aren't woods. They span for miles just in the direction I can see. This isn't even a forest; it's closer to a jungle. That's not the really weird part, however. This . . . whatever it is . . . is an insult to science. It's all wrong in every way. It makes no sense. There are the expected evergreens and standard deciduous trees, but interspersed between them are palm trees and heavy jungle foliage that should never be able to survive in this dry climate and have no business growing next to each other.

I gape at this impossible forest. Every different type of tree and foliage sways in perfect unison, picking up and slowing down in speed at the same time. I lick my thumb and hold it up. Nothing. There isn't so much as a calm breeze in the air. So why are they swaying? My biologist's heart, feeling great offense, demands I investigate further. Who needs some academy? What was I worried about, a monarchy or something? At this moment, all I care about is the impossibility that is the Radiant Woods.

I am reminded of my other worries, however, as I take a single step closer to the woods. I can feel my grief mana react. It wasn't the capital. This is what I have been reacting to. I am reminded of something Diana, one of my first friends from the House of Penance, said once: "Why the woods? Because that's where all the monsters are!" Are there people still alive in there? Supposed heretics with either broken or altered bodies?

I have to find out. I now have two fundamental aspects of my very being demanding I enter the woods. I hardly think about it as I start walking toward them. It's supposed to be full of monsters, but I can handle monsters. Right now I feel like I could handle the fucking king. My power is only growing as I walk. Mana courses through my body, demanding I use it. An intense pressure builds beneath my skin with every step.

"Lillith, where are you going?" Autumn calls out, and I realize I have walked maybe fifteen yards from the wagon. Shit, I can't just bail on the academy now. What was I doing? At the same time, I can't ignore this. I have to find out why my mana is reacting to the woods this way. And yeah, studying the impossible ecosystem would be a bonus. I hesitate, unsure of what to do for a moment as I look back at Autumn.

Her face pales and her eyes bulge. "L-Lillith, RUN!" she screams, and I whip around. Emerging from the woods is a monstrosity far more repugnant than I have ever imagined. For some reason when I heard *monsters*, I expected goblins and kobolds, or giant wolves or something. This is something more eldritch than *Dungeons & Dragons*.

This is a huge gelatinous mass consisting of slightly translucent, pink flesh. It looks like it has some kind of sparse fur all over its body, and it is running toward me with incredible speed. I say "running" because that's exactly what it is doing. It is . . . a blob, but as it moves, it forms multiple arms and legs to propel it forward. As each limb leaves the ground, it is absorbed back into the mass and a new one forms, higher up on the body. The way it runs, its body rotates like it's rolling toward me while also bounding on its multiple limbs.

It's fast, faster than horses can run. It's all right, I can fight it. I have never been more powerful. I try to form a spell to push it back, but my extra mana doesn't work. The spell just . . . dissipates. Fuck. I try forming a stone and the same thing happens. I use force mana to decrease my weight and . . . it works. Well, all right, I can't attack it with magic, but maybe I can overpower it?

I forget all about commoners and nobility at this moment. "Wallace!" I yell. "Get the wagon and the twins out of here! I'll distract it!" I don't wait for a response, instead using force mana to lift myself into the air and try properly flying, or rather falling forward, for the first time. This isn't like that time in front of my family's temporary estate. I am using my empowered mana to fly at speed in the opposite direction of the wagon.

I get dangerously close to the abomination as I fly by it, making sure I grab its attention. As I hoped, it changes course and moves in my direction. Disturbingly, it doesn't turn but changes which side of its body the limbs grow from. As I pass it, I get a closer look and almost retch. I can make out veins through its translucent skin. Its "fur" is thin and seemingly just sticking halfway out of its body. No follicles, just an inch of fur floating in it and the rest sticking out. It appears to be vibrating or shaking as I pass it.

It keeps pace with me more easily than I thought. I could maybe go faster, but I don't think I could react in time if something popped up in front of me. I hit anything that fast and I'm gonna look a lot like the thing that's chasing me. Making a decision, I slowly reduce my speed and change direction, flying into the woods. There could be other monsters, but I can also lose it. I considered flying straight up, but it might give up and just go for the wagon.

I want it after me until the others get away. I briefly consider just floating the whole wagon, but I don't want the group to know exactly how powerful I am right now. Besides, it would probably panic the poor horses to death. No, it would be best to lose the monster in the woods and circle back. I can catch up then.

With that, I enter the Radiant Woods.

CHAPTER FIVE

The Radiant Woods

I fly into the woods and immediately slow down. I no longer have the space to move freely through the air, and I don't want to find out how *Lillith vs. Magic Tree* ends. Instead, I ease up on the force and allow myself to land while maintaining momentum. I end up jumping a few times like a rock on water before I am moving slowly enough to transition back to running.

I hazard a glance behind me to see the flesh beast hasn't slowed at all. It is now throwing its body from tree to tree in such a way that it seems to be actually speeding up. The unnatural way it never turns, just changes what can be considered the front, is uncanny in a way that my head can't quite process. Fuck, it's almost on me. It is leaping through the air with perfect precision and is only a couple leaps away.

Even worse, I now notice that the trees it touches are eroding where it makes contact. So much for overpowering it with physical force. I approach a pine tree and take a page out of Fleshy's book, pushing myself off it with all my strength, directly toward the monster. As it flies through the air toward me, I slide on my knees and lean back, traveling underneath it. I run back in the other direction with the few moments I've bought.

I scan the trees it eroded and spot a sturdy one. I rapidly erect an earth wall behind me, hoping to slow the monster and make a break for the tree in question. Again, I glance back, and I see the wall did in fact slow it down. A few more moments. This also confirms that while I can't attack it, I can impede it by affecting the environment. I try conjuring a series of boulders in the sky and letting them fall. They fail to form, but I'm not sure if that is a lack of power or the same problem as my earlier attack.

Physical attacks it is. I make it to the sturdy-looking tree I had been running toward and jump up to ram it with all my strength. I hit just about the eroded spot and it creaks but doesn't topple. I begin to punch it to little effect. It's thick and I am unable to move it at all. I didn't expect it to collapse with a single hit, but it should be weak enough to budge a little at least.

Another look behind me reveals the monster has leapt over the wall and is running toward me again. Shit, I need to act now. I'm about to give up on the tree when I realize I'm an idiot. I got caught up in not being able to use magic on the monster and tried to topple a tree with my fists. Tunnel vision strikes again. I turn toward the tree and conjure a stone wall behind it, ending just below its weak spot.

Then I bombard it with force on the other side, and a loud crack screams through the forest.

Finally, the tree comes toppling down. I erect another earth wall to block the flesh thing and jump on top of the wall I used to create leverage against the tree. I wrap my arms around it and try to dig my fingers into the bark with little success. Note to self, grow some extendable claws or something. I heave, lifting the tree up. It is *heavy*. It's moderately tall, but I'm surprised by how heavy it is. Grabbing it from the bottom is probably the worst thing to do as well, but I have no time.

With a herculean feat of strength and a little upward force mana, which thankfully works, I lift the tree and manage to swing it forward. Gravity takes over from the force mana just as I go from lifting to swinging forward, and just as the force spell dissipates. It does this because, just as I swing forward, the monster leaps over the other earth wall and into the trajectory of my swing. Thank God it opted for over instead of around again. It was the fastest and most likely choice, but it would have been bad for me if it had chosen the alternative.

The tree hits the monster and, much to my relief, sends it flying in the other direction. I don't hesitate and leap from my perch to run in a different direction. Which way did I come in? I try following the path of eroded trees but they just . . . stop at a clearing of flowers. And I am still in the middle of the woods. Shit. I probably should have predicted this. Wallace said monsters never leave the Radiant Woods. While this thing definitely broke that rule, I should have known he said that for a reason.

I look around a bit more and find nothing is familiar at all. The foliage is different. Where I entered, there were small patches of cactus flowers and tall grass. The clearing I am in now is covered in orange lilies and has stalks of sugarcane in irregular patches. It is truly bizarre.

Well, this fucking sucks. These, uh . . . woods, I guess . . . should at least have the decency to guide me back to the entrance with giant hollow logs and music. Well, at least I got that thing away from the wagon. I look around at the trees and stones but find moss growing on random sides of both. I look up and see the sun directly above me. So much for the easy which-way-is-north tricks.

I look up again and face-palm, realizing I can just fly. It's not like anyone is going to look up my dress. I quickly regret the action as I smear tree sap across my face. Great. I rub my fingers together, examining it. It's not quite right. It's not sticky in the way I expect and it's more brown than amber. That's odd. I guess it's not the strangest thing, but it certainly bears further examination.

A low growl rumbles nearby and I pause. I slowly look up from my hands to see another monster. This thing is more solid, although it still makes little biological sense. It has digitigrade arms, like a dog's hind legs, but its actual legs are more human. Well, they would be, if not for the gray fur growing from them. Its knees and . . . both elbows have claws protruding from them. The claws on its arms are on the wrong side as well; it looks like they will stab the creature if it doesn't keep them extended.

Its head is like a dog's—not a wolf but a dog, except that its snarling teeth are flat and curved, like tombstones. I don't have time to gape as it jumps toward me with a speed I couldn't have perceived anywhere but this forest. Its claws go from ten yards away to maybe six inches from my throat in an instant, before it stops and slumps over. It coughs blood as the stone spike I conjured impales it.

It's dead. It's a good thing I chose the internal aspect I did, or I would have been dead. I'm relieved not every monster in this forest shares immunity to my attacks or, again, I would be dead. A morbid curiosity draws my hand to the monster's body, but I don't get the chance to examine it. I feel dozens of eyes on me and examine the tree line around the clearing. Dozens of bizarre monsters are eyeing me . . . greedily? It's hard to tell with their varied and absurd anatomies.

The only things any of them have in common are that they look dangerous and they have started charging me. I fire what must be hundreds of stone bullets out in all directions as they close in on me, and many of them fall. I don't wait around to find out how many I killed, however, and launch myself into the air. Time to get out of here. Magic is disgustingly easy to use in these woods, and it's only a few seconds before I am floating above the forest, free from the danger below.

I groan. There is absolutely nothing but forest in all directions. I could fly for weeks without reaching the edge. My fascination is rapidly turning into frustration. This was definitely not my best idea ever. I look down at the monsters below me and see the trees are still blowing in the nonexistent wind but . . . they are all blowing toward me. From every direction they are swaying, even stretching, toward me.

Even more disturbing are the bodies of the monsters I've killed. I have to look twice and lower my elevation to get a better look. The orange lilies are growing on them. It even looks like some kind of vines are reaching up to the monster I spiked. What the fuck is that about? I want to investigate, and I almost do, when I remember the . . . slime I fought at first. So far it is the only monster I couldn't kill. In fact, it's almost too easy to kill things in these woods. I'm literally sick with mana, and actually entering the woods made it jump by orders of magnitude.

I am not sure, however, if there are more monsters like the first that will be immune to me. Better not to risk it. I decide to get far away from here and try landing in another, less populated spot. I pick a direction at random, completely unable to find north. After a while, I should be able to use the sun.

This theory fails me, however. After what feels like hours, the sun remains fixed firmly in the center of the sky. What the fuck? Okay, fucked up magic woods I get. I can get behind that; magic does weird shit and I respect it. But the sun isn't in the goddamn woods! Everywhere else the planet rotates on a regular schedule! Why the hell is it just . . . sitting there above this forest?

I also haven't come anywhere close to finding the border, and I decide to land for a while. As I descend into the woods, the trees reach out for me again and I shudder. I land in dense woods and see yellow roses growing up the tree trunks. They appear to be growing out of the bark like it's soil. Weird. I stand still for a moment, waiting to see if I'm going to be attacked again. Nothing happens, and I release the breath I didn't realize I was holding.

I begin to walk. I suppose there is nothing left to do but investigate. I'm not getting out of here without learning more about this godforsaken place. I have to admit, I am horribly curious as well. Don't get me wrong, this place is a nightmare hellscape devoid of hope and happiness, like if Nevada had a lot more flora. At the same time, however, I could imagine worse places to be stuck than a forest of biological curiosities to learn about. In Nevada, the only curiosity would be slot machines in grocery stores.

I am reaching out to touch one of the yellow roses when I am yet again interrupted. I hear muffled, whispered voices, and my hackles rise. I use sound mana to hide my footsteps and creep in the direction of the voices. After a few minutes, I can finally make out what they are saying.

"I don't know why she ran into the Collector-forsaken Radiant Woods!" I hear a man's voice whisper defensively.

"The question," a woman responds with irritation, "is why you followed her!"

"She needed help! Because she was protecting us!" the man protests.

"Yeah, she was, and now we are all dead. I don't know why she ran into the damn woods, but people don't come back out, August! I like her too, but this was suicide!" Autumn's voice answers.

"Then why did you follow me in!" August retorts, and Autumn lets out an irritated huff. These idiots followed me in? It sounds like they knew there was no going back too. Fuck, that's . . . well, noble. For the first time since I regained my memories as Annie, I am happy to see a pair of nobles looking for me.

I emerge from my cover to greet them and have to dodge a burst of fire and a block of ice as the startled twins immediately react to my presence.

"Woah there, slow down, guys!" I say, holding up my arms in a placating gesture. The two gape at me in silence for a moment, before they burst out in unison with concerned questions. It's not ideal that they are stuck here too, but it does feel good to see them safe.

As I try to answer their questions, a thought at the back of my mind bugs me. I was flying for hours, and they entered the forest at the same place I did. How am I running into them now? If the woods drop you off at a random spot, why did the flesh monster enter the same place I did? What are the odds in this seemingly endless jungle of madness that I would land so close to them? I feel uneasy as I reunite with my companions. Everything about this place is wrong.

CHAPTER SIX

Under the Hat

Sarafyna

So, what exactly should I expect?" I ask as we walk toward the nearest temple.

"No one is really sure, but you have nothing to worry about," my dad reassures me. It is finally time for the rite of confession, and I have been feeling anxious since yesterday. I'm not sure why; I just have a bad feeling. I do my best to shake it off, as all my older friends have done this and they are all fine. My mom used to undergo the rite once a month, more frequently than most, and she actually looked forward to it.

I certainly haven't done anything notable to confess, and I know I need to stop worrying over nothing. This isn't the first time I've had a similar anxiety and it always turns out fine. When I was a kid, a woman down the road from us gave me the exact same feeling, but everyone else had nothing but good things to say about her. Since then I have gotten the same feeling many times without it ever being validated.

There is no reason to believe this will be any different. I decide to distract myself with other, happier thoughts. "I know, thanks, Dad," I answer before asking, "How is the hat block coming?"

Dad smiles, recognizing this tactic of dealing with anxiety. He has been carving the first hat block for the shop. It'll be cheaper than buying one, and woodwork has always been a hobby of his.

"It's finished, actually. I was going to surprise you when we got home! Some of the neighbors have donated some materials as well, linen, fabric, and straw. You'll be at the shop making your designs real in no time!" he answers, and a grin breaks out across my face.

"Seriously? That's amazing! Remind me to thank everyone!" I exclaim. I am beyond excited at the news. The shop needs some work before I can sell anything, but I have so many designs to realize that I'm not worried about it. The more money we save on materials, the faster we can hope to make a profit and the faster we can get Dad out of the stables. He's getting older for a commoner, and I'd like to take over as the breadwinner if I can.

I can tell the distraction worked because as soon as we round a corner and see the temple, the ice gripping my heart is completely unexpected. Why am I reacting so strongly to this? It's just a confession! I haven't done anything terrible, and this temple was practically my mom's second home. I shake my head a bit and take a deep breath. *It's fine, Sara. Stop panicking over nothing.*

None of this works, and my anxiety causes a slight tremor in my hand as we finally enter the temple. Dad notices, and as a priest approaches us, he rubs my back. "It's okay, sweetheart, I promise. I brought your mom here for this rite all the time. It'll all be okay." I look up at him with slightly glassy eyes. At some point, I started holding back tears and I don't even know why.

"I know, Dad, I don't know why I feel this way. It just feels like . . . I'm saying goodbye. I don't know why, I just can't shake the feeling!"

He looks at me with concern and pulls me into a hug.

"I understand. Feeling anxious is perfectly okay. But this isn't goodbye, I promise. I'll be right here when you're done. If you feel anxious, just look at the wall in my direction. I'll be right here, waiting and praying for you, okay?" he reassures me, and I nod. Usually, that would make me feel better, but it doesn't. The moment is interrupted by the priest arriving.

"Hello, welcome to the temple of the Collector. Is there something wrong?" the priest asks.

Dad gives me the opportunity to reply but my voice gets caught in my throat. His concern deepens and he decides to help out.

"Sorry, my lord. This is my daughter, Sarafyna. She is plagued by anxiety, but there is nothing wrong. We have an appointment for her first confession today," he explains on my behalf.

The priest smiles knowingly.

"Oh, is that all? It's quite all right, this happens all the time. She probably took a few coins from your purse or kissed a boy a little too early. Don't worry, Sarafyna, the rite of confession is confidential. There will be no rumors about you coming from here. Its only purpose is to give you a clean slate before the Collector," he says in a friendly tone.

It doesn't make me feel better at all. Is that what it is? Do I feel guilty? I have let Dad work himself pretty hard for my dreams. I didn't know, but . . . it is my fault anyway, isn't it? Is that why I am so deeply and thoroughly terrified right now? It doesn't feel right but it must be. "Come with me, Sarafyna, can you do that?" the priest asks, and I nod. I don't get a chance to say anything to Dad before the priest guides me through the halls of the temple. I maintain eye contact with my dad as long as I can.

When we turn a corner that cuts him off from my view, my heart and legs protest at the same time. My heart falls into my stomach and it feels like it's trying to claw its way out and return to my father. My knees give way and I actually start to fall, but the priest catches me. Why is my body rebelling against me like this?

"Oh, don't throw a fit. What, have you been sleeping around behind Daddy's back?" the priest says, irritated. "Well, get over it, we'll keep your little secret, okay?

Just come along!" All the kindness and understanding has left his voice and my stomach churns. *That's not true, I don't know why my body is doing this!* I want to protest, but the words won't come out.

Another priest runs up and both priests grab an arm and pull me up, then drag me along the corridors. "This one looks like a handful," the new priest consoles the first.

"Tell me about it. Haven't had to drag a girl to confession in a while," the first priest replies.

The newcomer frowns and laments, "Well, with a pretty one like this, I suppose there isn't really any mystery what the problem is. I swear to the Collector, we get more cases like this every year. It's a godless country out there." The first priest nods in agreement, and the two drag me into a circular room, then roughly put me on a stone seat in the middle.

I feel control of my legs return and something inside me screams to run. To get out as fast as I can, damn the consequences. My breathing is coming faster and sweat is pouring down my face. It no longer matters that this is supposed to be nothing. I don't care that it's supposed to be routine. This is wrong, and I don't know why, but I know I need to get out. Everything depends on escape from this cold, stone room.

I stand up and begin to run, but I feel a sudden pain radiating through my body. It's like the feeling you get when you hit your elbow in just the wrong spot. My legs seize up after only a couple of strides, and my momentum throws me to the ground. My face collides with the stone and I feel something crack in my nose.

"Woah, we got a live one here," I hear a man say through a laugh. "She must have done something real ugly to do that!" I start to weep. I'm in pain, and for only a moment, I lose control of my body entirely. I feel some kind of pressure holding me in place, but I push back and regain control. I don't know how I push back, I just . . . do.

"Please, help me!" I beg through the blood running down my face as I climb back to my hands and knees. "There is something wrong with my body!" I feel the same pressure and pain as before in a greater quantity and push back harder, breaking free again. "PLEASE!" I beg.

"Fuck, it's not working, get Father Medici!" I hear a voice yell, followed by scrambling. The pressure keeps coming back, but it grows easier to break out of until I hardly notice it anymore. As I finally regain my feet, I stumble. I am about to run again when priests from all around the room run to me and physically hold me, forcing me back onto the chair.

I don't understand what is going on, but I have never felt terror like this. I just want to go home. I want to make my hats and talk with my dad. I want to sit in my favorite chair and eat, but I can't push back against the physical force the same way I pushed off . . . whatever had been controlling me before. "Please," I whimper, "I just want to go home . . . I just want to go home . . ."

"Quite the heretic we have here," an elderly man says as he approaches me. "Now, where exactly did you learn divine magic?" he asks, and I look up at him. He is glaring at me. What did I do? I didn't do anything.

"I don't understand," I say, and he backhands me.

"This isn't a game, girl. Tell me who taught you divine magic, and tell me now," he insists. I look back at him, terrified. This isn't what's supposed to happen! It's supposed to be easy and quick. It's supposed to be a routine ritual!

"I'm sorry, I don't know any magic!" I respond, desperation coloring my voice. "I don't know what I did, I want to go home! Please, I'm sorry!" At this, I feel the strongest pressure yet and I have to fight to push the pain back. The older man's eyes widen.

"She's demon spawn," he announces, and my eyes widen in return. Demon spawn? What is he talking about? I'm just . . . me! The daughter of a stableman. A hatter! I don't understand!

"I'm sorry, my lord, there must be some kind of mistake! I'm just a hatter! I don't know anything about magic or demons or anything! I swear!" I beg, but he is looking at me with horror.

"You know what must be done. Deal with it," he orders the other priests. They descend on me. It is not long before I am completely tied up and gagged. Together, they carry me through the winding corridors of the temple. I look in the direction I believe my father is waiting, but it provides no comfort. They take me out a side door and toss me into the back of a covered wagon. A few of them follow me inside, and others seem to circle around.

I feel the wagon begin to move. Where are they taking me? I struggle to move with my arms tied behind my back and my legs tied together. The priests don't stop me from moving, however, and I am not too far from the back. I manage to throw myself toward the exit, but not far enough. My body gets halfway over the back rail and my face sticks out the curtain that covers the back. I feel the priest's hands pulling me back in, but before they can, I see my dad.

He looks confused and is talking to another priest just in front of the temple. He glances over, and our eyes make contact. For the first time in my life, I see cold fury contorting my father's face. I don't see anymore, however, as I am thrown to the other side of the wagon. "Sara!" I hear my father scream. "Sarafyna, I'm coming! Let her go! Let my daughter go!"

This carries on. His anguished cries and attempts to reassure me follow the wagon through the city. At the speed we are moving, he must be running like his life hangs in the balance. With his health, it will kill him to keep this up. He does anyway. His shouts slowly grow quieter, but anytime we stop they grow louder again. I hear his screaming for what must be at least an hour, and the sounds of the city fade before he does.

Then, finally, all I can hear is the horses, the wagon on the road, and my own soft sobbing.

CHAPTER SEVEN

Pursuer

So you are saying you came in hours away from here?" Autumn asks, and I nod again.

"Yes. After I fought off the flesh . . . thing, I flew for hours before finding you here," I answer, and the twins share a skeptical look.

"We entered at the exact same spot, Lillith," August challenges, "and flying takes immense and complicated mana. There is no way you could do it for hours!"

I roll my eyes. I am getting a headache and all my muscles feel sore. I suppose that will happen when you swing a giant tree over your head.

"In this forest, I have as much mana as I need to do just about anything," I answer, "and you have surely figured out that we are nowhere near the edge of the forest!" The twins exchange a look again and I get the feeling they are having a silent conversation.

"All right, I'll give you that," Autumn agrees. "But it's still hard to believe you could use that much mana. Even the king can't reliably fly, especially for so long . . ."

Arguing with Autumn and August is an interesting experience. They seem to take turns like some kind of tag-team wrestlers. The two who usually bicker and trip over each other can coordinate quite suddenly when they agree.

"He can't, or he doesn't?" I ask, and they pause, which I take advantage of. "Look, I wasn't just walking around in circles for hours, okay? And it doesn't matter really, because the end result is the same! We are nowhere near where we came in, and something drove us back toward each other."

The two give each other that look again.

"All right, Lillith, fair enough," August says. "That just leaves us with one question, I guess. What do we fucking do now?"

Finally, I can agree with him. The situation is bad, but not hopeless.

"Well," I reply, "what we need is information. The flesh . . . whatever . . . left the forest, right? Which means it's possible. All we need to do is figure out how." I reach out to a yellow rose and it seems to stretch to touch me as well. Creepy. This whole place seems to want to touch me.

"You think so, huh?" Autumn intones, unimpressed by my evaluation. Okay, yeah, *we need to know how to leave* isn't exactly wisdom that will be passed down for generations. Still, I'm working on it.

"Give me a minute!" I insist. "Can you . . . what's the word for it . . . scan things?

Figure out what they are made of, how they work?" I inquire. I've been trying to examine the things in this forest since I got here, but I've been foiled every time.

"Uh, we can feel if there is mana inside something, and maybe figure out its aspect," August answers. That will work well enough for my purposes. I'm likely the only person who understands the inner workings of the world well enough to actually analyze something's genetic makeup. This is a magical forest, however, so analyzing the mana could very well be enough.

"That works for me. I figure it's magic keeping us here, and it's magic holding the sun in the sky. If we figure out what kind of magic, we can get out. So, we analyze the magic in everything. The flowers, the trees, even the monsters if we run into them," I explain.

The twins give each other a look and then nod to me.

"Well. I have no other ideas. I have to warn you—we aren't that good at making out aspects we haven't grasped yet," Autumn hedges.

Well, I'm not too worried about that. Three of us will still find more than just I would. I cautiously reach out and finally make contact with one of the flowers. While it had been reaching for me, and its siblings are still doing the same, it doesn't do anything to me on contact. At least nothing I can discern.

"I can't guarantee it's safe. Everything here seems . . . alive," I say, "but we aren't getting out of here by playing it safe. Do what you can, and tell me if you figure anything out."

"I don't want to alarm you, Lillith," August says behind me, and I tense up. Are there monsters nearby? What's wrong? "But all plants are alive," he finishes. I take in a slow, deep breath through my nose. I'll admit I've made dumb jokes in bad situations before, but he needs to phrase them better. I just about blasted the area around us with stone bullets.

I pull my hand away before I can push mana into the flower and turn around to tell him so, and my eyes widen. Before the twins have a chance to react to my expression, I have thrown us all in the air with force mana. The twins scream in unison and I can't tell which voice belongs to whom. It doesn't matter, and I keep flying up. The trees feel impossibly tall, far taller than they felt last time, as we are pursued by the abomination of flesh I thought I had lost.

It throws itself from tree to tree, rapidly elevating behind us. I see the limbs it's creating are far more muscular than last time and its speed has somehow increased. We finally fly above the trees, and the monster throws itself after us. I put more mana into the elevation, enough that I worry I will break someone's neck if I use more force, and we barely avoid the beast's attack.

It creates a disgustingly long limb that extends to reach out to me. Before it can grab me, its body thankfully begins to fall and the hand at the end of it swipes in a last-ditch effort. It misses by a literal hair, a few strands of its sparse fur brushing against my boot. As it silently falls back into the woods, I sigh in relief and slow our ascent, allowing us to come to a stop in the air.

The twins look like they have just been fired out of a cannon, which, to be fair, they kind of have. Autumn's hair has lost its perpetual perfection and has turned into something of a tangled lion's mane. I suppose mine probably looks similar. She is gasping for breath, and August is actually puking into the forest below. Fair enough. I allow them to get their bearings.

After several moments, August wipes his mouth on his sleeve and looks up at me. "Collector, Lillith. A little warning next time?" he protests, and I stare at him, nonplussed.

"August, we survived that by the skin of our teeth. Your warning was either flying up in the air or getting swallowed by an acid monster." I see him preparing a quip, but we are both distracted as we look at Autumn, who is gaping at our surroundings in horror.

"She was right, Augie. There is nothing. Nothing but these Collector-forsaken woods for . . . ever. There really is no getting out of here . . . We . . . we are never going home . . ." She spirals and I try to head her off.

"No, Autumn. Remember that thing got out. There is a way, and we are going to find it. We'll find a way out." I give August a meaningful look and he seems confused for a moment, then realizes what I am indicating. I'm not getting through to her and she has started to hyperventilate. He might be able to talk her down.

"Yeah, Autumn," he chimes in, doing his best to follow my example instead of hers. "We are with Lillith of Endings! If she got out of a marriage with fucking Baldwin Tudor, she's not going to be taken down by a few trees!" I shake my head at him. Leaning on me isn't what she needs.

As her rapid breathing increases, I see him realize this and shift gears. "No, Autumn, that's not right," he says. "Do you know how I can be certain I'm going to get out of this? Because I have you. You have never let me down before. You have always gotten me out of trouble, our whole lives. And you have me to do the same for you. You are going to get out of here because I am going to take you out of here. And I'm counting on you doing the same for me."

This speech calms her a little, but not enough. I notice his hands shaking and I realize his emotional state is not far from hers. If he hadn't needed to puke, or if his first thought wasn't to make a joke, he would probably have broken down at the same time. I need to do something. My strong suit is making people angry, not making them feel better. The closest thing to comfort I typically provide is justice.

I decide distractions are the best I can offer. "Let's move on," I say, breaking the awkward silence. "We'll figure out how to get out of here once we are far, far from whatever that creature is." The twins vehemently agree, and I fly us in a randomly chosen direction. The flight is mostly quiet and lasts at least two hours. The sun, of course, refuses to move.

After the quiet and our slower speed allow everyone to gather their minds, Autumn breaks the silence. "Listen, Augie," she says, "about when we were attacked by that thing earlier . . ."

August perks up and turns in the air to face his sister.

"Yeah?" he invites.

"When we flew up in the air suddenly, you know . . . It's just . . ." She trails off.

"Go ahead, Autumn, you can tell me."

"Well, the thing is . . ." she starts, then a broad grin splits her face. "Your squeal was even higher than mine!" she finishes with a laugh. I join her as August's face turns bright red.

"Th-that was Lillith!" he insists as Autumn and I laugh harder.

"As if!" she challenges. "I saw you!" I see August turning an even brighter red and glancing at me. Hey, man, if you wanted to save face in front of me, you probably shouldn't have tried to blame me.

"Can I give you some advice, August?" I ask, then continue without waiting for an answer. "Just lean into it. You screamed. Squealed, even. So what? It was surprising! Anyone would have, and it was kind of funny. Own it." He looks at me skeptically and I laugh. "I'm serious! Do you know what really manly people never have to worry about?"

"What?" he asks, looking away to hide his blush.

"How manly they look," I answer. "Seriously, just be a person. People scream when they are scared or startled. If you'd laughed it off, or just screamed again, we would have all laughed and it would be over. Now? Now we know you are embarrassed, and we are going to make fun of you forever."

"It's true," Autumn agrees. "You simply aren't going to live it down. But don't worry, I'll protect you the next time Lillith startles you," she teases.

"Gonna be hard to do while you're squealing yourself," August retorts, and I smile. It looks like the twins have recovered from their brief panic. Now I just have to convince myself they weren't right. That and avoid panicking about that mana-invulnerable flesh monster. It followed us somehow. Or found us, and for some reason, it wanted us specifically. I shudder at the thought. I need to learn about these woods and get out of here as soon as possible. I decide to interrupt the twins before they devolve into bickering.

"I think it's safe to descend now," I say, and they look at me, concerned. "I know, I know, but we have to at some point. Come on, it looks like there is running water over there." The twins assent to my plan, and I slowly lower us back into the woods, near what looks like a river.

I almost immediately regret this, as a chorus of shrill screams greets us the second our feet make contact with the earth.

CHAPTER EIGHT

The Banshee

Pained, horrified screams assault us as we land. I throw up a sound barrier in all directions before it can do any damage. "Collector, did you land us in the third plane?" August complains, removing his hands from his ears. We all instinctively covered our ears, but the sound went right through them. Had I been any slower I suspect our eardrums may have burst.

"Maybe. The theory does ring true," I answer, rubbing my own ears. I certainly hope I can heal tinnitus, because there is a good chance all three of us have it after that. August and Autumn groan at my poorly timed joke and Autumn glares at me.

"Lillith, you're great, but your jokes are awful. Obviously, we landed in the wrong spot. We should find somewhere else before it starts again," she complains, and I shake my head at the same time August nods in assent. He then pauses, gaping at me.

"Lillith, you can't seriously want to stay here. What if that happens again? I, for one, don't particularly want to lose my hearing!" he protests. I hold my hands up placatingly.

"First, I don't think it stopped. I am protecting us with sound mana," I say.

"Sound mana??" Autumn interrupts me. "Lillith, we are fourteen! Exactly how many aspects have you manifested? Didn't you grow up a commoner? Did Lord Godfrey have you in a cell studying magic?" she marvels. I often forget how long it takes younger mages to grasp new aspects. A thorough understanding of an aspect makes it easier to aspect, which has always given me an advantage. At my age, however, one or two is usually the limit. It's not until attending the academy that students become more well-rounded mages.

"That doesn't matter right now," I deflect. "I am good at aspecting mana, yeah. But what matters is the screams."

Autumn just gapes, and August looks frustrated.

"Right, the screams that tried to make us bleed from the ears," August chimes in. "The screams we should be getting far, far away from! Yeah, those are what matter right now, we agree completely!"

I groan in frustration. I understand the instinct, but we are already safe from the sound. We don't need to flee!

"August, those screams are coming from someone!" I say. "Those clearly pained screams are coming from multiple someones! We can't just leave without finding out who!" He has the decency to look chastised, if not entirely convinced.

Autumn tags in. "They are coming from some*thing*, not some*one*! No person could make a sound that loud! We aren't going to find anything but another monster!"

"You know that, do you?" I snap at her. "In this forest, these impossible woods, you are completely certain that's not a person?" Whatever is causing that screaming is happening now. Whoever, or whatever, is doing it could be suffering. I can't leave these two behind because they need me, but I can't just force them to come either. I am growing angry with the delay.

August apparently does not pick up on my sense of urgency. "Even if it is, that's not our job, Lillith! Our job is just to survive until we see our families again! We aren't equipped to deal with whatever is over there, whether it's a monster or it's being hurt by one!"

I scowl as I turn to him.

"Then whose job is it? When someone, or even something, is suffering, and there is no one but you who can stop it, whose job is it to help them? Nobody else is going to come along, August! We are it! We are the only hope for . . . whatever is over there! If that is the sound of genuine anguish, it is either getting our help or continuing to suffer. Do you understand?" I lecture, my voice rising as I do. "Now, will you two just fucking come with me so I can protect you at the same time?"

The twins are pale faced, and they pause to look at each other but nod in assent. Their expressions are a battlefield of guilt, fear, and apprehension, but they steel themselves and follow me. I feel a little guilty myself at the back of my mind, but I don't have time to examine why. I adjust the sound bubble to disrupt but not block all incoming sound and the screams make it through.

It is quiet enough that it is no longer painful, and I run in its direction, the twins close on my heels. I idly notice marigolds blooming along our path as we run, and after a moment we emerge from the trees at the edge of a slow-moving river. It's bisected by a small island, maybe five feet in diameter. The water around the island is shallow enough to wade through, and in the center is the source of the screaming. The sight of the woman is forever burned into my memory in an instant. Her arms are tied behind her back, but it's the way her legs are secured that is horrifying. Tree roots grow from the ground and twist around her legs and over her waist, keeping her standing. A few of the roots have burrowed into her skin and I can see them pulsing like veins under her flesh.

She has no clothes, but her skin looks so much like leather that it makes no difference. Where her breasts would be, her chest is marred with irregular and poorly healed scars. None of these things is the detail that secures her such a permanent spot in my mind, and the scream is not coming from her mouth. Not her original mouth, in any case. Her mouth is sewn shut with thick roots, and it is silent.

The screams are coming from a series of mouths that have grown up and down her body. Her leathery flesh is parted at random locations and screaming lips, teeth, and tongues torment not just us, but her. The only things that remain untouched are her chestnut hair and her tired eyes, which watch us with resignation. A moment of shock paralyzes us, but then the woman's eyes widen, and I freeze, trying to interpret the look.

"LILLITH!" Autumn screams, and I whip around to see a catlike monster with ten legs pouncing on us. I immediately crush it under force mana, protecting the twins and killing it instantly. The three of us stand in shocked silence for a moment, until I realize the sound spell is keeping us dull. I surround the woman's body, excluding her head, in a sound bubble, and her eyes fill with relief. I then release the bubble around us and the forest comes alive.

The sound of movement is everywhere. I scan the tree line and see dozens of eyes reflecting the light the river allows into the woods. "Stay close to me!" I command, and I get to work as the twins comply. First, I try to surround us with a shield of force, but it fails. "There might be a monster I can't use magic on here, stay on your toes!" I warn.

I bring the twins into the water with me and toward the island. I send stone bullets in all directions, shredding monsters as they charge toward us with no regard for their own safety. Massive stone spikes erupt from the ground as I skewer larger monsters. What looks like a troll dies immediately as a massive crab scurries around it, its legs briefly climbing up against the body in its rush to reach us.

I use precise force mana to pull both of its claws off. One I use to sweep in a circle around the island, which we have now reached, killing smaller monsters in its path. The other I drive through the crab's main body, skewering it and pinning it to the forest floor. I have no time to rest, however, as different kinds of flying creatures are descending on us. I throw a massive wave of heat mana into the air to intercept them. With the power of my mana in this forest, it boils them in the sky and the smaller ones literally pop, raining blood and sinew down on us.

I hear August retching behind me, but I have no time to focus on it, leaving him to Autumn. The use of heat mana gives me an idea, however. I begin to combine earth and cold mana in the forest around us. The ground itself freezes in all directions, for miles. This is not the cold of ice but of an absolute absence of heat. The creatures still in the forest flash freeze on contact, their frozen limbs tearing from their bodies as they insist on continuing their attack.

This assault keeps up for what feels like forever, but I never grow tired or run out of mana. In this forest, I feel like a goddess of destruction—an idle thought that invokes pride and sickness in equal parts as I tear through the bodies of our attackers. With the ground assault effectively halted, I am able to focus on the flying monsters. I notice their number increasing and I continue to fight. I'm not sure how much time passes, but we are surrounded by bodies long before I am allowed any rest.

Eventually, however, the forest does run out of monsters. None of them were immune to magic like the flesh monster, and I wonder why my force shield dissipated. Finally, I turn toward the twins, who gape at me, terrified.

"W-what are you?" Autumn asks, fear contorting her usually elegant expression.

"H-how?" is all August manages, and I sigh. I suppose they have very likely never seen a mage use that much power before, and . . . it certainly wasn't pretty.

"I'll tell you what I can soon," I answer, trying to sound comforting but obviously failing. "But right now, we need to hurry. Whatever is controlling this forest seems to be actively after us."

"W-what do you mean?" Autumn stammers. I look at her pityingly. She's a kid. I forgot she is a fucking kid. Just a child on her way to school, and I dragged her into a massacre. Fuck. I actually yelled at them about our responsibility to help. It's not their responsibility, it's mine. They aren't the rich, ruling over commoners, not yet. They are just children.

They were scared children and I bullied them into coming here with me. Yes, I needed to protect them, but that doesn't really absolve me. I could have at least blocked their sight while I fought. I had the power to. Here in these woods, I don't know if there is anything I can't do. Unfortunately, I am starting to figure out why. I can protect them from that, at least.

"I'm sorry," I say, "this is my fault, and I will tell you everything I can. But first I have work to do. Please, trust me." Both of them nod. I can't tell if it is actual trust or fear, but I don't have time to discern which. They are staying still and safe. The monsters I killed are already being covered with marigolds. I need to examine them.

I kneel and gently touch the leg of an eagle-like monster I killed. I push my mana into it and scan its biology. My stomach churns. I do the same with parts from three more distinct monsters. Bile rises in my throat. I frantically grab a marigold, which immediately makes me feel sick in a different way, and scan it. A moment later, I let go in relief. The flower's genetic makeup was wrong, and I need to spend more time on it, but I am still relieved.

Finally, I stand and approach the woman in the center of the island. I notice the mouths on her body have closed, and her eyes are flooded with the exact emotion I most fear. Hope. "May I examine you?" I ask, and she nods. I gently touch her skin and flood her body with my mana. All my worries are confirmed.

I am reminded again of my conversation with Diana all that time ago. "Why the woods?" I asked. "Because that's where all the monsters are!" she answered. An interesting turn of phrase, and not one I think even she understood. People aren't banished here to be left for the monsters. People are banished here to become them. Like every other monster I examined—like every monster I had slaughtered—this woman has the genetic makeup of a human.

I want to puke, but I keep examining. It seems like her current . . . form is new. Extremely new. I can feel the residual effects of her body being changed, and even her more human attributes feel . . . fresh. This isn't something she has been dealing with since she entered this forest; this was for me. To torment me and to trap me.

Whoever . . . whatever is controlling this forest knew I would respond to screaming and knew I wouldn't leave once I saw her.

We flew for hours. In all directions. In completely clear skies. I had not seen a single bird or bug the entire time, but dozens, maybe hundreds of flying monsters ambushed me here? These monsters—these *people*—aren't just being tormented; they are being engineered on the spot to attack me. And that's the part that tortures me. They attacked me. Not to kill me, or even to hurt me, but for the same reason every spell but one worked.

My grief mana can only be used for the grieving, not against them. The only spell that failed during the massacre was the purely defensive one. The only spell that gave me the option of leaving them alive. These people didn't attack me to hurt me. Whoever did this to them wanted that, but it's not why they attacked. They came to me to die. I look up at the hopeful eyes of the tortured woman and every part of my being recoils. I have to help her.

"I am going to try to save you," I say, and her shoulders sag, tearing my heart in two. Nevertheless, I put my hand against her leathery skin and push mana into her. I try to force her body back to the shape of a human, directing it the way I direct it to make changes in myself. I push all the magic I can muster into her, but something fights me. Another magic, divine magic, keeps her in place. I push harder, more desperately, screaming as I try to save her, my eyes locked on hers.

I can't. The other mana is too strong, and she isn't cooperating. I couldn't even if she did cooperate; whatever power is opposing me is . . . insurmountable, even in this forest. I see her eyes pleading with me, and I have a sudden moment of clarity and pull my hand back like I just touched a hot stove. What was I just doing? This isn't what she fucking wants, this is what I want. It doesn't matter how much mana I have. Of course, the power of my mana is a fraction of what it was. I am not using it for her. If it had been a regular spell, it wouldn't have even formed.

Hot tears running down my face, I accept the request written in her eyes. I create stone bullets and fire them into her brain and spine to kill her as quickly and painlessly as possible. I then immediately collapse, vomit, and weep. The twins watch me with apprehension as I sob, but I can't reassure them right now. I can only cry.

I don't know how long I stay there like that, but eventually, a sound interrupts me. I look up and see something I never expected upriver. A wagon is stopped and a priest is watering horses.

CHAPTER NINE

Warriors of the Collector

I just stare in confusion for a moment. The emotional turmoil of the last battle and . . . what I had to do, followed by the mundane sight in front of me, gives me whiplash. The man looks completely at ease here; he isn't even bothering to look over his shoulder. Most wouldn't feel so comfortable and safe on a regular road, much less in a place like this. I gape for a moment, my eyes wide and fixed on the wagon.

After a moment, I look beyond the wagon and only grow more surprised. The forest has parted around a wide road. The forest that pulled us in to kill us, or perhaps me, is rolling out a red carpet for this priest. What are they here for? It doesn't elude me that this could be a way out, which is important while I have the twins with me, but in the grand scheme of things, information is more important.

I have a number of theories about how and why the Radiant Woods work the way they do, but investigation and data gathering come first. This priest could be the best source of data I can find. I figure I have two options. I can approach him directly for information. This seems like a less than ideal choice, all things considered. It's unlikely he is going to be on my side. There is a high likelihood that approaching him will lead to violence.

I suspect I would win any fight, especially since the forest couldn't do anything but incentivize monsters to attack me and keep me lost. I suppose I'll have to deal with divine magic, but even Baldwin would have been crushed like a grape if I fought him here. That doesn't get me any information, however. I also don't want to traumatize the twins any more than I already have, and I doubt they will understand why I killed a priest.

Of course, after today, *priest* is going to be the most dangerous fucking profession on this planet. If it weren't for people like Emeric, priests in the dark about the nature of divine power, confessions, and . . . this, I would just bar the temple doors and burn them all inside. They aren't like the city guards, where even the lowest level of participation requires complicity in slavery. Some genuinely just want to help people and don't realize who they are serving.

Nevertheless, I have innocent people's blood on my hands now, thanks to the atrocities of the temple. The blood of priests will replace it. I doubt a priest casually driving through the Radiant Woods is unaware of their nature, however. In any case, killing him in front of the twins may be a bridge too far at the moment, and again, if he's dead, he is useless to us. Option A is not ideal.

My other choice is to discreetly follow the priest until he leads us out of the forest. The problems with this idea are many. I don't know how the forest works yet. Is space being warped? Am I being manipulated with illusions? Is there some kind of instant teleportation happening, or are we in some kind of alternate reality? If we follow him and he suddenly disappears before we escape, we lose everything. No information and no way out.

Another thing to consider is that priests are the ones, to my understanding, who banish people to these woods. In other words . . . there could be a person in that wagon, or worse, a person lost in the woods who has already been left behind. If I hide and follow the wagon out, even if I'm successful, I might end up abandoning them. Basically? I have to approach, and I have to keep him alive.

All this consideration is a moot point, however, when Autumn looks up and spots the wagon. "A-Augie, look, a priest! He can get us out of here!" she says excitedly, shaking his arm. The two have been huddled up, holding their knees and burying their heads in their legs.

August looks up and then at where his sister is pointing. "Thank the Collector!" he exclaims, and both scramble to their feet to run toward the wagon.

"Wait!" I try to stage-whisper to them, but it's too late. They are running toward the priest, and worse, the priest is looking toward us. His eyes widen as he sees us and the gruesome scene surrounding us. I don't have time to react in turn as I am rapidly warming the area around us and using earth magic to stabilize the ground. As the cold recedes, it isn't as dangerous as when I first cast the spell, but who knows what magically cooling it to that level did to its structure?

I manage to finish in time and the twins are safe. I follow them and notice the priest banging on the side of the wagon and glaring at us. As I suspected, it seems we are not as welcome as Autumn may have hoped.

"Hello!" Autumn exclaims. "I'm Autumn of Forrester, and this is my—" She freezes in place. I feel the familiar uncomfortable feeling of divine mana wrestling with my will and I shrug it off. It barely takes an effort at all.

I walk past the frozen twins and threaten the priest as four other priests pour out of the wagon. "If you want to live, let them go, now," I demand. I give him a cold glare and he smirks at me.

"So, you are demon spawn, are you? Do you think you are the first we have dealt with? Do you think just because we are priests and you can fight off the Collector's will that we will bend to your empty threats?" He laughs. "If you could, you wouldn't be here in the first place. Trust me, it will be easier if you just submit. We'll be gone before you know it and you can go back to obediently waiting for the price of your sins."

I raise one eyebrow at him.

I suppose that's as much confirmation as anything that the priests force people into the woods. What did he mean by *demon spawn* though? Just an excuse for supposedly God-given powers failing? He should know about endoaspected mana, although I suppose that doesn't always allow people to defy divine magic. In my case, it's likely because of what my aim was when I aspected it. The term must have something to do with whatever propaganda is used to recruit priests for this work.

The other priests join the first, and one in slightly more ornate robes addresses him. "What's going on here?" I peg that guy as the boss.

"Mementos, brother," he answers, and I tilt my head. "Careful, one of them is demon spawn. Looks like she has been using her abilities to make the older mementos fight each other." At the end of that explanation, he gestures at the scene behind us. Most of the people and debris have been covered in flowers, but there is blood in the water and a few corpses are mountainous.

"Cute trick, girl," the new priest says, "but it won't help against us. We are warriors of the Collector. We are many, and we are mighty. Your devil magic won't work on us any more than our divine magic works on you. Just go back into the woods, and we won't have to hurt anyone. Our business is not with you."

"So are you in charge, then?" I ask. This will be a lot easier if I know who I need to leave alive. If I had any doubts before, they have been dispelled by this conversation. These priests know what is happening here.

"The Collector is in charge," he answers, and I roll my eyes. "But I am supervising this group on his behalf, yes."

"Good." I nod and use force mana to throw the priest controlling the twins in the air so hard that he's out of sight in under a second. "So you can answer my questions, then," I retort as one of the many and mighty warriors of the Collector dies from the impact of force before ever hitting the ground, and the twins regain their autonomy.

". . . brother, August Forrester," Autumn finishes, then pauses, noticing the sudden shift in the environment. "What . . . is going on?" she asks, confusion coloring her face and voice in equal measure.

"Kill them!" the lead priest orders, and powerful spells form around all four of them. I don't bother preparing a spell to block the light, water, and earth spells they are preparing; instead, I simply crush and absorb the mana they are using with pure mana of my own. Both twins have taken a step back as they see the priests attempt to murder them, and August actually falls backward. I idly catch him and prop him up with force mana until he regains his footing.

"Try to hurt them again, and die," I intone, inviting no argument at all. "Now, we came here for help. I simply have a few questions for you. There was no need to attack us on sight like that." I try to remain as patient as possible, but I do not have much patience to spare today. For the twins' sake, I'd rather not escalate this . . . right now. At least not until I can help them understand what the priests are doing here.

One of the other priests snarls, "Do you really think we'll just bend over after a couple of tricks?" and throws a hidden dagger toward Autumn. I'm surprised by how fast he throws it and realize he must have some body modifications of his own.

It's no matter, however, as I stop the dagger in the air and let it fall to the ground. I then give the offending priest the same treatment as the first, throwing him into the distance with violent force.

"Uh-oh, blasting off again," I quip, then give the remaining three priests a chance to process what just happened. "This isn't an empty threat. Try to hurt them, and you die. Now, what are you doing in the forest? Do you know how to get out, and can you take us?"

"W-what's happening?" August asks, his voice wavering. "I don't understand, why are they trying to kill us?"

"I'll explain later," I answer gently, "but I won't let them hurt you." I see his concerned glance at me and add, "I won't hurt you either. I'm just trying to keep everyone safe, I promise." I can tell they both remain apprehensive, but I can't help that.

"I won't answer your questions," the head priest addresses me, "and I won't leave you alone. You are all here for a reason, and your threats mean nothing to me. The Collector will provide for us, as he always does, and he won't allow you to harm us."

I look at him like he's an idiot. "He just fucking did, you moron," I retort. "And he will again if you try to hurt my friends again." His face just steels at this and I groan inwardly. Fucking zealots.

"He allowed you to move them, but this is his forest. They will land safely. You can't assault the Collector's servants in the Collector's domain!" he blusters, and my brow furrows in thought. The Collector's domain, he says. I wonder if that is true, or if it is religion claiming responsibility for something that was already happening. It could be either, although the way the woods allow the priests to traverse them suggests one more than the other. Of course, that could be explained by the source of divine magic. I need more data.

I decide to point out the obvious hole in the priest's theory. "My friends are in control of their own bodies—that first priest's magic is gone. He's dead."

The head priest glares at me but the other two share a concerned glance.

"You freed them with your devil magic," he insists, and I groan. I notice Autumn's eyes widen at the conversation as she starts connecting dots. We are interrupted by a thumping in the wagon, and I lean over to look behind the priests.

"What's in the wagon?" I ask, crossing my arms. They must have brought a wagon this size for a reason, and it seems not everyone came out to greet me.

"That's the business of the Collector," the head priest dismisses, sniffing. He is trying to put on an air of indifference, but I can see the concern pulling at his eyes. "Now, you may leave. We will have mercy on you today, given you leave us to our business."

I let out an entirely unamused laugh.

"You mean you can't figure out a way to kill me," I retort, and begin walking toward the wagon.

"Stop her!" the head priest commands, and all three priests try to form spells again. I crush their mana again, then drop one priest in a pit I open below him, holding him against the dirt with force mana. The other minor priest, who tried to distract me by casting an earth spell of his own at August, I kill by twisting his head around with force. I am trying to keep it clean, for the twins' sake.

I flip around toward the head priest, but he isn't casting. What is he . . . I get hit in the head by a rock. August and Autumn are attacking me. What the fuck? *I know I scared you, but these guys are trying to kill and control . . . Oh.* That's why the head priest stopped casting. I have the ground swallow him as well, this time closing the pit around him and crushing him to death. I need to stop getting into fights in this forest, it's too . . . easy. A girl could get used to this kind of power, and I really don't want to get tripped up by that.

The twins stumble as they regain control of their bodies again. Well, I killed the leader, but I still have one priest. Maybe he will help me. In the meantime, I walk around the wagon to look inside. I find . . . corn. Boxes and boxes of corn. This confuses me because, as far as I'm aware, corn hasn't been created in this world, at least not in this region. Also because . . . why?

I get a glimpse of a priest's hood ducking behind a couple of the boxes. "Come on out," I call. "Corn is no place for a mighty warrior." There is a moment of silence, then the priest emerges from his hiding place. Two things immediately strike me as odd. First, he is a child. Younger than the twins and, well, me, I guess. He is maybe eleven at most. Second, he has the milky eyes of someone who was blinded by an infection.

CHAPTER TEN

No Rest for the Wicked

I stare for a moment. The boy is obviously blind. Well, it should be obvious. I suppose I can't lean on visual biological cues in that way mere moments after tossing a couple of men into the great beyond with my magical powers. Still, the child behaves as if he can't see. This alone doesn't surprise me; I'm aware that people like him are often brought here. What catches me off guard are his priest's robes.

"Please don't hurt me!" The boy trembles, his eyes beginning to water. It takes me a second to realize he is talking to me, and I allow the silence to drag for too long before coming back to myself.

"Shit, no, I'm not here to hurt you," I say. "I'm here to help, if I can. Can you tell me why you are here?"

The boy fidgets in his robe for a minute before shaking his head.

"N-no," he stutters, "I'm not supposed to . . ." He holds a hand to his terrified face and reaches out to the canvas of the wagon to get his bearings, then begins moving toward the side of it, looking for stability.

"That's all right," I answer before asking, "Is there a reason you aren't supposed to tell me?" He fidgets more and moves one foot back, nervously trying to come up with an answer. I give him time, leaning back to see Autumn and August whispering to each other. I feel a pang of guilt at the haggard look the twins share. They are far too young to process today's events, and I am responsible for the worst of it. I can't think of what else I could have done, but I didn't do right by them anyway.

I return my attention to the boy as he answers me. "Brother Neville told me I could never, ever tell anyone or the Collector will punish me . . ." he explains meekly. I suppose Brother Neville is probably the priest I gave a rapid burial. I think about how I want to approach this for a minute, then I look at the boxes of corn and climb into the wagon, taking a seat opposite the boy.

"Are you hungry?" I ask, digging through the bag on my side for a snack. I'd rather not waste the little I have since I don't trust any food in this forest, especially after examining the flower earlier, but I do want the kid to be comfortable. He hesitates for a moment, then nods. I pull out some jerky and pause. "I have some food for you. If you hold out your hand, I'll give it to you," I offer. The boy hesitates for a moment before extending an open palm toward me.

I gently press the jerky into his hand, and he pulls it back to begin eating it. He tears into it like he is starving and I raise an eyebrow. I wonder how long it's been since he's been properly fed. "It's all right if you don't want to tell me," I say calmly. "You don't have to do anything you don't want to do. Do you want to know a secret about the things grown-ups tell you though?"

He doesn't stop eating, instead just shrugging at me. I find his reliance on non-verbal cues interesting and decide the infection that blinded him must have been relatively recent. "Sometimes," I begin, "grown-ups tell you things to keep you safe. They understand things a little better and want you to be happy and comfortable. They want to protect you." I pause for a moment to allow him to think through what I'm saying. He has likely been told similar things in the past.

"Other times, however, grown-ups tell you things only to keep themselves safe. If they hurt you, or do something that makes you uncomfortable, they might tell you to keep it a secret no matter what. If someone hurts you, or threatens you, they might want you to keep it a secret for their own sake, not yours. The secret is grown-ups do bad things just as often as kids do, and they want those things to be secret just as much as any kid would," I continue. I've never been that good with children. I like them, but I am not talented at communicating with them. I hope I'm doing okay.

His brow furrows, and I decide I might be pushing too much. "Of course, you don't have to say anything to me that you don't want to. Take your time, and if you change your mind, let me know, okay?" I ask, and the boy nods reluctantly, holding out his hand hoping for more food. I hand him some more jerky, then realize I have been an idiot. "My name is Lillith, by the way," I add in an attempt to cover for my mistake. I want to make him comfortable but I never even asked for his name. "Do you mind if I ask who you are?"

He yanks the jerky back, but he answers me. "Peter," he says, and I relax. He is either warming up to me or he is so focused on food he forgot how nervous he was. I'll take it either way.

"Nice to meet you, Peter," I respond with warmth. I then take out a few more pieces of jerky and put them in front of him. "I'm leaving some food for you here," I explain, guiding his hand to the spot. "I have to go talk to my friends now. Will you wait for me?" I wait for him to nod again, then I climb out of the wagon.

I cautiously approach Autumn and August, who tense up as they see me. I glance down at the pit I created earlier and see the remaining priest struggling against my force mana. I sigh; I have to handle one thing at a time. I leave him and walk over to the twins. "Hey," I hazard, trying to put them at ease with my tone. It has little effect.

"Lillith, what the fuck is going on?" Autumn demands, and I wince.

"It's . . . a lot," I answer. "I know. And I want to apologize. I . . . shouldn't have dragged you into that fight earlier. None of us should have been there," I begin, but August cuts me off.

"Why did those priests try to kill us? Why did everything keep jumping around like that? Why did you fucking kill that woman earlier?" The last question hits me like a fist to the gut. These two have lived a fairly comfortable life together. Before today, even the common troubles most people have were alien to them, and suddenly monsters started exploding around them before priests started controlling and trying to kill them. It's going to take a lot to explain today's events.

"Well," I begin, "there is a lot to answer about all of that, and I don't know if we are safe to discuss it right now. Will you try to trust me until we get out of this forest?" I ask, echoing my sentiments from earlier. The twins glance at each other and I add, "What I can tell you now is this forest is trying to kill us. That was a trap earlier, and it won't be the last one. I want to get us out of here safely, then I will answer your questions."

The twins communicate in silence for a moment, then turn to me. "All right, Lillith," Autumn apprehensively agrees, "but when we get out, I want you to answer all our questions." I nod in assent and the two stand, a bit shakily, to join me.

"For now, we need to move on. I don't know if the sky is safe anymore. I think we should take the wagon. This road could lead us out." I return to the pit and raise the priest out with force mana, then address him. "Do you understand what will happen if you try to hurt one of us?" I ask, and the priest reluctantly nods, venom in his eyes. I release him and let him fall to the ground in front of us.

He coughs, having struggled against the soil while I spoke with the others, and clambers to his feet. "What do you want from me?" he asks, and I rub my temples, when Autumn cuts in.

"Why did you try to kill us? We only wanted help!" she yells at him, and he glares back at her.

"Priests don't help mementos," he answers indignantly. "You are here by the Collector's will. Once we realized you were traveling with demon spawn, killing you became the safest option."

"Mementos?" I ask, my words competing with August's. "Demon spawn?"

The priest ignores me and answers August first. "Her," he says, pointing at me. "Women born of demons who use demonic magic to fight the Collector's divine power."

I roll my eyes while August's widen.

"My father isn't a demon, just a dick," I quip. "And I resisted your divine magic using regular old mana. Just an endoaspected mana that prevents you from controlling me, like faith mana." I see a flicker of realization in the priest's eyes before they harden again.

"Liar!" he accuses. "I would have been able to see endoaspected mana!"

I groan as the twins look at me with suspicion. It's not my fault grief mana turns invisible! Actually, it probably is. Mana aspects behave in response to your understanding of the aspect. Something about my interpretation of grief is hiding my mana. Nevertheless, it wasn't intentional!

"The invisibility of the mana is part of the aspect as well, as is its potency," I respond. "Now, can you please tell me what you mean by *mementos*?"

"As if you didn't know, demon spawn," he spits, and I rub my forehead in frustration.

"You're right, I am lying to you, trying to trick you into telling me something I already know. You have foiled my plans to gain knowledge I already have. Surely the Collector has a seat at his right hand reserved for you and your righteous wit," I intone. "Now that we have established that you have seen through me, do you mind answering anyway?"

"A memento is someone like all of you," he scoffs. "Heretics against the Collector who have been given as offerings to him. Left in the Radiant Woods as punishment for rejecting his teachings and his perfect design."

Okay, maybe I kind of did know what he meant. I was just surprised by the word choice. The priests assumed we were banished here for heresy. In my case, I probably would have been, but that doesn't change the fact that he is wrong.

"Wait, you think we are heretics??" August blurts out. "We weren't banished here, we just stumbled in! I swear, we are loyal servants of the Collector!"

The priest just raises his eyebrow.

"Loyal servants of the Collector traveling with demon spawn? I am no fool. I know heretics when I see them. You are still standing side by side with a priest killer!" he cries.

"You tried to kill us first! Are we just supposed to die??" Autumn asks, voice bursting with indignance.

In answer to her question the priest asks me, "Well, that's not true at all, is it, demon spawn?" the priest asks me as

"No, you stole their minds from them, then you tried to kill them when I told you no. That's still on you, you fucking moron," I answer, annoyed he is trying to use *not submitting to mind control* as a justification for trying to kill us.

The priest opens his mouth to respond, but we never hear what he has to say. The flesh beast that has been pursuing me flies out in front of me and tackles the priest, limbs forming to strangle and tear at his skin. He screams as his flesh corrodes on contact and freshly formed fingers burrow into his eyes, throat, and mouth. The monster's body morphs around the man, cutting off the sound of his screams, and I can see him struggling through its translucent flesh for a few seconds. Then, as suddenly as it started, his struggle stops.

We stand in silence as the monster dissolves the priest's body inside of it. It doesn't turn, but its limbs are reabsorbed into its body, and a mouth begins to form on the side facing me.

CHAPTER ELEVEN

Autonomy

I freeze, my mind traveling a thousand miles a minute. I consider throwing us in the air like I did last time. However, the monster is feet away from us and dozens of yards were barely enough last time. I have to save the child as well as the twins, and force alone won't be safe while he is inside a loaded wagon. I can't do it, not fast enough. What if I get them in the air and it kills me? I might as well kill them myself.

Can I draw it away, like the first time? No, it'll just choose the easier prey. I just watched it devour the priest; there is no reason to believe it will find me specifically interesting when there are other close targets.

Fuck, what do I do?

I am vaguely aware the twins are screaming while the priest is . . . digested, and my eyes briefly flick toward the wagon to see if Peter is investigating the noise. I'm relieved to see he hasn't appeared, which in retrospect makes perfect sense.

The monster finishes forming a mouth of sorts, and I remain frozen in indecision. I can't attack it with magic. Can I create a chasm between us that it can't cross? No, it's between me and the wagon; I'd be abandoning Peter. Maybe I can create domes of earth around all of us? No, I wouldn't be able to see Peter, and the monster wouldn't go away. Maybe I can stop light from bouncing off the earth? But we'd still be trapped and separated.

The flesh beast's malformed mouth tries to speak, but no sound emerges and its entire body . . . vibrates? No, shudders. It tries to form more distinct lips but it's like it's not certain how they should look. I continue trying to think of a way to get everyone out safely. Why do I have time to think of a plan? Why hasn't it attacked us yet? Can it not move while digesting? No, Lillith, it's obviously trying to communicate with you, you idiot. Think, why would it do that? It never tried that before. Actually, wait, why doesn't my magic work on it?

My mana has only failed one other time, when trying to defend us from the monsters'—people's— assault earlier. Purely defensive magic does work against this one, however. I interrupted it with a stone wall earlier. *Why? Think, Lillith, why? Why did they attack you before? You know that—they wanted to die. But why that way? Why not kill each other, or themselves? Some of their bodies were formed in such a way that it would be hard not to at least harm themselves, so what role did I play in it, and why is it different this time?*

The monster tries to speak again and fails to create sound a second time, its body shuddering. I focus on its lips, but they don't move in a way I can make sense of. Okay, attacks fail and defense works on this monster—no, this person. That's the opposite of every other person in this forest. So their intent is different. Their grief is driving them in a different direction. Actually, I don't think my grief mana should stop me from attacking someone just because they are grieving. It should only fail if I am using someone's grief as a tool against them. I should be able to cast regular spells with pure, unaspected internal mana.

I feel the twins behind me. *Good, they aren't running; they know it is safest with me.* I think one of them is speaking to me, but I can't quite process what they are saying. *No, pure won't work,* I'll be too slow, too weak. I won't be able to react in time. Think. Why is it . . . are they attacking me? Are they attacking me at all? They tried to catch me, but if defensive magic worked . . . that means I am not working against their intent. Only attacking them, trying to harm them, is working against them. So do they want something else?

No, don't be an idiot, Lillith, you just saw them eat a man. They are definitely attacking . . . no, wait, they attacked *him.* This is a person who was brought here by priests and abandoned to become . . . this. Maybe they recognized that? They could be hostile to priests but not us! No, wait, I can't gamble on that, it's too dangerous. Think, dammit, what do I do? I feel someone shaking my shoulder but I shrug them off. I don't have time for that. I have to figure out a way to get everyone to safety and get out of the forest.

Wait! Out of the forest! The priests come and go, and so did the flesh . . . person. Then it clicks. Divine magic is the easiest way to transform the body. *The Collector's forest, transformed people, priests able to freely come and go . . .* Finally, exactly one resident of the forest is able to transform their own body, leave the forest, and get to me no matter how far I go? It has divine magic, it has to. They have to. They can get us out! No, they are the ones who brought us here; they don't . . . No, that's not right. I brought us here; they came to me outside the forest for some reason.

My mind is about to collapse from trying to work through the problem in front of me, and the fleshy mouth has started repeating the same two movements, over and over. I feel a harder shake on my arm and August's voice finally gets through to me. "LILLITH!" he screams.

". . . What?" I ask quietly, wide-eyed, still in something of a daze, and I see relief wash over him.

"Lillith, I think . . . I think it's trying to say *help me.*" A sort of horrified curiosity colors his face.

I look back toward its . . . their . . . mouth and look closely. They are trying to mouth words, he's right. Two words, though their mouth doesn't move like a normal mouth. But it has formed some sort of disembodied tongue that moves with it. *Help. Me.* He's right. They want my help. Why did they chase me like that? Why try to grab me with their corrosive touch?

"Help you?" I ask, and their body shudders again, but differently. "Help you how?"

They pause. After a moment, limbs grow out of their body but don't do any-thing. They want my help changing back? Well, that seems obvious, but . . . I can't, I already failed. Whatever is changing the people in this forest is too strong. Besides, they can modify their own body, so why do they need . . . Oh, of course! They can make a mouth but not sounds! I steel myself, my racing thoughts finally slowing and deciding on a course of action. It's a risk, but it feels right.

"If this doesn't work," I whisper to the twins, "get the boy out of the wagon and try to get away. I think I know how to help them." I start to step forward but I feel both twins holding me back. I could pull away easily, but I don't. Instead, I look toward Autumn.

"What are you going to do to it?" she asks.

"I don't know how to describe it," I say with a shrug. "Can you trust me one more time?"

Autumn studies my eyes for a moment, concern and fear warring for control. I see her come to a decision, look past me, and nod at August. The two let go of me, and I walk slowly toward our pursuer. I hold my hand out, hesitating for a moment before placing it on their flesh. I immediately feel burning, agonizing pain in my hand, which pulls a scream from my lips. I fight through it, pushing my mana into them.

I grit my teeth, a scream continuing to escape through them as I examine . . . her. She's a woman, well, probably. In any case, she likely used to have female anatomy. I can't exactly read DNA, but I can feel the pattern her body wants to have. That's what she is missing. She can change her body on her own. Somehow, she is able to fight the force of the forest I couldn't overcome. But she doesn't understand anat-omy. She can make limbs, kind of, but she can't form her body the way she wants it.

She doesn't understand where her organs go, or what they do. She doesn't even know what organs she has. She is desperate to fix herself and has the power to do so but not the knowledge. But I do. I don't know how she knew I would be able to help her, but I am probably the only person in this world who can. I pulse my mana through her, using all the power at my disposal to put her body right.

The force I have been wrestling with fights back, and I can feel it has the power to overwhelm me, to crush me like an ant under its heel, but the woman helps me. She fights back with her own divine mana, and I feel the opposition shriveling away from our combined abilities. She is . . . powerful. Far more powerful than Baldwin ever was. With all my power in this forest, working directly for what she wants . . . we are the more powerful force, and I can see her body shrinking and taking shape.

The pain in my hand starts to dull, but I scream with effort and keep manipu-lating my mana in every cell of her body. As we form vocal cords for her, I hear her scream join mine. It feels like hours pass us by as we fight to give her body back to her. The sky darkens and I feel the atmosphere crackle as lightning strikes a tree near us. A moment later, we are in a clear part of the forest again.

We jump around the forest and rebuild her, piece by piece. I can feel the fury of the Radiant Woods as we defy it, but the woman stays one step ahead of it, moving us faster than it can attack us. I block acid rain with force and find myself in a field of flowers a moment later. I finish forming her vascular system and the woods fight back.

We race through apocalyptic storms and clear skies as we defy the forest and a woman's body takes shape in front of me. I am relieved to discover her brain is unmolested, likely to keep her aware through her transformations, and I help reattach it to her newly formed spine. We war with the forest on two fronts until, finally, a woman stands before me. The sparse auburn "fur" has collected on her head in a short pixie cut.

Her face is gnarled and her joints seem wrong, but she is undeniably human. I look around and find the twins and the wagon still here. The forest has let up on its attack, and we are now surrounded by lavender trees. I don't know how she managed to bring us all here, but I am extremely relieved she did. I can't pick out an age for her; it seems there is more precise work to be done before she is who she once was. Lumps and benign tumors grow over her eyes and stick out all over her body. "I'm sorry," I say. "I think it will take time to do more than this, time we don't have. Are you okay?"

Her mouth opens and an uncomfortable rasping assaults me. She grits her teeth and clenches her fists, then tries again. "I—I'mmm oookaaayyy . . ." She groans. "Thhaaank yyoouu." I don't know if there is something wrong with her vocal cords or if she simply doesn't remember how to use them properly.

"I couldn't have done anything if you weren't . . . well, a badass," I retort, exhausted. She tilts her head in confusion and I decide to move on. "I'm Lillith, it's a pleasure to meet you, uh . . ." I say, a question clear in my tone. August and Autumn approach us cautiously, eyes wide and jaws slack.

The woman sits down, equally exhausted, and answers with what I assume is her own name. "SSSaaaraaaafffyyynaaa."

CHAPTER TWELVE

Sarafyna's Sorrow

Sarafyna

I don't know how long it has been since that day. The day of my first confession, when the priests dragged me away. The last time I saw my father. I know I was on that wagon for weeks. I was given food once a day and was allowed to relieve myself only when one of the priests needed to as well. I remember, at the time, I wanted nothing more than to finally get to wherever they were taking me. I gave up on going home a few days in and just wanted to be allowed off that fucking wagon.

I was so young. I can't recall how many times I've wished I never left the wagon and the care of the domineering priests. When I was finally freed from them, it was only to be abandoned. The priests put a bag over my head and shoved me out of the still-moving wagon. I fell hard against the ground and my face was quickly surrounded by fast-moving water. The pain and the panic overcame me, and I convulsed, trying to get up on my knees.

They hadn't bothered to untie my hands and feet, and I grew certain I was going to drown. My body was mostly on dry land, so I should have been able to pull myself out, but with my limbs tied and the water overwhelming my senses, I was consumed by panic. I thrashed and struggled with all my meager strength but I couldn't break free. The water just kept coming and I couldn't breathe; I just wanted to breathe! Rope cut into my flesh as I tried to pull myself free, but I wasn't strong enough.

Blackness crept into the corners of my eyes and I felt myself going. That was it; I had been left there to die. Then, in a second, the ropes around my ankles and wrists just . . . snapped, and I was free. With the vestiges of will I had left, I pulled myself out of the water and scrambled to my feet, pulling the hood off my head and getting my first proper look at my surroundings. I could barely take it in. I was surrounded by plants I had never seen before, trees that made no sense, and lilies growing around my feet.

I stood by the riverbed, confused and anguished. Why? What was the point? Why spend weeks dragging me to this place just to leave me here alone? I sat down on the riverbed, amongst the impossible lilies, and wept. I missed my home. I missed my father, my run-down shop, and the hat block I had been excited to see after the confession. I didn't understand. Why was this happening to me? I had never done anything to anyone.

The silent forest didn't answer me. There wasn't so much as a cricket or a squirrel to give this place life. Just the foreign plants and the unrelenting river. I wept there for hours. I wailed like only someone confident in their solitude ever could. I wept and wept until my throat ached and my eyes felt blistered. Perhaps I would still be there now, forever locked in that bed of lilies, except eventually, my hunger overwhelmed my emotional agony.

My stomach felt like it was eating itself, and the sickness of hunger drove me to my feet. I didn't know what I could find to eat, or even if I would. But I reached out for this tiny purpose and grasped it like it could pull me back to my happy life in my quiet neighborhood. I couldn't grasp what was happening, but it was a reason to move forward and do something. First, food, then maybe a way home.

I didn't have this purpose for long, however. I had barely walked fifteen paces to the tree line when fruit began to grow out of the trees in front of me. I stared at it blankly for a moment, and a branch shook as if in offering. Confused, I reached out and plucked the purple fruit from the tree. I examined it with apprehension, but my growling stomach drove me to try it. I took a single bite and was shocked by its splendor. I had never eaten something so delicious in my life.

I devoured it in moments and quickly accepted another. This one was equally flavorful but far meatier, and I felt myself filling up. The tree offered a new fruit, however, and I felt that same pressure the priest exerted over me encouraging me to continue eating. Suddenly, the fruit felt like lead in my stomach. I pushed against the pressure, but this time I couldn't shove it off. I felt my hand accepting another fruit, and I greedily inhaled it.

I ate fruit after fruit, struggling against my own body as my stomach protested the excess. After a dozen or so pieces, I finally felt the pressure ease up and the fruit stopped growing from the branch. I doubled over, certain I was going to puke, but my body refused to comply. Feeling sick, I stumbled along the river. I had to get out of there. I walked and walked but found nothing new.

Eventually, I decided to take a risk and enter the forest. I figured I would have food, whether I wanted it or not. Eventually, if I walked long enough, I figured, I should reach the edge of the forest. I ventured into the woods and wandered. And wandered. And wandered. The sun was unmoving and the day never-ending. I didn't know if I was maintaining one direction or not. Though I felt I would never be hungry again, I walked until my stomach and fatigue forced me to stop. I ate when I was hungry. Water appeared when I was thirsty. Thick beds of lilies appeared when I was tired.

I don't know how long I traveled like this. I slept and ate dozens of times. Hundreds of times. I don't remember when the changes started. All I know is one day, my jagged, untrimmed nails had turned to claws. Another day my teeth had grown and sharpened, stabbing me when I bit down. The fruit lost its enticing flavor the more I fought against it. Every bite tasted like oil. I continued my days of wandering. I was forced to eat and I discovered new changes in my body.

I never stopped fighting. Every time I felt that pressure, I pushed back with my entire being, and every time, I lost. I stopped picturing my old home. I stopped imagining seeing my father again. Instead, I held the image of my old body in my mind. I focused on it as I rested. Occasionally, I would wake up and some of my old self would be back. Like when I was a child and I wished to have smoother skin or longer legs and would wake up with the changes I wished for.

I started to suspect it wasn't luck as a child and it wasn't the forest's mercy now. With determination, I focused on my body all day, every day. I focused on the feeling of pushing against the forest, and eventually, I learned to fight the changes. One day I managed to remove an extra joint in my arms, and the forest punished me. Rain that burned my skin fell from the clear skies. I fought back.

I changed my skin so the rain didn't hurt, and thorns formed instead of lilies when I was tired. I changed my flesh to burn the thorns and thick mud tried to suffocate me instead. I didn't stop fighting. I thought I was winning. While wandering, I started to feel the forest change around me. I felt the same pressure that always tormented me acting through the trees and the flowers. I learned how changes felt, and how to react to them.

I knew when the burning rain would come, when the thorns would form, and when the earth would try to swallow me. It was almost like I could feel something physical approaching me. One day, I used my own will to simply . . . step out of the way. I found myself in an entirely different part of the forest. I saw plants I'd never seen and I felt the rage of the forest.

"You can't escape me."

I knew I had done something the forest never expected. It tried to assault me again, and again I shifted through the forest with an act of will. It could no longer hurt me. I was able to step aside when it wanted to feed me its poison. I could move freely throughout the forest. I still needed to eat, so I changed myself. I could touch the forest and steal its energy. I could dissolve the plants with a touch and take their power for myself.

"You belong to me, Sarafyna."

The more I did this, the stronger I became. I was faster, smarter, and the pressure of the forest had a harder time gripping me. One day, I felt a new pressure. It was similar but . . . weak. I shifted to it. The energy wasn't next to me but a few hundred paces away. I ran to it and discovered a group of priests in a familiar wagon. We all froze. I considered asking them for help, but . . . rather than hope I felt rage. Rage like I'd felt at the Collector when he took my mother from me. I could have followed them out of the forest, but I felt them exerting pressure on me and my vision went red.

"No one will help you."

I intentionally formed the claws I had gotten rid of and tore through one's throat. Some part of me felt horror at what I was doing but . . . that was Sara. That was the hatter who lived with her father. I was something else. I was fury. I was hate.

I was Sarafyna and I burned with loathing. I extended my arm in a fleshy mass and caught another priest's head, dissolving it into my body. I felt the priest's power flow into me, return to me. It was my power. It felt like the life that they'd taken from me. It felt good.

"This won't save you."

I heard screaming and the priests scattered. I wouldn't let them go. I shifted through the forest and cut them off, consuming them, tearing them, dissolving them. I ate like the forest forced me to eat fruit, gorging myself on the lives of these small men. No more would they abandon helpless girls in this . . .

"Hell. You are in hell, and you belong here."

They would never throw a child in a wagon while their desperate father chased them to the edge of the city. One by one I hunted them, and they felt the fear they had given me. I found them and then they felt nothing. I consumed them all like so much steaming meat and my fury grew. This wasn't the last time. More priests came, and more priests were hunted. Sometimes the forest protected them; sometimes it failed. I grew stronger and the forest couldn't punish me anymore.

"Do you think you are winning?"

This continued. For days. For months. For years. I don't really know. But the war continued. One day, I felt something new, an edge. A border. An end. The end of this relentless torture.

"There is no home for you out there."

I shifted to it, and . . . emerged from the forest into the night. The first night I can remember seeing in a lifetime. I had escaped and I felt true joy for the first time since I stood in front of that old shop with my father. I wanted to literally leap for joy, but . . . I couldn't. That's right, I had no legs anymore. I had nothing. I couldn't face my father like that. I wasn't worried; it was a long time since I had taken control of my body.

I tried to change back, but . . . I couldn't. I couldn't . . . remember. I didn't know how. I didn't know what I should look like. When had I started adapting only to the forest's attacks instead of maintaining my body? It must have been years. I tried to form an arm, but it was wrong. I formed a leg, but I couldn't maintain it. I could build temporary, fake limbs, but that was it. My joy was drowned by anguish. I couldn't go back. I had gone too far, in more ways than one.

"This is the only home left for you."

With the agony of hopelessness, I turned back to the forest. I used my temporary limbs to pull myself back to the only place I could ever belong again.

"Welcome home."

CHAPTER THIRTEEN

Sarafyna's Solace

Sarafyna

I was alone, excepting the priests, for so long. I didn't realize I wasn't the only one here. When my abilities grew, however, I started to notice other presences in the forest. They weren't priests; they didn't have the energy priests had. Each of them was isolated, and as I observed the movements of the forest, I realized it was keeping them that way. If they ever got close to each other, the forest would shift around them and keep them apart.

I must have passed by some of them dozens, no, hundreds of times as I wandered the forest. But the forest couldn't hide them from me anymore. I shifted to one of them and found them only a few hundred paces away. I didn't have the precision to land next to them, and the forest moved them away before I could get to them. I followed and the forest reacted. It was the same sick game it played when I hunted priests.

I shifted again and used my temporary limbs to close the distance in an instant. The forest still kept them from me. It was faster than it ever had been when moving the priests, like it cared more about keeping me from its other victims than keeping me from mine. I pushed harder. I learned to use the trees and landscape to propel myself faster. I pushed myself to my limits and further, day after day, until I finally reached my goal.

I shifted and closed in on the other presence until I was right in front of them. It was . . . horrifying. I had never seen my reflection; I'm not sure I would have been able to handle it. In a sick way, that's exactly what I found myself looking at. Not literally—this person's monstrous form looked completely different from mine—but their eyes were familiar. Their legs had been shortened and their back bent, and joints had been added into their arms. This form forced them to constantly crouch but didn't provide them the support to do so. They looked like they were constantly struggling not to fall over.

It wasn't their body that reflected mine, however. It was their desperation. The agony, the sorrow, and the hopelessness. They looked surprised to see me, but they didn't react past that. They said nothing, and they did nothing.

"You won't find any friends here."

I tried to approach them, but I felt the forest exert pressure on them. They opened their mouth and began to scream and I shifted back. The message was clear. Back off, or they suffer. I realized they couldn't fight back like I could. I resigned myself and moved back into the forest, leaving them alone. I was furious. I wasn't allowed to even grieve with someone else. I thought about the look in their eyes before I left. The hopelessness and the longing I recognized creeping over me every day. The desire for it to just . . . end.

"That will never happen."

I knew the forest wouldn't allow it. It wouldn't let anyone out so easily. It had complete control over everyone but me. At that moment, I decided I would never let it win. One day, I would burn it to the fucking ground. I wouldn't give up and I wouldn't resign myself to hoping for death. I would be the great enemy of this . . . what was the word? . . . hell. I would grow stronger. I would fight harder, and I would take everything from it.

I began to devour the forest with greater vigor. I absorbed its power, day after day. I learned to tap into it. To grow my own flower beds and trees. I hunted priests whenever I could. I got stronger and better at finding them. The forest was becoming my domain. My hunting ground. I owned it nearly as much as it owned itself. In exchange, I gave up more humanity each day. I hated myself for it, but I didn't matter anymore. I feared what I was becoming, but so did the fucking forest.

I lost my connection to anything but that one goal. I lost the ability to see, to feel what I touched, or to taste. I didn't even breathe anymore. I could still feel the energy of the forest and the energy of the priests. I realized the other residents of the forest had another energy I could see them by, but the forest suppressed it, tried to hide it from me. It didn't matter; I wouldn't bother them again.

"You can't hurt me. You are mine."

I thought I had given up my past life entirely. I thought this was all there was left for me. Consuming the forest until it was gone.

But I was wrong.

The monotony of my life broke in an instant. I felt something, an energy like I had never encountered before. Something . . . just out of reach, no, just outside the forest. It was . . . hope.

It felt like a cozy room on a rainy day. A savage storm thrashing in rage and a mother's safe arms in the center. It cried out to me; it invited me. It wanted to give me everything I had ever lost. It carried the promise of my father, of my hat shop, of my old forgotten home. More than that, it carried the promise of fire and blood. It wanted to scrub the stain of my loss from this world. It offered to hold me in one arm while it crushed the forest's life with the strength of the other.

I felt life again. I felt my future and my past like they existed for the first time in years. I wanted more. Whatever this energy was, it convinced me I deserved more; I could have more. I shifted. I ran toward it. I wanted to bask in it. For the second time, I left the forest.

"You are mine, Sarafyna. I will kill her."

I felt its attention on me, I felt its energy reach out to me and . . . dissipate. I ran toward it as fast as I could and it ran. I followed and it shifted. I didn't understand. It invited me but it fled from me. I followed and it changed direction. I adapted and . . . it entered the forest. I couldn't understand, but I followed. I made sure I entered at the same point and used every tool I could to close the gap. I threw myself from tree to tree, absorbing their energy as I did.

It suddenly shifted directions and moved toward me and I felt pure joy until . . . it missed me. It passed directly under me and ran the other way. I felt the energy reach out around me again, but once more it dissipated before it could get near me. I just wanted to touch it. A moment later the energy somehow created a wall between us. I didn't care; I leapt over it.

Another wall was created and the energy stopped in front of me. It seemed to have started attacking the forest for some reason, and I was filled with glee as I could discern the forest's pain. The energy pushed into a massive tree and I felt the forest tear and rage. For the first time, I felt all the other presences in the forest gathering in one place. The forest was bringing them together for some reason. I didn't care what it tried—I could tell this energy wouldn't be stopped.

A tree was torn from the forest, and the energy . . . threw it at me. I felt myself being thrown across the forest and my heart cried out as I flew away from the energy. I crashed into a cluster of trees and slid across the forest floor as I landed.

"She rejected you!"

It . . . she? She couldn't have rejected me. She was inviting me. She was offering me help. I could still feel her energy, but . . . she had somehow thrown herself into the sky. I tracked her through the forest and followed her wherever she went. I could shift to her, but . . . I'd just find myself in the sky. Instead, I followed her from the ground. She would land eventually.

I was right, she did land. I was about to shift to her, but I felt something else. Two more presences. They had a similar energy to the other victims of the forest but . . . more alive? I felt the energy, or the woman, approach them. I suddenly remembered the same energies had been near the first time I felt her. I realized they must be her friends. I had forgotten about friends. I paused for a moment and just felt their energies interact. I longed to be one of them, but I waited and observed.

Until I felt the forest reaching for her. It wanted to take her from me. I felt her reaching back and panicked. I shifted to her and ran to close the remaining distance at full speed. I strengthened my limbs to leap faster, but she was too quick. She threw herself and her friends back into the sky. I couldn't let her go. I threw myself between the trees and followed her, even throwing myself into the sky after her. She was too far. I reached out an arm for her, and as it failed to reach, I extended it. I grew it to the limits of my ability and almost touched . . . but the earth reclaimed its hold on me and I began to fall. She was gone again.

I didn't understand why she was fleeing me . . . but then it clicked. The other victims in the forest couldn't feel energy like I did, so maybe she couldn't either. To her, I was just . . . whatever I was. Of course she ran from me. I had turned myself into a monster whose only skill was killing. I needed to communicate with her.

I continued to track her and noticed something disturbing. The forest was doing something. It was gathering its victims in one spot and . . . changing one of them. Adapting it. I examined its intent more closely and realized it was making the victims an offer. It would let them near her. Near each other and . . . it wouldn't protect them. Like me, they looked like monsters, and if they attacked her, it would let her kill them.

It was preying on the one hope it had left them in order to hurt the only hope I had left. This made me furious. *She could help you!* I don't know how I knew, but I knew. She could help me too. We could help everyone, together. Eventually, I felt her land and the trap sprang. She didn't run from these ones, for some reason. She fought them. But she was stronger than the forest expected. She overpowered everything it threw at her. She hurt it directly and its fury grew.

The fighting went on and on and she was untouched. As the battle drew to a close, I noticed something. Priests had entered the forest. The forest shifted them to her. It wanted to enlist them as a new attack but . . . she was too strong. I felt as her friends ran to the priests and she followed. I felt when the priests tried to use their pressure on them, and I shifted nearby to protect them but paused. She was fine. She shrugged it off as easily as I did.

To my immense glee, she threw one of the priests into the sky with enough force to kill him in an instant. She seemed to engage with the other priests a little before easily killing them as well. All but one were dead in seconds. I began to understand the furious storm surrounding her warm core. She left the final priest alive but trapped, and she hovered at the back of the wagon for a while. I couldn't understand—the wagon was empty except for some kind of food from the forest.

I was going to move to stop her from eating it, but she didn't. She just waited there for a while, then went and spoke to her friends. Eventually, she freed the remaining priest to speak to him. I worried she was going to leave the priest alive, and I wanted to prove I was her ally. I ran. I ran with all my strength and took the priest. I absorbed him and used all my power to form something I hadn't used in years. A mouth.

This time, she didn't run, and I tried to speak with her, to ask her for help. No sound came out. I didn't know how to make sound. I shook in frustration. I tried again and again but created no sound. I focused on forming my lips, but I had no air to pass through them. I tried forming a tongue. I couldn't make a sound, but I could try to mouth the words.

Help me. Help me. Help me help me help me help me. I couldn't tell if I was shaping the words right. I grew desperate, and her friends ran to her. I don't know how I could tell, but at a certain point, I realized she had understood. A change in her energy told me she knew I wanted help, and she wanted to help me. After a moment, she approached me. She put her hand on me, and I finally felt the embrace of the hope she offered.

CHAPTER FOURTEEN

Escape and Tension

I want to build a bed of lavender and collapse on it. Helping this woman was like a balm for my soul after the day I've had, but it was also the most exhausting thing I've ever done. As a former grad student, that is not an insignificant thing to say. Alas, I have far too many things to worry about to sleep. Peter is still waiting in the wagon, probably terrified, the twins have probably been traumatized for life, and this woman, Sarafyna, likely needs the expertise of a few professions that don't exist yet.

More important than any of that, however, are these fucking woods. I want to burn them to the ground and salt the filthy earth, but after the fight I just finished with it, I know I can't. Not yet. It took everything Sarafyna and I had together to overcome its will, and that was with her body's full cooperation. We'd never be able to do the same for any victims like the ones I . . . encountered earlier. The undertaking of finding every single one of them, convincing them we can help them, and gambling that we actually can? It tears me apart from the inside out to admit, but it's far beyond me. For now. At the moment, I need to get Sarafyna and these kids out of here. If there is help to be had, I want to get it for all of them. I have at least one unpleasant conversation to have with everyone and I need to know they are safe. I can't tell how old Sarafyna is, but she needs protection just as much as the children do, if for different reasons. I feel a boiling rage as I watch her rubbing her hands against her face and head. Hers is a story I don't know, but it crushes me all the same.

In any case, we need to get out, and I think she can get us there. I feel sick; today has been one of the worst of my life, but I have been trying to sound relaxed and comfortable so she will feel the same. It's hardly enough to ask her to transport us out, however. *Hey, I know you just now got your human body back for the first time in who knows how long, and I know you are exhausted beyond belief, but I'm gonna need you to do me a favor real quick* doesn't sound quite right.

I do need to ask her somehow though. I open my mouth to speak to her, wanting to at least get properly acquainted before asking, but this worry resolves itself. Without warning, she jerks her head up and looks around. Her eyes are . . . swollen over, but it seems like she can still see somehow. I don't have a chance to ask her what the problem is before the forest shifts around us and we find ourselves just outside the tree line, about four hundred yards from what looks like a public road.

"Sssorryy," she apologizes, "it wwwasss goooiing t-to at-tack uuussss."

I look at her with a hint of disorientation for a moment, then I notice the trees shaking, and decide it's time we move on.

"Thank you, Sarafyna," I gently encourage, and she just nods absent-mindedly. She seems . . . out of it, like she isn't certain this is reality. It will probably be that way for a while, if it ever changes. "We need to get away from the woods now. Will you . . . come with us?" I offer, and she hesitates. Out of the corner of my eye, I see a horrified look assault Autumn's face and I wince. I really need to sit down and talk to the twins.

Sarafyna looks directly at me, despite her eyes being unusable. "M-mmooonnsssterrr," she answers. My stomach churns. I understand the fear. We can . . . probably fix her up better without the forest's interference. There was something weird about her, and I don't think she is only referring to her appearance. I glance at the twins, who are glaring at both of us, and I remember the priest she devoured.

"No," I answer, "not from what I've seen. You're no monster. I can feel what you are. It radiates from you like a fire in a winter storm. You are hurting. You are in more pain than anyone should ever have to bear. But you are strong enough to come back. I don't know what you had to do in there, but I know what I saw you do. Fighting back doesn't make you a monster. What happened to your body certainly doesn't make you a monster. I don't think you are a monster. You are safe with me," I promise.

She looks at me, then at the twins. I follow her gaze and see the horror in their eyes. "They are kids, Sarafyna," I say, "and they don't understand . . . what happened to you. I will talk to them. Can we get away from the forest first?"

Hesitantly, she nods, and I give the twins a meaningful look, promising I will explain myself when we are safe. They look more than a little skeptical, but they don't have anywhere else to go. A petty part of me wants to be irritated with them, but they are children. They were chased by what looked like an eldritch abomination and watched it eat a man. I can only ask so much of them.

"August, can you drive a wagon?" I ask, and he just stares at me like I asked him if he wanted tea in the middle of a battle. "I'm sorry. I really am. Today never should have happened to you two. But it did. We have weeks to work through it, and I promise I will keep you safe. Right now, I want to get as far away from these woods as we can, so can you drive a wagon?" I ask again, more insistently.

After a moment, he snaps out of it. "Y-yeah, I can do that." Well, that's something. We have a way to get to the capital. I nod and walk around to the back of the wagon.

"Peter, are you okay?" I ask, and realize he is hiding behind the corn again. "It's safe, you are safe," I assure him. For a moment, I only hear nervous shuffling, but he does emerge again, holding his hand against the side of the wagon to guide himself.

"Is it over?" he asks.

I nod before realizing I am an idiot.

"It's over," I answer aloud. "We are leaving the woods."

"The priests?" he responds, clear apprehension in his voice, his body tense.

I hesitate for a moment.

". . . Gone," I finally say. "It's just me and a few friends now." He visibly relaxes, slumps down onto the seat at the side of the wagon, and starts crying into his sleeves.

"It's all right," I say. "I've got you. May I hug you?" I want to comfort him, but suddenly wrapping my arms around him is more likely to cause panic than anything. He nods, almost eagerly, and I pull him into me. I allow him to cry for a minute, but I have to attend to other things. I gently release him and say, "We are headed to Visenar, the capital. Can you tell me where you are from?"

He shakes his head. "I don't know what it's called." I remember how long it was before I even knew the name of Satusmor. Most commoners don't travel much, and the city they are raised in is their whole world. "But it doesn't matter. I wasn't allowed to go home anyway," he adds bitterly. That's right, he was probably in a house of penance before here. Sarafyna too. If I brought him home, he would just end up back in the forest.

"Would you like to come with us?" I ask. He allows the question to hang in the air for a moment before answering with a question of his own.

"If I'm with you, will I still have to go to the temple?" I frown slightly at his fear and apprehension. He is too young to be this afraid of anything real, but he's right. Still, he seemed to respect the rules the priests gave him. The combination of obedience and fear of the same group paints a grim picture of the poor kid's past.

"No," I promise. "In fact, I'd really prefer you didn't." I can see relief and hope dancing across his face. After another moment, he shrugs.

"All right, I'll come with you," he acquiesces. I sigh in relief and start looking around the wagon. Aside from the corn, I find the priests' luggage.

"I'm glad to hear that, Peter," I respond as I dig through the priests' things. "We'll be headed off soon, so make yourself comfortable. And don't try to eat the corn." I doubt he would, as corn is pretty hard to eat raw, but you never know. I find what I'm looking for and pull out a more casual priest's robe. I pat Peter on the shoulder to reassure him, then climb out of the wagon.

Sarafyna is still naked. It's not exactly risqué with the current state of her body, but she still deserves the dignity of clothing. "Here," I say as I approach her. Her eyes are still covered, but she extends her hand to meet mine, accepting the robe. "I realize it's probably not exactly your style, but it's something." She immediately begins to pull the robe over her head. It is fortunately fairly baggy, so it doesn't get too tight anywhere.

"Th-thankss," she says. She seems to have an easier time speaking than a minute ago and I'm relieved she is getting the hang of it again. I'm fairly certain she has everything she needs to speak normally, which indicates it has been a very long time since she has tried.

"Come on," I invite, and lead her to the wagon while August familiarizes himself with the horses. "Peter, this is Sarafyna." She suddenly jerks her head toward the wagon as Peter stands.

"Pleased to meet you. I'm Peter," he says, bowing a little and only missing her direction by a little. Sarafyna is frozen, just staring toward the wagon without response. Peter looks concerned and asks me, "Um . . . is she there?"

I examine Sarafyna in concern.

"Is everything all right?" I query, and she shakes herself out of her apparent shock.

"It'ss okayy," she answers, even more clearly. "Nice to mmeeet yyouu, P-Peter." Interestingly, her nod also misses Peter by just a little. I understand she probably can't see right now, but she seems to know exactly where the rest of us are. Interesting. "Aare wee at the wagonn?" she asks, and it's my turn to jump.

"Right, sorry, let me help you," I say, then climb up into the wagon to help guide her into it. Autumn has approached and is glancing between me, Sarafyna, and Peter with a mixture of fear, concern, and disgust. As Sarafyna successfully climbs into the wagon, I wonder at the extent of her sight—and the nature of it. She jumped between trees with pinpoint precision when she had no eyes at all, but now needs help climbing into the wagon. "Come on up, Autumn." She gawks at my invitation.

"Look, Lillith, I don't know how—or why—you made that . . . thing look human, but I am not riding in a wagon with it. I can't believe you are letting it near that boy!" she practically snarls. I see Peter and Sarafyna start at the same time, and I groan.

"You have it backward. I didn't make her look human, Autumn," I say. I wanted to hide the nature of the forest from the twins as long as possible, or at least until they had time to process today's events, but the situation has changed. "The forest made her look like a monster. She has always been human," I explain.

"Wait, what? What are you talking about?" she protests. "It was chasing us, it killed that priest! It . . . ate him!" She looks horrified and I can tell she has more to say, but we need to get away from the woods.

"I get it, I understand. I understand why you are scared, and I promise I won't let anything happen to you, but it isn't safe here. Tonight, I will explain everything. About the forest, about Sarafyna, and about the priests. All right?" I have been asking her to trust me just a little longer all day, through horror after horror, and I can see that trust is close to breaking. The fear of the forest is stronger, however, and she reluctantly nods. "Thank you. If you like, you can ride up front with your brother."

She seems relieved and runs around to the front of the wagon. I climb into a spot where I can see the front seats from the back. August has also taken up his position in the driver's seat and I call up to him, "Are we ready to go?" He looks back toward me and reluctantly nods.

"Yeah, I can get us out of here," he agrees, and I nod back.

"Good, let's find a place to camp, and I will explain everything I can to you."

He simply nods, and we finally depart, driving away from the godforsaken forest. I glare back at it. I will return, and it will not survive my next visit. I idly pick up a piece of corn and push mana into it. I don't know what I was expecting, but it wasn't this. I have to bite my tongue and fight back vomit as I realize what it is I'm holding.

"D-don't eat that!" Sarafyna exclaims, and I jump. Apparently, she can see what I am holding as well. I have a feeling I know how she is seeing, but I'll have time to ask her about it as we drive. I'm impressed by how quickly she is regaining her ability to speak. She didn't have a throat an hour ago, but she spoke fairly clearly just now.

"You couldn't tie me down and force me to eat this," I assure her, and I mean it. I would sooner eat shit, or even a pear, a thought which makes me shudder. She seems to relax as I put the corn back. "The first thing we are doing when we stop is burning all this." She relaxes a great deal at that promise.

"Thank you," she says. "For everything." She seems entirely back to normal. This woman is adaptable as fuck.

"We didn't quite finish—we can try to completely heal you now, if you want," I offer, and she actually smiles a little.

"I'd like that," she warmly agrees. I hold my hand out. She gives me hers and I push my mana through her. There is no one fighting us now, and I am still partially empowered by the forest, if not to the same extent. I am able to fix a few more things. Her joints straighten out, which is a fascinating thing to watch. The growths all over her, however, do not. I can't seem to affect them at all. They resist my magic like the woman in the forest did. "I'm sorry," I say, "I don't think I can do any more than that."

She just smiles at me again. "I had a feeling," she says dismissively. "Don't worry. You have done . . . everything for me. I can handle the rest on my own . . . eventually." I know more about the human body than she does, but it seems she knows more about the cause of the growths. I just nod.

"Glad to hear you getting the hang of the new pipes," I say casually, and she gives me that same gentle, heartbreaking smile. I want to hear her story, but it would be better to hear it with everyone present. We ride in silence for what feels like a half hour or so. Eventually, August stops. It is time to set up camp and start a dangerous conversation with the twins.

CHAPTER FIFTEEN

Campfire Stories

We set up camp in silence. The priests, being a larger party, had more tents than we needed. We set up three. One for Autumn and me, one for August and Peter, and one for Sarafyna. That arrangement may change depending on how this evening goes, but three tents will do in any case. Since we are still near enough to the forest, and I have Sarafyna and Peter here with me, my mana is still quite powerful. It takes very little time to get the entire camp set up.

The twins avoid both Sarafyna and Peter for different reasons as we set up. They clearly fear Sarafyna, and I suspect they just don't interact with younger kids often. I find the priests' travel supplies, which, upon inspection, prove safe to eat. I make food for Peter first and get him settled in his tent. Instead of gathering firewood, I build seats in a circle with earth magic, then use light mana in the center and heat mana in a bubble around camp. I use a sound barrier to prevent Peter from hearing the upcoming conversation as well.

The twins wait for Sarafyna to choose a seat, then find their own on the opposite side. I sigh and sit in the remaining seat. We all sit in silence for a few moments, staring at each other, waiting for someone else to speak first. I am about to break the silence when the twins, overcome with anxiety, beat me to it.

"Who is the kid?" August bursts out.

Autumn immediately follows this up with, "What's wrong with his eyes?"

I open my mouth again to answer but they don't let up.

"What was up with the forest?" August adds.

"What were those monsters?" Autumn continues. They keep this up for a while, alternating questions in rapid succession. August, then Autumn, then August, and so forth.

"How did you use magic that powerful?"

"Why did you kill that woman before?"

"Did you have to kill the priests?"

"What do you mean that . . . thing has always been human?"

"How did we get out of the woods?"

"Why couldn't we before?"

I hold my arms up to indicate I need them to slow down. "Hold up! I'll answer all your questions, all right, just give me a chance to!"

The two, mouths still open, pause for a moment. They give each other that look I have grown familiar with, then nod together.

"All right," August agrees, "but I reserve the right to interrupt you with more questions."

I rub my temple but nod in assent. Having won a moment of quiet, I pause to think through what I want to say. They look at me expectantly and I take a deep breath.

"I think," I finally begin, "the best place to start is with Peter. The kid, as you said. More specifically, with your question about his eyes."

"Fine, what's wrong with them, why can't he see?" Autumn interjects, genuine curiosity in her voice. I turn to look at her and plan my question out before I speak.

"He's blind. By the looks of it, probably due to an infection. He was probably born with sight, but not everyone is. There are any number of reasons someone might be blind," I explain, and this time it's August's turn to interrupt.

"People aren't just . . . born without sight, Lillith! The Collector wouldn't deny someone sight from birth! I've never heard of anyone being 'blind' before!" he protests.

"Right." I nod along. "You haven't. You've never heard of anyone without sight, or hearing, or the ability to use their legs. Have you ever wondered why?" I ask.

"Because it just . . . doesn't happen. We are designed with eyes to see and ears to hear. Why would the Collector even give us legs that didn't work?" Autumn challenges.

"All right," I allow. I don't want to get sidetracked by religion, and it doesn't matter for this point. "So what about people like Peter? What about people who lose these abilities later? Have you ever heard of someone with just one arm or leg? What about someone who has lost their eyes? Even just one? Have you ever met anyone like that, ever?"

This question is met with silence and I can see the twins' brows furrow in unison. "I didn't think so. Of course you haven't. Almost no one has. It's not like you don't know what a sword is. You know that weapons, spells, and wars exist. You know not every injury is lethal, and not every injury can be perfectly healed. So why have you never seen someone who was disabled in any way?"

The twins look uncomfortable with this line of questioning and August responds, "You're right. We haven't. And I can't explain that, but what does it have to do with . . . everything?"

I nod at him. "It has . . . everything to do with today. Because those people don't just disappear. They are easy to hide, sure. No one wants to think about them. No one wants to help them. They are inconvenient and uncomfortable. But they don't just disappear." Then I begin to tell them about the houses of penance. The old, neglected homes for those who society has decided it doesn't want to worry about.

I tell them about Diana and Ozzy, victims of the disregard of the rich. I tell them about Abby and her mother, who were abused and owned by Baldwin. And I tell them about the priests. The divine magic that steals people's minds and tries to rule their bodies. I tell them what Diana said about the residents of the House of Penance and how the priests eventually collect them. I tell them how they feared being healed and being abandoned in the woods.

The twins dutifully listen, disbelief, disgust, and horror chasing each other across their faces. "So you are saying," Autumn answers, "the temple is taking these people, controlling their minds, and eventually abandoning them to be killed by the monsters?"

"They threaten them with that and leave them in the woods anyway?" August adds. My heart breaks. I didn't want to tell them what their mistake was. These were the terrified children who huddled behind me as I slaughtered monsters. They would never be the same after that, and knowing what had really happened? No child their age should be exposed to knowledge like that. But they have a right to know. Especially if I am going to ask them to keep my secrets, they have a right to know why.

"No," I answer, unable to keep the boiling venom from my voice. "I told you, didn't I? Priests' magic is used to change people. To rule their bodies. To own them and dement them in whatever way they want. Divine magic can be used to impose their will over other people's flesh. The temple doesn't abandon people to the monsters. The temple abandons them to *become* the monsters."

I watch confusion turn to horror, then anger as they process the claim. "No," August denies. "That's not true. That can't be true. You're wrong. You're fucking lying! How could you possibly know that!"

I shake my head as he speaks. "I'm sorry, August," I answer, "but it's the truth. I examined the bodies the same way I examined the flowers. Those were human beings, distorted by divine magic. They were victims of the temple, abandoned to . . . hell." In the corner of my eye, I notice Sarafyna start and turn her head to me, but I continue talking to the twins. "What do you think Peter was doing in that wagon? Why do you think the priests attacked us? Why do you think you lost time when speaking to them?"

"The Collector would never allow that, not from his own servants!" Autumn protests. I was waiting for this question. For much of this life, I wasn't sure whether the Collector was real or not. I am now inclined to believe he is. My leading hypothesis, in fact, is that we just met him. I don't have enough data to substantiate this, but I certainly can't dismiss it either. That is not the correct answer for this situation, however.

"One thing you'll find, with servants of gods," I start, strategically planning my response, "is you can't necessarily trust them to actually serve their god. At least, not with the dedication with which they serve themselves. That's not universal, of course. Emeric is a very kind priest and I doubt he has any idea about this. But when you prop up a man with the authority of the omnipotent . . . it becomes pretty easy for that man to use it to elevate himself instead. Just because you have faith in the Collector doesn't mean you have to trust priests."

This seems to placate Autumn a little. I'll ease into the idea that her god is a tyrant worthy of death, assuming she still speaks to me after tonight. August is about to ask another question, but Sarafyna speaks up for the first time. "May I say something?" she asks. The twins tense up and Autumn is obviously going to deny her until I see realization dawn. She put the pieces together about who Sarafyna is now.

"Please," I invite, and Sarafyna nods.

"What your friend is saying . . . well, I don't know about all of it, but I think it's true. I was never sent to a house of penance. But if you'll listen, I can tell you my story."

The inherent question goes unanswered for a moment, but the silence is broken by August.

"All right, I'd like to hear it," he says. That is an excellent sign. There is another brief moment of quiet as Sarafyna takes a deep breath.

"A long time ago," she begins, "I was just a girl who wanted to open a hat shop . . ." She goes into a story that sends directionless adrenaline through my body. My nails draw blood from my palms. I nearly vomit when she tells us she survived off the fruit of the forest. Her story is a hard one to listen to, and with each new pang of grief comes a fresh wave of fury. At a certain point, my control over my mana falters, and I see the twins' eyes widen. Beads of sweat form on their foreheads under the pressure of my mana, and I have to take deep breaths to regain enough control to suppress it.

The twins don't seem to enjoy the story any more than I do, and I can see it is getting through to them. August seems to realize first who it was that freed us from the Radiant Woods, and Autumn a moment later. On the occasions Sarafyna mentions her father, I can hear her voice waver. At their core, the twins are kind people. A flesh monster couldn't imitate the suppression of emotional agony like this, and I can see her humanity is growing harder to deny.

The end of her story is met with silence. I want to wrap my arms around her like a hurt child, but I can sense she wouldn't welcome being touched right now.

"I—I'm sorry," Autumn finally says, tears fighting against her words. "I shouldn't have called you a thing. I was just—"

"It's all right," Sarafyna cuts her off. "Anyone would say the same."

I remember her calling herself a monster earlier. There is more meaning in that than the twins realize, I think.

The conversation goes on for several more hours. I struggle to explain why the people in the woods attacked us and why I killed the last one. Sarafyna struggles to explain why she killed the priest. We support each other, and eventually, the twins seem to run out of questions. We sit in the heat of my magic in quiet for several minutes and I regret not starting a fire. This is warmer and cleaner, but a fire somehow would have provided more comfort.

"I . . . need to think," Autumn eventually says, and August nods. "If it's all the same, I'll share a tent with August tonight. We need to talk."

I understand and simply nod. The two shamble in exhaustion to an empty tent. Sarafyna and I sit in silence for a while longer.

I want to help her understand she isn't a monster, but I think I should let her sleep first. Eventually, she speaks up. "I think . . . we have a lot to talk about," she says.

"I think we do," I agree.

"But I haven't slept on a bedroll in . . . I don't know how long. There will be time," she says, and stands. I stand with her and guide her to the remaining empty tent. Before she enters, she turns to me. "Lillith, thank you," she whispers, then disappears inside.

I stand in the quiet camp for a while. Today was . . . eternal. I sit back down. Leaving the sound barrier up, I eventually open my mouth and scream. I have been pushing it down all day. The people I killed today, the things I learned . . . they are just . . . Too. Fucking. Much. So I scream. As loud as I can and with all the emotion I have been suppressing all day. I scream until I have no energy for it, and allow it to morph into quiet crying. I couldn't even name a specific thing I am crying about, but I need it.

There are times in life when you carry a cry around with you and it needs to find its way out. I don't want to carry this one any longer. I finish the cry for the people I killed in the woods. I cry for Sarafyna. I cry for Autumn and August. I cry for everything that happened in Satusmor. I finally let it out, and the tears do all they can to heal me. I spend at least an hour there, letting the light go and only maintaining the warmth.

Finally, I get up and move to the wagon. I throw the filthy corn out, surrounding it with walls of earth for now. I don't want to disturb any of the others, and I curl up to sleep in the back of the wagon.

CHAPTER SIXTEEN

Moving Forward

I wake up before anyone else. I kick myself for not arranging some kind of watch schedule last night, but I don't know if any of us could have really managed it anyway. Based on the moon, it doesn't look like I slept more than three hours. My entire body is sore in a way it rarely has been in this life, and my eyes bear the scars of a night of crying. I rub my neck and observe the camp. It remains quiet.

I decide to make breakfast, if there is any to be had. A quick search of the priests' belongings reveals some travel rations but nothing fresh, which makes sense. It is what it is, and I collect what I can use. There is at least enough for a few weeks of travel, but I expect we are a bit farther than that from the capital. We'll hunt if we run out. We certainly aren't eating that fucking corn.

In fact, before anything else, I open a hole in the earth I used to store the corn. I flood the makeshift storage container with heat mana. This close to the Radiant Woods, it takes little effort to incinerate the lot of it. I then bury the remains far under the earth and wash my hands of it. The priests must have partially been in the forest to collect it, which puzzles me now that I think of it.

If Peter was there to be abandoned, why collect the corn first? In Sarafyna's story, they just threw her from the wagon without even stopping. I don't want to think about what they wanted gray-matter-enhanced corn for, although I have a theory, but the wrinkle about Peter elevates the issue for me. I glance at his tent with narrowed, puffy eyes. I need to hear his story.

My worries are interrupted as Sarafyna emerges from her tent and approaches me.

"You're up early," I greet her. "I don't mind if you sleep longer. I have things handled here."

She gently shakes her head as she approaches me.

"I don't sleep much anymore. It hasn't been safe in a long time, and . . . my dreams aren't as kind as they once were." I can understand that better than most, although her nightmares are likely much worse than mine. I gather some of the priests' wood in a firepit and use heat mana to light it.

I use force mana to hover stale bread and hard cheese over the flames and allow them to toast together. "Fair enough," I answer. I continue preparing the food, adding some for her. If she has something to say, she will. She just sits next to me for a few moments before speaking again.

"You . . . have a unique perspective on the world," she says, and I smile. That's an understatement in this world. "I told you, yesterday, what I felt from you. Why I came and found you. I can still feel it, you know." I glance at her and raise an eyebrow. "I know you've helped me more than I'd ever hoped already . . ." She trails off and I understand.

"We're already even," I answer the unspoken concern. "Without you, I would never have left those woods."

"You wouldn't have been there in the first place without me," she challenges.

I scoff.

"I thought you said you could feel the emotion in my mana? We both know I was always going to end up there," I retort.

She tilts her head in acknowledgment, conceding the point. "That's what I want to talk about, actually," she says.

I suppose I can understand that. I don't answer her right away, however. Instead, I pull the bread covered with the now-melted cheese toward us and offer her a slice. She can't see it, but I see the moment she realizes what I am offering her.

She gratefully accepts and hesitantly takes a bite. She chews for several moments before continuing, and I see water running down her cheeks. I suppose this is probably the finest meal she has had in years. I let her enjoy it for a while, and she slowly eats the entire thing. After wiping her face with her sleeve, she speaks again. "I'm sorry," she says. "It's a small thing, but it's something I thought I had lost forever."

"You didn't lose it," I say with vitriol. "It was taken from you."

She nods and I see her fists clench.

"You're right. And that's what I want to ask you about. It was taken from me. Everything was," she says. I can hear anger rising in her voice as she speaks. "My father, my dreams. Even my visits to my mother's grave. And the people who took it all have names. They have homes . . ."

I feel her pained fury as she speaks, and I answer her question before she has to ask it.

"Not for long," I say. I'll help her. I was never going to let people like that continue to draw breath anyway, and they are a major obstacle to my own plans. She and I talk for the next few hours. She describes the men at her confession to me and answers some questions I have about the woods. Some of her answers alter my strategy a great deal. Eventually, she and I make a few plans together, and as the sun rises, I see a genuine smile from her. I can't offer her complete safety and security, but I can offer her justice.

The light wakes the twins first, and they emerge from their tent as well. They awkwardly approach the fire and sit down with us. "Autumn and I talked about everything last night," August says, "and I'll be honest. We are scared. We don't understand everything, and we just . . . don't know how to make sense of it . . ."

Autumn cuts in as he trails off.

"But we at least understand why you did what you did in there. We know we are safe with you . . . both of you," she admits. "And we want you to know you can trust us. We need more time to think everything through, but we won't do or say anything to hurt either of you."

I give them a half smile. They could be lying because they are afraid of me, but I don't think they are. They really are good kids.

"Thanks," I respond, "that means a lot to me. So you'll keep traveling with us?"

They both nod and I release some tension I have been carrying. That will make things a lot easier. Peter emerges as well at this point and comes to join us. I begin preparing food for all of them and they eat breakfast in silence. Peter remains too nervous to speak, and I don't blame him. I wonder if Sarafyna and I can heal his sight. I'll have to ask her later. If he lets us anyway. I'm also not certain Sarafyna has ever tested her abilities on someone else's body—at least, to do anything but dissolve it.

"August, we need to head east," I finally say, breaking the silence. He looks at me with confusion.

"Visenar is north," he says. "We still have to go to the academy, Lillith."

"I know," I answer, shaking my head. "Look around you. We are nowhere near where we entered the woods. I spoke to Sarafyna this morning, and we came out in the wrong spot. We have to go east to get to Visenar." He gives me an odd look at this explanation, but eventually just sighs deeply and accepts it.

We pack up the camp and load everything in the newly empty wagon. We don't have many things of our own, so it's easy to do. I'd kill for a bath, but there is no water near us excepting August's ice mana, and expending enough for a full bath would exhaust him. With nothing more to do, we find ourselves on the road fairly quickly. Autumn has elected to ride up front with August again, and the rest of us sit in the back.

I decide to spend the ride practicing magic. I really want to master my radar spell, and I could use a few more aspects. I have been having trouble aspecting mana recently. It feels like I've hit some kind of bottleneck, and new aspects slip through my fingers like oil. I focus for a long time. I want to add water mana to my tool kit, but I just can't seem to manage it. I don't understand the difficulty, as my understanding of the concept should be more than thorough enough.

This goes on for hours, and I feel my mana growing weak as our distance from the woods grows. I am becoming frustrated when I hear Sarafyna speak.

"Peter, would you like us to heal your eyes?" she asks.

I'm glad to hear she was thinking the same thing I was, and I look toward Peter to see his response.

"Y-you can do that?" he asks, awe in his voice.

"I think so," I answer, "if you are okay with it."

"B-but the priests said only they could . . . and you got rid of the magic food . . ." he splutters, and I furrow my brow.

"I have the same power the priests do," Sarafyna says encouragingly, but I cut in with a question.

"The magic food? You mean the corn? The stuff you were hiding behind before?" He tilts his head, then decides to answer my interrogation first.

"Yes, ma'am. They said they needed it to make me better. It's part of my—" he starts before cutting himself off and slapping his hand over his mouth.

"Peter, do you know how you went blind?" I ask. "Do you remember getting sick, or hurt in any way, before it happened?"

He looks concerned and doesn't answer. Sarafyna seems to have picked up the urgency in my tone and remains quiet as well. I decide to ask another question. "Did you ever live with a bunch of other people who were hurt or injured in some way? Maybe older people or anyone who had similar problems to yours?"

He tilts his head again before shaking it. "No . . . I've never been anywhere like that. We were all just blind . . ." He trails off. That doesn't sound like a house of penance. There is something more going on that I need to understand.

I've just opened my mouth to ask another question when I am bombarded by mana. The wagon suddenly jerks as well. We aren't under attack; it's not that kind of mana. No, we are all perfectly safe. It's no wonder the wagon jerked—this must have taken August by surprise as well. This amount of mana isn't at my level, but it is far more than the twins have. The wagon comes to a stop, and after a moment, the twins poke their heads into the back of the wagon and gape.

I don't blame them. I'm slack-jawed myself. Everyone but Peter stares at Sarafyna. I knew she was a powerful divine mage, but this isn't divine mana. I have never been able to perceive divine mana if it wasn't directly interacting with me. This is regular magic, pouring off Sarafyna in waves. She is a mage surpassing a lot of nobles in power.

CHAPTER SEVENTEEN

The Road to Visenar

D o you mind suppressing that!?" August exclaims, and Autumn's face mirrors the question. I have an entirely different question, but I'd like to ask it in private. The division between divine magic and regular mana is a little fuzzier for the twins, but as far as I know, the two are entirely unrelated. They can interact, but they are different types of energy. Based on her story she shouldn't have mana at all.

I decide not to correct him, however, and answer for her, "Sorry, August, I'll take care of things back here. For now, try to focus on the road." As I speak, I use my mana to contain hers and protect August from the pressure. He relaxes a little and turns back around.

"You should really warn us before doing shit like that, you scared me halfway to the third plane!" he complains. Autumn looks at us for a moment longer with a suspicious look before turning around. I'll explain it to them later, but I'd like to speak to Sarafyna privately first. I surround us with a sound barrier and she furrows her brow.

"What's the matter? What's that for?" she asks, and partially answers my first question before I can ask it. She can see the sound barrier. She can't see, but she can see my mana. Even I can't see mana with my eyes closed. Actually, she saw my mana from a distance before she had eyes at all—that much is obvious in hindsight. I review our interactions in my brain and pick out a few things.

She can't see Peter. She could see the trees of the forest. She can see me and the twins. She noticed when I was holding the corn, which didn't have any mana in it that I noticed. "Did you know you are a mage?" I ask, beginning my gentle interrogation. As far as I can tell, she seems confused. She answers to the best of her ability, but it becomes clear she doesn't have a thorough understanding of mana or divine magic. She understands people have different energy, but not the specifics.

This leads to another long conversation about the Radiant Woods, and I form a few more hypotheses about them. The most significant thing I learn is that Sarafyna could see the other victims while she was in the forest. First, this means the forest suppresses and hides the mana of its victims. This explains why her mana suddenly became apparent when we got far enough away. It also means she can see suppressed mana.

Finally, it isn't just her; everyone who's abandoned there becomes a mage. I suppose she would not have sensed anyone who did not become a mage, but she saw enough I can assume the forest is giving them mana somehow. Few commoners have magic, and there is no way enough nobles were banished to the woods to account for the number of magical "monsters" there. None of them cast any spells against me, but of course, having mana doesn't mean being able to use it. Like how possession of a human mind doesn't indicate the ability to code, read, or practice any other learned skill. That has some grim implications, but it could be useful in the long run. I have to assume the forest gives the victims mana and hides it, or at least, hid it while I was there.

"Well, that's . . . something," I finally say. "For now, I'll have to teach you to suppress your mana. And I'd like to do a few experiments. I've been assuming you had the same divine mana as priests, but there are some discrepancies. They seem unable to detect divine mana, but you can. They can't detect suppressed mana either, and yet again, you can. Is this a question of power? Does divine magic have aspects like mana does? Is it because of your mana? We don't know enough about divine mana to guess, and the only priest I really know doesn't have it. Is that all right with you?"

She nods. "I don't mind. I don't have much left to work toward, so any step toward what I do have, I'll take." I wince. I should probably try to think of a way to help her aside from getting justice. That's not the kind of thing anyone should be saying so blatantly. She needs something else to care about. That's when our earlier conversation pops back into my head and I drop the sound barrier.

"Sorry about that, Peter," I apologize, "we had something important to talk about. Did you have any time to think about our offer?" Sarafyna seems to remember at the same time, and I see her body language brighten a little.

"It's all right, ma'am," he answers, hope in his voice. "If she can do what the priests can, I think it should be okay if she helps . . . I, uh . . . would like to try, if . . . you're still offering . . ."

I grin broadly. With his fear of the priests and his insistence on obeying their previous orders, I worried he would turn us down. For once, someone is just going to let us help them. I look at Sarafyna and she nods. I put my hand on Peter and Sarafyna doesn't move.

I push my mana into him and feel Sarafyna's intent alongside mine. She imposes the basic concept of healthy eyes, and his body tries to comply, slowly. For my part, I try to address the cause, which seems to be bacterial keratitis or something similar. I can't find evidence of an injury that could have caused it, but I can help heal it. I don't have the same level of power I had in the woods and I grow weaker with every moment, but weaker isn't weak. It's slow, but with effort, I can feel the combination of our abilities healing him.

It seems we lack the ability we had in the woods, however. Sarafyna seems to struggle more with changing other people than with herself and I am just less powerful. I notice sweat pouring down her face and withdraw my hand. "That's all we can do today, I think. How do you feel, Peter?" I inquire.

He looks directly at me and squints his eyes.

"I can . . . I can see something!" he blurts, and I grin. I catch a slight upward flick on Sarafyna's lips as well, but it doesn't reach a full smile before Peter follows up with "It's just sort of blurry colors, but I can see a little again!" With that news, her mouth turns back down.

"I'm sorry. I wasn't strong enough . . . I wanted to do more—"

I cut her off.

"That's normal. I had an . . . ex with divine mana once. He couldn't make significant changes in a single day. We have time; we'll do more," I promise, and both of them seem encouraged.

"I can't wait . . ." Peter says under his breath, and I affectionately rub his back.

"You courted someone with divine mana? Was he a priest?" Sarafyna asks skeptically. "How did that go?"

"He had too much of a temper. One day he completely lost his head and I just dropped him," I quip.

"That makes sense. I certainly wouldn't trust a priest with anger issues." She scowls. That's the understatement of the century. "Should have killed him . . ." she says under her breath.

"I'll tell you the whole story later, when we have a little more privacy," I promise, and she tilts her head at the chuckle in my voice. I have a feeling she'll appreciate the unabridged version.

Sarafyna's mana is the last major shock for the next couple of weeks. We slide into a bit of a routine. Neither I nor Sara sleep long, and we often discuss plans while the others sleep. It is on one of these nights that I discover she does in fact appreciate the entire story of my engagement to Baldwin. I even tell her about my grief aspect. She can kind of discern it anyway, and even if I couldn't trust her, she would have more to lose from coming forward than I would.

In the mornings, I help her practice suppressing mana. This takes a lot of work, but she makes progress every day. She is the fastest student I have had so far; it's not long before she can successfully hide it without my help. We also explain the difference between divine magic and mana to the twins. This is a bit of a risk, as they learn more about Sara, but less of a risk than them realizing it at the academy after we hide it from them.

After that, we help Peter recover his sight. He looks forward to this every day and sits down, practically shaking with excitement, while we are still practicing mana suppression. By the end of two weeks, he can see as well as the twins can. "I can see the grass!" he exclaims as we finally get his vision back to normal. He runs away from my hand and hugs Sarafyna. She is the one with "priest magic" and gets most of the credit for his healing.

He doesn't shy away from her appearance at all, which is a pleasant surprise. She is making progress on this herself, but it is slow going and not perfect. On the wagon, we practice on our own. Sarafyna has been tackling the tumors all over her body. She understands something about them I don't and prefers to work on them alone. Her right arm is the first area she heals. It now lacks the large tumors, although her skin strongly resembles a bad burn scar. I suspect this is true farther onto her torso as well. In a month or two, her entire body will still look disfigured, but in a more manageable way.

I wonder why she didn't heal the ones holding her eyes shut first, but I allow her to keep her reasons to herself. In my case, I give up on aspecting a new type of mana. I've hit a wall and I figure the academy will help me past it. Instead, I continue to alter my own body. My poison blood is useful with enough preparation, but I'd like a similar option for unexpected combat. I don't want to be caught unaware like Baldwin. As such, I have been growing retractable fangs.

It's slow, and extremely uncomfortable, but in a few months, I will be poisonous *and* venomous. If I ever lose magic, I will still be deadly. This takes focus and time but isn't too difficult. In the meantime, I also practice my radar spell. It has two problems: my light mana is visible to mages unless there is a lot of grief in the area, and when it is invisible, I can't see the returning light signals.

The first problem I eventually solve with a trick that should have been obvious. My imagery has been wrong. Instead of sending out light mana in all directions, I create a point light. The mana is in a single spot and radiates light in all directions. I consider converting the light into visible light as it reaches me, but I don't care for the results. I can't use it passively this way. Other people will see the light, but I won't if I'm not facing that direction. What I need is three-hundred-sixty-degree feedback at all times. I don't quite master it, but I get closer.

The twins start to warm up a little over time as well. August even begins to banter with me a little again. I'm certain Autumn has something she wants to say, but she seems to want to say it while we are alone and is biding her time. I don't push; I'm just glad they are slowly returning to their lively selves. At the end of two weeks, August calls back into the wagon.

"You were right, Lillith! I see it! I can see the capital!"

CHAPTER EIGHTEEN

Goodbyes and Greetings

What do you mean? Where exactly is she going to go?" August asks, completely taken aback. Sara and I spoke about this a couple of weeks ago, but it hasn't occurred to the twins.

"Think about it, August," I answer. "She has no papers and no one to vouch for her but us. She wasn't with us when we left Satusmor and . . . look at her. We bring her through that gate with us, and best case she goes straight to a house of penance."

He looks uncomfortable, and Autumn tags in.

"Even so, we can't just . . . leave her out here!" she protests. I'm a little surprised by their objections but perhaps I shouldn't be. They haven't spoken to Sara much over the journey, and when we first met, they were overtly hostile to her. Once they understood she was human, however, they changed the way they interacted with her completely. They aren't friends, but they have compassion for her.

As such, the idea of leaving her outside the city is, of course, horrifying to them.

"It's all right," Sara chimes in. "You aren't 'leaving me out here.' I am parting ways for now, that's all." I'm often surprised by how even-tempered she usually is. When she speaks of the temple and the woods, I can taste the venom in the air. The rest of the time she is remarkably mild. Her tone and willingness aside, however, the twins are not to be deterred.

"That's the same thing, and we can just sneak you in!" August insists.

I awkwardly rub the back of my neck. He's probably right—we could—but there would be no point. For everything to work right, she kind of needs to stay outside the city for a while. I can't really tell them that though. They were pretty shaken by the concept of penance houses and what happens to people in the woods, and I think I can trust them not to talk about what happened. There is, however, a decent gap between asking them to keep that a secret and *these are our plans for high treason against the crown; pay them no mind.*

"I'm not ready to go back yet. Not to this city. It's no longer my home," Sarafyna says. "I'm not . . . whole yet. I need time, that's all. Can you give me time?"

The twins' faces soften at that. Masterful move, Sarafyna. Or, you know, completely sincere move. I hadn't realized she was actually from Visenar as she is implying. Of course she would have a hard time in the city right now, especially in her current state. It's also true that she needs the privacy of the wilderness for a while, but this is likely another reason she suggested this. I offered to let her stay with my family, but this is a better plan anyway.

"Are you sure?" Autumn verifies, and Sara nods. The twins give each other one of their *consultation* looks. "All right, if this is what you want," Autumn reluctantly agrees. "I'm sorry we couldn't know each other better, and . . ." She trails off.

"Thank you for getting us out of the woods," August finishes, and Autumn nods enthusiastically.

Sara gives them a gentle smile. "You are the ones who brought me out of the woods. I'll be grateful to you for the rest of my life," she responds quietly.

The twins and I are about to respond when Peter speaks up, his wide, fully functional eyes filling with water.

"Can I come with you?" he pleads, and Sara gives him a wide grin. The two have gotten closer than any of us have on this trip. Peter sees in her a savior and a new family. Sara sees in him a past she could have had, and an opportunity to save someone from becoming her. I'm not surprised he wants to go with her. Honestly, it's not a terrible idea. He is, of course, welcome to stay with my family as well, but this could be better. He doesn't seem to have a family or life to return to, and she will take care of him. He is, of course, welcome to stay with my family as well, but this could be better.

Sarafyna might be all right on her own, but she needs something other than revenge to live for and if she doesn't look after Peter, I'll have to sneak him in. I think she will probably put more into caring for and raising him than a lot of other people in the city would.

Autumn interjects to contradict my acceptance. "Absolutely not, I am not leaving a child in the wilderness. Not a chance," she insists. Well, that is a fair enough reaction.

"Why not? Sara will take care of me, right, Sara?" he asks, looking to his friend for confirmation.

"I will, if that's what you want," she promises. I can tell she wants him to go with her and my heart warms.

"You can't even see him!" August argues.

That's not going to be the case for long, however, and I'm not terribly worried about it. He could, in fact, be her eyes in the meantime. I decide this argument isn't going to go anywhere helpful and elect to sidestep the whole thing.

"Now, come with us, Peter. It will be safer for you with us," I say, apparently agreeing with the twins. He looks directly at me, betrayal flooding his face, before he perks up.

"Well, okay," he agrees, not arguing anymore. The kid could use some practice lying. Fortunately, the noble twins aren't conditioned to expect commoner children to lie or disobey, and they were behind me when I winked at him.

"We will have to hide him, of course," I say. "Gonna be hard to explain where we got a kid in priest robes." The twins seem satisfied and Autumn mutters something about crazy people as Peter settles down. I go to say my goodbye to Sara quietly. We hug for a long moment. "Don't worry," I whisper a promise to her. "If he's here, I'll find him."

She gives me a hopeful squeeze. "Thank you, Lillith, for everything," she responds before withdrawing from the hug. "Goodbye, everyone, thanks again!" she calls out, waving goodbye to the group. Peter, very suspiciously, does not say goodbye in return. The twins don't seem to notice though.

"I'll get Peter hidden, then I'll join you two up front," I say as we start to get loaded up on the wagon again. August cocks an eyebrow at me.

"Why?" he asks. "There is so much more room back there."

I shrug at him.

"They'll be more likely to search the back with people there," I lie. It's a terrible one that doesn't make sense, but the following truth buries it. "Besides, I want to catch up with you two. What, you don't want me around?" I ask, obviously feigning offense.

"Well, suit yourself. Not gonna be a lot of room up here with three people though . . ." he warns, and Autumn smacks his arm.

"What are you implying? We take up hardly any room at all—we are dainty ladies!" she challenges. This isn't my favorite type of joke, but I can only expect so much from them right now. I'm just glad they are joking with me at all. The twins devolve into the type of senseless argument only siblings understand, and I say a quiet goodbye to Peter.

"Take care of her," I say. "She needs you as much as you need her."

"I will," he says. "Promise to come visit us?"

I hold a pinky out to him. "Give me your pinky. Where this is from, it signifies the most sacred and unbreakable of promises." He gets a solemn look before accepting my pinky with his own. I shake it up and down, then give him a hug. "Goodbye, Peter."

"Goodbye, Lily," he responds. I send him off while the twins are distracted and climb onto the front seat of the wagon next to them.

"He's all set," I say, and we set off together.

It is still several hours before we reach the massive city, and we make friendly conversation the entire way. It's not like it was at the start of our journey, but we're moving forward. We mostly talk about what we'll do when we reach the city. Initially August is all about touring the academy and Autumn just wants a decent meal. Once I mention my first goal is a bath and a change of clothes, the twins immediately amend their plans to match mine.

We finally pull up to the gate and the guards stop us. The two of them eye up Autumn and me, and I roll my eyes. The closest one approaches and addresses August. "Papers, please," he intones. Riding in the front and in our ruined clothes, they likely can't tell we are nobles. They usually can't tell with me anyway, but the twins would normally be waved through with their expensive traveling clothes.

"We, uh, don't quite have them. We got waylaid on the way from Satusmor and lost our luggage," August explains sheepishly, and I face-palm. We are at the wrong gate to be coming directly from Satusmor. I should have coached him before we got here. The guard smirks, then gives Autumn and me a greedy look. We obviously look like criminals, and criminals are just future slaves. I shudder at the thought.

"You are coming in the west gate on your way from Satusmor?" He signals to his partner. "I don't think so. No papers, and more than a little suspicious. Let me guess, escaped slaves? Or did you steal the wagon from your employer? I'm going to have to ask you all to dismount the wagon and come with me."

"What, no, we are—"

The guard cuts him off.

"I'll question these two personally," he says. "Hold the boy here," he orders the other guard. His partner is about to protest, but I've had just about enough. No need to let this go any further.

"I'm Lillith of Endings," I announce, forming stones above my hand and floating them around in a circle. "Whatever you are thinking, I suggest you drop it. We aren't the criminals you are hoping we are." I mean, I am, actually—I'm about as criminal as someone can be in this world—but that's beside the point. I glare at him and his face pales.

"A-apologies, my lady," he says.

I roll my eyes. We are doing the same damn thing we were a second ago, but suddenly they've gone from getting their shackles ready and belts unbuckled to bowing their heads. Fuck monarchies, man.

"Shut up," I snarl, already tired of this man's presence. "Just let us through the fucking gate." Now is not the time for it, but this particular guard is going to get a second visit from me.

"Right, my apologies, my lady," he says, waving to his partner. They stand out of our way and a confused August drives us through the gate.

"Damn, Lillith, that was pretty harsh. He was just doing his job." Autumn seems to have picked up a more negative vibe than her brother and she doesn't join him in reprimanding me.

"He was trying to arrest us and make us slaves," I explain, fatigued.

"It would have been sorted out long before that happened. You are the duke's apprentice. We weren't in any danger," August argues.

"Right, and what if I wasn't? What if the same thing happened and we weren't mages or nobles? What then, August? Why exactly do you think he wanted to talk to Autumn and me first?" I lecture. It's not exactly his fault he doesn't understand what just happened, but the exchange soured my mood.

"I, uh . . . I don't know, maybe he wanted to make sure you were safe? You were traveling alone with an unknown man; he might have wanted to ask you about me where I couldn't hear," he proposes, and I groan. He didn't even notice the way the guard was undressing us with his eyes.

"Is that what you think it was, Autumn?" I ask.

She looks down and whispers, "No, I don't think so."

August's eyes widen and he halts the wagon.

"I'll kill him," he snarls, and whips his head in my direction. "Why were you so gentle with him?"

"Not right now, you won't. You could probably get away with it, but you'll have to kill a lot more than him first, and no one is going to check your family name before they try to kill you right back," I say. He's not wrong to want to challenge the creep now that he understands, but he should be a little more strategic than attacking him in front of the city gates.

"Come on, you could tear that guy apart in seconds!" he protests.

"You're right, I could." I nod. "But having the ability, even the right, to do that doesn't always mean it's safe." I'll take a closer look at Stary Gary later, but right now we need a place to rest. Besides, he is just one of many. "Just get us to a hotel for now. We'll talk about it there."

"A what?" August asks.

"An inn, sorry. Creep put me in a bad mood. I'm all out of sorts," I answer.

With that, August begrudgingly nods, and we enter the city proper. I have a lot to do, but I need some proper sleep first.

CHAPTER NINETEEN

Reunion and Pastries

The following day I find myself awkwardly waiting in the foyer of a massive mansion. I would have come here eventually, but I had planned to run a few other errands first.

My intent was to seek out my family as soon as I had gotten some sleep and a bath. That plan only went so far, however. Perhaps predictably, announcing the name *Lillith of Endings* and forcing my way through the gate did get reported up some chain of command. As such, my breakfast at the inn the next day was interrupted by a courier with a so-called "urgent package."

I was a bit surprised I was found so quickly, even with the scene at the gate. The inn I had chosen for myself, which the twins reluctantly followed me to, was less than prestigious. We could have thrown our names around to get a free room, but I steadfastly declined to do so. After a long argument about proper accommodations, followed by a longer argument about where Peter disappeared to, I spent some of the priests' meager travel expenses on a night's stay, a lackluster meal, and a bath for each of the two rooms.

The next morning, I was eating an omelet and bread with water and lamenting the lack of seasoning. Spices are far more expensive here than in modern America. At first, this didn't bother me much. In medieval England, spices were quite a luxury. Then I learned that in this world, they were actually much easier to find, particularly in this country. No one had to travel to India for them or deal with international trade. However, like soap, they were hoarded and turned into a luxury good anyway. You can't even grow them yourself or you'll be charged with some bullshit crime about disrupting the market or whatever.

What was I talking about again? Oh right, while I was stabbing at my food, fuming about simple goods being denied to commoners, I saw the courier come in and loudly announce they were looking for Lillith of Endings. I raised my hand and waved him over, getting a few sidelong glances from other guests at the inclusion of a family affiliation in my name. The urgency of the delivery was explained, and I gave the nervous courier a generous tip. The nosy twins examined the package with growing confusion as I pulled out a Danish and a note.

That's how I found myself here in this entryway, waiting to speak to Godfrey. The Danish was, to be fair, delicious. This didn't make me feel better though. Nobles often like to justify their standing in the world because they smell better, their food is better, their clothes are better, they are more successful, etcetera. This is all true . . . because they withhold simple goods and knowledge from commoners and intentionally create that gap. The sweet and welcome taste of the pastry after the bland breakfast only makes the contrast more obvious. That and coming to this luxurious estate from that run-down inn. It's not gonna stop me from eating it, mind you; my sweet tooth is starved. I am gonna make them easier for everyone to get though.

"Lillith, what in the three planes is going on? What are you doing here?" Godfrey, my supposed mentor and sponsor for the academy, exclaims as he appears through a doorway. I remain seated as he enters, much to the chagrin of a few passing servants. I am still astonished when I see his mana. The man is a force of nature.

I finish chewing and swallow, then look at him like he's some kind of idiot. "Eating a Danish," I quip. He rubs his temples.

"Glad to see you haven't changed," he groans. "You are weeks early, Lillith. You came in the wrong gate. You look like something chewed you up and spit you out. I'd like an explanation!"

I did look like that. I had tried to clean the clothes in the leftover bathwater last night, but I still only had one outfit since losing my luggage.

"Well, ya got me. By all accounts it doesn't make sense," I joke, shrugging.

He gives me an unamused stare. I miss when people understood my references. Although, he probably wouldn't think it was that funny right now anyway. I sigh and tell the best lie I discussed with the twins last night. "We were attacked by highwaymen," I explain. "I let the coachman get away with the luggage and fought them off, then tried to use magic to catch up but . . . we got lost."

"What kind of magic?" Godfrey asks, raising an eyebrow at me.

"Oh, you know, my force magic," I half lie. "I can use it to decrease our weight so we move faster and tire more slowly. That and the lack of luggage and I suppose we made better time than I thought."

He looks at me suspiciously for a long moment.

"And you got so badly lost, you got to the city from the wrong side? This is a big city, Lillith," he challenges, and I force a sheepish blush.

"I got a little distracted, okay? We wandered off the road a bit to find some fruit—you know how I feel about sweet food. We couldn't find the way back. But, hey, we made it, didn't we?"

"Highwaymen, you say?" he inquires, his eyes narrowed. "Highwaymen that attack obvious nobles with magic ability? You know, the king is pretty harsh on banditry, especially that which targets noble parties. He sends knights to hunt down anyone who tries it. There aren't a lot of people willing to risk it. In fact, I haven't heard of nobles being set upon on the roads in, well, decades now. Not by a group like that anyway."

I expected he might be suspicious of the story. "Well, you know the Satusmor government has been slacking off lately," I say, and he nods. I honestly don't know if he knows that; it's possible it's beneath his notice. On the other hand, he's right. Commoners don't attack nobles. They don't even attack the kids, because they don't understand magic, and as far as they know, any noble kid could kill them with a thought. It's one reason nobles don't bother with guards when walking around town. A silk shirt is as clear a deterrent as walking around with a shotgun and body armor. It's possible the trouble in Satusmor isn't below his notice.

On the other hand, no one in Satusmor has the magical ability to challenge nobles yet and the troubles are sort of . . . muddy there. It could just look like a general failure of governance to people as high up as Godfrey, who left the city well before anything got serious. It doesn't matter, however. I was going to have to mention our old home's struggles; if he had heard, it would seem weird if I didn't. Plus, it will lend legitimacy to the lie. "With enough money from the right people, I could see a few brave and unscrupulous souls taking up the profession. Especially if the people paying them were related to the former city lord . . . it would be easy to believe they wouldn't be punished. In any case, it was a moot point by the time I was done with them," I add, sending the blame in the safest direction I can think of.

"Ah," Godfrey responds, "I suppose the Tudor house does have some surviving members." This sounds like an acceptance, but I have trouble telling how convinced he is. It will have to do for now. I considered meeting up with Wallace, the coachman, on the way to the city, but I'd have had to deny civilization to the twins longer and I could use the extra time to arrange some things first. I'm not just in this city for my studies, after all. I will have to intercept him at some point and convince him not to talk about the woods, but I have time for that.

"And the wagon you drove in on?" Godfrey asks after a moment.

"Found it abandoned near the Radiant Woods," I answer. This is a weak part of the story, but I figure the temple will probably go looking for their priests at some point, and it could make sense, taking Sara's story into account. This way I've already explained it before they ask any questions. "Anyway, here I am," I say, holding up my hands, one still holding a half-eaten Danish, like I am presenting myself. Godfrey grunts and shakes his head, then sits down next to me. He pulls his own Danish from . . . somewhere . . . and begins eating with me.

"You are going to be a real headache, aren't you?" He sighs.

I grin.

"I've no idea what you mean. I'm a proper lady now, didn't you hear? An upstanding student of the academy," I retort, feigning offense. Yeah, though. I'm going to be a huge headache for him. I kind of like Godfrey, and I hope I can get him to come around, but . . . what's the church metaphor about camels and needles? The rich and powerful, especially the fucking royal, do not like giving up that wealth and power. When I help take it away, I can only hope we don't end up being more than a headache to each other.

"Right, and I'm sure you've grown well-mannered and respectful too. Well, it's no matter. I suppose we should get you registered at the academy. They aren't expecting you yet and won't have your dorm ready. At least you'll have more time to choose your classes. I'd like to discuss that with you—there are some classes I recommend you take."

"Dorm?" I ask. "Why wouldn't I just stay with my family?" I fully intended to live with my parents while here. A dorm room could be . . . inconvenient.

"Ah, well, that is a bit complicated. Your family's estate is pretty far from the academy. You'd have trouble with the commute, I fear."

I raise an eyebrow and respond with a serious tone. "Are they okay?"

"It's fine, they are fine," he assures me. "It's just . . . some of the women they insisted on bringing with them . . . draw a little attention in the noble quarter. They selected a humbler home in a less prestigious part of the city."

I relax. That makes sense. I approve, actually, and I'm glad to hear they are still with some of the women we freed from Baldwin.

"I see," I accept. "Well, fair enough. I'd like to see them tonight though. It has been a while." I don't mind visiting the academy first, but I do miss my family. I also, uh, need a couple of favors from men I trust. I need some fucking pants, armor, and a mask. Things women have a hard time buying.

"Now, as far as classes," Godfrey begins, "I know you'll want to enroll in some combat classes, but I don't recommend trying. They aren't designed to be coed and . . . well, you won't be welcome." I roll my eyes but I don't protest. I'm not actually interested in those classes. I'm attending to learn more about magical item enchantment. Yeah, combat classes would be helpful, but I just don't have the time.

My understanding is the academy is more like a university than a high school. I have to pick a major and gear my classes toward that. This seems to be more or less what Godfrey wants to explain, and I nod along. It's honestly more my element than anywhere else has been. I have no reason to push back much. Godfrey and I are both interested in me learning enough to make new discoveries rather than get really good at winning duels. I don't fight by the rules they'll teach anyway.

I also have the advantage that I don't need to actually graduate. Recognition from the university isn't going to matter much in a few years, I suspect. Godfrey is pleasantly surprised when he hears which classes I am most interested in. Conversely, I am disappointed by the number of prerequisites my classes need. They make sense, but come on, man. I'm pretty sure I know more complex math than any professor here.

It doesn't matter though. I won't have trouble with the first classes, at least. Once we are finished with our pastries and Godfrey is done convincing me to do what I already planned to do, we depart for the academy.

CHAPTER TWENTY

Facinley University

Godfrey and I arrive at the academy grounds in the finest carriage I have ever seen. Even here in the richest part of the city, we get a few glances as we step out. This is partially due to how ornate it is and partially due to the contrast with my current attire. Godfrey provided new clothes for me, but he also knows me. Alongside the overly expensive dress he offered, there was also a far plainer choice. It's probably not a mystery which I put on.

I have nothing against pretty dresses—I like them, actually—but they just aren't practical. I mean, I have nothing against their nature. Neither the wealth nor labor practices involved in their creation are likely to impress me. Either way, I favor clothes I can move and work in. As such, I leave an impression not unlike a farmer walking down the red carpet. Whatever, they can scratch their heads all they like. I am more interested in the campus itself.

It is massive and circled by a towering wall. We have to pass through a gate just to get inside, and it's guarded by actual knights, with mana. I hope I have longer between classes than I often had as an undergrad or I am going to exhaust myself running between them well before I learn anything. It does remind me of a college campus in a weird way. There are a number of buildings forming a bustling community. Signposts direct students and visitors to various named buildings divided by school of study. This much is extremely familiar to me; I thrive in this shit.

Where it differs, however, is scale. The size of the campus and buildings baffles me. The cost of both baffles me even further. Were it not for the ever-present air of stress and anxiety, I would wonder if this was an extension of the royal palace. The architecture is grand to an excessive degree. The huge, ornate buildings aren't what really shock me so much as the garden. I say *garden*, but I mean the whole damn campus. An idyllic and well-tended garden connects every single building and lines every exquisitely decorated walkway.

I would expect a garden a fraction of this size to be a crown jewel of a royal palace. It is maintained with magic, which I can tell from the mana radiating off each plant but also because it would be impossible otherwise. I now understand why Godfrey bothered to offer me the pricier dress. He knew I wouldn't choose it, but it was actually on the simple side for a setting like this. Christ, how many people could we help just with the money and magic that goes into maintaining this campus?

Give us a damn quad with some trees and distribute food and healing instead, you jackasses. I sigh to myself as I walk with Godfrey between bright flowers and perfectly manicured hedges. For a second, I think people are staring at my simple dress, but their looks are more worried than judgmental. Then I remember the immensely important and powerful mage escorting me. Right, I always forget he's not the simple bookseller I met years ago. I suppose that's why Baldwin had him there. The rich know no better way to put someone in their place than to force them into a customer service job.

I ignore the curious looks, and most students seem to lose interest after a moment anyway. We are an oddity together, but they all have other worries. I was actually expecting more . . . well, magic. There are students in secluded corners practicing small spells, but for the most part, people are just . . . hurrying or socializing. A few are taking notes in what must be incredibly expensive notebooks. All in all, it feels like a disgustingly pretty university.

Finally, we arrive at what must be an administration building, and I scoff as Godfrey turns what look like ivory doorknobs. We navigate a confusing labyrinth of halls and finally arrive at . . . an office, I think? The extravagant fountains and water-fall wall combined make it feel a bit more like a luxury hotel room. I'm clued into its true nature by the mahogany desk and the smartly dressed, redheaded woman sitting behind it. As we enter, she stands and politely tilts her head to Godfrey.

"Welcome, Lord Godfrey, we weren't expecting you so soon. I apologize for the state of my office!" she says. I look around, confused. The room is spotless. I decide to shrug it off. I suppose she is probably hedging; if there's a complaint, she's already answered it.

"Please, sit down, Lady Cateline," Godfrey answers, waving off the apology. "I believe I mentioned I have an apprentice. I am here to get her properly enrolled. I'd like to introduce Lillith of Endings. Lillith, this is Cateline of Roul, the headmistress."

Cateline gives me an appraising look and my eyebrows climb my forehead. I suppose the office should have clued me in, but I am surprised to see a woman with so much authority in an official capacity. I've seen women running shops and the like, but it's always a shop that belongs to a man.

Noble women do get more opportunities, but headmistress? I wouldn't have guessed that.

"I'm not familiar with the house of Endings. Where do they hail from?" she asks once she is done eyeing me.

"Satusmor. Hers is a new house, established not more than a year or so ago," Godfrey explains, and Cateline nods. "May I leave her with you for now? I have a few other things to attend to."

Damn, he's leaving me here? How am I supposed to find my family's house after this? I don't know where shit is in this city, man. I narrow my eyes at him but he doesn't notice.

"Of course, my lord. She is in good hands. I will personally get her registered," Cateline assures him.

"That's very kind of you, thank you very much. Lillith, I'll speak to you again after you are settled in here," he says, waving to me before unceremoniously leaving. *All right, man, watch me get a Danish with pears in it next time you ask. That'll teach you.*

"Another one, huh?" Cateline asks as her blue eyes scan me again. "I hope you are better behaved than the other common-born student this year," she scoffs.

Godfrey, come back—I think you accidentally took this lady's manners with you on your way out.

"I'll do my best to exemplify more admirable behavior," I promise, referring to exactly the type of behavior she wants me to avoid.

"See to it that you do, child. Now, have you considered which classes you'd like to take in your first year? Did Lord Godfrey advise you on what your options are?" she inquires.

I nod. "I don't suppose you have any kind of advanced placement tests?"

"We do not," she says with an unamused look. "I'm certain Lord Godfrey provided you with some very fine tutors, but so do many other students on this campus. I assure you; you are not as far ahead as you think, if at all." I suspect she is wrong, but oh well. Maybe I am somehow wrong. It wouldn't be that shocking if advanced math was simply not accessible to my usual crowd. The architecture in this city certainly suggests that.

"Very well. Yes, I do have an idea of what classes I'd like to enroll in," I reply.

She pulls out a few papers to help me schedule my classes. She is fairly short and impatient with me, but I suppose this probably isn't usually her job. Still, I'm not the one who told her to do it. Nevertheless, we do get a schedule planned out. When we are done, I am enrolled in Introductory Mathematics, Basic Mana Aspecting, Potestian Government, The Collector and the Aggregation, and The Science of Mana.

Two of these teach necessary knowledge to effectively combat the government and temple, and the rest are requisite classes for what I actually want to learn. Unlike at an Earth university, there is no graduate or undergraduate program, and there is no such thing as a major. This means I can pretty much take whatever classes I want, although students' parents often more than influence what they enroll in.

The schedule isn't bad and I should have plenty of time for . . . extracurriculars. Especially if they don't keep too close an eye on attendance.

Cateline looks over the schedule approvingly. "Sensible choices. You are already less of a headache than the other one," she says, rolling her eyes. Every time she mentions this other commoner student, I want to meet them more. The main session of classes won't start for a few weeks, however. Maybe I'll meet them then. "Come along, I'll show you to your dorm room," she adds, and leaves the room, not checking to see if I am following.

I briefly entertain the thought of just ignoring her—something about her just irks me—but there would be little point in that. I follow her out of the room and across the campus to what looks like a series of mansions positioned against the exterior wall. She leads me into one of them and explains, "This is where you will be staying. Each unit houses four students and a small staff. Your room will be on the second floor."

Right. Of course the dorms are actual, fully staffed mansions. Why wouldn't they be? She leads me past a room with ELEONOR OF RENATUS engraved on an ornate placard, up the stairs, and to a similar room. This one, however, is labeled LILLITH OF ENDINGS. As we enter together, I'm immediately aware that it is nicer than any I've ever slept in. The closest I've ever seen was the room I killed the Lord of Satusmor in. A concerning thought occurs to me as I recall the knights guarding the campus. "Does the gate to campus close at night?" I ask, and she eyes me suspiciously.

"They do" is her curt response. "And a lady of your age should have no need to pass through them too frequently. Anything you need can be found on campus. If you leave too late, you will be locked out for the night. You have been warned."

Well, goodbye giant room. You were too big for me anyway. Getting locked on campus at night simply isn't an option. I suppose I could try throwing myself over the walls, but . . . renting a room seems easier.

"And I am only going to warn you once, so pay attention," she preemptively reprimands. "You are NOT to bring any boys back to your room. We do not stand for behavior like that on campus grounds, and disciplinary action will be swift and harsh."

"All right, thanks for the clarification," I say, and she gives me a sharp nod. There was never any danger of me bringing one of the children at this school to my room to do anything even slightly suggestive. They are literal children, and bringing any kind of boy back is even less likely. That's one thing she legitimately doesn't need to worry about.

"I'll leave you here to get settled in," she says. "Try to get your things moved in today unless you have other appointments with Lord Godfrey. And . . . please wear something more appropriate when you attend classes." She gives me a disapproving once-over with her final words, and I look down at my modest dress and bodice.

"Oh, I'm sorry, is this too tantalizing?" I quip.

She just rolls her eyes again and mutters something about commoners under her breath. I get the feeling she would have slapped me or something had I not walked into her office with a duke. I was doing pretty well not being a smartass with her. Unfortunately, my persistent inability in either life to find clothes that aren't "inappropriate" to *someone* triggers something in me. Oh well.

Well, I'll store some stuff here, I suppose. For now, I desperately want to go see my family. I visit my private washroom, steal all the soap, and head out of the "dorm." I have no fucking clue where Godfrey went or how to find my family, but I see no sign of him coming back soon and I'm burning daylight here. With that, I depart the campus and head toward the nearest tavern. I figure Godfrey is probably still tracking me, and if he's not, I can learn the layout of the city.

I briefly lament not having Sarafyna to show me around the city, then sigh and begin my search.

CHAPTER TWENTY-ONE

Home Is Where the Heart Is

I get maybe twenty paces from the campus gate when I hear a voice behind me calling for Lady Lillith. I turn and see one of the knights guarding the gate running up to me. Apparently, they had been told to keep an eye out for me, but I had slipped past them for a moment anyway. "Yes?" I ask, and the man slows as he catches up to me.

"My apologies, Lady Lillith," the man huffs. I raise an eyebrow. I get he is wearing armor and all, but he is a damn knight and he barely ran at all. Perhaps the campus isn't quite as protected as it appears. Well, I can work with that. "Lord Godfrey asked me to give you this if you left before he returned," he explains, holding a note out to me.

I accept it and give him a curt nod before turning around and leaving him there. I open the note to read it as I walk away. *Lillith, in the likely event you leave before I return from my short errand, I have left a carriage with instructions to take you wherever you need to go . . . within reason,* the note starts, and I have mixed feelings. On one hand, that was thoughtful of him. On the other hand, I'm detecting some passive-aggressive snark in there and I don't appreciate the tone. On a more serious note, I don't like the idea of using one of Godfrey's servants. Worst-case scenario, the man is a literal slave. Best case, he is paid and treated well but I am still acting like a noble lady with a personal servant. Both ideas make my skin crawl to different degrees. *I've also left a small portion of your house stipend, although your family uses most of it. I suggest you buy materials for classes and a few new dresses. I understand you have an allergy to presenting yourself with dignity, but there is a dress code to attend to, I'm afraid. I have included the details below; you will simply have to suffer through it.*

I scowl. We *simply* have differing opinions on what is dignified. I do need to learn some of the things this campus teaches, however, so I will indeed have to suck it up.

I briefly deliberate between my desire to keep a low profile on campus and my desire not to spend ill-gotten tax money on something useless like an extravagant dress. That's when I remember I don't have to follow those rules. My mom has grown to be a competent seamstress; all I have to do is pick a rich asshole to steal high-quality materials from. I won't look as ritzy as some women, but I should meet the minimum to blend in.

I scan the rest of the note and it's similar advice until I reach this relevant portion: *The coachman has been given directions to your family's home, so he can take you there whenever you are ready.* That's what I'm talking about! I swear, that man put details about fancy dresses first just to screw with me. I follow the note's directions and find the coachman waiting for me. As I feel his mana radiating off him, my concerns wash away. The man is a moderately powerful mage.

I remember that for particularly prestigious nobles, the closest aides and servants are often themselves nobles. Positions such as that are actually competed for in a duke's house. I didn't think that extended to coachmen, but on reflection that's probably not this man's primary role. Based on the way he is looking down his nose at me, I suspect he actually outranks me. That's not hard to do in noble society, but it does make me feel less like I am taking advantage of someone. Besides, it's not like I never used a ride-sharing app in my last life. This city is massive and I have to live in the society as it is until I can change it. All in all, this is the best I can ask for.

I exchange brief words with the driver, who seems less than interested in polite conversation, and before I know it, I am on my way to see my family and a few friends they brought with them. I'm tired. Exhausted, really. After Satusmor and those fucking woods, and everything with the twins . . . I feel like I just crawled out of an industrial dryer filled with stones. Even the little sleep I get is plagued with nightmares. Now that I'm headed toward my loved ones, however, I finally feel genuine happiness. A few times on the ride I catch myself excitedly tapping my foot.

After what feels like forever, we finally pull up to what looks like a tavern and inn. As I exit the carriage, I raise an eyebrow at the coachman and he rolls his eyes at me. We are definitely in a poorer part of town, but we are also closer to the district's market than any residences. Nevertheless, the coachman parked off the road next to this building, so this must be where they are. I shrug it off and enter. I see Abby, the one-eyed woman who helped me kill Baldwin, eating with a group of women who were with us the same night.

I understand then and feel like an idiot. There are no grand estates in this part of the city, and these women would be in danger in a richer neighborhood. A tavern and inn has enough rooms for everyone, a huge kitchen and dining area, and exists in a more welcoming area in town. Honestly, it's a brilliant idea. This dirty common room full of people I trust and have been through hell with looks far more appealing than the luxurious room I just left on campus. Unfortunately, Godfrey is right. That ride took way too long to stay here while I'm attending school.

"Lillith, welcome!" Abby exclaims as she spots me. "Godfrey said you wouldn't be here for weeks!"

I smile at her. We don't actually know each other that well, but we still share a stronger-than-average connection through the history we do share. She is one of the only other people I know who doesn't add *Lord* to Godfrey's name. After Baldwin, I am not shocked her interest in respecting nobles has faded.

"Abby, how are you?" I ask, and she walks over to me. She is joined by several others, and I politely speak with them for several minutes. I really want to find my family, but I am actually glad to see the women we took in as well and I enjoy seeing them happy and comfortable. It's a bit weird that my brother Gilbert is technically their guardian now, but if someone had to be, I suppose he's not the worst choice. I don't think he would take advantage of them, but I will ask around anyway. He does have a . . . history with women, but it's one of a naive teenage boy more than anything. He seemed to legitimately change pretty much as soon as he was confronted with reality.

All in all, I don't completely trust him, but I think they are safer with him than most other options. This women-need-a-guardian bullshit isn't long for this world anyway, if I have my way. He is also my brother, and I love him, mistakes and all. I am excited to see him, Henry, and my mother. I have mixed feelings about seeing Edward. He has been, well, abusive for years now. He's also my brother though, and I still remember how close we were as children. I am nervous to see him, but our last conversations before parting were . . . well, not encouraging exactly, but not discouraging. I think there is hope for him in there.

My conversation with the group is interrupted as a familiar voice calls out across the tavern. "Lily, you're here!"

I look up and see the widest grin in history decorating Henry's face. Just being called Lily warms my heart. Peter had started to before we arrived, but the name sounds like music on the lips of long-absent friends. I return the grin. The brother I had put so much effort into saving from Baldwin is living a happy life with family, old and new. I break away from the group of women, who part for me, and run to hug Henry.

"You have no idea how good it is to see you!" I exclaim as he ruffles my hair before hugging me. From anyone else that would have felt condescending, but from him, it's just . . . my brother.

"You look like you came through the third plane to get here. I bet you have quite the story for us," he says, concern in his voice.

"You have no idea, man. I've been to hell and back. Where are the others? I'd like to tell everyone at once, if I can," I respond, looking around. I haven't spoken to any one of them since they left Satusmor. Communication is slow between cities for everyone but the richest nobles. I have seen Godfrey and Emeric use enchanted spheres that function as long-distance communication devices, but these are not common. They grow less common as distance increases, apparently, and only a few officials have spheres that are capable of city-to-city communication.

I learned this in Satusmor when I was expecting a much faster response to the Tudors' deaths. Apparently, with the city lord dead, there was a delay in communicating with the capital at all. Someone had to find Reynold Tudor's communication sphere before it could even be reported. Larger cities have more long-distance spheres, but they still have to communicate in relays to reach faraway cities. Travel is also uncommon among lower classes, and only very common for particularly important nobles. For this reason, even letters were out of the question.

The king travels almost constantly, but even he can only visit a few cities a year—and he was unlikely to help me send my family correspondence. I could have tried utilizing merchants, but they do nothing for free. As such, I hadn't heard so much as a peep from my family in a half a year, and they had heard nothing from me.

"Come on upstairs, everyone is in their rooms!" Henry says, and leads me upstairs, all the way to the third floor.

We stop at Gilbert's room first and Henry barges in without knocking, a chronic plague among my family members. Gilbert jumps and falls out of his chair. I gape at the room around him. There are papers with impressive drawings on them all over the room. I don't know how he afforded so much paper, but . . . he is getting pretty good. "You scared me half to dea—wait, Lillith??" Gilbert exclaims as he recovers from the shock.

"Hey, Gilbert," I say nonchalantly, "nice drawings."

His cheeks burn bright red, but he just climbs to his feet and comes to hug me.

"I missed you," he whispers to me as we hug.

"Missed you too, idiot," I respond. We move on and find my mom's room. She is sewing and talking to Edward as we walk in and responds to our presence without looking up.

"Hey, can you get some yellow thread? I'd like to embroider some yellow flowers on this. I think they'll match her hair," she requests, assuming it is either Henry or Gilbert who walked in.

"Sure, Mom," I respond. "Where is it?"

She stabs her finger with her needle before sharply looking up at me, her eyes wide. She looks good. I mean like really, really, good. I don't know that I've ever seen her look so alive. There is more color in her face and light in her eyes than ever. My pride-fueled dad absconding to who knows where and being replaced with all the women downstairs might be the best thing that ever happened to her. As she looks at me, tears well up in her eyes.

"Lily, you're okay!" she gushes, and I feel water running down my cheeks too. When did that happen? Before I know it, she is embracing me and somehow we are both crying.

"I missed you, Momma," I say quietly, and she holds me tighter. I don't know how long the embrace lasts, but it's healing. Oh god, is it healing. I feel like the last few months have taken years off my life, but nothing can cure a troubled soul like a loving mom's arms holding your head against her. When we do emerge, I notice our eyes aren't the only red ones in the room. Gilbert is strategically looking the other way and Henry is sniffling. Even Ed has complex emotions chasing each other across his face.

"L-Lillith," Ed stutters, "good to see you." That's honestly the kindest greeting I've gotten from him in years. It's not as surprising as I would have thought. They were moved here because Satusmor wasn't safe, but I was left behind and they had no way of knowing if I was okay. I'd have to give Godfrey a lecture about not keeping them updated. As far as they knew, I could have died by now. Even Ed has shown concern in the past when it looked like I had actually been hurt.

"It's good to see you too, Edward," I concede, and he awkwardly nods at me. I suppose that's the best I can expect. I promised Henry a story, but that's not what we need right now. Right now, we need to just be a family for a while. I decide to let the coachman know I'll be staying here tonight, and I spend the rest of the evening with my loved ones.

That night, I have a bland meal that tastes better than the finest food I've ever eaten while laughing with my family. I tell jokes that aren't that funny and my sides ache as I laugh at equally bad gags from my brothers. I go to sleep on a cheap bed and let myself feel like I am safe, like everything is all right, just for one fleeting night.

CHAPTER TWENTY-TWO

First Blood

Before the Radiant Woods, I'd never killed an innocent person. I've killed many people in more than one world, but always because that world would legitimately be a better place without them. In the Radiant Woods, I killed because those people didn't want to be a part of the world anymore. I didn't know that's why I was killing them, but . . . some part of me did. It felt off the entire time. The look in each person's eyes as they ran to me . . . flew to me . . . attacked me . . . Their claws were out, but in a way, I knew they were dull.

Or maybe that's wrong. It seems so clear as their faces visit me each night. I can see the agony and the plea on their faces with perfect clarity, but I don't know how real they are. Is that what I saw, or is that what I am painting on my memory of them? It doesn't matter. I killed them and they didn't deserve to die, even if they wanted to. I couldn't help them any other way. I know that. My mind understands that, but my heart doesn't believe it.

Part of me is convinced I could have saved them. Given them their lives, minds, and bodies back. Helped them seize their autonomy from . . . whatever that forest was, and healed them. That belief is what torments me every night. That part is what presents me with their faces in a parade of the tormented. A procession of my victims. I want to run away every night, and I do. But I just flee back to Satusmor. I run from the faces of the dead only to find more.

I am back home, during the time I spent alone. Without my brother, my mother, or Godfrey. When I had no one I could really trust. I can see the laughing face of Horrus, captain of the Satusmor city guard. I see the bodies he climbed over to find the golden ticket he thought they were hiding. The ticket I created. I remember choking the life out of Captain Horrus for what he did, and . . . I remember enjoying it. Not the act of killing itself, but the revenge. In my dream, I am outside my body, watching the smile on my face as he gasps for breath.

I take a sharp breath through my nose as my eyes fly open. My heart remains still, but adrenaline flows through my veins. A quick glance around the room and the minimal light leaking through the curtains reveals I have only been asleep for maybe three hours. That's the most I ever sleep, and the same dream that always wakes me up. It's a lie. I didn't smile as I killed that creep. Killing him was entirely necessary. I don't know why my dreams torment me with that version of events every night, but they are relentless.

The reminder of Horrus does serve one purpose, however. This city is full of people like him. It's full of their victims. There are slaves, houses of penance, the hopeless, and the abandoned on every corner. Each of them has a boot on their throat, holding their face in the dirt, just to elevate someone an extra few inches. I am here to remove them all. I'm reminded of the gate guard, the rapist, who wanted to enslave and use me as I entered the city. He's a small target, and his absence won't have a massive effect on the city.

It will matter a great deal to his victims, however, especially the future ones. His was the first face of the city's stain of corruption and authority I saw when I came here. It is only appropriate that he is the first I remove. I don't have my luggage, but I don't need it. My mother has a stock of simple, plain clothes for the found family we live with. Using light and sound mana to mask my movements, I dig through them and find a simple dress and cloak, which I quickly change into.

I leave the inn without waking anyone and enter the quiet night. This city is a large one and hard to travel through quickly during the day. Without electricity, however, there is far less activity at night. There is some, mostly criminal in nature, but the previously bustling streets are quiet. I can't hire a carriage, but I don't need one. I hadn't entirely been lying to Godfrey. With force, light, and sound mana, I can move through the city quickly and quietly despite its size. I can't quite fly like I did in the forest, but with my strength and agility and reduced weight, I move faster than a carriage when alone and unimpeded.

It still takes some time to traverse the city, but I arrive at the same gate I entered through. Tonight, I am lucky. As I observe the gate from afar, I see the same guard in the same place. I suspected I might; it's not uncommon for guards to work the same shift and post multiple nights in a row. I don't know the exact schedule yet, but I knew I would find him eventually if I came to the same spot. We had arrived late the first night as well, so it was likely this was his regular shift.

It's easy enough to walk right out the gate unnoticed. A couple of walls of illusion created by copying and moving light give me a narrow hallway I can walk through unseen. I could snipe him easily enough with a stone bullet, but I need to know for sure. The man hadn't been subtle, but he hadn't actually announced he was going to arrest us either. With the way slavery works in this world, *guard* and *slaver* are more or less synonymous. Nevertheless, it doesn't feel quite right to just kill them all on sight.

This isn't my old world. It's not reasonable to believe there is a way to be a city guard without full knowledge that you are going to be explicitly involved in slavery. But some part of me says *what if?* What if a child, believing his parents' stories about the importance and heroism of guards, joined the corps and has only ever guarded the gate, never making an arrest and never connecting the dots that they were associating with human traffickers?

Spoken out loud, it's not really plausible. It's not a secret who slaves are or who catches them. Guards don't get one post forever, and they all train together. They all know what their job is, and they all know the laws. Including laws that obviously only exist to make it easier to create slaves. They all have explicit orders on who they can and can't arrest. Anyone who objected wouldn't be a guard anymore. This very guard had even demonstrated that he will arrest commoners but not nobles.

Rationally, the entire profession should be fair game. I have killed guards before who were only running to stop me, but they were doing so after I killed a man they knew used slaves and raped servants. Their job, which they are trained and willing to do, explicitly involves practicing some of the greatest evils mankind perpetrates. They might as well be wearing Nazi uniforms.

But . . . what if I am wrong? I have always been conflicted about guards in this world. I don't have a great relationship with my father, but he was one of them himself, and he is my father. Part of me wants to believe they aren't as obviously complicit in slavery as they are. Besides, what if the gate guards in this city are actually an entirely different organization than the city guard?

What if they are just mercenaries guarding the gate? What if they can't arrest or enslave anyone and have no intention of doing so? None of this seems likely—the gate guards and city guard are the same in Satusmor, and I can't imagine nobles hiring outsiders to protect their gates, and it's literally the same uniform, but . . . who knows? To me, this feels like a pretty thin objection, but the smile on my face in my dream haunts me . . . I want to make sure I have a line. It may be an excuse, but there is no urgency, and I have time to check first. So I give this man a chance to prove me wrong.

I walk just out of sight, release my illusions, and approach the gate again. "Halt!" the man commands, and I stop. My hood is up and my head is lowered so he can't see my face. He could demand to see it, but that would just give me an easy out, and I could visit him another night. Reports would reach Godfrey, which would be troublesome, but it's unlikely to turn into a major problem if I don't kill him now. "What's your business here this time of night? Where are your papers?" he interrogates.

"My apologies, sir, I lost my papers on the road. I am just here to visit family," I answer. Immediately the guard scoffs.

"Lost them on the road, on foot, at this time of night? Right. Come with me, girl, I have a few questions for you." The excitement in his voice serves to verify my suspicions, but I follow him for now. This is basically the same thing that happened last time, minus the talk with August. He also seems to be in a hurry. "I don't know what you are involved in, but it's plain as day you are up to no good," he says as he signals to his partner and leads me into a small building just inside the gate. As all three of us enter, he closes and locks the door behind him, then asks, "What do you think I should do about that?"

I look around and see a few weapons, a desk full of papers, and an old bench. "I'm sorry, I really don't know what you mean. I am just trying to get to my family," I whimper, and he chuckles.

"I don't think you are going to make it, sweetheart. I can't just let a criminal through the gates. I have a job to do!" He laughs. "Unless, of course, you can convince me of your innocence . . ."

My stomach churns a bit. I was clearly not mistaken about this man's intentions.

"Criminal? I'm sorry, sir, I don't understand—I haven't committed any crimes, I swear," I plead, only to be met with more laughter.

"You illegally entered the city without identification or permission. I can't just ignore that, can I?" he retorts.

"But you brought me through the gate. I stopped when ordered, didn't I?" I reply, allowing more confidence into my voice. He doesn't notice.

"Well, I suppose that's your word against mine. Besides, I caught you sneaking around in the gatehouse, a building with classified documents and weapons. The penalty for that crime is death, not slavery," he purrs. "It's going to take a lot of convincing to get out of this one, sweetheart."

I hear rustling behind me and finally turn around and look up at the grinning man.

His pants are already around his ankles and he has barricaded the door. I feel bile rising in my throat and notice his face paling as he looks me in the eyes for the first time. Recognition and fear are the final emotions to color his face before a stone spear impales him and pins him to the sturdy door. To his left, his so-far silent partner meets the same fate.

I am far more powerful than I once was, and a simple stone spear takes little effort to conjure and propel. I glare into the first man's eyes as the light fades from them and blood splutters from his mouth as he uses his dying breath to call for help. He fails to make a sound, and after a moment, he is dead. His partner died first, and both men now hang limply from my spears.

I decide to dissolve the conjured spears, holding the men up with force mana. I replace them with actual spears from inside the gatehouse. It's best if it's unclear what type of magic killed them. It will already be suspicious to anyone who investigates that this happened so soon after I arrived, and I don't want to link this to myself any more clearly. Especially when more high-profile victims begin appearing and the nobility begins to care enough to look. Fortunately, I am not the only student to travel here at the same time. I would have waited longer, but . . . what if this fucking creep found another victim in the meantime? Instead, his corpse is pinned to a door with his pants around his ankles. That alone justifies the risk to me.

In the morning, these bodies will be found, and it will be reported up the chain of command, but not too far up. If my guesses are right, the nobles won't pay any attention to it anyway. Nonmagical, commoner murder victims have never been high on their priority list. With any luck, they won't put two and two together until much later. Dates aren't tracked as strictly here, and murder investigations are usually just a day of asking around. By the time my other activities are important, people might not even remember what day this happened. This could all be wrong, but that's part of why I did this tonight. To find out.

I pull out a bag I brought with me for this very purpose and scatter its contents on the floor. Garlic. This will be meaningless for the time being, which is for the best. But when the same thing shows up again in the future, it will help me cultivate a certain . . . image. And it will help let the nobility know there is someone, or something to fear out there. I can use that when the time is right. I will admit the choice of garlic is a bit on the nose, but I have been accused of being a dork before; I don't mind. After a moment of consideration, I search the desk until I find the entry logs, and I burn them. Godfrey already knows when I came in the gate, but perhaps that very fact will point away from me if he decides to look into this for some reason. It's the best I can do for now, and I slip out a window, then travel back toward my family's home. Tonight was something of a trial run. I will soon know whether my guesses were accurate or not, and can better plan more important outings around the response to this.

All in all, there are two fewer rapists in the world and I have a way to gather information. The gate is unguarded and will be for a while. With a little observation, I will find out how the city guard and nobility react to that, and how they investigate this type of crime. When it matters in the future, I'll have far more information. I also planted a little seed I can nurture later.

Now I just need to wait and observe.

CHAPTER TWENTY-THREE

Old Friends

Good morning, Lily!" a cheerful Henry greets as I come down the stairs for breakfast. I stare at him with half-lidded eyes, and he grins back at me.

"You know, I'm really glad your time in captivity isn't keeping you down," I respond, "but you could, I don't know, be a little more traumatized, at least in the mornings?" I don't mean it, and he knows I don't mean it. I am honestly astonished at his resilience and glad for him that he remains as happy as he is. I myself am an ugly mess of compartmentalized experiences I mostly cope with through action and gallows humor.

"Oh, shut up, I made breakfast, come join us!" he says, and I rub my eyes before following him. While I don't need as much sleep as most people, I do need some, and I haven't gotten much lately. It's been weeks since I killed the men at the gate, and I've been closely watching for a response from the city guard. I wanted to see how far up the chain of command it was reported and what sort of actions they took in response.

I had a few theories and expectations, and I needed the information. What they did, however, defied anything I had prepared for. I had been out all day and night, partially to prepare for classes, run a few other important errands, and mostly to keep an eye on the situation I caused. As far as I can tell, they did nothing at all about it. The bodies were disposed of and then . . . nothing. There was no investigation and no posturing. They didn't even replace them for a couple of days, which absolutely baffled me.

My best guess is I am missing something, so I have been staying out longer and later. Which is why I am running on an hour of sleep on the morning of my first day of classes. As nostalgic as that feeling is, it's no more pleasant than it was in my last life. I can, at least, run for a lot longer off an hour than I could then. I sit down at a round table with the rest of my family. Edward shifts uncomfortably while Gilbert and Mom greet me.

"Morning," I intone before stabbing some kind of meat with my fork and taking a bite. I scan the room as I chew. A few other tables are occupied with the women we sort of . . . adopted? That's technically exactly what we did, but it feels gross to use the word since they are mostly adults. They are all the women who were left without a guardian when Baldwin died. If we hadn't taken them in, they would have been assigned guardians regardless, and it probably would have been decided with what amounted to a quiet auction.

After a few minutes, Edward awkwardly stands up and brings his breakfast to another table where a new group is forming, and I raise an eyebrow while I chew. He hasn't been as openly hostile since I got back, or since Baldwin gave me the scar over my eye, now that I think of it. Still, I guess he still doesn't enjoy my company.

"He's not avoiding you, sweetheart," my mom promises, apparently reading my expression. "He's just . . . well, I'll let him tell you." I look at her quizzically, then shrug and return to my meal. "I have a couple of dresses done for you, by the way. I've no idea where you got the material, but they are some of the finest I've ever made." I awkwardly swallow so I can respond with an empty mouth.

"Thanks, Mom, I can't wait to try them on." I am waking up a little and manage to inject more life into this response. I truly am grateful; I did not want to waste money on overpriced noble dresses and a tailor. She saved me on that front.

"I saw them," Gilbert adds, "and the makeup kit you brought home. I have no idea how you afforded that, but the guys at your fancy school will think they're on the first plane. Mom did an amazing job!"

I laugh at that. I am pretty average, as far as I can tell. Maybe it's just because I look like a fourteen-year-old, but my highest aspirations are *moderately attractive*. Nevertheless, I understand the sentiment.

"Well, the guys at my fancy school can keep their first plane in their pants," I quip, "but seriously, Mom, thank you so much."

She smiles warmly at me. She had a harder time of it the last couple of years, and it's really good to see her so happy.

"It's no problem at all, Lily," she responds. "Honestly, I enjoyed it much more than the other outfit you asked for. That one was atrocious. Please, never tell me what you use it for; I don't think my heart could take it."

Henry and I choke a little at that. She is referring to my more practical clothes, which include a tunic and sturdy pants I can fit light chainmail under. They are more comfortable and formfitting than the same would be if I'd bought them from a tailor, who would never make them to my measurements. It also has a large hood and a simple mask that goes over my eyes.

The mask is more of a backup than anything, since I use light mana to obscure my face when I wear it. It also has gloves with steel sewn into the knuckles among other reenforced sections. This is what I wear when I am . . . making house calls to people like the guards. Or when I am acquiring finer fabric and makeup for school, of course.

"In any case, you did a great job on all of it, Mom. You have been a big help to me too!" Henry adds, changing the subject on my behalf. "My alchemy would be far more dangerous without the clothes you made for me!"

"Oh, the design for that was actually mostly Lily's," Mom responds, and the conversation moves on from there. My family has a basic idea of the sort of things

I do. They all know what really happened with Baldwin; we live with a group of people who were present for that story. They also have a decent understanding of what happened to Walter, but I don't share everything with them. This is for both our sakes. My mom would never sleep again and . . . I'm just not ready to talk about the Radiant Woods with them.

I finish my breakfast, then crack my neck and stand up. "I'd better head out," I announce. "We are pretty far from campus. My first class isn't for a while, but I need to get over there and get ready."

"All right, honey. Let me get your dresses for you," Mom says, wiping her mouth and heading back up the stairs.

"First day, huh? You gonna be okay out there?" Gilbert asks. "You need help with anything?"

"Yeah, actually, I could use an assistant today," Henry answers, and I smile at him. Well done. Gilbert always avoids helping Henry with his work and there isn't much he can do for me. I laugh as Gilbert's face twitches at Henry's opportunistic answer, then I go to meet my mom. She is already returning with the promised dresses.

"Thanks, Mom," I say, accepting them from her and giving her a quick hug.

"No problem, Lily, good luck today!" Her hug back is a tight, reassuring squeeze.

I head outside to be greeted by the impatient face of Godfrey's coachman. I shrug at him as he rolls his eyes, then I get on and enjoy the ride to the campus. I get a few odd looks as I enter the gate, but the knights don't stop me. I haven't changed yet, so I look extremely out of place, but I just ignore them as I head to my "dorm," where the nice mirror will make putting on makeup much easier. I am pretty out of practice, and I've never used this medieval version, so I want the advantage.

As I walk into the small mansion turned dorm, I'm met with two very different expressions on two faces. Autumn's eyes widen as she realizes we are rooming together, and I'm glad to see her. I suppose it makes sense. The twins aren't very prominent nobles, and while I have prominent backing, I am not either. I knew they grouped students by area of origin and rank. They don't group us by grade, however, as the other girl in the room looks about seventeen. She is looking down her nose at me like a skunk just walked into her room.

I shrug her off; skunks are cute and she should show them more respect. Instead, I focus on Autumn.

"Lillith! Are you in this dorm too?" she asks excitedly, and the other girl gives her a sharp look. I am glad to see she is excited, and time has helped heal the shock of our experience in the woods. I suppose a familiar face does a lot to close gaps in new environments.

"Um, do you know this . . . commoner?" the older girl says condescendingly, and I roll my eyes.

"Huh, oh, this is Lillith of Endings. Don't let the common dress fool you; there's a lot more to her than meets the eye," Autumn answers, and I laugh.

"It's good to see you too, Autumn," I say. "Yeah, this is my dorm, although you probably won't see me here much."

Autumn looks disappointed and the other girl looks relieved.

"Well, that's good to hear. Exactly how lowborn are you to dress like that?" the unfamiliar girl sneers.

"Just lowborn enough to be roomed with you, it would seem," I quip, and she looks like I smacked her across the face. "Anyway, I have to go get dressed. I'll catch up with you in a bit, Autumn." Autumn nods and waves as I head to my room.

The dresses my mom made actually are fantastic, and I won't lose out to anyone on campus. They aren't exactly comfortable, but my mom complied with my insane request to sew in pockets. It takes me a while to figure out the makeup, but I get it together. I think I look decent, all things considered, and I'm unlikely to stand out too much. I head down in the finest red dress I've ever worn and looking like a million bucks. I am, of course, so well-dressed because today I am attending . . . basic math.

The rude girl from before is absent, but Autumn is waiting for me. "Lillith, you look great!" she exclaims. Her blue dress is just as nice, and I realize she is going to class today as well. It's a bit silly how dressed up we are expected to be, but with the children of so many prominent nobles attending, there are a lot of behind-the-scenes politics at play here.

"Same to you; you're killing it," I respond, and her smile begins to fall before I add, "Which is to say, you look wonderful. Sorry, I suppose that's an uncommon turn of phrase here." She smiles again and accepts my explanation readily. Of the people on campus, she will be one of the ones more prepared for my antics. "I'm headed to math. I don't suppose you have the same class?" I ask. It's a core class for students our age, and it's not unlikely she will be there, as it is only taught in three different sessions.

Her face brightens and she nods excitedly. "I am! Do you want to walk together?"

"I'd love to! I'm glad to see you doing so well. How is August?" I ask, and we catch up while walking to class. All in all, it feels a lot like my undergrad days on Earth, excepting the black-tie apparel. As Annie, I would have walked to class in my favorite hoodie with *Bash Back* printed on the front in hot pink letters. Oh well, I suppose this dress does bring out my eyes.

"So, who was the ray of sunshine earlier?" I inquire as we approach the building our first class is in.

"Oh, that was Iris of Bonner, one of our roommates. Don't mind her; only Iris impresses Iris," she answers. I suppose there are probably more than a few Iris types on this campus. It's why I'm dressed like this, after all.

As we finally arrive at the theater-style classroom, I am met with August's familiar face. The three of us are looking for seats when a sneering voice calls out, "Lillith, what in the third plane are you doing here? Shall I call the knights to escort you off campus?"

I groan as I see who the voice belongs to.

I don't actually have that much against this kid. The last time I saw him, he was just a spoiled child being a spoiled child. Assuming he was unaware of the steps his father took against me, that's probably all he ever was. I still don't like him much, however, and I am not happy to see him here.

"Who is that?" August whispers to me, and I sigh.

"We used to be . . . friends," I answer tiredly, "a long time ago. Although I haven't thought of him much lately."

Hugh snickers at the description of our past relationship, and I rub my temples, already exhausted with this school year.

CHAPTER TWENTY-FOUR

Class Begins

We weren't friends," Hugh retorts. "We were courting. Until I decided a commoner was beneath my station. I got what I wanted from her anyway. You really shouldn't bring your pets to class—I don't think commoners are allowed here." I roll my eyes at the smirk on his face as he addresses Autumn. I see he hasn't grown more pleasant over the years. Also, gross dude. We were, what, twelve last time we saw each other? Why would you even want people to believe you "got what you wanted" from a girl that age?

"These classes are going to be tough with a memory like that, Hugh. I suggest you take careful notes," I intone.

He scowls at me. Interestingly, Autumn and August aren't the only ones to snicker at that. Hugh's face turns red.

"My memory is perfect, but thank you for your concern, common trash. I should have listened to my father when we were younger. He always had the right read on you," he sneers.

"If I recall correctly, I completely took your father's breath away," I retort, eyebrow raised. This only draws a confused look from Hugh, which confirms that he was not informed of the details of his father's death. The city guard, Baldwin, and Reynold were all aware of my role in Walter's death, so that is interesting. I suppose Baldwin didn't want any uncouth rumors about me before the wedding. After a second, I realize Autumn is blushing and Hugh looks furious, and I realize my mistake. Since only I know the true double meaning of that joke, I hadn't considered what conclusion others would draw. Oops.

"My father never touched you, idiot girl. That privilege was mine alone," he snarls.

"Of course he didn't. Much like you, his intimate interactions with me all ended when he woke up alone in wet sheets," I quip, then turn away to get my quill and notebook.

"I think I will summon the knights. I won't be able to focus with the stink of a commoner in the classroom with me," Hugh furiously threatens, and August steps in.

"What house are you from, that you feel comfortable threatening Lillith of Endings, the apprentice of the Duke of Facinley?" he asks.

Hugh's face pales and I groan. *Dammit, August, I was doing fine.* I really didn't want to fucking name-drop Godfrey. Now everyone in this damn class is going to pay attention to everything I do. I glare at August as Hugh stutters.

"He doesn't have a family name," another boy cuts in, likely trying to gain my favor now that he knows who my "backer" is. "He's from a family of merchants who bought their title and magic circle. They weren't important enough to be christened by the temple. He's just a wannabe noble trying to earn status by attaching himself to proper nobles." With that, Hugh thoroughly loses the support of the classroom, but I don't feel like I won.

I did piss off a sexist loser, but thanks to August, it went from a perfectly respectable verbal joust to throwing noble names around and shaming a kid for his status. His low ranking among nobility is not what he should feel ashamed of, and it's no victory to fall back on that. That and now I am going to have people hanging onto me just to get closer to Godfrey. I have gathered that Godfrey lost a great deal of respectability among upper nobility during his time in Satusmor, but he is still miles above the average noble house.

I give August a sharp look that only draws confusion from him, but we don't get a chance to discuss it as the professor enters the room. She is a severe-looking woman, which surprises me. Not her severity but her gender. So far, I haven't met a single male professor on this campus. This confuses me as much as my doctor being a woman when I was a child. In this society, I would expect both positions to be primarily men.

"Everyone be silent!" she commands with mana projecting her voice. She has her aura suppressed, but I can see a lapel with sound mana around it on her dress. The class quiets down quickly and takes their seats. Again, I am surprised. To this day I have not seen a man respond to a woman's orders with such respect, even a noblewoman. Excepting children with their mothers, I suppose.

"I am Clarrise of Cavallo. You may call me Professor Clarrise or Lady Clarrise. I will be teaching your Introductory Mathematics course this semester. I strongly suggest you pay close attention during my lectures. This course is a difficult and fast one, and it is a core requirement. In other words, if you fail this class, you will have to retake it until you pass, or you will not graduate. I do not care who your parents are, and I do not care how much mana you have. I don't care if the Collector himself is backing you. If you do not focus and work hard, you will fail this class," she lectures.

I feel my focus failing me.

I have heard this introduction a few times, and it apparently remains more or less consistent across worlds. I didn't attend with many nobles in my past life, but the sentiment is the same. She lectures for nearly an hour on what will be covered throughout the course, and I relax. It seems that, while students are assumed to have received tutoring, the expectations are fairly low. This year won't extend far past fractions, long division, and other similar concepts. Based on the culture and architecture I have seen, I suspect this world's knowledge of mathematics extends somewhere around trigonometry, but not all the way to calculus.

There is also no standard education system in place, so while at my age I would have been learning algebra, it's not surprising they are covering simpler concepts instead. In any case, I could do this shit in my sleep; I don't even need a calculator. That's what I expect, anyway, but when Professor Clarrise writes an equation on some sort of magic board at the front of the room, I realize a minor mistake. I recognize the numeral characters, but the other symbols are mostly alien. I had encountered a few when learning to draw magic circles, but I hadn't read more than I needed.

As such, I have no idea how to read the question. At a glance, I see the numbers are all listed horizontally while the unfamiliar symbols are stacked vertically on the right, but I can only guess what each means or how they interact. I'm not too worried about this; I have time to learn this notation before it becomes relevant to me. "You in the red dress, can you tell me how to solve this equation?" the professor asks. Well, shit.

I look at the board and the professor for a moment before I shrug and lean back. "I'm afraid I haven't got a clue," I answer, unworried. There is no point in trying to fake it; I might as well own it. Clarrise narrows her eyes at me and a subdued chuckle radiates through the class.

"Young lady, I suggest you take this seriously. I am not an easily amused woman, and brushing me off isn't going to result in positive marks," she reprimands me.

I wave my hand placatingly.

"Sorry, I mean I legitimately don't know how to read that. I don't understand the notation."

She raises an eyebrow at me.

"Your tutor never showed you basic mathematical notation? That is more than an oversight, that is open negligence. What is her name?" she asks, unamused.

I don't miss the assumption that my tutor was a woman, and a couple of puzzle pieces fall into place. I suppose teaching must be considered women's work. I don't know if that is because it involves working with children, if it's considered caregiving, or some other reason. It's interesting how sexism can be expressed differently, but I suppose it's all made-up social standards anyway. There is no reason it would manifest the same way across worlds.

"I never had a mathematics tutor, I'm afraid. My house is fairly new, and I have only had such opportunities for a year or so," I explain. I hear the start of a few snickers that are cut short as they remember who my backer is. That is going to get old fast. Although Godfrey will probably be pleased.

"Then you are starting quite a bit behind. I suggest you secure a supplementary tutor at your earliest opportunity, or you will most certainly fail. You are already in a questionable position and will have to work hard," she says firmly, and I nod along. From where I am sitting, I have to learn simple notation and everyone else has to learn a year's worth of math. I think I will have an easier time than she suspects. Hugh snickers and tries to whisper jabs at me, but I ignore him, which results in his face growing redder with rage.

The rest of class is uneventful, and I am not called on again. We receive an assignment, which is handed out as a sheet of enchanted tin. It seems it can be activated with aspectless mana and one equation will appear at a time. I am more interested in the workings of the magical item than anything else and I look forward to examining it. I have already seen more complex magical item enchantments today than I have the rest of my life combined. I suppose the academy is probably the origin point for a lot of designs, but I would expect them to be more widespread. Especially if they can hand out homework assignments on them.

Considering the opulence of the rest of the campus, however, it seems the academy is more important than I expected. Much of the kingdom's wealth must be invested in this campus. I suppose that explains why Godfrey wants me here. If the academy is so important, sponsoring a student who performs well may be better for his reputation than I thought.

"Um, I can teach you the notation, if you want," Autumn offers, and I am drawn out of my introspection.

"Thanks, I'll take you up on that!" I agree, and she smiles back. She also gives me that look she has been giving me since we escaped the Radiant Woods. I think she is looking forward to having me alone; it seems she may finally say whatever has been on her mind once we have some privacy.

"Okay, I'll help you back at the dorm tonight—does that work?" she asks.

I shake my head. "Sorry, I have something else to do tonight."

She looks disappointed and confused, and protests, "But . . . the gates will close. You'll have to come back at some point."

"Ah right. You may find me absent from the dorm a lot. I have other responsibilities . . . outside the campus walls," I explain as we walk away from the classroom.

She gives me that same look again, then nods.

"If you say so. Will you have time tomorrow?"

"Oh, uh, yeah, I have some time between classes. I have my science of mana and aspecting classes tomorrow."

"Okay, I suppose that will work."

"Anyway, I have something to do now, actually. I made a promise to a friend." I start to depart, but Autumn grabs my arm to stop me.

"Be careful out there," she whispers to me. "Stay safe, okay?" I see genuine concern in her eyes, and I soften.

"I'll do my best," I promise before leaving her there, still looking concerned.

I do have a promise to keep, however, and a few shops to investigate. A few hours later, and after several dead ends, I finally find a promising storefront. When not investigating the city guard, this is what I have been doing.

I examine the little dress shop in front of me. The street, the window, and the landmarks are all exactly as Sarafyna described. This has to be it. The shop that should have been hers and the window that should have displayed her hats. Here is where I will find my first clues about her father. I promised her I would find him, and this is step one.

I take a deep breath and enter the shop.

CHAPTER TWENTY-FIVE

Information Gathering

Nobles and the rich are the only people who are consistently clean. My hair, clothes, body, and teeth all out me as a noble the second any commoner sees me. This is particularly frustrating for me because these should not be signs of wealth. Merchants love selling something cheap to produce for a great deal of money, like insulin on Earth, and nobles love the optics. Nobles and royalty are not actually especially beautiful people. They are nevertheless perceived that way because they keep soap, shampoo, makeup, and fine clothes for themselves. It's, by design, become a feedback loop. Nobles get nicer baths, basic hygiene products, and cosmetics because they are "superior." Nobles look and smell better than commoners and are even generally healthier, then reference that fact as evidence that they are superior. The same system is used with education, mana, food, and anything else they can control. The worst part of it is, they even have the commoners reenforcing the idea.

I tried spreading the knowledge to make and distribute soap in Satusmor and was met with surprising pushback. Partly this is because they don't understand how germs and sickness work, and partly because when you spend a lifetime without it, you don't know how good it feels to use it. That and *this animal fat and wood ash is how nobles look so pretty* sounds like a snake-oil pitch.

The most important factor, however, is the very divide nobles want.

If a commoner does start cleaning themselves up, they start to look like a noble. Irritatingly, this is met with ridicule from both castes. Commoners treat other commoners like they are arrogant, suspect them of hiding wealth or wasting money, and ostracize them. Nobles treat commoners like they are stepping above their station and find petty ways to punish them. All in all, the average commoner finds it easier to maintain the status quo than challenge it. To them, it looks like little gain with a large social risk. It's like a minimum-wage worker saving up for a thousand-dollar watch. Their coworkers will laugh at them and the rich will sneer at them. Except this shit has a practical use, dammit!

If mana didn't promise such profound changes to people's lives, I probably wouldn't have been able to spread it either.

This is why, when I walk into the dress shop, the woman behind the counter splutters, "M-my lady, is there any way I can serve you today?"

I sigh internally but keep a smile on my face. This has happened all day. I did change out of my . . . school clothes before visiting any shops, but it doesn't matter. I am clean and I look like a noble. Nobles may still look down on me in this simple dress, but a commoner will spot me from a mile away. At the absolute lowest, I am obviously at least the maid in a noble's house, and they are sometimes nobles as well.

"I just had a couple of questions, if you don't mind?" I ask in my best talking-to-my-prick-boss voice. Not the snarky one, the overly polite and friendly one they all misinterpret as "respect." I want to let her know I am not here to throw a fit, and so far, this tone has helped. She still looks worried, but I perceive a slight release of tension.

"I . . . I don't know if I have any dresses that will be up to your standards, but I can bring out my best ones. A-and of course I don't mind answering any questions you have about them, anything you need, my lady," she says.

I hold back a groan. I want to tell her to just call me Lillith. Or Lily, friend, buddy, lil fella, or anything else that isn't *my lady*, but I remember Wallace and hold myself back. It will only stress her out more.

"Not about the dresses, actually, but about the shop. I'm looking for a friend, someone who used to own this same building," I explain, and she looks confused and worried.

"Uh, I'm sorry, my lady, but I don't think that's possible. My husband has owned this shop for nearly ten years now. You would have been very young when I bought it. Is it possible you have the wrong shop?" she asks before paling and adding, "N-not that I don't think you know what you are talking about, I'm sure I am just wrong about your age, I . . . I'm sorry."

"No, no, it's perfectly possible you are right and I am mistaken about the shop. This is the most like the one I am thinking of, however. Do you know anything about the previous owner?" I ask, trying to reassure her and move forward at the same time.

"I . . . no, my lady, not much. I'm sorry," she responds. When my face falls, she hurries to add, "We bought it from the town guard, though. I believe the previous owner must have had his assets seized by them after being arrested. You may be able to learn about them from the nearest barracks!"

I perk up at that. It's pretty terrible news for Sara, but it is a lead. I can't track it down at the moment, but it's somewhere to start. From what I know about Sara's father, he was a good worker. If he was the last owner and he is still alive, he will probably be a slave now. The records of slaves are well-kept to prevent their escape.

"Thank you very much, ma'am," I say, even bowing slightly, and she looks at me with wide eyes. She is like Wallace and responds to my presence with more fear than some other commoners. She has probably had a pretty bad encounter with at least one in the past. I put a few tin coins on the counter before excusing myself.

Now I have two reasons to visit the guards, and that is what I will do tomor-row night. For now, I need to find a place to sleep. The campus gate will be closed by the time I get back to it, and I need somewhere I can go to regularly. As I am contemplating this, I walk by another shop and something in the window catches my eye. On a whim, I enter and pay a generous price for it, then return to the road to hail a carriage.

Sometime later, and after finding a secluded spot to remove my dress and reveal my more practical clothes, I find myself at the perfect inn. It is still in a poorer part of the city, but richer than my family's inn and much closer to campus. A little watching and waiting and I discover it is used for a few seedy things that both nobles and commoners might partake in. It has a gambling den in the basement with a common and VIP section, and it is used for buying and selling green mist and black-market potions.

In other words, a noble in more common clothes and a mask will not be out of place here at all. The owners are discreet about their clients, and the guests aren't discreet enough about their friends. Inside, I walk up to the counter to ask for a long-term room and am greeted with a question. "What's with the mask? No one cares who you are, kid," the man asks.

"Oh, I know. It's just, it's terribly comfortable; I think everyone will be wearing them in the future," I quip, and he rewards me with a gruff laugh.

"Suit yourself. What can I do ya for?" he retorts. I tap my chin thoughtfully.

"How much for a room?" He points at the wall behind him with his thumb. I see a tiny piece of paper pinned to the wall with prices listed, off to the side of the menu for the tavern. "Sorry, how much for a room indefinitely?" I ask.

"If you wanna stay long term," he grunts at me, clearly bored, "you gotta talk to the owner. For now, just pay the regular price until you can make arrangements with him."

I put my coins on the counter, and he pulls a key off a rack on the wall and tosses it to me.

"Room's on the third floor. Meals aren't included. Don't let me know if you need anything," he explains, and I chuckle. The contrast with the woman at the dress shop is astounding, and honestly, I like it better this way. Even nobles here won't want to call attention to the fact that they have been here. They won't be arrested or anything, but it wouldn't be a great public-facing image and they wouldn't be welcome back. It's also possible this guy is a minor noble himself; he is cleaner than the average commoner and greasier than the average noble. I suspect he has made his status unclear on purpose.

I move up to the room and unpack my things. This will do nicely. The window faces an alley and it even has a small bath. This will be much better than the fancy mansion the academy provided for me. My own little Batcave, so to speak. Once I have everything in place, I head back downstairs and order a meal. The food is actually seasoned for once, a benefit of going to a place nobles frequent. It's not bad, honestly. As I eat, I listen.

Most people talk about topics of little interest to me, although a couple casually boast about cruelties they have committed or witnessed and I make note of them. My ears really perk up when a couple of guards complain about a new assignment, however.

"My unit is being sent after the fucking traitors," the first guard complains, halfway through his second pint of beer.

"Shit, that's pretty dangerous, isn't it? Shouldn't they be sending knights after them? We aren't really equipped to deal with them!" the second guard responds, shocked.

"They do, but knights are too obvious. Some bullshit about mages being able to spot mages or something. They are using us to set up traps. Fuck, man, I don't know if I can do it. Maybe I should retire," Guard One explains.

"That's not right. I swear we bend over backward for those noble pricks. We never investigate anything they do, we act as personal security for them, we even give them free slaves, but do they give a shit about us? No. The minute some of their own start causing trouble, they send us at them like cannon fodder," Guard Two laments.

"Shut up!" Guard One orders under his breath. "Complaining about our assignments is one thing. Complaining about nobles is another. We have it better than slaves, and I want to keep it that way!"

"Oh, please, no one is going to turn us into slaves. They need us too much," the clearly drunker Guard Two retorts, much more loudly.

"You idiot, nobles come here. They don't need us specifically!" the cautious guard insists, and the conversation devolves into a meaningless argument.

This provides me with two pieces of information. First, there is a group of noble traitors, possibly rebels, in the capital. Either people have traveled from Satusmor, or more likely, considering the implied danger, there is an antiroyalist faction of nobles here. Second, this is well-known information. Maybe not to every commoner on the streets, but the guard who was too cautious to complain about nobles had no problem talking about the assignment. In other words, it's either not a secret or it's a poorly kept one. I'll have to investigate them, but if I play my cards right, they might be very useful to me. One more thing to investigate, and another reason to visit the barracks tomorrow. I finish my meal and head back up to my room. I spend the rest of the evening working on my magic and body modifications before going to sleep late into the night.

Starting tomorrow, this is going to be a very interesting year.

CHAPTER TWENTY-SIX

Happy as a Hatter

Sarafyna

Lillith insists I'm not a monster. Meeting her gave me my life and body back. She freed me from what I thought would be an unending torment, and in a short time, I have grown to trust her more than nearly anyone I've ever known. I don't know if that is pure gratitude or the result of the overwhelming energy I feel whenever she is near, but I have never felt so safe as with her. I even agreed to a lot of her ideas that . . . well, in the past, I would have run from her and asked for help.

That is to say, I believe her when she says she doesn't think I'm a monster. It's just that . . . she is wrong. She didn't merely help me take my body and life back, she helped me take my mind back. All that time in the Radiant Woods, I had to shove my humanity to the back of my mind to survive. As the hours, weeks, and years blended together and I stopped relying on sight and sound, I became something else. The world turned gray and bland, and I melted into it. I flowed with the Radiant Woods and barely thought about anything before the end. Lillith's energy made me think, for the first time in years, about seeing my father again. When I started resembling a person again, my mind began to clear and I was able to make sense of my time in the forest. I remember the rage that compelled me to hunt the priests. I remember chasing them down like rats and devouring them. I remember consuming them and using them to grow stronger. They are still with me, even now.

They are long dead; their souls have long departed this plane. Their bodies maintain some of their will, however. It's why Lillith couldn't heal them. She said she can only help a person change their body with their consent. Well, not every part of my body is mine. She said I have divine magic, which can change bodies against their will, but mine doesn't seem to work like that. It's easier for me than her, but even my divine magic can't smooth the skin made up of my victim's flesh nor the bits of the Radiant Woods that resist the form I tell them to take. I can condense and suppress it. I can hide the actual size I am capable of reaching, only leaving evidence in my deep footprints. But I can't make it . . . me.

They are no longer the giant welts they once were. I can see again, with my actual eyes, for the first time in forever. Instead, my entire body appears to be covered in burn scars, like it has melted—which I know because I can see again, with my actual eyes, for the first time in forever.

So Lillith may say I'm not a monster, but she is wrong. When I was still a child, an innocent girl excited to open a hat shop, I would have feared me. The monster with other people's bodies melted into her own. I would have nightmares if I even imagined a creature like me.

It disgusts me, what I have done. I am terrified of the person in me that, blinded by rage, hunted and dissolved the objects of my hatred. When I think of the priests, however, the little girls at their first confession not knowing how close they are to a fate worse than death . . . I don't regret it. That's what really makes me a monster. I am repulsed by what I have done, and I am going to do it again. I am going to scrub that mind-raping filth from the surface of this world. Lillith knows I am going to continue to kill and hurt people. She even plans to do the same. But she can't feel their skin warring with her own. She can't feel their fear and pain as they dissolve.

She can't tell me I'm not a monster.

Then there is Peter. He reminds me that I am not only a monster. I gave him something he had lost as well. And he gave me the same. Not just his sight—he is grateful for that, but it's not what really healed him. I am his family now, and he is mine. Lillith said she would find my father, but I don't know if he is even alive. I refuse to get my hopes up about seeing him again. I stopped hoping for that a long time ago. But Peter is like a little brother. He cares about me, and he isn't afraid of me.

I can't imagine another child seeing me, even knowing about me, and not fearing me. I got the feeling that boy and girl we traveled with were kids and I could feel that they feared me. Even after they apologized to me, they still didn't feel safe around me. It's a strange thing to be pitied and feared by the same person. Peter doesn't pity or fear me, as far as I can tell. I can't . . . sense it from him like I can with the others. It must have something to do with mana, but that doesn't matter. What matters is he loves me like a sister or even a mother. He relies on me. His happiness is the one purely good thing I can contribute to the world.

I can't make my hats. I'll probably never even wear one again. But I can make Peter happy. As I watch Peter sleep, I fiddle with my fingers, growing and removing claws, teeth, and eyes to practice. This is one of the things I have been getting good at. For Lillith's idea to work, I need to form my body at will. Now that I have been reminded what it means to be human again, I can get back to it on my own. I don't know what will happen if I change myself too much or for too long, but changes like this are becoming easy.

Regular mana, on the other hand, is not. I haven't been able to control it or so much as tilt my head toward a single aspect. Lillith tried to help me with this, but even with her guidance, I made no progress at all. That's fine. My so-called divine magic will be enough.

As I am thinking about what I need to do and wondering if I will be ready when the time comes, I feel it. Lillith's energy is nearby. Well, sort of. She is near the drop spot outside the city walls. She says she suppresses her mana, but if she is close enough, I can always feel her. I don't know why this is, and according to her, that guy she killed with divine magic showed no signs of a similar ability. Nevertheless, I know she is near.

I gently wake Peter, and he looks up at me and rubs his bleary eyes. I give him a moment to adjust to the dark before speaking. "Hey, kiddo, it's time," I whisper, and he nods.

"All right," he agrees, and begins gathering his things. Lillith left us with the remains of the priests' provisions at first, but she has been bringing us regular supply drops since. I could hunt a little with my abilities, but she honestly knows a lot more about what is safe to eat and what Peter needs to be healthy. Her support has kept us safe this entire time. "Okay, I'm ready, Sara," Peter says, and I hold my hand out for him. We walk out of our little cave and into the open air, hand in hand.

"How did you sleep?" I ask, squeezing his hand gently. I am grateful to have him here, but I also worry about him.

"I slept okay, thanks," he answers, and looks up at me with concern. "I wish you would sleep more as well . . ." Sometimes I think he worries about me even more.

"I don't need sleep so much these days. I'm too magical." I smile at him and he pouts. The lighthearted deflections are apparently wearing thin. He's right to worry. I feel completely lost, all the time. Without the goal of dealing with the priests and the joy of taking care of him . . . I don't know if there would still be a place for me in this world. There is no hat shop waiting for me anymore. No warm home. No future. Peter can feel that, or at least that I feel that. We walk in silence the rest of the way to the drop point.

As we approach, I move the foliage hiding the supplies and my breath catches in my throat. I can't believe what I am looking at. There is the usual crate of food I am always impressed she gets past the gate guard. The clean clothes and the soap she insists will keep us from getting sick if we use it. On top of that, however, is a simple, round box. It's not the nicest I have seen, but it is unmistakable.

With it comes a sense of excitement I thought I had lost. That childlike sense of wonder I was certain the Radiant Woods had stomped out of me. It's small, and it's the tiniest spark, but it's there and it's so warm. My hands tremble as I lift the lid on the box, and one of them covers my mouth when I first see the contents. I feel tears running over my fingers as I look at the beautiful hat inside.

It's a simple one, with a curved brim and a couple of cloth flowers sewn into the top. I haven't seen one in so long, I have almost forgotten the joy they brought me. Somewhere, deep down, Sarafyna is still alive. I don't know why Lillith decided to include this with our supplies today, but I clutch it to my chest and cry. It's not much, it shouldn't be much. It's just a little thing. But even now, she is still pulling me back to humanity.

"What is it, is everything all right? What's wrong?" Peter panics and puts his hand on my shoulder. I just turn and pull him into a hug.

"Everything is perfect, Peter. There is nothing at all to worry about," I promise, and he returns the hug. "We are going to figure everything out, I think."

He looks up at me as I let him go. He looks between the simple hat in my hand and my red eyes and tilts his head. He opens his mouth to say something but closes it again, just nodding. Then he opens his mouth again and asks, "Are you happy?" I hear the hope in his voice and nod vigorously. I have tried to fake more happiness than I have felt while staying with him, but you really can't underestimate the emotional insight of children.

"I am very happy. I don't know why this is what did it, but yes, Peter. I am happy," I answer. He gives me the widest, most childlike grin I have ever seen. We pack up the supplies and begin making our way back to our cave. "I'm sorry, Peter. I haven't been being honest with you; you're right. I should have known you could tell. Thanks for bearing with me."

"It's okay. I don't really mind." He beams. He is obviously excited to see me actually happy, and it has a feedback effect. He grows more energetic and I can't help but rise to match him. "Why are you so happy about it though? It's just a hat," he asks, confused but still grinning.

"Just a hat? How dare you! You clearly have no idea what you are talking about. There is no such thing as 'just a hat.'" I laugh in response, then launch into a long-forgotten tirade about how much personality a hat carries and what it says about its wearer. I regale him with old stories of the love that goes into crafting them, and while he doesn't seem that interested, he smiles and nods along as we walk. It feels like a dam has broken as the passion I locked in a dark corner of my mind flows out again, and I couldn't stop if I wanted to. I revel in the feeling of it running through long dry veins.

When we arrive at the cave, Peter pauses and I turn to look at him quizzically. "I haven't been honest with you either," he admits, and I kneel down.

"Oh? Is there something wrong?" I ask with a smile still on my face. He looks at the ground and kicks his foot nervously. My smile begins to fade a little. "It's all right; you can tell me," I encourage him, and he looks up at me awkwardly.

"When you found me, I wasn't being left in the woods," he admits. "I had been living with the priests . . . for years. They said I was there to get their magic . . . They promised they would make my eyes better if I became one of them . . ."

CHAPTER TWENTY-SEVEN

Blind Leading the Blind

I sit on a log outside Sarafyna and Peter's cave. I have mostly been dropping them supplies as needed, but on my last visit, Sara was waiting for me with a serious look on her face. She brought me back here to listen to Peter, who is currently avoiding eye contact with me.

"It's all right, Pete, you know we can trust her," Sara reassures him, and he kicks his feet in the dirt.

"Take your time, Peter," I add. "Just start whenever you're comfortable." I am dying to know what they want to tell me, but pushing him will only make things worse. After a few moments, he finally starts in a whisper, growing louder the longer he speaks.

"It started with my first confession. I wasn't scared or anything, but I didn't want to go. But my papa said all boys had to at my age. Oh, this was a couple of years ago, I think. I asked him why girls didn't have to go until they were older, but he just told me I'd understand when I was a grown-up. Still, I didn't want to go. Something about it made me feel all twisty inside. They made me go anyway. My mom took me while my dad was working, and I only felt worse when we got to the temple.

"Mom made me go in anyway, and the priest who met us was nice. He gave me a cracker with actual sugar in it, and I put it away for later, when my stomach felt better. The halls of the temple were confusing, and by the time we got to the room with the stone chair, I couldn't remember how to get back to my mom. The priest smiled at me as he brought me to sit down, and I started to think I was just being a baby, but . . ." He trails off.

Sara rubs his back as he struggles to find the words to speak. I frown as I start to guess where this story is going. After a heavy silence, Peter sniffs and continues. "I don't remember what happened. One moment I was scared, hoping the confession went quick. I hadn't done anything that bad so I thought it might be fine, but . . . I'm not sure. One moment, priests were circling me, and the next . . . everything was dark. I couldn't see anymore and I started to panic. It got hard to breathe and I fell out of the chair, trying to find the light.

"Someone grabbed me and picked me up, and I cried for help, but they just brought me somewhere else. We were walking for a long time, it felt like, up and down stairs. But it never got any brighter. I was so afraid and lonely. I wanted to go back home. I wanted to be with anyone at all. I cried and begged to go home, or for someone to light a torch, but they ignored me. After a while, they stopped and told me to sit down. I reached out, trying to find a chair, and found my hands on something soft instead. Once I sat on it, they announced they had a 'new disciple,' and a bunch of voices responded all at once.

"They left me there, and a whole lot of voices surrounded me and scared me. There were people all around, asking for my name and how old I was. They were all boys, which I guess made sense 'cause I realized later the soft thing I was sitting on was a bed. The others told me I lived there now and I would be there for a long time. I didn't understand—I lived with my parents, they would want me home. But I didn't know how to get there. I fell over on the bed, crying like a baby, and the other boys left me alone.

"I fell asleep like that, and I don't know how long I slept, but I didn't feel any better when I woke up. Things were like that for a long time. Every day a priest would come down and feed us. He would tell us stories about the Collector and reward us with treats if we asked or answered questions. They told me I was supposed to be a priest myself when I grew up, that I'd been chosen by the Collector as a servant. I didn't think I wanted to be a priest but . . . for some reason, the thought made me happy.

"That was my life for a couple of years. I got to know the other boys. Some new ones and a few that had been there for years longer than me. We became friends but . . . I still felt lonely. Eventually, becoming a new priest was all I cared about. I only felt comfortable when the priest was telling us stories and offering us treats. The older boys even said, when we proved our faith to the Collector, the priests would take us on a trip and we would be able to see afterward. Oh, right. None of the other young boys could see either. The room wasn't dark—I found out the Collector had broken our eyes as a test of faith, they said.

"But the older boys said they could see. The priests said my parents were really happy for me, and I could see them again when I was a priest. This seemed normal. Well, sort of. It seemed normal because nothing else did, and what the priests said was the only thing that made sense. So I worked to prove my faith. I always asked the most questions about the stories. I started answering them for newer boys. I didn't even notice how hazy everything felt after a long while.

"Then, finally, I proved my faith. The priests said I could go on the trip. I left the other boys and went on a long wagon ride. It felt like forever, but one day it suddenly changed. I had grown used to how foggy my brain was, but it started to clear up, slowly. It was kinda like how if you hold your head under the water in the bath, the sound gets all funny, but when you come back up it gets better. The fog just cleared. I started to miss my parents again, and it didn't make sense they wouldn't say goodbye before the temple took me.

"Odd things I always pushed to the back of my mind started to come back to me. Like how they never let us talk to our parents. But things were still weird.

Before, I really wanted to be a priest for some reason but didn't understand why. For a few moments, that went away entirely and I was back to normal. But then suddenly, it came back but different. All the smells and sounds changed around me, and the fog was controlling me again. After that, instead of wanting to be a priest, I just really wanted to make the Collector happy," he says, and pauses for a moment as he struggles to recall exactly what happened.

As I listen to his story, I go from horrified to hopeful. From his description, it sounds like the priests' control wavered when they approached the Radiant Woods and was reasserted by the woods themselves. The implications of that open up a lot of options. I can't chase them down at the moment, however, as Peter continues his story.

"Anyway, we went around collecting . . . whatever that stuff was. The stuff in the wagon you got all worried about. They said eating it would make me an apprentice priest and give me the Collector's blessing. They spent a long time on that, but then . . . there were a lot of scary noises. The priests stopped and climbed out of the wagon, then I heard arguing and fighting and tried to hide. I guess you know the rest. That's when we met. At first, I was scared of you. But you said you could help me see, like the priests could, and they were gone so I went with you, Miss Lily.

"After more scary noises and more hiding, the fogginess started to go away again. It went faster when I was near Sara, and I started to remember things again. The older boys saying we shouldn't want to be priests. Saying we couldn't trust the priests and we shouldn't feel so scared and alone all the time. I even realized I didn't feel lonely anymore. When I was around Sara, I felt safe. And scared. I remembered the others telling me that, after their trip, they tried to find their parents, and their homes were either missing or they had been forgotten.

"I didn't know how I had managed to ignore that when they told me. It seemed so big and important once I could think clearly. But it was then that I realized I didn't have a home to go back to. Because I believed the others. I don't know if my parents are still around, but I know they won't have a place for me if I find them." He wipes tears off his cheek as he talks, then finally meets my eyes. "I'm sorry I didn't tell you before. I wanted to but . . . I was afraid. You and Sara, you don't like priests much. I was scared you would hate me too. But . . . I trust Sara."

I look at him in thought. "It's all right, Peter. We don't hate you. Thank you so much for telling us."

Sara wraps an arm around him. "You did really well, Peter. Thanks for telling her; you'll be glad you did," she says, and he turns to hug her.

My mind races. It sounds like it's not just the woods. Even Sara's divine magic can free people from the temple's control. As far as I know, she didn't do this intentionally. I know the Radiant Woods didn't intentionally erase Peter's conditioning. Of course, Peter couldn't see, so it's only a hypothesis, but it's a promising one. His experiences seem to support my theory that mind control can't withstand divine magic from a more powerful source. If I am right, when someone under the influence of divine magic approaches a stronger divine magic, or even acquires divine magic of their own, the control should fade or even vanish entirely.

This does, however, replace my worries with a new one. "Peter, I'm sorry, do you know if this is how all priests are trained?" I ask, worry nearly throttling me. I had thought divine magic didn't work on priests, especially divine priests. If they are themselves mind controlled, they are victims as well. If mind control works in a chain like that, eliminating priests may not only be ineffective long term, but it might be monstrous. I make eye contact with Sara, who is clearly worrying about the same thing.

Peter scrunches his face up in thought. "Um, I don't know for sure, but one of the oldest boys didn't think so. He said he was one of the first to be recruited from confession. I didn't think much of it—it's one of the things I ignored at the time—but he said priests started going missing a few years ago, and they started using boys like us because of that," he explains, and I let out a breath.

I spend the next couple of hours questioning him. From what I can tell, it's not as bad as I worried. It seems like once an apprentice priest has divine magic, they can think clearly again and other motivations are used to indoctrinate them the old-fashioned way. As color returns to my face, it drains from Sara's even further.

"They started doing this to children . . . because priests started disappearing?" As she pleads for confirmation, Peter nods.

"I think so, yeah." Sara looks sick.

"Lillith, I have to save Peter's friends. I have to save them as soon as possible," she begs.

"Of course we are going to help the others," I agree, holding up a placating hand, but she shakes her head.

"No, I'll do this one. I know you have other things to worry about right now. I have to do this myself," she insists, and I tilt my head but agree. I would like to go with her, but she was dangerous to me even in the Radiant Woods. She can handle this. And she is right. We spend the rest of the evening making plans so I can meet her and help her transport the kids safely.

It's strange for me to plan to just . . . go back to class after hearing that story, but it's the best move right now. I start altering my plans even further as I make my way back home.

CHAPTER TWENTY-EIGHT

A New Friend, an Old Worry

No, I'm quite serious." Leo laughed. "The kitchen staff caught me in the middle of the night, in my underwear, halfway through the cake. My father was absolutely furious!"

I laugh along with him, enjoying the moment of peaceful revelry. Across from me in one of the campus restaurants is Leo, the infamous "other commoner" Cateline had been complaining of. I encountered him this morning as both of us crept onto campus when the gates opened.

"I can't say I blame you. I too catch a glimpse of my inner madness when presented with half-decent desserts. Who cares about green mist? The food commoners are forced to eat is the real crime," I respond, to Leo's emphatic concurrence. "So what did he do?"

"Oh, he was furious. Yes, the state I was in, and in front of other people, was one thing. But honestly?" Leo leans in conspiratorially. "I think he just wanted a bigger portion of the cake himself. He had a sour look on his face for a week!"

I chuckle at this. Leo was a pleasant surprise this morning. I don't know why he was off campus, but after our initial exchange, we had clicked like old friends in an instant. I don't even know how it happened, but we had shared secrets no one else knew by the time we made it to breakfast together.

It's no mystery why the headmistress hates him. He's so bright, alive, headstrong, and thoroughly not a noble. He isn't like the twins, who I grew to like as we traveled simply because we were together and they weren't horrible people. He's the friend I always had but hadn't met yet. I didn't have grand plans for him to help me end the monarchy; I just liked talking to him.

"Well, honestly, it could have been a lot worse than some sour looks. Eat half of my cake and there is going to be some violence," I quip, and Leo waves me off. We continue to chat idly, almost as if I wasn't planning someone's murder in the back of my mind, while I wait for Autumn.

"This restaurant is so surreal," Leo says after a lull in the conversation. "It's bigger than my house and it's just here for students?" I can't say I disagree with him. I've stopped at food trucks and little build-a-burrito places at my old universities hundreds of times. As Annie, I only ever stopped at a place like this to throw a brick through the window. This restaurant doesn't even charge us. I mean, it does, but they just send the bill directly to our sponsors. I benevolently directed Leo's bill to

Godfrey with mine. The man can afford it, and if I have my way, this academy won't have the chance to settle most people's accounts anyway.

"I couldn't agree more. Between you and me, I may liberate some of their spices for my family," I say conspiratorially, and Leo leans in with interest.

"Lillith, there you are!" I turn around to greet Autumn. "You, uh, are going to stop by the dorms before classes, right?" she asks.

"Yes, yes, I know. I need to dress to impress. Can't learn the science of mana without accentuating my assets, right?" I respond, rolling my eyes. "I'm headed there after breakfast—we can walk together if you like."

"You know how we present ourselves reflects on our sponsors, Lillith. For Lord Godfrey's sake, you should probably dress up before coming here next time." Autumn sighs. I shrug; she's right in a way. I don't represent anyone but myself; I don't care if someone wants to claim me and my accomplishments, but I also don't want the attention I have likely been getting all morning. "But yes, I'll walk with you. We can make plans for tutoring later!" She beams at me.

"Yeah, I just got carried away with—" I start before trying to gesture to Leo and realizing he is gone. "With, uh . . . that's weird . . ." Autumn looks past me.

"You know, you could have waited for me." She pouts as I look around. I guess Leo isn't comfortable around other nobles yet, so I shrug it off. He might not seem like the type to do anything but speak his mind, but I have a couple of guesses as to why he might avoid nobles. I'll ask him later.

"Sorry," I apologize, "you know how I am with sweet food." I gesture at the pancakes in front of me and she nods knowingly.

"Yeah, I probably should have guessed." She sighs. I feel no shame in how easily she accepted that excuse. Growing up as Lillith, I hardly ever got anything with flavor, much less sugar. So what if I enjoy the chance at it now? She sits down next to me and orders her own breakfast. We make pleasant conversation, but I don't connect with her like I did with Leo.

I do, however, trust her. She has earned that, and it's enough to provide a different kind of comfort. They are the same age, but one is a kindred spirit while the other feels more like a student I am fond of. She doesn't eat a huge portion of pancakes like I did, demonstrating at least one area where her wisdom surpasses my own, and we are on our way to our shared dorm before long.

"Your Science of Mana class ends around the same time as my Household and Estate Management class—do you want to meet at the dorm to catch up on your math?" she asks. I raise an eyebrow at the class she is taking, but I suppose it is likely a common one for noble ladies of her standing.

"Sure, thanks for the help," I agree. "You are a true hero." She smiles in response. Considering our typical dynamic, she is clearly excited to teach me something, and I see no reason not to let her enjoy it. Her glee doesn't last long, however, as that familiar worry creeps back across her eyes as she looks at me.

"Actually, Lillith, there is something else I want to talk about as well. Will you have time for both?" A little aimless panic dances through my muscles at her tone, but I rein it in. It's good she is finally getting whatever it is off her chest. That tone just always precedes uncomfortable conversations, and anxiety is a trained response.

"Yeah, I have a good gap between classes. I'll lend you an ear," I say, and she seems to simultaneously relax and tense up at the same time, like one worry is replaced with another and she carries them in different places.

"Thanks, Lillith. I'll see you then, but you seriously need to get ready. Your professor will probably kick you out if you look like that." She gestures at my simple dress, which I wear over my more practical clothes.

"Yeah, yeah, I got it." I wave her off before heading up to my room and putting on the elegant silver dress my mother made. I get my makeup done faster today, and it's barely an hour later before I am sitting in another theater-style classroom. None of the students from my math class attend this lecture, as it isn't a core requirement and few people have an interest in how mana works on a base level—most favor classes on how to use it.

"Hey!" the excitable girl next to me says. "I'm Vanessa of York, I don't think we've met! Are you a first year? This is a pretty hard class, I'm impressed you are taking it already. Let me know if you need any help, this is my second time through, so I have a pretty good idea what the course is gonna cover. Did I mention I'm Vanessa? Nice to meet you!"

I jump a little at the energy and sound attack she ambushes me with, and I pause for a moment before answering.

"Um . . . nice to meet you, Vanessa. I'm Lillith," I answer, remembering just in time not to extend a hand for a shake.

"Lillith as in just Lillith?" she asks, tilting her head. "Are you from a recently raised merchant family or do you have an affiliation? You should really use your entire name when introducing yourself, I know it's growing more common to just use your given name, but that's the thing, common is exactly what it is! We are ladies of Potestia, and we should behave as such! Besides, how will you find the right house to marry into if you don't announce your own?"

My mood sours at this new wall of sound and I answer, "Endings. I'm Lillith of Endings. My house is newly christened, in the last year."

"Oh," she says, then looks away awkwardly. She doesn't respond with the whole "dirty commoner" spiel but with the condescending and judgmental look boomers and losers give to tattoos. She pretends I'm not still looking at her before turning to her other side and repeating her first attack on a new and unsuspecting victim. I just roll my eyes and look toward the front of the room. A few minutes later, a severe and elderly woman with the tightest topknot science is capable of marches into the room. Everyone goes quiet as she silently scans the class.

"I am Judith of Dawson. I am an expert in mana of all types and aspects and the foremost expert on mana science in Potestia. This will be an extremely difficult and trying year for all of you. I see quite a few familiar faces. To the new faces, I must warn you. There is a reason for that. Two-thirds of you will fail this class. If you look to your left and right, only one of you will be here at the end of the year," the professor says.

I nod along to a standard introductory speech. I understand what she is saying. If you don't focus and study and all that, you will fall behind. It's probably true and I have seen it happen many times. It's probably even more important to tell this to kids at this age. This is a university setting full of high school–aged children. Still, some part of me wonders why, when your job is to teach something, you would brag about barely clearing a thirty percent success rate. It's the petulant part of me that was once an undergrad, and the calculus teacher in me tells her to zip it.

The rest of the class is uneventful. Much like my math class, this is the introductory class. The day when we get our syllabus for the year and hear all the speeches about what is to come, the teacher's homework and makeup and exam policies—all that stuff that is very important and extremely difficult to pay attention to. I do notice the girl from earlier, Vanessa, whispering to her new friend and glancing in my direction, but I just let it wash over me. No point starting anything over it, especially if this is a class I'll need to focus on. My past life doesn't give me an edge this time.

Sometime later, we are dismissed, and I stretch my hands above my head and yawn before collecting my things. I notice some guy eyeing me as I stretch and I present my middle finger to him, which he finds thoroughly confusing. Finally, I head to the dorm to meet Autumn.

She is waiting for me in her room, which is decorated primarily with red and has quite a few cute stuffed animals displayed around it. I haven't actually seen a stuffed animal in this world, and it warms my heart a bit to see them until I realize why the first ones I found were in a noble girl's room.

"Hey, Lillith," Autumn says with apprehension. "Look, I know I said we would study math first, but I really need to ask you something."

"Uh, hello," I respond, indicating I'm slightly annoyed I wasn't allowed a single word before she sprang that on me, but I say it softly enough that she knows it's more of a friendly irritation than a legitimate one. "Go ahead. It'll be better if you aren't distracted the whole time, so ask away."

She takes a deep breath before fixing a resolute stare on me. "You know as well as I do things were getting pretty bad in Satusmor before we left," she begins, and I nod. They were getting different, anyway, if not actually worse for most people. But things were less comfortable and it would have been pretty stark for nobles. "But I can't get it out of my head. With the Radiant Woods, and everything you said back there . . . what you said about the House of Penance . . . the way you reacted when you heard that . . . woman screaming . . ." She trails off and my still heart sinks.

"I even know you helped kill the lord there," she continues after a moment, "and it's just . . . Look, I'll just say it. Did you have anything to do with everything else that was happening there?"

CHAPTER TWENTY-NINE

Two Worlds

I immediately surround us in a sound barrier and Autumn tenses up while glancing at the mana. "All right, Autumn, we can have this conversation now. Honestly, I should have been expecting it, and I should have brought it up before we got here, probably back when we were around the fire with Sara. I'm sorry," I begin, and she waves me off before I can finish.

"I'm sorry, but can you just answer the question?" She gives me an almost pleading look, and I hold back a grimace. She won't let me talk to her about it first; here's hoping she will after I answer. I briefly entertain just lying, but . . . it's just as big a risk as telling the truth. It's not like I can just kill her, so I am either going to lay my cards out on the table or hide them. If I lie now, I lose her trust forever when the truth comes out. I can live with that at a certain point, but . . .

If I lie and delay this confrontation but have no goodwill, I'll have to bolt, and I'll have to take my family with me. That is a lot of people to hide. It won't be impossible to do what I need from that position, but it will be hard. If I tell her now, I still might have to run, but I have a chance of keeping her on my side. That may be an excuse because, well, I want some fucking friends. People I can really rely on with things that matter, and I want Autumn to be one of them. She is a kind person, and if I can make her understand, she will want change too. Maybe not in the same way, but she will want it.

"Yes," I reply quietly, fixing my eyes on hers. "Will you let me tell you why, and how?"

She stares back at me while emotions war across her face. The tension in the air is palpable and the silence stretches . . . and stretches. I awkwardly look around and jump a little as I realize there is a stuffed animal less than a foot from my head a little behind me and to the left. The stuffed cow stares at me with simple black eyes and my cheeks turn a little pink. I recover quickly and am actually glad I was startled as Autumn suppresses a giggle.

"That's Wilburt, don't mind him," she apologizes before her face softens toward me a little. It was a small moment of levity, but it just might carry my entire future on its back. She polices her face and the tension returns, but it's more flexible. "All right, Lillith. Say what you need to say. I'll listen," she finally agrees, and I breathe a sigh of relief.

"Thank you, Autumn. I know it might seem weird, and it might not make sense, but I want to start with a question. You said things were getting bad in Satusmor before we left. Can you tell me what you mean by that?" I ask.

She furrows her brow.

"What do you mean? You were there the whole time; you know what was happening! What kind of question is that?" A little of the tension returns.

"I know, but please, try to answer what I'm asking, what I'm really asking. *Getting bad* implies that things were going from a better state to a worse one. Can you articulate how that is the case?" I ask, then hold a hand up to stop another irritated outburst. "I know, it seems obvious. Please just play along for a minute!"

She examines me with blatant irritation before deciding to trust me. Certain experiences can earn you this kind of trust from the right people. "All right, fine. Parts of the city practically turned into war zones. The government nearly came to a halt. When we did get a new lord, he had to execute a huge number of the city guards! A few people even got attacked near my estate!" she explains, punctuating each point with a sharp breath, and I nod along.

"Parts of the city were war zones, and a few people got attacked near your estate. There is an interesting contrast there," I respond. "Did you ever see one of these war zones?"

"What? No, of course not; why would I go anywhere near somewhere like that? Are you saying they weren't there? Lillith, I'm not an idiot. They were more than some rumor!" she protests.

I shake my head. "No. They were real. It definitely happened," I concede. "What I want you to think about is why you never saw them. Because they didn't happen anywhere near you. Because, at least while we were there, no one was targeting you or anyone like you."

"What does it matter if I was the one targeted? People were hurt, Lillith!" she protests.

"Do you know how it all started? Do you know what I actually did? What turned the streets of Satusmor into war zones?"

"What? You are saying you weren't just involved, you started the whole damn thing??"

"Yes! By drawing a fucking magic circle for commoners! For the people who are left to rot until they are sacrificed to the Radiant Woods! For the children who are only alive because they learned to steal, and scrape, and find just the right shelter during winter storms. The ones who hadn't already starved to death! The kids whose frozen bodies hadn't been burned so fucking nobles wouldn't have to deal with the rats and the stink and the stains of their failure! It all started because I gave a bunch of people something you probably got as a goddamn birthday present!"

"Look, I get it! I have had a comfortable life! I didn't have to fight to survive! I accepted that the world wasn't what I thought it was when you dragged me out of those woods with a woman I thought was a monster. But that doesn't mean you can just . . . indiscriminately distribute weapons to children! Some of those people were dangerous, you know they were! And you gave them their weapons!"

"Weapons? That's what you think I gave them? Fucking weapons? You might understand that people have had harder lives than you, Autumn, but you still have no idea what you're talking about. Weapons. What I gave them was a fucking chance! Mana may look like a weapon to you, but that's because you'll never need it for anything else. Yeah, you'll use it for other things. Otherwise, they wouldn't have let you have it at all. But you'll never *need* it."

"So what, you created an army of child soldiers to fight back? Like that is a better fate for them? You can say it has other uses, but it's still a weapon, Lillith!"

"That's easy to say. You've never wondered if you would live to see the next day because you couldn't feel your fingers and there was no heat nor families willing to share theirs. You've never found a friendly and familiar face wounded and bloodied because there was nowhere for them to hide from the hail. You've never gorged yourself on dirty water to trick your stomach into feeling full. You have had the tools to protect people from that your entire life! But no. What if they use it as a fucking weapon?"

At my final words, there is a pause, and Autumn looks conflicted, but she digs her heels in. "But they did, though, use it as a weapon, didn't they?" she asks, fixing a glare on me.

I sigh. "What do you think the first mana to be aspected was? What do you think was changed the most, when commoners got mana?" I ask.

Autumn clicks her tongue. "I'm getting tired of this game, Lillith. Just say what you want to say!"

"Fine. It was earth. Light. Water and plant life. The first thing that changed was that farmers were able to produce more food. They were able to supply poorer districts and pay the city's taxes. The starving didn't have to search so hard to eat. People found places to sleep or made their own. Kids had warmth on cold nights."

"Right. And that devolved into street brawls and executions because, what, kids were too well-fed?"

"Yes! Because desperate children got a taste of something better and believed the promise that, with magic, it would be given to them. Because the city guard believed it too and wanted to take it away from them. Because, despite your concerns, it is really hard to turn mana into a weapon when you have been denied an education and a chance to practice. Because they had a chance to be on equal footing with the nobility, and that was dangerous."

"What are you talking about? Children with mana do become nobles! You are an example yourself! Why would that be dangerous?" she challenges.

I decide to approach this from an angle she will understand.

"The same reason you aren't allowed your own name. The same reason you aren't even allowed to fully use your brother's, Autumn *of* Forrester. The same reason you will never be the head of a noble house, have full authority over your own money, or be allowed to actually own anything. The same reason you will be required to have a guardian for the rest of your life."

"Look, I'm as frustrated about that as you are, but that's just the way things are. What does it have to do with what you did?"

"Because if you were in charge of yourself, if the law applied equally to you and you had the same education and magic as the men in your family, you could say no. Think of when a man four times your age pays too much attention to the top of your dress as you bend over and you feel his eyes crawling over your skin like leeches. If you were truly on equal footing as him, you could tell him exactly where to shove it. No one could tell you it was an overreaction. No one could call you emotional and bitter and feel safe dragging you through the mud while they apologized to the 'noble and upstanding gentleman' for your behavior."

I see this, at least, is hitting home and I press the advantage. "If your life, your finances, and your ability to survive and live your life aren't dependent on someone else, they lose so much power. How many women have you seen in unhappy marriages? How many never would have married the man they did if they had full authority over it? How many would leave their husbands if they had somewhere else to go? If they wouldn't be rejected and ridiculed and spit on by everyone they knew for it? If the powerful don't own you, you can say no. You can marry a man who cares about you, or a woman. Or not get married at all. They would have to actually be decent people to get laid, and they are terrified of that."

I watch understanding dawn on Autumn's face. This is clearly something she has considered or been frustrated by before, and the context of the conversation connects some dots. She does look a bit shocked and scandalized when I suggest marrying a woman, but she doesn't address it. "So you are saying commoners are the same, right? If we don't withhold magic from them, we don't have the power to control them."

"Not just magic," I respond. "Housing. Food. Shelter. Fucking soap! They have to do backbreaking labor for all of it, and all we have to do is roll out of bed. Then we fucking charge them for the privilege and spend half the money they work for on our own comforts!"

"All right, I'll give you that, but honestly? That work needs to be done! Someone has to do the farming and the cleaning, Lillith."

"Yeah, but people don't need a sword to their throats to do it! I don't know if you noticed, but sex serves a vital purpose too. Women still don't need to be socially blackmailed into doing it with men they despise! People can take care of each other without a boot on their throats! And I don't know, maybe more people will clean their own shit if there is no one to threaten into doing it for them."

"That's not really the same thing. I understand what you're saying, but you are being naive, Lillith. Maybe you are right, and the violence in Satusmor was because of vindictive nobles and greedy guards. I don't know. But I'm not an idiot. However hard it is to use mana as a weapon, some people figured it out. And you aren't giving anyone an 'equal footing' without inviting violence. Without putting more people in danger."

"You're right. Some people did. They didn't live long, because they didn't understand the gap between them and the nobles they attacked. And a couple of them even lashed out at innocent people with misdirected rage. I killed one of them with my own hands. But yes, things are going to get violent. If it weren't for the temple, they would have grown violent sooner. Because things won't change without it, not here. Not in this country, and not in this world. But when you use the backs of men to elevate yourself, violence is their right."

"And what about me? What about my parents?" Autumn asks, her chin tipped up. "What happens when things get worse? Will they be safe or are all nobles on the chopping block? They are good people, Lillith! They are kind to their staff and they don't even use slaves! They are even charitable, and they might die because of what you did! Because of your recklessness and naivete, they could get hurt! If anything this conversation only scares me more!"

"You are a good person, Autumn. I do believe that. I believe you care and want to help the same people I do. But there isn't another way to do it. And I'm sorry, I really am, but your parents know what commoner lives are like, and they are still rich. They can still afford a staff to be kind to, and they still receive tax money earned from the labor of slaves. And you have spent your entire life benefitting from the same things."

"So, what, you are saying you will trade our safety for commoners'? I do want to help them, but there has to be another way!"

"No. We have been trading lives for comfort for thousands of years. I am ending the fucking trade! The current state of affairs is already you trading human beings, their lives, and their autonomy for your own benefit. For *our* benefit. And you are terrified of losing the security that trade has always bought you. It's not really your fault. You're fourteen. You've never known anything else. But whenever I say a world where we don't hold people's lives, bodies, food, and minds hostage is possible . . . whenever I say we don't need a sword at anyone's throat to survive, two types of people tell me how naive I am. Tyrants who are comfortable holding the sword, and cowards who are too afraid to fight it. So you need to ask yourself which one you are."

Autumn looks at me like I slapped her. For all intents and purposes, I did. What I said was harsh, especially for someone her age. But this isn't something I can tread lightly with. I am helping people fight back, whether she agrees with me or not. She needs to understand the gravity of what is happening, beyond individual families. "So because my family is rich, it's okay if they die in pursuit of your goals?" she asks, tears forming in her eyes.

"No. Because your parents are rich, they have the ability to contribute more to either maintaining this filthy society or fighting it. What I'm saying is I hope you will fight it," I answer.

"Then they will just be in danger of being killed by the other nobles! Even if they do nothing, they are in danger, and I have to worry for them every night! There is no option where they are safe!" she sobs at me.

"I'm sorry," I respond, "but that's exactly the point. That's the world everyone else already lives in. It's the world most people always would have lived in, even if I had never done anything. That fear you have now is one that most people fight their entire lives. It's a fear the most dangerous and disgusting people in this world feed off of. And I am going to do something about it."

At some point, she started pacing, and at this she slumps back into her chair and folds her arms on her desk, crying into them. "Just . . . go," she orders, and I nod, slowly standing and walking to the door. I pause and look back.

"For what it's worth, I don't want to hurt you or your family. I hope you, and they, will help me fight the people who do," I say, but she doesn't respond, and I leave the room.

That could have gone better. I had so much more I wanted to say and so many things I could have said better, and I'll have to be prepared to run, just in case. But it could have gone worse as well. I'll give her some time alone.

As I head down the stairs, something occurs to me and I swear to myself. I still don't know how to read the fucking math notation.

CHAPTER THIRTY

Regrets

Had to steal something decent to wear? Resorted to creeping through your housemates' rooms, have you?" Iris sneers as I descend the stairs from the direction of Autumn's room. She is in the sitting area adjusting her makeup and waiting to be insufferable, apparently. I am never really in the mood for this shit, but right now? I could smack that smarmy look right off her face.

"I wouldn't worry, Iris. As long as I am searching for something presentable, your room will remain safe," I retort, and she snorts at me.

"I don't think you would really fill out one of my dresses, sweetheart," she quips as I cross the room.

"I guess that makes two of us, Iris. Now, if you'll excuse me, I have a class to get to," I respond tiredly. I honestly feel like shit after my meeting with Autumn, and I need to get out of here before I pull someone's hair out.

She gets a sour look on her face before brushing it off and continuing to apply blush to her cheeks. "I suppose that poor Forrester girl was your best bet. The Collector knows the Renatus girl can't dress herself. Although Autumn has nicer dresses than that, if you are going to steal, you might as well take something less . . . embarrassing," she taunts just before I leave the room. I whirl on her and slam a fist into the wall beside me.

"Here's an idea: How about you shut your fucking mouth while opening it is still an option?" I ask through clenched teeth. She insulted a few too many people I care about and I am not in the mood. Instead of responding, she stares at me with wide eyes. I pull my hand from the now slightly displaced and cracked bricks and storm out before she can say anything.

Well, that was stupid, but at least it shut her up. I carry an emotional cloud with me to my next class. I sit down in the back, choosing a seat near the door. No one tries to talk to me before class starts this time, my mood clear enough to deflect any unwelcome friendliness. I can't stop picturing Autumn, crying with her head resting on her arms as I left. I really fucked this one up. I feel like I started off well, but . . . she is a child. She is an innocent and kind girl who is worried about her parents.

Just because I am right doesn't mean I was right to treat her that way. I got carried away and who knows what state I left her in. There were better ways to communicate what I needed to without scaring the shit out of a naive girl. I groan inwardly, my elevated tension from discussing the state of this world synergizing with my guilt over scolding a child into tears and leaving me completely unfocused.

The professor for my mana-aspecting class enters and half my brain does a double take. She is tall with curly brunette hair and looks about thirty or so. She is, well, hot. Ugh, my defenses are completely down right now. This is not something I can let distract me. I need to focus.

"Good afternoon, class. I am Lady Kyra of Hayward. This year, we will be examining the process of aspecting, de-aspecting, and altering mana," she begins, and I start to tune her out a little. The first day of classes is pretty much the same regardless of class. As I watch the professor, my mind drifts back to Autumn.

I need to talk to her again. I need to apologize, while still explaining why commoners deserve access to mana. I didn't even talk about the mind control almost all of them are under, the main reason things turned out the way they did. More importantly, I left her afraid. I trusted her because I wanted a friend, and I left her sobbing and picturing her parents dead. I need to go back as soon as the fucking class is over.

I try to adjust my focus to Professor Kyra and succeed, in a way. I watch a brown curl bounce in front of her tan eyes. I wonder how she got her medieval eyeliner so perfect as I hyperfocus on her red lips. As my eyes drift to her pronounced collarbone, then to the curve of her . . . *God dammit, Annie, er . . . Lillith. Whoever you are, this is not the fucking time for this!* I am seriously off my game. Yes, I need to stop thinking about Autumn until I can do something to fix my mistake. If I have to distract myself, why can't it be with the content of the lecture and not the figure of the woman giving it?

Usually, I don't allow my mind to wander like this. Yes, I notice attractive women, but I don't typically focus on it more than on what they are saying. With the way I punched the wall earlier and now this? I am losing too much of my carefully cultivated control. I'm more shaken than I thought. I really let myself get carried away with Autumn. I have been holding everything in with an ever more strained thread and today it snapped. I let go and let it all fall out and crush Autumn under its weight.

Now I am cracking bricks at slight provocations and drooling over my professor. Fucking great. Just as I am resolving to just leave class early and go apologize to Autumn, my internal lecturing is cut short by another girl's voice. "Hey, gorilla girl, I think she's asking you a question!" I jump, looking around. Sure enough, the girl who spoke is staring directly at me.

Gorilla girl? I look down at my partially exposed arms and raise an eyebrow. Yeah, I am toned, muscular even, but come on. I'm hardly a body builder. I suppose the line for "too buff" is much lower in this world, at least for women. Although no one else has said anything like that, so maybe it's just this girl's problem.

"Hello? Young lady, are you with us?" Kyra asks, and I look back at her sharply.

"There you are. A little early in the year for the vacant look, isn't it? You can daydream on your own time. Do not waste mine in the future."

My cheeks flush a little as I am reminded of the daydream in question, but I just nod.

"Sorry about that, just having a rough day," I apologize. I could probably come up with a sharper retort than that, but the least you can do after checking someone out is be polite to them.

She gives me a curt nod.

"Now that you are with us, why don't you help me illustrate my point? Would you care to share what aspects, if any, you have access to?" I pause. I'd rather not share that, but I suppose it is fairly normal to only have one at my age. People will see me using others, so I should share a few of them.

"Sure," I answer. "Currently, I have aspected light, sound, force, and heat."

She nods and begins to speak. "Light and sound are common starter aspects. You will want to de-aspect them this year so . . ." She trails off as she looks back up at me sharply. "I'm sorry, you have four aspects?" Maybe sharing four was too many? Oh well, too late now.

"Uh, yes?" I respond hesitantly, and her face hardens.

"There is no point in lying, young lady. You will have to display every aspect you have access to during this class . . . Or did you mean those are all of the aspects you have used in the past, but not exclusively the ones you currently have aspected?" Her tone shifts mid-sentence and I try to decide how to respond. I have read about de-aspecting but never really saw the point. Essentially, aspecting mana is willing mana to take the form of something you are familiar with. It is imposing your will on mana and mentally defining its characteristics.

De-aspecting, on the other hand, is scrubbing your mana of any trace of an aspect. You clear it from your body and intentionally release your mental image of it. Once you do this, you can no longer create mana of that aspect as needed. Always seemed like a waste of effort to me, but perhaps . . . It's too early to draw this much attention, so I decide to adjust my lie to meet the professor's expectations. "Uh, yes, sorry. I originally aspected light and sound, and now have force and heat," I answer.

"That makes more sense." She nods. "Having two aspects at your age is already quite impressive; perhaps someday you actually will have four. That is extremely rare, but it is not impossible," she says before moving on with her lecture about mana. The lack of silly pride that can come along with praise from pretty girls is an excellent sign. I am regaining my sense of focus and control. I have found something new to think about. There is some kind of limit on the number of aspects one person can maintain before they have to de-aspect one to learn another.

Clearly, this limit is not four, or even five, as she implied. It certainly explains the difficulty I have had recently. Counting my internal aspect, I have nine. Perhaps that is my limit at the moment? I spend the rest of the class half listening and half planning my next move. I can probably drop cold mana; all of its effects can be mimicked by manipulating heat mana. In fact, there is no reason not to treat them as the same thing. I might be able to combine others as well.

Perhaps light and sound can be . . . I don't know, wave mana? Although light is also a particle. There are a lot of things to consider. One day of class and I have already figured out something important. This is definitely going to be my favorite class, and not just because of the professor. I don't come to any solid conclusion before Kyra dismisses us and I am brought back to reality. Oh right, Autumn.

I head directly back to my dorm, where I knock on Autumn's door, but there is no answer. In fact, the door has been left ajar and it swings open, revealing a dark and empty room. Shit. I quickly leave the dorm and begin searching the campus. I don't know her class schedule, but I guess I can ask around. Most people don't know her, but after a while, I get lucky and come across August.

"Lillith, I was just looking for you!" August greets me with a huge grin on his face. He is speaking to a couple other noble boys I haven't met yet, but I earned his full attention just by walking up.

"Hey, August," I say, suppressing the concern in my voice. "Have you seen Autumn anywhere?" His smile falters a little and I feel a bit bad. The poor kid obviously has a crush and I just brushed him off to ask about his sister. It's a little tough to care at the moment, however.

"Uh, no, sorry. Her classes are over for today, so she could be anywhere. Have you checked your dorm?" he asks.

I nod. "No luck. I'll go check . . ." Then I spot the disappointment climbing onto his face. "Oh, I'm sorry. You said you were looking for me—did you need something?"

He blushes. "Uh, well, you see, there's this party, it's being thrown by Prince Kallon, and I, uh . . . I thought I might . . . escort you . . . to it?" he practically pleads, and I go to give him a polite refusal when something occurs to me.

"Will students be the only ones in attendance?" I ask, which paints his face with confusion.

"Uh, no, there will be quite a few prominent families there. No one would want to miss the prince's party, right?" he responds.

I bite my lip. "Okay, here's the deal. I am very sorry, August, especially if I have completely misread the situation. I am really not interested in courting anyone. I would be more comfortable just making friends," I answer. His face falls, embarrassment and dismay meeting in his eyes.

"Sorry, August, sounds like you aren't man enough for her!" One of his friends laughs, and I glare at him.

"That's decidedly not the problem. He does have a better chance than you ever will though," I retort before returning my attention to August. "I would love to hear more about this party, however. I'll go with you as a friend, if you like," I concede, and his expression brightens. A room full of the most powerful people in the country? I can hardly say no to that. I don't mind hanging out with August a bit either.

August gives me more details about the party, and we make plans together before I leave him to exchange friendly insults with his rude friends. That was helpful, but I still need to find Autumn.

Godfrey

I take a long pause to digest the story just told by the girl in front of me. I have spoken to her before, when she confirmed Lillith's . . . suspect story of their trip here. The new version of events simultaneously makes more and less sense. I get the feeling there are still things Miss Forrester is hiding from me. How they escaped the Radiant Woods, what happened to the monster that chased them in, and several other details.

I suppose it doesn't matter much, however. What matters is her story of Satusmor. I haven't been keeping a close eye on events there, but I suppose I should start checking reports from the communication relay here. It's rare for serious issues to arise, but it shouldn't surprise me that Lillith managed to cause one. If anything, it would have made less sense if she didn't. A full rebellion, however? Few people have ever tried that. Now we have two at once? Something is strange about that, but this . . . this is good.

I can use this. I initially thought Lillith would be an excellent asset to the country, with her unique ideas and magic circle. Overpowering a mage like Baldwin at her age speaks to more than genius. Having her in my corner was always going to change things, but this is even better. If I play my cards right, I can transform things completely. Lillith isn't wrong that this country needs change, even if she isn't right about how to do it. I knew that even before Baldwin and his little friends managed to . . . enslave and humiliate me as they did.

It is going to be delicate, but with this "true king" nonsense combined with Lillith spreading magic to commoners . . . I can leverage both to make actual, practical changes. This country needs a real leader. It doesn't sound like Lillith will ever really understand as I hoped, but she is still young and naive. In the meantime, I need to keep a much closer eye on her.

I look back at the red, tired, puffy eyes of Autumn of Forrester. "It's all right, Autumn. I will keep your parents, and everyone else, safe, I promise," I console her, and she nods weakly.

"Th-thank you," she practically whispers. She hasn't touched the tea or Danish I had brought for her. The poor child is clearly feeling guilty, but there is nothing to be done about it. She did the right thing. "Don't . . . don't hurt her," she pleads. "She is a good person, I just . . . I just . . ." She starts to sniffle again and I nod.

"It's all right, Autumn. I won't hurt her," I promise. And I won't. I need her to keep doing exactly what she is doing.

CHAPTER THIRTY-ONE

Violent Investigations

Another one tried to escape today, huh?" a weaselly little guard asks as he and his partner arrive to relieve the day shift.

"I dunno if *tried* is the right word, not with that pathetic performance!" a scrawny guard chortles in response.

"You couldn'ta cleaned up the mess? How long's he been layin' there for? He stinks!" a stocky man, one of the relieving guards, complains, and the two on-duty guards roll their eyes.

"You know the captain hates it when we clean 'em up durin' the day! It upsets some of the customers. Besides, he wanted to leave him as an example for a bit. After the beating the captain gave him, I doubt we'll have another runner for a while." The scrawny man laughs while the new guards grumble. The stocky one walks through the gate they are guarding. He enters the yard on the other side and approaches a crumpled, bloodied man in the center.

Before he can take more than a few steps toward the body, an invisible force collapses around him from all sides. In an instant, he is reduced to the steaming meat whose value he never surpassed in life. His blood compresses to a small box before the force is released and his remains paint the other guards. Horror and shock barely have a second to grip their faces before something impacts the weaselly guard's side, then head, and he collapses on the ground, small wounds on his left being mirrored by gaping holes on his right.

The scrawny man tries to scream for help while the remaining guard begins to run. No sound escapes, nor does the fleeing man. Instead, their heads are forced against each other with enough force to crack both open and kill them instantly. I walk through the carnage I created in under ten seconds and approach the body in the courtyard. I have arrived at one of the "dungeons" in the city and I can already feel my mana swelling.

I chose this location because, while it isn't the largest, it is the last point slaves pass through before they are handed off to noble families. This is where prisoners are transferred after they have been requisitioned, and where they live until their new masters pick them up. The guard captain in charge of this facility will have the answers I am looking for. I kneel down to the man in the dirt and my heart sinks. One of his eyes is swollen shut, but the other is open. There is no life behind it.

The blood oozing from him and pooling around his body is congealed and sticky. He has been dead for hours, left to rot in the sun until the guards can be bothered to drag him to the pit they use for cremations. My teeth grit behind my mask of darkness, a wall at the front of my hood that allows light in but not out. Based on the wounds and what those guards were saying, the captain beat this man to death for trying to escape. I slowly rise to my feet and approach the nearest of the two buildings.

The captain will have an office in the main building, but he isn't my only target. No one who works here is walking away tonight. They want this place to be inescapable? I can do that. I surround the entire facility with a force-and-sound barrier. It takes immense power to maintain it, but the grief surrounding me seizes my heart and floods my veins with hyperdense mana. It's almost too easy, which only serves to stoke my cold fury.

In this moment, I forget all about my worries with Autumn. I never found her, and I never apologized. I never got the chance to explain, in a way she would understand, why it is so important to share mana, and other resources, with the common people. I started to, but I got carried away by the moment and forgot I was talking to a child. She would have understood that I am not just . . . attacking innocent people but fighting back. But none of that matters at this moment. Tonight, in this dirty backyard, there is only me, the cold body of a desperate slave, and the people who left him there.

I make no effort to hide myself, physically kicking the door of the building off its hinges and walking into what looks like a small barracks. Five soldiers in various states of undress gape at me from different positions around the room. There is a brief moment of quiet as I scan the room for weapons and hiding spots while the men try to process what is happening. The two closest guards react first, jumping into action and reaching for their spears. Their spears meet them halfway. The first man falls to the ground with a spear in his throat, and the second crumples over as he is impaled by his own weapon.

I don't wait for the three remaining guards to come to their senses. One man is beginning to rise from the lower bunk of two beds when I collapse the structure, crushing him. Another is skewered on a stone spike from the ground while I twist the final man's head around, breaking his neck. After my last experiment, I have decided it will be far better to make it clear a mage is responsible. I continue to move through the barracks, and several other guards are given the brief chance to choose between fighting or fleeing before ultimately meeting the same fate.

Some part of me recoils at how easy this has become. I have always been willing to kill when necessary, but it has always been accompanied by a struggle. I don't want to think about when I became capable of massacring men with barely a thought, but the hesitation is drowned by the image of a beaten and bloodied corpse, still fresh in my memory. I steel myself and continue my gruesome march. It's not long before the crunching and cries of the men are traveling faster than I am, and the remaining guards attempt to flee before I ever make it to them. It won't save them any more than it saved the man they left to rot in the dirt.

As I exit the building to pursue the last of the slave catchers, my force shield deflects the first counterattack. Heavy wood javelins splinter and bounce away from my left side. I turn in the attack's direction and see a finely dressed couple glaring at me, the man still extending one arm. Powerful mana radiates off both of them and I clench my fists. I wasn't expecting anyone but staff at this hour, and I haven't fought many other mages. I don't think I have much to worry about with the current state of my mana, but I have no idea if they have their own endoaspects.

The man forms and propels another javelin and I examine it. I have never seen mana of this brownish color, but it's fair to assume it is wood mana or something similar. The mana travels with the weapon, which reveals he is propelling his weapons by manipulating them the entire way. This is less efficient than my own projectiles, which I propel with great force from the point of origin like a bullet. He won't be able to keep it up for long or fire as frequently. I begin to take a step in their direction when vines radiating with olive mana erupt from the ground and attempt to bind my feet.

They struggle against my force mana, and I see the woman grimacing with focus. I take a step forward anyway, pulling the vines from the ground with mana and physical force. The woman stumbles as control of her vines is wrestled away from her, and I get closer. If this is what they are capable of, they won't be an issue. I can't say for sure why they are here, however, so I have to speak with them.

"What are you doing here?" I interrogate them with a voice amplified and disguised by mana. The two of them look a little taken aback and give each other a look.

"I should be asking you the same question!" the indignant man retorts, firing off a few more attacks which impotently bounce off my shield.

"We are stopping a murderer and rebel. We are serving our king!" the woman adds, and I rub my neck with frustration. Instead of asking again, I envelop them in pure mana, crushing their own auras before I use force to bind their arms to their sides.

Their eyes bulge and the man shouts, "Who are you? Why can't I see your mana? What do you want?"

Instead of answering, I walk closer. I am not nearly as powerful as I was in the Radiant Woods. I am stronger than I am on campus, but if I am able to overpower two mages so completely, they must be fairly low ranking. I've met many other students on campus who would give me more trouble than this. "I asked a question first, and I don't want to ask again. What are you doing here?" I demand.

I watch the calculations behind both of their eyes as they decide whether they should answer me. I encourage them by increasing the pressure of the force holding them in place, and the man decides whoever I am, it is probably someone more important than him.

"I-I'm sorry, my . . . lady," he says, glancing down at my feminine figure to verify the title he should use. "W-we are just here for a new maid! We lost one and just needed to fill out our staff!" Unfortunately for him, that's the wrong answer. I do need a little more information, however, so I clench my teeth and respond.

"Lost one?" I ask, already knowing the answer to the implied question. "So why are you here at this hour? And why yourself? Why not just requisition a replacement?"

"We have requisitioned too many . . ." the woman begrudgingly admits under her breath. "We aren't an important house, and we've . . . lost several servants recently. We are here to bribe the captain for a few extra—"

I've heard enough. A twist of force and both bodies fall to the ground, lifeless. I want to puke just listening to them. I don't even want to think about why their other slaves are "lost" so frequently, but whatever it is, these two will never be responsible for it again.

I turn around and spot the remaining guards. One man appears to have broken his arm attempting to muscle his way through the force barrier. The other two have teamed up to dig their way under it. With almost no effort, I fire stones into each of their skulls, then turn back to the main building. Walking through it boils my blood.

Since I entered through the back of the building, I start in the slave quarters. I am in a large room lined with cells, each with an abused slave inside. There are men, women, and children crammed in each. Collectively, there must be thirty or forty of them spread through about fifteen cells. All of them are naked, bruised, and dirty, with the exception of a woman who is chained to a post in the middle. She has been clothed and bathed, and I realize she is likely the maid the dead couple came here for. Can't present merchandise in the state the rest of them are in, after all.

None of them react to me, and when I look at any of them, they look away like they fear reprisal from eye contact. Where is this fucking captain? I leave them where they are, for now, continuing to search the building. I encounter a few more guards, who I dispatch with little effort, and eventually find what I am looking for. I slowly enter the captain's office and circle the desk, where I find the man curled up with his hand over his mouth, hiding while his men fight. Yeah, that checks out.

I reach down, pull him to his feet, and throw him into his chair. "Pull yourself together," I order, not bothering to disguise my voice. This man won't live to testify about it anyway. "I have a few questions for you."

"P-please, you can take whatever you want! J-just let me live!" he pleads, and I smack him upside the head.

"Focus. I just told you what I want. Answer my questions—can you do that?" I say, voice packed with impatience.

"A-and then you'll let me live?" he snivels.

I roll my eyes.

"Tell you what. Answer my questions, and I will give you a chance. That's the best I can offer you."

"W-what chance?" he whimpers.

"There is a man in your yard. I hear you are the one who beat him to death; is that right?" I ask.

Confusion tints his fearful face.

"Y-yes. He tried to escape! He was just a slave, a criminal! I didn't do anything wrong!" he insists, and I suppress the urge to kill him here and now.

"A slave. A criminal. You and your friends patrol the streets of this city. You pull the poor from the homes they can't pay for. You outlaw any method they find to survive, and you drag them here for stealing bread or trespassing in a stable on a cold night. Meanwhile, you leave the rapists and murderers alone. I mean, arresting them would take actual effort, right? You don't even investigate the nobles. You make the commoners choose between 'crime' and a slow, lonely death. Then use the choice to live as justification for stripping them, beating them, and enslaving them," I practically growl, and it's clear on the captain's face he has realized his mistake.

I don't give him a chance to change course before I continue. "You know the difference between you and a criminal?" I ask. "A criminal is willing to take a risk. Some of them are evil people. Some of them just want to survive. But all of them are willing to put their necks on the line. You do just as much damage as the worst of them. More, actually, but only because you licked the right boot and let its owner pat you on the head. You are willing to hurt, and abuse, and destroy . . . so long as you are safe. And what happened the first time you were actually in danger? You curled up and hid. So you want to know what makes you different from the worst criminal you ever enslaved? The absolutely most despicable person you ever sold for a profit? They had a fucking spine."

He stares at me, eyes practically bulging out of his head. I continue once I see he is too afraid to respond to me. "So, here's the deal. You beat that man to death, and your guards laughed about it. So if you answer my questions, here is what I will do. I will hit you. Ten times. I won't use any spells, just my fists. If you live through them all, you can walk out of here. If you don't . . . well, I guess you will see what I mean about how you compare to criminals."

I see him, still scared, glancing at my arms and legs. I am short, I have a woman's voice and body, and I see him decide he can live through ten hits. "A-all right. I can answer your questions," he agrees, and I lean forward.

"Right answer," I whisper, and move on to my interrogation. He doesn't know as much as I'd like, but I do end up with two logs. A record of the slaves who have been requisitioned over the last couple of decades and a personal record of his under-the-table deals. This will help me find Sarafyna's dad, and it provides a fairly comprehensive list of future targets.

"All right," I say when I am done. "Stand up. Now is your chance to walk out of here, if you really are of superior stock to the people you sell." He does as I say, and I see hope in his eyes as I crack my knuckles. He opens his mouth to say something, but I swing before he gets the chance. My fist connects with his rib cage, and he flies into the wall behind him before collapsing on the ground.

I slowly approach him as he struggles to stand before collapsing and coughing blood onto the floor. His eyes roll over to me and he starts trying to crawl away. I'm actually impressed; I thought the first hit would have killed him. "That was a warm-up, but I'll count it. Nine more, Captain," I say before picking him up by the back of his shirt and pushing him against the wall. "Prove you have a spine. Don't try to run early."

I let him go as he leans against the wall. He coughs again and blood drips out of his lips. He grips the wall and tries to pull himself away from me, but I swing again, this time connecting with his head and crushing it against the wall. He falls again, this time dead. I wipe my fist on his shirt and collect the logs, contained in several sizeable journals. It's going to take a while, but I am one step closer to Sarafyna's father.

I don't linger long after scattering a little garlic around the scene, storing the journals in a bag, then returning to the slave quarters. I have a long night ahead of me, and Sarafyna isn't the only person I need to help tonight.

CHAPTER THIRTY-TWO

Rumors

I rub my temples as I walk to meet Leo for breakfast. It's been two weeks since I last spoke to Autumn, and she has been avoiding me. At first, she just gave me a worrying, wide-eyed look, but now she looks down and chooses a seat across the class from me.

Her sweet, oblivious brother has noticed her acting weird but has managed to miss its connection to me. He excitedly chats with me about the prince's upcoming party whenever we meet, as if his sister isn't clearly upset with me about something. I've tried to apologize to her but have consistently failed. She is drawing a boundary, and I have to respect that for now.

I have a way out for my family. For myself as well, if I need it, so I just need to wait and hope everything doesn't blow up. Two weeks without knights arresting me at the gates is a good sign, and I think it may be all right. I just need to worry that my friend won't talk to me.

Of course, it's not the only thing I have to worry about. One guard may not have been enough to get the knights on my tail, but I can't be certain of that moving forward.. My first kill wasn't investigated because there is something I don't understand going on between whoever this rebel group is and the city guard. Now that they are finding nobles dead, however, the stakes have become real to them.

News travels slowly in this city, and more slowly in this country. Even more slowly than on medieval Earth, which is confusing given the existence of magic. But news does travel. I have had to exercise more caution than before, taking winding routes to and from campus.

Visiting the houses of penance in this city hasn't been easy either. Considering how slowly information proliferates, priests seem to be far more aware and up to date than even the royal knights. Rather than the forgotten and ignored dumping grounds the houses of penance once were, they are now guarded at all times.

Priests are far more dangerous to me than regular mages. I can break free from divine magic, but it grows harder the more priests I am fighting. That and, to be perfectly honest, a battle for control over my own body is far more terrifying than a fight for my life. Just remaining calm and collected is a challenge when fighting priests.

I am making progress, however slowly, but the houses are no longer safe places to share magic. I have so many things to plan for and be careful of . . . so many people to protect and usher to safety. Thank Christ for Sarafyna, or I would have collapsed from stress weeks ago. I have actually gotten to see her and Peter regularly recently, and it's quickly becoming one of the highlights of my nights.

Much like meeting Leo in the mornings is becoming a highlight of my days. I don't unload any of this on him. He has an entirely different kind of battle to fight, and this isn't one he would be good at. But we provide each other a safe place to just . . . relax.

Sarafyna offers me complete trust and safety, a shoulder to lean on in my darkest moments, and the support I desperately need. Leo, on the other hand, offers me quiet and laughter. A single meal each day where none of it matters and I can just . . . eat with my friend.

I arrive at our favorite restaurant, a secluded little diner built to target students of lower standing, and walk in to see Leo already waiting for me. A smile paints both our faces as I join him at a two-person table in the corner.

"Good morning, Lily!" he says happily. "How have you been doing with the notation?" He has been teaching me in Autumn's stead and doing a decent job of it. His mentor apparently ensured he got appropriate tutors ahead of classes, in stark contrast to *some* other commoners' sponsors.

I hold up a hand and wobble it back and forth to indicate I am still so-so on it. "I've gotten the hang of the basics, but I'm a little fuzzy on a couple bits. Like how you indicate one portion should be evaluated first," I answer. The basic operations were easy to learn. They just have different symbols I had to memorize.

The system seems pretty similar to postfix back on Earth. The operands are listed first, followed by the operators. Interestingly, operations are separated by a space, and all operators are stacked at the end. Numbers with multiple digits are also vertically stacked, with the first digit on the bottom.

It's a bit annoying to read but not terribly confusing. Nevertheless, complex algebra requires more tools than I have learned, and it's frustrating not to understand them. Leo laughs at me.

"Your class doesn't need any of that yet—you know everything you need to! Why are you in such a rush to get ahead?" he asks before taking a far too generous bite of pancake.

"You don't understand. I have to know how it works. I just have to," I explain poorly, then take a slightly larger bite myself. He looks me in the eyes and accepts the silent challenge. After a few moments of chewing, he answers me.

"You are right, I don't understand. You are stressing out about concepts years ahead of you! You gotta relax, Lily," he insists, his next bite exceeding mine.

"Because," I say, my face somber and my tone serious, "I can't know that it exists and not know how to do it." I then stare him directly in the eyes as he chews, skewer a full pancake with my fork, and try to stuff the entire thing in my mouth.

As I struggle to chew and refuse to break eye contact, he bursts into laughter and spits out his bite, at which point I lose my straight face and join him, trying not to choke.

We get quite a few stares from the other low-ranking noble kids at nearby tables, but we always do. We laugh and joke for the rest of breakfast, and all too soon I have to say goodbye and head to my math class.

Lately, my life has felt like the different panes of a stained glass window. A moment of joy followed by a moment of sorrow followed by a moment of intense violence and rage. Each moment driven by a Lillith in a different state of mind and clearly divided. As I walk into class and watch Autumn hurriedly shuffle to the other end of the room, I feel the glass of my happy morning shatter as my world is engulfed in melancholy.

This is reality. The world I belong in. The carefree moments of kindness do me a lot of good, and they are what Leo needs, but . . . these reminders of the gravity of my choices are important too. I just wish they didn't have to pull my heart from my chest each time.

I shamble to the back of the class to take a seat, deftly dodging an attempt from Hugh to shoulder check me. I don't really know what he hopes to gain from these attempts to harass me, but not letting him test his strength against mine is a kindness I extend to him for my own sake.

"Just focus on learning how to add, Hugh," I call after him as we pass each other. "Enough math, and maybe you can put two and two together about your luck with women."

"I'm the one who can read the question—maybe you should be the one focusing!" he retorts, and I roll my eyes. I haven't been asked to publicly solve a problem again, and the myth of my incompetence persists. It doesn't really matter much in the grand scheme of things, so I leave it as is. Some part of me does want to show off and make him feel like an idiot, but . . . that would be a bit childish.

I just take my seat and sigh as August walks in, glancing between me and his sister. He is clearly deliberating about which girl to sit next to, so I just point at Autumn to indicate the clear choice. He looks a little hurt, but I don't feel too bad. She needs his support more than I need his goofy crush.

He hasn't pushed at all since I told him I wasn't interested, which is a huge relief, but he can't hide the hope in his eyes. He doesn't let it keep him down and happily joins his twin near the front. Shortly after he settles in and fails to cheer his sister up, Professor Clarrise enters the room and calls for silence. She quickly receives it, but instead of beginning her lecture, she scans the rows of students until her eyes settle on a cocky but not particularly important boy in the middle.

"Randull," she calls to him, and he startles, finally giving her his full attention. "The headmistress has asked to see you. You will be excused from class for the day."

"Um . . . why?" he asks, eliciting a raised eyebrow but, curiously, no reprimand from Clarrise.

"It's regarding a personal matter I don't believe you would like me to announce in front of the class. You are excused, young man," she replies, finality evident in her voice. Randull awkwardly collects his books and makes his way to the front entrance of the classroom. As he leaves, I spot two knights waiting to escort him to the headmistress, and I'm not the only one.

"Is he getting arrested? What did he do?" a boy seated in front of me whispers to the girl next to him. She subtly shakes her head before whispering back.

"No, I don't think so. The same thing happened to a girl in one of my other classes last week. Didn't you hear anything about that?" she asks.

"No." The boy shakes his head as he responds. "What about it?"

The girl leans in conspiratorially before replying.

"She hasn't come back since. Later, I heard both her parents were murdered! And they weren't the first—apparently, another noble couple was killed along with a whole barracks of guards before that!" she confides, and I begin paying far closer attention. I don't hear many campus rumors since I do most of my eavesdropping at my chosen inn. Perhaps I should do more here. Of course this would be one of the first places hearing about me. Children of every noble family in the city attend this school at one point or another.

"Murdered? You can't be serious . . . By who?" the boy exclaims a little too loudly, and our professor shoots a death glare in our direction as she has started her lecture and is not amused by interruptions. The two students act as innocent as they can for a few moments until her attention returns to teaching us painfully simple math, then the boy repeats his question more quietly.

"No one knows!" she whispers. "Although my brother is a knight, and he says the killer is definitely an earth mage, and . . ."

"And??" the boy eggs her on impatiently.

"And at every scene, they have found bits of garlic sprinkled near the bodies. It's the weirdest thing! Well, actually, there is one thing more peculiar about it . . ." she teases, and the boy nearly falls from his chair in frustration.

"What? Garlic? Why? What could be stranger than that?" he responds.

She looks around as if she wasn't surrounded by listeners and happy to be overheard.

"The slaves!" she answers, a scandalous expression on her face. "Apparently, all the slaves in every household, even dozens being kept by the guards, vanish from every scene! The knights have searched the city and not one of them can be found!"

"All of them? Surely they just took the chance to hide in the nearest slums, right?" the boy responds, and she shakes her head.

"That's the thing—apparently, they never would have made it there, and even after searching, not a single one turned up! It's like they turned to smoke and vanished from the map! My brother says they were recruited by some rebel or terrorist group, but if you ask me? The serial killer is a demon and the slaves are all some kind of sacrifice!" She practically giggles. While this girl is not exactly endearing herself to me, this is extremely useful information. If her brother is a knight involved in investigating, perhaps I should get to know her better.

I decide to introduce myself at the end of class. A girl with direct information about the investigation into this "serial killer" and a clear desire to share it is more than I ever could have asked for.

CHAPTER THIRTY-THREE

Confidants

I look in the mirror appraisingly before leaving my dorm room. I look exactly like a thirty-year-old woman trapped in a teenager's body. Which is, you know, fair. Nevertheless, it doesn't look quite right to me. I am wearing at least three YouTube tutorials' worth of makeup and maybe the most extravagant pink dress I have ever seen. The puffed sleeves would make Anne Shirley proud. I have some simple ruby jewelry on as well. It's not quite as excessive as it should be for a party thrown by the prince, but anything too distinct might be recognized by its original owner.

The red does complement my eyes and the dress well, however, so I am hoping that makes up for it. I also used heat and force mana as a magical curling iron. I look a bit silly and very rich, two words that perfectly exemplify me. More seriously, I look exactly like I will be expected to look. Like a noble girl emulating older women. I give myself one last once-over, sigh, and exit my room.

"I hear you are going to meet the prince with August," Autumn says as soon as I emerge. I freeze for a moment. She hasn't spoken directly to me for a couple of weeks, and I actually get my hopes up at her gentle tone until I turn and see the concern on her face. This isn't about me. Of course she is worried about her twin. "He's really excited about this, you know. Please . . . I don't want him to get hurt. I know you aren't interested in courting or anything and . . . I don't want him involved in . . . whatever you have been doing at night."

I give her a serious expression as she awkwardly hugs her arms to her sides and fights the urge to look away from me. "I know, Autumn," I respond as gently as I can. "I won't hurt him. I was up front about my interest. As far as my other . . . activities, he is as oblivious as ever. I won't involve him, I promise."

At this she does look away, some tension releasing from her shoulders.

"Why are you even going to this? It doesn't seem like your kind of party," she asks, a hint of accusation in her voice. I think of the vial Henry made for me that I have tucked in my sleeve, filled with the distilled poison from my blood, which I plan to spike a few drinks with. I suppose the accusation is fair, although the poison is entirely harmless without the activating protein. I even had it extracted so no one would unknowingly be drinking human blood. Nevertheless, I was planning on doing something there, and I am getting in with August's invitation.

I groan inwardly as I realize I am, in a way, involving August. Shit. I suppose I'll have to sneak back in after we leave if I want to keep the promise I just made. It'll be a bit riskier but I should be able to swing it. At the very least, I can rub elbows and secure my own invitation to future parties. It's not like this shit will stay in their systems forever anyway; I'll need to do this multiple times.

I nod at her. "You're right. I wasn't arrested and executed weeks ago, which means, despite the way I snapped at and scared you, you didn't turn me in. You have extended a lot of trust to someone you haven't known that long; it's only fair I do the same. I was going to do something. Nothing dangerous, but I was using this invitation to do it. I didn't even think of it affecting August. That was thoughtless and unfair of me, so I won't do that, not like I planned. I will make polite conversation and get my own invite for the next one. Does that work for you?" I ask, and she looks down.

"R-right," she answers. "Thank you." She turns, and I call after her before she leaves my sound bubble.

"Autumn, wait," I plead. "Can we talk when I get back? I . . . owe you an apology."

She seems to shudder but she gives me a slight nod, then continues to her room. I smile a bit to myself. Finally, I will get a chance to make things right. I descend the stairs only to be met with a snort from Iris.

"What are you all dressed up for? You look like something that belongs in a novelty doll shop!" she chides. I look at her with feigned concern.

"Oh, you didn't get an invite from Prince Kallon? I would have thought, considering our relative standing, you'd be the first stop he made!" I gasp as if shocked and her eyes widen.

"You liar! You aren't seriously going to the prince's party!" she protests.

"No," I answer, rolling my eyes, "I am going ironically." I shake my head and begin to walk past her, but she pushes herself between me and the door.

"Where do you think you're going? I refuse to accept that someone with such common blood is allowed anywhere near Prince Kallon! Not when I wasn't invited!"

I sigh. This girl really hasn't said one thing worth listening to since I met her.

"Perhaps your nose was raised so firmly in the air, you simply didn't notice him offering the invite," I quip. "Now, if you'll excuse me, I'd like to go." She glares at me for a moment until I give the crack in the brick behind her a meaningful glance, and she winces a bit. She then picks up her dress and storms off to her own room. Thank the Lord for that. Now, to go to a party full of people just like her. I leave the mansion and find August waiting for me.

"Lillith! You look radiant!" he says in greeting.

I sarcastically bow.

"Thanks, you don't look bad yourself. I'm sure you'll be the talk of all the ladies at the party."

"All but one, I'm afraid," he jokes, a badly disguised hint of sadness in his voice. I give him a courtesy laugh, but it's followed by a bit of awkward silence as we walk. The party is being held in the prince's "dorm" on campus, so we don't need a carriage to reach it. "I'm sorry," he says, blushing a little bit. "That wasn't that funny, was it?"

"Not really, no," I answer, and he looks down before building up the courage to ask the question that has probably been on his mind since I shut down his romantic intentions.

"Can I ask . . . is there a particular reason you don't want to court anyone or . . . is there something about me that makes me unacceptable as a partner?" he practically pleads.

Poor kid. I remember being an awkward teenager with a crush. Actually, my teenage body is probably not unrelated to my lack of focus in my aspecting class. At this moment, I make a possibly rash decision, but probably not a terribly dangerous one. Not with August, anyway. His sister knows about my treason; he'll probably have a milder reaction to my sexuality. Probably. I knew a few people in my past life who would have proved that guess wrong.

In any case, Leo already knows, and August has a good heart. I don't mind easing his self-consciousness a bit. I throw up a sound bubble before speaking. "First of all, just for future reference, no one needs a reason not to want to date someone. Just not wanting to is reason enough. But honestly? A little of both," I answer, and for a moment, he looks like I slapped him until I raise my hands placatingly. "It's not what you think. There are reasons I don't want to court anyone for at least four years, but you would think I was insane if I told you what they were. The reason I'm not interested in you, however, I can share, if you can promise not to tell a soul."

"Date? What? Wait, never mind. I don't know what the big secret is, but I can promise that, sure. Tell me straight—what exactly is wrong with me?" he asks. I take a deep breath. I'm actually nervous. It's funny; no matter how many times I do this, I still get flustered every single time. Probably because it has gone so poorly so many times. The image of my first set of parents flashes through my head. Those assholes actually invited our pastor over to exorcise me when I was a teenager. This is unlikely to go the same way though, so I push through.

"There is nothing wrong with you. With either of us, really. But . . . August, I just don't like men, that's all." He looks a little offended and I realize that came out wrong. "No, I don't dislike men, not on principle. I mean I'm not attracted to them. Romantically or sexually. I like women."

At this, he stops walking and just stares at me.

"Are . . . you serious?" he asks, his voice cracking a little. "Like, you . . . I can't even picture how that would work—"

"I'd rather you didn't try, actually," I interject, and he chokes a bit, then turns pinker than my dress, realizing what he just said, and waves his hands to assure me that's not what he meant.

"No, no, I just mean . . . you know, courting and marriage. Besides, isn't that . . . heresy? Wouldn't it be an insult to the Collector's design?" he asks, genuinely confused.

It is a question, not a statement, but I nod anyway.

"Maybe. But *the Collector's design* was the same excuse the priests used to abandon people to torture in the Radiant Woods. I don't know if that's really the best metric to use here, man," I answer honestly. This throws him off even more and he pauses.

"So, what, are you saying the Collector is . . . evil?" he asks, eyes widening.

I shrug. "I don't know. Honestly, I have a few theories, but I don't have any idea for certain if he exists, much less how involved he is in what the temple does. But think of it this way. He is supposed to be an all-powerful deity, right? How important is it, on a cosmic scale, that I look at girls the same way you do?" I challenge. He pauses to think about it.

"So . . ." he begins, "you mean it doesn't make sense for him to care? But why would everyone say it does?"

"Same reason they throw people in the woods to suffer," I answer. "In fact, there are probably more than a few people like me in there right now. What I am saying is that either he really does care, and he is a petty tyrant, or the priests are mistaken or lying. People are fallible, August. And they love to control other people. However you feel about your faith, doesn't it make more sense that some asshole is grossed out than that an omnipotent god gives a single shit?"

He processes this as we walk for several minutes, and I keep the sound bubble up just in case. Right as I think the awkward silence will kill me, August finally speaks up. "So . . ." A wide grin breaks out on his face. "How about that Professor Kyra? Easily my favorite class." I reward this response with a full laugh and he joins me. The awkward tension evaporates just like that, and we chat happily for the rest of the walk. "Really, though, there isn't anyone at all you are interested in? I mean, I know you can't openly pursue it, but there must be someone, right?" he pokes, and I chuckle.

"Like I said, I have other reasons courting isn't appealing to me at the moment." I let him shrug and start to change the subject, but I add in, "Although, I've been visiting Sarafyna a lot lately . . ."

He gives me a double take and I give him a sheepish smile. I am honestly more than a little surprised that went as well as it did. This is not a progressive world, and my particular community is very likely handled the same way as the disabled community. Of course, August and I have been through some unique experiences and he wasn't exactly impressed with the houses of penance either.

Speaking of Sarafyna, part of me worries about her. She has her own plans tonight, and they are far riskier than mine. I look in the direction of the temple she is likely already visiting and nervously bite my lip. I need her to be safe, and this is the first time she has risked actually fighting someone with her newly honed divine magic. I am pulled out of my worries as August speaks again, however.

"Well, here we are," he says, gesturing at the very obvious small castle in front of us. "Dorm room" indeed. "I probably should have asked this earlier, but do you know any formal dances?" he asks, and I shrug again.

"I can do the washing machine," I answer, and he examines me.

"The washing . . . what? Why would you even want to know a dance about washing something?" he asks, utterly befuddled.

"What? I like Selena, you have a problem?" I ask, and he just chuckles.

"Lillith, I have no idea what in the third plane you are talking about."

With that, we present August's invitation to the knight at the door and enter the castle. As we make our way to the reception hall, I grow physically weak. August struggles even more and I have to hold him up. When we enter the main hall, the reason becomes clear. A young man, maybe a year or two my senior, is making polite conversation with a group of nobles, each trying to act unaffected.

This boy is even more formidable than Godfrey and his aura has far more of an edge to it. Like Godfrey, he looks like he doesn't belong in this world. In an instant, I know that if I fought him anywhere but inside the Radiant Woods, I would die. There is no question about it. There are no tricks I can use. No clever plans. If I face him as I am, I will end. I take a deep breath and enter. This must be Prince Kallon. I can't kill him. No way. But, unless he plans to end the monarchy himself, I am going to.

CHAPTER THIRTY-FOUR

Chewing

Sarafyna

I feel empty. Not hollow, exactly, but like something I have always carried has been torn away and I am what's left. This is how it feels to walk through the city I grew up in. It hasn't really changed, not in any meaningful way. Not to the people who live in it. To me, however, it has lost everything familiar. The baker whose bread I could never afford is gone. The new homes are old and the old homes are older. Even the little creaking gate on the walkway to my old house is gone.

The house itself has been painted, and the absence of my kindly, smiling father screams from every silent window. If I close my eyes and listen, drowning out the rest of the world, I can hear his feet, pounding against the pavement as he chases my wagon. I can hear his voice crying my name and begging my captors to give me back. I don't know why, of all my memories with my father, many of them happy and warm, this is the only one that will come to me with any clarity. I shudder and push it away. Lily says she has a lead on him. The little part of me that still feels hope can hold on to that for now. I don't need this sickening memory.

I shouldn't have come here, I know that. It's not what I came into the city for, and it has nothing for me. It's just a street now. None of the secret spots I hid in as a kid exist anymore. The smells are different and the warm comfort of home it always offered is just . . . cold stone and rain. Part of me wants to knock on the doors. Try to drag someone or something, anything I recognize, into the night air so I can confirm my childhood was even real. But I can't do that. I have to stay hidden, and if I showed anyone my face, they would reject me anyway.

Well, anyone but Lily. She seems completely unbothered as far as I can tell. She has that . . . darkness spell over her face every time I see her, but I can still somehow feel her emotions. Maybe she is disfigured too—that would certainly explain both things—but honestly, I think she just doesn't care. Thinking of Lily, I am reminded of why I am in the city. I turn my back on the old neighborhood that moved on without me, and I walk into the rain.

I take the same route I nervously took so, so long ago. Images of my last walk with my father flash through my head as I take the same turns down the same roads. I remember how nervous I was. The promise of my hat block and Dad's hand on my shoulder, ushering me along. I have to stop as I realize I am not remembering that foreboding feeling as I approach the temple. No, this is the same feeling, but it's not a memory. I can feel it again. It feels like the grease on a spoiled piece of meat. I suppose some things are exactly as they once were.

My heart beats against the inside of my chest when I finally reach the temple. I don't want to be here. This was the last place I went before my life ended. I never wanted to return here, but . . . if what Peter said is true, I have to. I have no choice. I take my hat off for a brief moment and slap the sides of my face in an attempt to force focus into my head. I have to do this. Finally, I replace my hat, privacy veil and all, and take a deep breath. Then I enter the temple.

There aren't many people around, but I can feel the ones who are. At least the ones with either mana or divine magic. I walk through the empty halls to the main sanctuary. It is the only fully public location, and it's in the center of the building. If I want to scan the entire complex, that's the place to do it. I enter the room, a round sanctuary with an elevated stone altar in the center, surrounded by pews. I take a seat near the middle and concentrate. There are quite a few priests here, but none are active. The area where I can sense them must be where they sleep.

There are large gaps between them, the intervals fairly regular. Then there are a couple walking through the halls in the other direction. So far, all of them are far too powerful to be the people I am looking for. Wait, there is one priest . . . he's coming this way. My heart races and I take short, shallow breaths as I feel him walking closer and closer. I am allowed in here, and there is no reason to be afraid, but I can't help it. I practically jump out of my skin when I see him enter the room from the opposite side. He looks right at me, then starts in my direction.

My eyes widen and sweat drips down my scarred face as he approaches me. It's a good thing my dress is drenched with rainwater, or the nervous sweat staining my clothes would be more obvious. I am glad Lily managed to find this veil. I can see through it fairly clearly, but it obscures my marred face unless someone gets extremely close. I do not want my features to be seen right now.

"Good evening, my lady," he says, giving me a gentle bow. "It's awfully late, and quite a night, to be presenting yourself to the Collector. Is everything quite all right?"

It takes a conscious effort to keep my body in its current shape as he asks me this. His polite tone, his feigned kindness, and his saccharine smile fill me with rage. He's older, by a decade or so, but I will never forget his face. This is the priest who took me from my father. The man who pretended to be kind . . . until the witness was gone. The man who threw me in a chair and subjected me to mind rape and banishment to hell.

"My lady? My lady! Are you all right, my lady?" He panics, but I am far away. I want to scream. I want to run. I want . . . to kill. Then, a moment later, I find what I am looking for and I remember why I am here. They are a floor or two below me. Dozens of little souls, each with a seed of divine mana. Other boys like Peter, the children I came here to save.

"I'm sorry," I practically whisper, and the priest relaxes. "I've had an awful time of it."

"That's all right, my lady. The Collector is watching over you. Tell me what's on your mind," he offers.

"It's funny," I answer, fighting the urge to puke, "you don't remember me, I suppose. You were the first priest I ever met. You brought me to my first confession."

He looks confused at the revelation and puts his hand over his chin and mouth in thought.

"A noblewoman? Why did you want a confession? I'm very sorry, my lady, you are right; I remember no such thing."

"I didn't suppose you would." I nod. "I was just a girl then. A scared child. But my mother always took such comfort in the temple, before she passed. Any temple. She said they were sanctuaries. Little bastions of safety in a terrifying world. That's why I came here when I was young. I came for the comfort my mother always felt." The slithering snake of a priest nods sagely.

"Sounds like your mother was a wise woman," he replies. "Is she why you are here tonight?" I don't answer for a moment. Instead, I drink in the emotions of the children, trapped somewhere below me. Their confusion, their fear, and their sorrow. Most heartbreakingly of all, their hope. The one emotion only the youngest have. And of course, their faith.

"What do you do with their parents?" I ask, turning my head to look directly at the priest.

"Pardon, my lady?" he replies, genuine confusion coloring his voice.

"The children. The ones you pull from the poorest parts of town? The ones you blind and train to do your bidding? The ones whose lives and sight you return as a reward after taking them away?" I inquire, my voice perfectly polite.

He freezes, then his face hardens.

"Ah, so you are one of those. This happens sometimes. They are supposed to investigate the families first, but occasionally we miss a relative. Who was it, your sister? Brother? Ex-husband? I see now. You are no noble. Just an angry child here to rage at the Collector's will. I don't know where you got your information, but I wouldn't worry. You'll see whoever it was soon enough," he tiredly explains to me.

I feel a familiar fury as he speaks. So unconcerned. So detached. I begin to see the red I thought I left in the Radiant Woods. "My mother said the temples were the Collector's little sanctuaries, but she was wrong, wasn't she?" I say, fighting with everything I am to hold myself together and remember my humanity. "They are his mouths, aren't they? And you, you are his teeth. Drawing in little, frightened girls. Pulling them from their fathers. Taking little boys from their mothers. And chewing. Breaking us down with slow, deliberate bites until you leave us to be digested." I feel tears running down my cheeks and I hear it again. My father's feet hitting the cobblestone. His desperate cries. His gasping breaths as he runs for far longer than his body can take.

I am coming apart at the seams. The monster that rampaged through the woods wants control, and I can barely keep it inside until . . . he grabs me. His firm hands grip my shoulder hard enough to bruise and that's as far as I can go. I form a mouth on my shoulder, full of rows of razor-sharp teeth, and bite. Through the fabric of my dress and through his fingers. There is a moment of silence before his body processes what just happened. Then, just as he screams in pain and falls to the ground, I stand and remove my hat and veil. "W-what are you?" He gasps through sobs of pain as I walk toward him, and he tries to scramble backward with his one good hand.

"I told you. I am a scared girl who trusted you. I came to you because I believed you were safe, and you dragged me to the Radiant Woods to suffer. Because you couldn't control me. No, you could have, really. I was an impressionable child. But your divine magic didn't work. So it wasn't because you couldn't control me, it was because you couldn't magically control me. It was because you simply couldn't conceive of putting effort into it. That's how little my life was worth to you," I answer. He looks at my auburn hair, then my face. I see the moment he remembers me, and I feel his divine mana try to control me.

I shrug it off and he begins screaming. "Help! Help me! Demon! There is a demon in the sanctuary!" he cries. More priests will definitely hear him, but the part of me that cares is too far away. Right now, I am the Sarafyna who survived the Radiant Woods. I am the hunter the Collector himself can't stop. And this man is prey. He tries to form some kind of spell, but I do the one thing I have learned with my mana and crush his under its weight. He tries to stand and run, but I extend one arm and it grows.

A mass of flesh pins him back to the ground, and I extend it all over his body. "Please," he whimpers, realizing no one will get here in time to save him, "please . . . I am sorry! I don't . . . I don't . . ." He trails off and I glare at him, my mouth extending to snarl at him.

"You don't what?" I snap at him. "You don't understand? You don't know what's happening? You just want to go home? Yeah, I understand." Then I form more mouths, all along the flesh that pins him to the ground, and each of them eats. This is when he starts to truly scream, and I cover his mouth with the flesh from my extended arm. His eyes bulge as my mouths chew, some shredding his flesh with teeth like blades and others crushing and mashing with teeth like stones. I glare at him and my fury grows. It consumes me, and it consumes him.

I stare him in the eyes until I see the light fade, and just like that . . . I come back to my senses. What am I doing? I just . . . tortured him to death . . . This isn't . . . who I want to be. I feel my mana and divine magic grow as my body digests the man. I also feel the priests running toward me. What did I do? Killing is one thing. I have seen the good Lillith has done by killing, but what I just did was . . . something else.

I look down at my bloodied hand and my shredded dress. I ruined everything.

I can't save anyone now. I have to run. I have to get out of here and save myself so I can try again later, because . . . I am a monster. I thought I left this part of myself back in the woods but it's clear now. Sarafyna is truly dead.

I take the nearest exit to the outside and begin morphing and contorting my body in one of the ways Lillith taught me. It's gotten easier, even more so after . . . eating that man. Before long, I have compacted my body into a fleshy bird and am flying away from the temple.

I'm not sorry that priest is dead. But it doesn't feel like he is the only person I just killed.

CHAPTER THIRTY-FIVE

The Party's Over

Leo

I don't know what to do next. I see Lillith every morning now. We often enter the gate at the same time, and when we don't, she always meets me for breakfast. This is . . . probably more than I should ask for, but still. Whenever one of those nobles shows up, I feel like I'm on the outside looking in. Lillith is one thing, but they . . . they are dangerous. I don't know why she can't see that. They are no safer to her than they are to me. I understand wanting to trust them, but Lillith comes from the same background as I do.

They will never really accept us, and we will never be safe. Even when they act kind. When they reach a hand out to help. They are always looking down when they do, and there is always a condition attached.

I'm not far from campus, and as I think about what Lillith is doing, a little noble girl, maybe five or six years old, runs past me. I see it before it happens, but I'm too late to stop her. She steps on her too-long dress and falls face-first onto the cobblestone. After a moment of quiet, she begins loudly sobbing and I run to her side and kneel to help her up.

"Ouch, what happened?" I gently inquire, trying to behave calmly, like nothing is actually wrong and my concern is minor. In reality, she looks awful as she looks up at me with red eyes and blood running from her nose. She hit the ground pretty hard. With kids, however, they will often match the tone you set. If I panic, so will she. So I remain calm. She looks confused for a moment as she examines me, but it's brief.

"I—I was pulling my sock up but Momma didn't notice, so I ran to catch up but I stepped on my dress, and, and . . ." She trails off before wiping her nose on her sleeve and hurting her sore nose again. At this, she starts crying and I pull out a handkerchief to begin gently wiping the blood. Just as she is calming down, a woman slaps the cloth from my hand.

"What are you, some kind of pervert? Get your hands off my daughter! How dare you touch her?" she practically shrieks before grabbing her daughter by the hand and dragging her off. The child looks back at me, but I hear her mother scolding, "Don't talk to strangers like that!" The mother glares over her shoulder at me and I slump. I'm so tired of this. As the pair disappears around a corner, I come to a decision. I can't keep going like this. I have to see if Lillith is still at the dorm.

I don't know when she leaves, but I have to try before I lose my nerve. I stand up, turn, and return to campus.

Lillith

The pressure of the prince's aura is intense, but as unbelievable as it seems, he is holding back. Not as much as he could be—he is letting enough power out so everyone in the room knows where they stand. I don't know why he even has a knight at the door. His aura is clearly how he is really weeding guests out. Only people with a certain level of mana will be able to tolerate this for any amount of time. For the first time in a while, I unmask some of my aura.

Not all of it—like the prince, I only release as much as I need to. It would be more comfortable to protect myself with the full force of my aura, but I don't want to explain why it's on par with the mana of a family a hundred or more years old. I also have to hide the mana still gathering at my tattooed circle that answers the question. It is enough, however, and I can move around the room without feeling exhausted as I push back against Kallon's ambient mana with my own. August releases his aura as well, but his is weaker than mine.

"You all right, bud?" I ask, and he nods, a bead of sweat rolling down his face.

"Never been better," he replies through a forced smile. "I can already tell this party will be loads of fun."

I chuckle before responding. "Hang in there; my bet is he will rein it in after a while. This is just to scare away undesirables, like me," I quip.

August looks up and down at my calm demeanor while he grimaces.

"It's doing a great job of it," he jokes, and I laugh, then extend my aura a little more, adding my own to his and allowing him to relax. He sighs in relief. "Thanks for that."

"Any time. Now, let's mingle, shall we? It's a party, after all," I say, and we push our way into the crowd.

"Right, maybe I can find a nice lady who'll want to dance with me, eh?" he suggests.

I give him a skeptical look.

"August, you didn't even know what a blind lady was when I met you, I doubt you're gonna find one here," I joke.

"I mean, I guess not but why . . . Wait, hold on . . . Hey!" he protests, and I laugh.

"Seriously though, they'd be lucky to dance with you. I wish you luck!" I encourage him, and he rolls his eyes at me.

About half an hour after the party starts, I am proven correct as the prince suppresses his aura a bit, maintaining the sense of unreality around himself but allowing the rest of us to breathe. I suppress my aura, and August is free to leave my side. This choice greatly increases his chances of finding a dance partner and my ability to get a feel for the other nobles in the room.

With the heavy aura released, the party starts in earnest and the conversation becomes far livelier. I slowly make my way through the crowd, making polite conversation and introducing myself. I'm pretty far out of my element here, but I do all right. I get a good sense of some more important nobles and recognize a few names on my list. It makes me feel a little sick, the happy and friendly smiles I get from the slave owners. Some of them are nearing adulthood and their worldviews are growing more concrete.

I do encounter some hope, however, as I finally make my way to Prince Kallon and overhear the conversation he is having with another noble. The man he is talking to is one of the few who seemed unaffected by the pressure earlier, although he now looks a bit disheveled. Not like he has done anything serious, but his hair is messy and his clothes aren't tucked in all the places they should be. Considering his exaggerated hand gestures as he debates the prince, the reason for this is obvious enough.

"We rule by the mandate of the Collector, Dominic; certainly you aren't questioning God?" Kallon protests.

"No, of course not, you are missing the point!" The man, Dominic, waves him off. "It's about obligation! It's about the future! I am not questioning if we should rule, I am questioning how!" He looks about seventeen or so and, now that I look at him, fairly similar to the prince. He must be a close relative, especially if he is openly challenging him like this.

"By the Collector himself, you sound like Uncle Godfrey!" Kallon sighs before accepting a drink from a passing waiter, a man with an impressive aura of his own, I notice. "Are you going to hide in some backwater city too?"

Dominic sighs himself. "Grandfather has made his mistakes, I'll acknowledge that, but that doesn't mean he is wrong!" My ears perk up a little. So he's Godfrey's grandson, that's interesting. What's more interesting is Godfrey has apparently been questioning the method of the royal family's rule. *His* family's rule. Did the prince of Potestia seriously just call him 'uncle'? Is that in a colloquial sense or is he *that* kind of duke? I suppose I've never actually spoken to him in depth about any of this, but the way he helped cover for me in Satusmor makes a bit more sense with both revelations in mind.

"Our family's rule has kept Potestia prosperous for thousands of years! It would be foolish to start experimenting now!" Kallon complains.

Dominic shakes his head and waves one arm back and forth.

"That's exactly the problem! Thousands of years, and everything is exactly the same! Have you ever wondered if things could be *better*? Faster travel, more immediate communication? What if we could have cleaner cities and stronger soldiers?"

"Dominic"—Kallon shakes his own head, a sympathetic smile on his face—"you have lost track of your own argument! What does that have to do with the treatment of commoners?" He laughs and Dominic growls in frustration.

"Because, Kallon, we are limiting possible advancement! If only a small portion of the population has access to magic and education, only a small portion of the population has the chance to make new discoveries! Grandfather was inspired by a commoner, and he says he discovered an entirely new type of magic circle!" Dominic insists. Kallon bursts into laughter. I click my tongue a bit myself at the way "Godfrey's" discovery was framed. He doesn't even know how to draw the damn thing.

"Godfrey is an insane man whose old age only degraded his mind further while he was hiding away," Kallon replies. "He didn't discover anything! Especially not from a commoner. Dominic, they are bumbling idiots. They can't read or wash themselves, much less make new discoveries in magic. These ideas are just childish. Don't worry, you'll understand someday. It may not be easy; learning can be painful! But you will learn how the world works!"

I get an immediate headache, and when Dominic rubs his temples, I can see he feels the same way. I probably won't exactly find an ally in this man, as he wants to change how the monarchy rules and I want to remove the monarchy entirely. But at this moment, I feel his pain. "Learning can be painful," Kallon said. Arrogant little prick. I swear, being condescended to by an honest-to-God idiot is the true pain. It's not even directed at me, or someone I completely agree with, but it still hurts. Kallon has clearly never bothered thinking about anything but his own superiority.

The two argue like this for some time, and I never actually get the chance to introduce myself to either before the party comes to a close. I barely had to avoid dance requests all night and August clearly had a good time. I had hoped to sneak back in after leaving with August, but I'll get another opportunity to slip my little gift into the drinks. This won't be the last party, and I think I have a few leads on possible escorts that I don't mind implicating in some treason in the future.

It wasn't a waste either. This Dominic, and apparently Godfrey, are influential people who, if I heard right, support sharing magic, at least to a degree. That is extremely useful information. I'm in a decent mood as I help the clearly drunk August back to his dorm. I pretty easily carry him inside, where a couple of his dorm mates cheer as I make my way to his room with their directions. I prop him up on his side in bed, then depart, to the same roommates' boos. I give them a smile and tell them to fuck themselves, then head toward my own dorm.

I'll finally get to apologize to Autumn and move forward. I'm a little nervous and remind myself not to let myself get carried away this time as I ascend the stairs in our shared mansion. I take a deep breath, then knock on the door. There is no response and my heart sinks. Did she change her mind?

"Autumn, are you in there?" I call, and I'm met with silence again. It is pretty late; maybe she is asleep. I am about to give up when I hear it. She's quiet and muffled, almost imperceptible, like there is something covering her mouth. I do hear her voice, however, and I hold my ear to the door. Then she says it again. "Help me . . ." she struggles to beg.

I don't hesitate. I kick the heavy oak door off its hinges and barge into the room. Inside stands a man, clothed in a deep navy blue with a mask over his face. He is holding one hand over Autumn's mouth and a knife in the other.

CHAPTER THIRTY-SIX

Sense Emotion

I don't hesitate. Processing what is happening isn't an option. The man's eyes widen as the door flies open, and his knife-wielding hand rises to her throat. Before the door even lands, I am moving across the room. I use force mana to force the intruder's hand against Autumn's collarbone, which is enough to prevent him from drawing the blade across her throat, and in a second I have both his hands gripped in mine. I throw them both away from my friend with all my strength and use force mana to throw the man through the window, then pull Autumn into a hug.

"Are you all ri—" I begin before heaving us both to the side. The man, who somehow stopped himself only a few feet away, threw a knife at Autumn's back, which I barely manage to avoid. She screams and I prepare for the next strike. I use mana to decrease my weight and increase my speed so I can recover and fight without pulling Autumn with me. I'm surprised when I see he hasn't made another move. I stand between him and Autumn, and he seems to have waited for me to recover for some reason.

I take advantage of the brief moment of uncertainty. He is a tall man, towering over me, and he's already brandishing a new throwing knife. That's not what worries me, however. I can overpower a larger man easily enough. What worries me is his aura. He is powerful, more so than almost anyone at the party I just left, excepting the prince and presumably Dominic. I have been fighting with an advantage for a long time now. In every battle I fight, I am surrounded by the grieving and oppressed. People who need my help and whose presence empowers me to help them.

Here, in the middle of a campus full of the rich and powerful, I am just . . . me. Sure, there are at least one or two grieving people . . . somewhere near me. And of course, I am not a weak mage. I have been accumulating mana for years and now surpass any noble family that's been around for less than a century. None of this changes the simple fact that stands before me. I am, for the first time since Baldwin, completely outclassed.

I hold up my fists and take a combat-ready stance anyway. Power isn't everything, and I have a few tricks up my sleeve. I feel a pang of fear as I think about trying to win this fight, and to my horror, his aura grows denser. He has a fucking fear-based aspect. I take a deep breath to calm myself and push the fear down. The mana remains still, and I get my fear under control. I am the picture of focus and I drown out all other emotions with determination, which . . . causes his aura to grow more. Fuck, what kind of aspect is that?

Fine, if that's the case, I won't think. I'll just fight. If his mana is stronger, I'll just beat it out of him. I charge him, swinging a fist and sending force toward his feet to throw him off-balance. He dodges my swing easily and pushes against my force with his own pure aura, strangling my mana. I stumble over his extended foot and he calmly walks past me, going straight for Autumn. As I recover and turn, Autumn screams. The man is forming his own spell. Its color is similar to my force mana but its nature feels different.

I throw force mana at him that he easily deflects. At the same time, I create a loud screeching with sound mana. He can deflect my mana but not the effects created by it. As he smacks his hands over his ears, I push Autumn to the side of the room with force. He flicks his finger and my sound spell is squashed like a grape. I am already running to tackle him, but he leaps over me like Peter fucking Pan. It's not like a force-propelled jump—he literally glides from the ground into a flip over me and gently lands on the other side.

I turn on my heel and he is already casting a powerful fire spell in Autumn's direction. I throw myself between the two, casting an air spell as I do. This one is a vacuum where I deny the passage of air at all, like I would with sound or light. It takes a lot more mana to maintain as vacuums really don't like to exist, it turns out. At the same time, I put a sound barrier between it and myself. This puts the fire out before it can hurt either of us, and the rival mage quickly stops casting.

The combination of the sound it makes beyond my barrier and the nonmagical air pushing us while working to fill the space finally throws the imposing man off-balance as he lurches forward. A large number of stuffed animals, Autumn, and I lurch a bit as well at the brief gust of wind in the room. It only lasts a second before the vacuum closes, however, and our movement is minor. I hope it is enough as I push myself forward with the momentum and try to hit him with a quick jab. It's not as strong as a hook, but for me, it doesn't have to be.

This all happens in a second, and my knuckles are a breath from crushing his skull, but with the same mana as earlier, he gently pushes himself to the side and slides down my arm. The asshole then wraps his arm around my waist and spins me, tossing me across the room. None of his movements are sudden or rough like mine; everything he does is like a dance.

"Fuck!" I yell in frustration while Autumn screams and tries to form her own fire spell to fend off her assailant. He crushes it mercilessly under his mana and begins forming a new spell with a type I haven't seen before. "All right. Enough of this *Crouching Tiger, Hidden Dragon* shit!" I snarl, and reduce my weight, then create an explosion of force behind me. I launch across the room toward him.

Again, he dodges to the side and I fly right past him. The stones I conjured behind me don't, however. I launched them in multiple directions to maximize my chances of hitting him. Two of them collide with his side and cut deep into his flesh while I collide with the brick wall. Before launching myself, I pump mana through my body, reinforcing myself with both pure mana and painful internal force. This stops any bones from breaking, but I feel the crack in my nose as brick meets cartilage.

Blood runs down my face as all three of us recover from the exchange. He is faster than I am, and a new mana rapidly conjures two steel blades over Autumn. I try to push them with force mana, but my frustration and pain combined with Autumn's fear have empowered the man even more. He crushes my spell without so much as a glance. How many fucking aspects does he have? I watch the steel blades fall, ready to bisect Autumn, and I panic, throwing myself between the two.

Crushing mana inside my body is still beyond him, and so my reinforced body manages to block the blades. From killing anyone, in any case. Both blades still bite deep into my flesh and bone, and I cry out in agony as they slow. They cut over half an inch into my forearm and push me back into Autumn, forcing her against the wall.

"I don't want to fucking hurt you. Now, get out of my way," sneers the vaguely familiar voice of the attacker. He then takes advantage of my disorientation from the pain to grab a handful of my hair and roughly throw me across the room. I collide with the bed frame, which collapses with the impact. Panicked, I dig my way out from the splintered wood and grab the edge of the rug the man is standing on. I pull it with all my strength, and the man actually stumbles, falling to the ground. The combination of his bleeding side and the lack of mana in my attack finally took him down.

I try to regain my feet before he does but immediately stumble to one knee. I look down at the sharp pain that lost me my balance and find a nearly foot-long shard of wood from the frame lodged between two of my ribs. I feel a familiar blackness edging into the corners of my eyes and fight it off with sheer force of will. If I pass out here, Autumn dies. I don't know why he wants me alive and her dead, but it's the only advantage I have.

It's too late to attack him since I stumbled. So, gripping my side, I run to Autumn instead, putting myself in his way again. As he recovers his feet and clutches his own side, he sighs. I see him forming a powerful spell when everyone feels it. The pressure of an even more powerful mage. I didn't use all those sound spells for no reason. Help is coming and we all know it. The man glares at me, grabs the wood splinter in my side, yanks it out, and flees through the window.

I immediately cough up blood and grip my side. It is bleeding profusely, and I have to use heat mana to burn the flesh and stop the blood before I lose too much. I look around, fighting for consciousness. The new mana is still approaching, and I move quickly. I don't know what this is about, but it's an opportunity. I retrieve a small bag of garlic and sprinkle it on the ground. I know they have noticed this little calling card, and if I'm going to get my ass kicked, I might as well get an alibi out of it.

Barely a second after I hide the pouch, Headmistress Cateline storms in. She takes one look around the room, glares at me, and begins directing a parade of mages to search the area. She instructs one to get a doctor and I let myself collapse. I don't pass out, but I just . . . lie there and wait for help to come. Fuck, this hurts.

"Th-thank you, Lillith," Autumn whispers, and I roll my head in her direction to look at her. I don't have the energy to really keep my eyes locked on hers, but I hold my hand in a weak thumbs-up.

"Anytime, kid," I wheeze before erupting into coughs. That's not good. Something is ruptured in there. The world starts to wobble a bit, and I try to put my other arm over my eyes, only to stop as I see two foot-long blades still wedged into it. Instead, I just close my eyes. After an eternity, the doctor arrives and I am hoisted onto some kind of stretcher. As they carry me out of the building, I see Leo rushing to my side.

"Move aside, child," Cateline orders while literally pushing him over with mana. He crumples on the ground in pain, and I try to glare at the woman but lack the energy to put real emotion into it.

"Don't do that to him," I groan, and she suddenly jerks her head to me, pure disgust on her face.

"What did you just say?" she sneers before pressing one of the blades further into my arm with her thumb.

I find the energy to cry out at the pain. I am not reinforcing my body anymore, and the sharp blade cuts through me like butter.

"I said," I struggle to answer through gritted teeth, "don't fucking do that!"

She holds her thumb in place for another second, and then as suddenly as it came, her rage melts away. She waves to the doctor to take me to be treated and stays to speak to Leo. I want to help the kid out, but I can't do anything but be carried away right now.

I want to pass out, but two thoughts keep me fighting to stay awake. As the blood runs from my mouth and nose, I curse internally. First, I'm pretty sure I just fought a fucking bard. Warriors exclusive to royalty. Second, they are going to try to measure my fucking pulse.

CHAPTER THIRTY-SEVEN

Reconciliation

I manage to fight off sleep for the duration of my initial treatment. It's an unpleasant choice to make in a world without effective anesthetics, but I have to pump mana through my blood to simulate a heartbeat. Eventually, they actually bring a priest in to help heal me, which is less helpful than they expect. The priest, who has no understanding of biology, does the same thing Baldwin did and just tries to form my body into an image he has in his mind. If I hadn't made changes to myself, this would work. Instead, I have to fight off his intent to keep my enhancements intact. My fangs are almost useable, and I don't intend to lose them and my blood poison right now.

All this together results in a decidedly unpleasant treatment, a lot of teeth grinding, and enough pained eye watering to leave my eyes red and puffy.

And so I find myself in front of Headmistress Cateline looking like some kind of pale, bloated fish. She eyes me appraisingly from behind her desk, and I can see the disapproval written across her face. If not for my current state, she'd see the same on mine. I haven't forgotten her thumb on the knife in my arm.

She looks through a few papers before looking back up at me. "So, Autumn of Forrester, Eleonor of Renatus, Iris of Bonner, and you, Lillith of Endings," she intones, maintaining eye contact with me. "No one of particular import in your dorm. And yet, a mage with enough power to avoid our knights and sneak onto campus targeted you, of all people. Would you care to enlighten me as to why?"

I don't even have to lie, not really.

I can think of multiple reasons someone would target me, but Autumn? She's just a cute kid trying to live her life. "I don't know why that man was there," I answer. "I wish I did. I'd actually like to avoid being thrown around like a rag doll in the future, if possible."

She just gives me an unamused look.

"Can you tell me how you survived, then?" she interrogates me. I lean my head back in exhaustion.

"Barely," I quip, and she just glares at me expectantly. "I don't know. I don't think he was trying to kill us. Whatever he wanted, it was something else."

"And what might that be?" she practically accuses, an eyebrow raised.

"I couldn't say, but tell you what? I'll ask the guy next time I see him," I retort.

She smacks her papers onto her desk with a loud thump to illustrate her frustration with me.

"This is not a game, Lillith. Your tone and behavior are unacceptable. The company you keep is abhorrent, and you are developing behavioral issues. I expected more from Lord Godfrey's apprentice. You are going to embarrass him," she reprimands, and I roll my pained eyes. She'll further injure a beaten child and that's conducting herself like a noble lady, but I have breakfast with Leo and I am disgracing Godfrey. She seriously needs to get over this shit.

"Believe me," I say, "I am the architect of my own behavioral issues. And I honestly can't tell you anything more about our attacker. I would love to have them out of the picture, so I would tell you if I knew anything."

She examines me for a long moment.

"If it were up to me, I would expel you right now just for your attitude. You are lucky to have Lord Godfrey supporting you, and you should appreciate him more." Apparently, she is more concerned with my lack of respect than with the man who attacked her students. "As it stands, I will suspend you instead. For causing a violent disturbance on campus. You and Autumn will be banned from campus for two weeks. It would be longer, but your aspecting class is scheduled to measure students' mana levels at that point. This will not happen again, do you understand?"

I just start laughing at that. It's all I can do. What a fucking piece of work. It's fine, I'd rather heal up around my family anyway. The laughter makes her angrier, and I should hold it back, but I just can't. I'm exhausted, in pain, and this shit is just too much. Sometimes it's all you can do. The rest of our conversation is less than productive, and eventually, I am sent to the dorm to collect my things. Here, I find Autumn, sitting on the floor and clutching her knees in front of my door.

She has been crying herself, and I can understand why. Teenage girls aren't supposed to have to fight for their lives from assassins. I feel a pang of guilt. She was clearly the target, but the assassin's efforts to keep me alive make it clear it was not unrelated to me.

"You all right, Autumn?" I ask gently, and when she realizes I am there, she throws herself to her feet and wraps her arms around me.

"I'm sorry, Lillith, I'm so sorry!" she sobs into my shoulder, and I rub her back. Has she been blaming herself for my injuries?

"No, Autumn, I am. I don't know who that guy was, but if it's anyone's fault he was after you, it's mine. I am so sorry. And I'm sorry about how I handled that conversation. I could have addressed certain aspects of it, particularly with your parents, a lot better. Will you give me another chance?" I ask, but she just starts sobbing harder. So I hold her and let her get it out. If there is something I know as well as anyone, it's what it feels like to need a cry. Sometimes, you just carry it with you. For days, weeks, years. A good cry can wait just beneath the surface, weighing you down until you just . . . set it free. Surviving an assassination attempt at fourteen will definitely do it.

It's a good while before she calms down, but I don't mind. Once she does, I bring up the awkward reality of our suspension. They aren't going to let us stay here forever. "So, uh, I don't know if they told you about our suspension . . ." I trail off but she nods, wiping her eyes on her sleeves.

"I know," she answers. "Lady Cateline told me . . ." I see all the concern I expected behind her eyes. I address it before she can.

"I know you have no place to stay and might be nervous about renting a room alone. My family's home is . . . below the standard you are used to. But it's safe, and you are welcome there . . . if you want," I offer. She looks up at me with wide, red eyes. Then, for some reason, she begins sobbing again.

"Th-thank you, L-Lillith!" she responds through sobs. "Y-you are too nice to me . . . You fought so hard, and . . . and . . . I'm sorry!" I just hug her. My own eyes water. It's my fault, and she is beating herself up so much.

"Of course I fought. You are my friend, Autumn. I already hurt you. I scared you. And then you were attacked, probably because of me. I should be the one saying I'm sorry." I try to reassure her, but it doesn't help. We go around like this for a while before she calms down again.

Finally, she responds to my offer.

"I would love to stay with your family."

"We'll be happy to have you." I give her a gentle smile. "Come on, let's get your things."

We go about the work of packing, and several hours later, we arrive at my family's makeshift home. The other women we are sheltering are scattered around the first floor. There are fewer of them now, as many have been evacuated, just in case. I think Autumn will still have to share a room with me, for now. It's the best way to protect her if she is attacked again anyway. We are all closer to our emergency escape route this way as well.

In the corner I spot Edward, smiling and chatting with a blonde woman. I narrow my eyes as I realize she has always been there when Ed has chosen to chat or eat with our guests instead of the family. Then I recognize her dress as the one Mom was making with Ed when I first got here. Perhaps he really wasn't avoiding me . . . He then spots me and hurriedly looks away. The woman he is with crosses her arms and says something under her breath I can't quite understand. The two seem to have a light disagreement that consists of her scolding him, and I take note of it for later.

I am quickly distracted as the rest of my family comes to greet me.

"Lily, what a pleasant . . . What happened to you??" my mother exclaims when she notices my bandages and awkward walk. She rushes to my side to examine me more closely. Gilbert and Henry shake their heads with concern, but both are familiar with some of the fights I have found myself in.

"I heckled an angry minstrel," I joke, and she gives me that unamused look only moms can manage.

"I know you do some dangerous things, Lillith. It scares me to death just to think about, but I don't try to stop you. I understand why you do what you do. The least you can do is be honest and serious with me," she scolds.

"You're right, I'm sorry, Mom." I nod. "Sometimes a joke is just how I keep things from getting to me," I say apologetically. "To answer that, let me introduce my friend Autumn." I gesture at her, then tell the story of the fight. My mom looks like she is having heart palpitations, and the concern on my brothers' faces is clear as well.

"I'd hate to be that guy when you find out who he is," Gilbert half jokes.

"He must really be something if he managed to beat you so badly," Henry adds, and Autumn nods along.

"You have no idea," she says, and the entire group kinda looks at each other, wondering how much the others know.

"I'm Gilbert, by the way. It's a pleasure to meet you, Lady Autumn." He bows and she politely curtsies in response.

"The pleasure is mutual, Lord Gilbert," she responds formally, and Henry and I both practically choke.

"Yeah, Lord Gilbert, the pleasure is mutual." I laugh, and Gilbert blushes at the friendly but mocking tone.

"We don't really use titles like that," Henry explains with a smile. "I'm Henry. I'm happy to meet one of Lily's friends." She fumbles this curtsy, blushing a little. Henry doesn't miss it and his cheeks flush as well. Mom comes to their rescue.

"Well, we are very happy to have you, Autumn. I'll get everyone some tea," she announces before running to the kitchen.

"Autumn and I have some things to talk about, so we are going to head up to my room. We need to get her unpacked anyway," I say, and my brothers let us go. "Tell Mom she can bring the tea up!" I call behind us as I lead Autumn to the room I usually sleep in when I stay.

When we get there, we sit down on opposite beds and face each other. We are quiet for a while, then we both start to speak at the same time, tripping over each other in our attempts to end the awkward silence. Then we both try to concede to the other and delay the conversation again. Finally, my mom drops off the tea, a nice blend I . . . acquired . . . from a richer family's home, and we finally manage to speak to each other.

"I feel like . . ." I begin as Autumn takes a sip of tea. "I feel like when we last spoke, I got too caught up in the *whys* of what I am doing and didn't explain enough of the *whats*." She looks down and doesn't respond, so I continue speaking. "First, I'd like to tell you more about Satusmor. What I did, what I wanted to do, and what went wrong."

CHAPTER THIRTY-EIGHT

How Many Times Can We Say No?

I don't want to be a violent person. I am—violent—but I don't want to be. I am violent to fight back. On my own behalf, and on behalf of others. I kill in self-defense. Defense from immediate violence and defense from structural violence. This is something I started to talk about before, but . . . I didn't do it very well.

"This is where I failed you. This is where I left you crying and fearing for your loved ones. I am so sorry. I want to do better. Not just with you, but with everything. Because I don't want to be a violent person. In another world, where I had a better chance, I would resort to it far less frequently. I don't want to hurt anyone . . . Well, that's not true. That's what I tell myself, but it's a lie, and I want to be honest here. There are people I want to hurt. People who see pain as a revenue stream, who inspire depths of grief and rage that I just . . . But, sorry, I'm getting distracted again.

"The point is, I don't want to organize an army and lead them in a war against the nobility. I don't want to drag every noble through the streets and execute them in the public square. In fact, what I want is a world where violence is not the shadow behind every corner and the collar on every neck.

"I just want a world where people take care of each other. Where homes and hygiene products aren't withheld from anyone. Where people aren't things. I just want people to be treated as people. Not tools that are owned. Not objects to be manipulated and coerced. Just . . . people.

"That is what I set out to build in Satusmor. Not an army. Not a group of raiders and avengers to make the nobility pay. For certain people, there was no avoiding violence. I knew this. But it wasn't the goal. The goal, and the way it began, was to start with just one city where people were treated as people.

"Not an easy thing to do in a country ruled by a king, but I thought I had a chance. In part because this country makes no sense. The more I learn about it, the less sense it makes. Communication between cities is slow. Travel is rare. Both far more than makes any sense. Even then, I knew we barely had any trade between cities. This is weird, but it gave me an advantage.

"It gave me a chance to change one city without the entire country crushing us. And at first, it went well. Great, even. But, as you know, it failed. Things went wrong for four reasons. Two of them I expected and was prepared to respond to. One of them I knew about but had to live with. The final problem I should have expected—I did, but only to a minor degree. I had no idea the extent to which it would poison anything and everything I tried.

"I started with the poor. The homeless and abandoned. The people we lock away in the corners of society and ignore so we don't have to feel uncomfortable or guilty. This wasn't part of any plan at all. I just had the tools to feed and clothe them, and they needed it.

"Anyone with a fire and a loaf of bread faced with starving and freezing people would offer to share what they have. And if they could teach them to start a fire of their own, they would. I understand, in hindsight, and with the versatility of magic, that in the case of mana, this may seem more like giving them a sword. But anyone who denies them the fire because *if they know how to make fire, they might burn someone's house down*? Well, that person has simply never been so cold.

"But, after that, I moved on. I killed the man who was trying to force me into a marriage, and I killed his father who gave him the authority to do so. At the same time, I cut the head off the snake in that city.

"For a while, there was no real direction behind the guards or the few knights in the city, and the different nobles in town couldn't agree on who was in charge. I was free to move about and act without too much fear of an organized response.

"So I went to the farmers and the ranchers. It is amazing how much power is granted by food distribution. If one man had absolute power over all magic, but another was the only one who could ever create food, the man with bread would be king.

"I shared magic with them and some of them agreed to share food with others. They learned earth and plant magic faster than anyone else learned any aspects, the effects of working with both for so long. They produced food faster than ever, and it changed lives. They could provide for the extravagant feasts of the nobility and the needs of the commoners without working themselves into an early grave. Street kids agreed to help them handle the larger harvests as well. And this did work close to how I'd intended . . . at first.

"Next, I went to vendors. Not large merchants but bakers and tailors. People struggling to survive selling basic goods. Then I went to women. Women looking for an escape from marriages and guardians who abused and violated them. Even some noblewomen were looking for somewhere they could live without a guardian. I helped all of them find new homes and introduced the idea of magic healing, to little effect, unfortunately.

"This is how I spent the early months, after Godfrey left and before things got bad. And I helped people, or rather, people helped each other. It's the best I've felt since I was brought into this world. It was easier than it ever would have been without magic. Magic makes self-sufficiency an almost obvious way to live.

"But it couldn't last. It wasn't long before I started running into problems. The first was the most obvious. I was alone and . . . I'm just not good at this. I can put my neck on the line any day. I can take a hit as many times as I need to. But getting people to work together effectively and long term? I'm, well, a failure. I can give an impassioned speech, but truth be told, a lot of people just don't like me. They don't like each other, and I'm ill-equipped to help with that.

"The second was that people are people. For every person happy to be given new tools for survival and new people to rely on, there were more than a few eager to grasp onto power themselves. Some already had a tiny taste of it in their little gangs, clubs, or marriages, and they craved more. Others respond to being beaten down with fantasies of holding the club themselves. These are the ones who caused a scene. The ones who tried attacking women and picking fights with each other and guards.

"Then, there is violence. Structural violence. Authority. The kind of violence that is used against commoners every day. When rapists are willfully ignored or children are denied food. The violence of taking a home away from someone who can't afford it, of forcing people to degrade themselves for their supposed betters or face eventual death. The violence that is authority, because that's exactly what authority is. It doesn't always look that way. But that's what it is. In all its different forms, whether from a kind leader or a cruel one, it always boils down to how many times you can say no.

"A cruel leader will become violent the first time. A kind one will take longer to get there, but eventually, it ends in violence. If there is no violence, then there was never any authority in the first place. It ends in enslavement, imprisonment, execution, or a slow death by starvation and abandonment. As we learned on the way here, it sometimes ends in the Radiant Woods. It's in authority's nature.

"So, when the guards wanted magic for themselves and only themselves? Well, that was a question of how many times we could say no. When we didn't need degrading jobs to feed ourselves and the richer nobles had to take care of themselves, and they told us we had to come back? How many times could we say no? When we stopped paying the prices for wood and meat and didn't pay merchants just for carrying it to us? Well, you get the point. That's what I mean when I say I am violent defensively. Even when I am the one who goes looking for a fight. Even when rapists kneel in front of me and surrender. Because, once I let them go, they go back to telling people that *no* isn't an option.

"That's what I was doing. Not organizing an army. Not creating my own little magic soldiers to fight and die for me. I was giving people a chance to say no, and connecting them so they could lean on each other instead of on people who hated them. I did this knowing that it would lead to violence. I did this fully prepared to fight. Because I knew opting out was never an option. We are commodities, and by living and supporting ourselves, we were stealing.

"So as soon as Lord William showed up and reorganized the city leadership, they came for us. Mostly the city guard. We were still below the notice of the powerful nobles, and I was the only one with enough magic to be dangerous to an armed and trained soldier. The guards captured people and tortured them. They raided the houses of penance and discovered my magic circles. They started learning magic of their own, and being the most familiar with weapons and pain, they learned to use it faster than any of the other commoners. Like the farmers and their plants, the guards found their own cruel aspects with terrifying speed.

"That's when things truly fell apart. The nobles didn't want the guards having magic any more than us. Just like us, the guards were a tool. So Lord William sent the few knights in the city after any commoners with magic, guards or otherwise. Meanwhile, the guards kept coming after the rest of us. The guard captain, Horrus, was the worst. He was like a hound with a taste for blood. He had figured out magic quickly, and he was cruel. He took pleasure in hunting us down.

"When he found the first house I went to, he . . . well. Anyway. He was cruel. So when you heard there were battlefields in the city streets, that's what you were hearing about. People who just wanted a life of their own being hunted down for saying no. None of this was insurmountable. It would have been easier if I weren't so inadequate. If I had organized better or communicated more frequently or just been fucking faster, maybe the few friends I had wouldn't have . . . But that's not the point. Even with someone like me, only good at fighting, we could have been okay. We could have fought back.

"But that leads us to the final problem. The catastrophic issue that pulled everything apart. At first, I thought it was normal. People stopped trusting each other. They became paranoid that everyone was leading the guards back to them. The farmers started to grow too afraid to distribute as much food. Fights broke out and groups fell out. This is normal when you are being hunted. It's normal to an extent anytime a new group forms. But . . . it kept getting worse.

"I found barns, full of rotting food managed by distrustful farmers. Families broke apart, turning on each other. Even houses of penance devolved into chaos. It was worse than anything anyone had ever warned about in a world without the rule of law. That may make sense to some, but it's a silly thing to believe. Or it should be. People turn on each other in stressful situations, but not like this. This wasn't just my bad organizational skills, and this wasn't the stress of a more powerful enemy.

"See, this is another thing that makes no sense about this country. One country, for thousands of years. One royal family, the entire time. All the scheming and plotting of the most power-hungry people in the world and there has never been so much as one upset, much less commoners fighting back on a meaningful scale. That just doesn't make sense, especially in the early years when mages weren't as powerful.

"It was confession.

"Most commoners, in every city in the country, go through confession. Not everyone—some find ways out of it—but it doesn't need to be all of them. And they go through it regularly. So when one priest dies, the effects don't end. The idea of mistrust in other commoners is built into our brains during confession. It is wedged in there by a hostile and invading force and kept there under the pretense of piety.

We are programmed to rely on our supposed betters. The harder we fight back, the more it takes effect.

"We were never allowed to opt out. We were never allowed to take care of each other. Even our minds were their property all along. I knew this violation would hurt us, but I didn't realize how thorough it was. That was the nail in the coffin. That was my biggest failure."

Autumn has been letting me speak uninterrupted, but as I grow quiet and she sees my eyes start to water, she moves over to my bed to put her hand on mine. "So, what did you do?" she asks, and I take a deep breath.

"Well. There was only one thing I could do," I answer, preparing to tell the rest of the story. At least, the parts I am ready to talk about. "I went to church."

CHAPTER THIRTY-NINE

I Want to Do Better

I'm not like Sarafyna. I can't spot a user of divine magic from a mile away. And I lived with a priest. As far as I can tell, a lot of them are just . . . people. People like you who worship the Collector and want to do the right thing. Not all of them use divine magic to manipulate the populace and keep us in our place. I don't think many of them even know about it. So I had to go to the temple. I lived with a priest and he was a genuine, kind man. He cared about children more than anyone. Given some recent . . . revelations, I can be even more certain he doesn't know everything his leaders are up to," I begin again, and Autumn interrupts for the first time.

"W-what revelations?" she nervously interjects. I can see she is struggling to process everything I have said, but the things I'm saying about the church are the worst. I pause before responding, worried about upsetting her further, then decide to just get through what I am saying first.

"I'll . . . get to that in a bit," I respond awkwardly, scratching the back of my head. "For now, I'd like to get to the end of this, if possible." She looks frustrated and anxious, but she reluctantly nods. So, I continue. "Right . . . So, even knowing the temple was responsible for keeping people in submission and suffering and slavery for as long as they did . . . I couldn't just lock the doors and throw a torch through the window. Because, unlike the guards, they aren't open about their atrocities with their subordinates.

"So I did something I really, really didn't want to do. I went to confession. I was exempt, as a noblewoman, but I went anyway. It's hard to describe what that experience was like. It was almost better when I couldn't remember it. The feeling of sitting in the center of a group of people trying to worm their slimy little fingers into my mind was repulsive. It feels like being licked. Like they were crawling under my skin and looking for a comfortable place to burrow in.

"It was all I could do to identify the priests responsible. I could feel their intent, the beliefs they tried to force into me. It was everything I feared. Paranoia, hatred, and even disgust for all the people I wanted to help. Admiration and love for the people above me. A desire to bend the knee to the lords and ladies above me and to trust the temple above all else. They tried to take me away from myself. I had to refuse and play along at the same time.

"It worked though. I found them. I burned their faces into my mind in place of the sickness they tried to put there. But they don't all go to every confession. So I had to go again. And again and again. Each time felt like standing naked in a room full of people laughing and ridiculing every flaw they perceived. Except it was my soul that failed to meet their standards, not my body. But I kept going back until I recognized every single offender, every single time.

"At that point, there was only one thing left to do. Free the minds of my friends. So I went looking for the priests who had surrounded me and tried to own me. Who had done the same to children all over the city. I followed them. I learned when they would be alone and when they would be expected. And one by one, I removed their tentacles from the minds of their victims. It was . . . grueling. As I said, while I recognize violence as necessary, I don't enjoy it.

"There is only one way to end that magic. I don't have another option; I want you to understand that. The entire world is built to prevent change. From the country to the individual. There is no hope of rehabilitation, only endings. But priests . . . priests are hard to end. Divine mages can heal themselves, and their bodies fight injury more than ours do. Depending on their level of ability, it can take quite a bit of effort. So I had to poison them first, then corner them when they were alone. Or I would be dead now and everyone in Satusmor would still have a mind rapist in their heads.

"It was . . . grueling. As I said, while I recognize violence as necessary, I don't enjoy it. It was . . . a lot. Slow and . . . hard to stomach. It makes me sick just to think about it. But . . . it worked. Not at first. There were too many of them, and they had done this too many times to too many people. But once every priest who ever controlled a person was gone, the victims had their minds back. They were in charge of their own actions and emotions again. Once I had removed enough, a lot of people changed. Not as much as you might think, but enough.

"The priests were subtle. Their long-term control mostly only extended to what they perceived as potential dangers. Dangers to them or to the kingdom. People only grew suspicious and violent with each other once they had stopped relying on either religion or government to survive. Or rather, once people found an alternative, the priest's control insured it would fall apart. But with enough divine mages gone, that last step became possible again. People were willing to work together. Without mind control, the idea of sharing extra food and getting extra help started to look attractive again.

"But, of course, a lot of the damage was done. The control was gone but the memories weren't. People still remembered every farmer who let food rot while they starved. They still remembered every friend who turned on them and every cruel word they lashed out with. The division was there; it wasn't easy to heal. I couldn't have what I almost had before, but some small communities still managed to emerge. Small groups of people who had a taste of a better life, who wanted to give it another shot.

"They are the ones who gave me hope for Satusmor. The ones who distribute food when the guards aren't looking and share their homes or shelter women hiding from their guardians. It wasn't enough. Not to survive long term. Not in a world built to make that type of life impossible. But it existed and, to my knowledge, still does. Things were quieting down when I left Satusmor. I failed there. I rushed things. I didn't have enough help. I didn't take the reach of the temple into account. And people got hurt. But it doesn't have to be that way.

"I'm only telling you this because I want to be completely up front. I want you to understand what I have done and why, even the things that look . . . less than honorable from the outside. And because I want you to understand the lengths I will go to, not just to help the victims of this country but to make sure I am only doing what is necessary. I won't be tearing through the houses of nobles and executing anyone I see. And I won't stand by while anyone else does.

"Even though they benefit from the state of commoners, they didn't choose to be born a noble. Even though the temple is responsible for violating so many people, I understand individual priests don't know this. And the guards . . . Well, the more I investigate them, the more it seems like complicity in slavery is universal. But I am putting effort into confirming that. All this is to say, as long as I can help it, innocent people are safe. I am not targeting your parents or anyone else like them.

"At the same time, all the violence you are afraid of? It's already happening every single day. This country wades through fresh blood with every step it takes. It's so thick in the air I can hardly breathe. It's how the common people are controlled, and it's how we force people to serve us and clean our mansions. I intend to end that, but I don't control everyone. I can organize people, or I can try, and I can try to show them a better way of doing things. But not everyone will listen.

"That's what I was trying to tell you, before. Things aren't safe. Not for most people. Most people are living one mistake away from starvation, homelessness, and death. Many others are trying to survive after that mistake. They can be turned into a slave, killed, or beaten, on a whim. The world is everything you are afraid of it becoming, and it always has been. It just looks peaceful because you were born into a group that is protected by it. At the end of the day, it does keep a small portion of the population safe, just at the expense of the rest.

"And yeah. Removing this system is going to take that protection away. And for people who have lived with it their entire lives, that is terrifying. I haven't known you that long, but I don't think you are the kind of person who wants to feel safe by maintaining that constant state of violence and fear over everyone else."

I finally pause, giving Autumn a minute to process everything I have said. She does look conflicted, but she isn't crying into her arms this time.

"And . . . that's everything that happened?" she finally asks.

"No. That's . . . a quick overview, but it's not everything. I lost people. I saw them get hurt because of my mistakes. Because of my failures. I really don't want to talk about the specifics of what happened to them, but I will. If you need me to," I allow. And I would. Eventually, I should. These realities deserve to exist outside of my nightmares. But . . . I will always want one more day where I don't have to say it out loud.

She doesn't speak for a long time, and we just sit next to each other on my bed. Eventually, she sniffs and stands up. "Well, Lillith. That's . . . a lot. But thank you for telling me. I don't really know how to respond right away. But . . . can I just ask one question?" she asks.

I nod. "Sure, if you aren't tired of my voice," I reply, trying to hide the tension in my shoulders.

"You said you want to do better," she begins, "which means you are going to try again. You probably already are, somehow. So, the way you are doing things this time. Will we be safe? August and I, and the people around us?"

I look at her for a moment, trying to decide how to answer. She doesn't break eye contact, silently insisting on a response. "I know what my mistakes were. I won't repeat them. I am being more careful. I am getting help. And I am moving more slowly. For the next couple of years at least, you will be as safe as ever. Things won't look like they did in Satusmor . . . but . . . this has to end, Autumn. It can't go on. It just can't. And ending it won't be bloodless." I see the worry starting to paint her face, so I hold up a hand. "But," I add, "I have a safe place. I can keep anyone you need safe when that time comes. Just say the word."

At this, I see a thousand pounds lift from her shoulders.

"You promise?" she asks again, and I hold out a pinky, which she raises an eyebrow at.

"Sorry, you grab my pinky with yours. It's the most sacred kind of promise." I chuckle through an awkward smile. And just like that, the tension breaks and she finally laughs. It sounds like music and my heart grows lighter. Then, just as I think things can start to get better, I see a new expression on her face and my mood dampens again.

"Lillith, there is something that I . . ." She trails off and then another thought occurs to her. "Wait, what were the recent revelations about the temple?" Oh right. The kids. Peter confessed his actual affiliation with the church to Sarafyna, and it made bile rise in my throat. And . . . she had gone to help his friends last night. And . . . I was supposed to meet up with them. Fuck.

"Shit, I am sorry, Autumn, but you just reminded me of something urgent I have to do. Can you hang out here for now?" I ask. She tilts her head.

"Hang out? What does that—"

I cut her off.

"Sorry, no time to explain. Just . . . stay here. Get to know my mom. I really need to go," I explain as fast as I can while rapidly changing into my more practical clothes. A moment later and I am out the door, rushing to get to Sarafyna.

CHAPTER FORTY

The Safe House

I rush to our agreed-on meeting place, but I have little hope I'll find her there. I was supposed to be there fucking yesterday, and she would have had a group of children with her. She would have had to take them back on her own. Without me to watch everyone's back, that wouldn't be impossible, but it would be extremely difficult. I know I missed it because I had to fight a much more powerful mage, but even so . . . I have just been talking about wanting to do better.

Yet I literally forgot about a bunch of abused children who need my help. If ever there was evidence that Sara and I can't do this alone, this is it. I curse as I ride in the wagon I have rented for the purpose. The driver is going as fast as he can, but the roads are still too busy for me to move freely and without attracting attention. The ride feels like it takes weeks, but I am just impatient. Finally, we pull up to the corner I directed the driver to, and I rush off, flipping him a large coin as a tip.

Then I move as quickly as I can without everyone seeing me. Unfortunately, I am already a woman dressed in pants and leather armor. Running about with magic spells would basically be crying out to the world that something suspicious was up. I don't know how much the authorities know about me. As far as the chatty girl from my math class knows, they don't have much aside from my preferred targets and that I leave garlic when I kill. I haven't left any targets alive, but not every servant has wanted to come with me. They could easily have a description of my clothes.

So I move through the alleys, using illusory walls when I have to pass busy roads. This is an extremely high risk. If someone passes through one, all sorts of alarm bells will go off. My illusions duplicate existing light, so I can't make unique images. So when the wall goes up, it may look, to anyone paying attention, that the people in the road suddenly got slightly closer to them. Most will dismiss the discrepancy as a trick of the eyes, but I nevertheless have to move quickly when I use them.

With this, I manage to arrive at a humble house just outside the temple. I bought this house under a false name and was planning to rendezvous with Sara once we were both done with our tasks. It is close enough to the temple that Sara should have been able to move the kids here without being spotted, if they were quick. They wouldn't have had to move in the open for very long at all. It's also small enough that no one would think to search it for such a large group of people.

It's one of several similar safe houses I've set up around the city, and if they are still waiting for me, they are in the basement I excavated with earth mana. I rush inside and down the hidden hatch. Sara is not there, and neither is anyone else. I search for signs of them but find nothing. As far as I can tell, Sara never came here in the first place. Considering the hatch above was closed and covered, if she did come here, she left the same way she came in. That would be extremely odd.

As I am looking around, I hear faint voices. No one should be here and my hackles immediately rise. Using sound mana, I use a similar trick to my illusory walls and duplicate the sound above me. This way, I can hear the conversation without sticking my head out. "Did you say she went in here?" a man says, and my heart sinks.

"It looked like it. Just a little while ago. Do you think she has something to do with . . ." a second man responds, and I narrow my eyes.

"A suspicious woman in men's clothes, skulking about an abandoned . . . shack like this the night after a high priest is murdered? Yeah, I think she has something to do with it. Are you some kind of idiot?" the first man sneers.

"Sh-should we go in?" his friend asks, nerves clear in his voice.

I look up at the uncovered hatch and then to the center of the basement where the most dangerous secret I have sits. I can't allow them to find this place. It would ruin everything. But they are priests. Hard to deal with, especially if they haven't been dosed with my blood poison yet. I feel the roof of my mouth with my tongue. The fangs aren't ready yet, but . . . they are close. If I focus all my mana on this one change, while I am here in this house, I might have a chance.

Instead of climbing the rope ladder I have in place, I leap up out of the hatch and close it, using a sound bubble to hide the clang as it slams shut. Then I cover it with a rug and sit down to focus. Up here, I don't need a spell to hear the voices. It's a small building and they are just outside. "No, we should ignore it and go about our merry way," the more abrasive man retorts. "Of course we should go inside! Do you want to report to Medici that we found a suspect and ran away?"

"N-no, it's just that . . ." The timid man hesitates. "You didn't see the body. Whatever did that . . . it's not human. I just . . . I don't want to go like that . . ."

I keep one ear on the conversation as I focus every ounce of my mana to manipulate the makeup of my body. I am just a breath away from finishing my fangs, and I need them now. I grit my teeth. Typically, I can't feel the changes as I make them. Rushing it like this, however, is a different story. Even though I have very little left to do, the pain is excruciating. I audibly growl as I force the mana through my veins, trying to put those last pieces in place. I feel the flesh fold and contort around the new, needlelike teeth. The taste of copper fills my mouth as loose skin bleeds and the fangs taste air for the first time.

"Oh, just shut up," the abrasive man rebukes. "You'll be fine. I want to find this killer and show them who they're fucking with."

At that, the door swings open. I open my eyes and see both priests enter, the larger of them practically being dragged by the smaller one. There is an awkward moment as we all stare at each other, and sweat rolls down my forehead as I try to force new venom through freshly grown channels into my already bloody fangs. For a brief moment, I wonder if I can talk my way out of it. These could just be regular priests, after all, and I wouldn't be the first woman in town to walk around in pants. They would consider it weird, sinful even, but as a noblewoman, I would probably get away.

I quickly dismiss the idea. If they have a description of the killer in the rumors, they'll never let me talk my way out of it, and I'm wearing a mask with magical darkness surrounding my face. I either show my face and hope they don't think it's weird, or I handle this now. It sounds like Sara had to kill one of them last night as well, which is not ideal and probably ruins any chances of explaining my behavior away. If they aren't divine mages, however, I might be able to run. They have an aura, so they are mages, but it's only the divine magic I am worried about.

This worry is shortly dismissed as I feel the familiar discomfort of having too much blood drawn. At least one of them is using divine magic on me. I growl at the violation and glare at them, allowing the red of my eyes to pass through the light barrier in my hood. This is primarily a scare tactic, and it works. They each have a varying level of horror on their face before I leap from my spot and throw my shoulder into the smaller man. This isn't typically the choice I would make, but since the larger man is clearly also the larger coward, it seems like the thing to do.

I hold back enough to leave him alive, but he flies into the wall and I hear a crack. I then turn to the side and swing a fist at the remaining priest. He is still terrified but he raises his arm in time. It snaps as my punch makes contact and he is immediately knocked from his feet. I have to rely on physical attacks while my mana is all focused on my fangs, but I still have the advantage. Then, while both priests are down, I make one last push, and just like that, everything clicks into place. I can feel the fangs move without a thought, not unlike my own fingers. Venom flows smoothly through them, causing a slight tickle. Extending, retracting, and killing with them is as easy as breathing. My latest enhancement is complete.

I examine the priests as they recover. As I feared, both of them are rapidly healing. Two divine mages. Well, it's too late for them now. I throw a sound bubble around the building with my now-useable mana. I feel the slithering of their divine magic continue to assault me, but I throw it off easily enough. The smaller man's eyes widen as he stands. "Demon!" he yells, and the larger man actually yelps, like a kicked dog. Both begin to form spells I recognize and I immediately move to the more dangerous of the two, forming a spell behind me as I do.

Elemental magic is the most common as it is the easiest to understand. The smaller priest is forming a stone dome around himself while the larger priest begins to throw fire at both of us. It's not a terrible plan, blocking me in and protecting the priest I am fighting while roasting the entire area with fire. But it is far too late. I use a thin vacuum to disperse the fire behind me, creating a wall of flames between their caster and me. It also obstructs his view and allows me to deal with his friend.

With the steel in my gloves and my current strength, I swing a fist and crack the stone dome in front of me. I tilt my head, surprised it withstood the hit, then punch a second time. It shatters and I use the same hand to grab the hiding priest's throat. He is already completely healed, but not for long. I pull him toward me, grab one of his arms, and bite. My brand-new fangs tear right through his robe and into his flesh. As I pull my face away, I immediately see the effects. His divine magic can't keep up.

His eyes bulge and his arms slump. If I weren't holding his throat, he would be vomiting. Without his healing, I no longer have to worry at all. I bring my other hand to his head and snap his neck. Then I throw his corpse through the wall of fire and into the other priest. The fire immediately stops as my other opponent screams and falls backward, scrambling to throw his friend's body off him.

By the time he succeeds, I am already on him, my fangs tearing into his neck. As I stand, I can see the yellow-purple discoloration around the puncture wounds, and he stares up at me, holding his hand to the wound. His healing has stopped too. I see the veins in his face bulge and his eyes grow bloodshot, then he vomits all over himself. Rather than leaving him to what will clearly be a miserable death, I use force mana to snap his neck as well. Then I gasp and let myself fall on my ass.

I need a fucking break. But first I need to clean this up and find Sara—I want to know what happened. I pull the two bodies into the basement, where disposal will be easy. It still takes me nearly an hour to clean everything up. Anyone investigating this house, which the larger priest may have told more people about, will do more than raise an eyebrow at all the scorch marks and whatnot. The anxiety eats at me while I clean, but eventually, I am done and can go to Sarafyna outside the gates.

This time, worries aside, I move slowly and deliberately toward the door. This whole fight was just the result of another failure. I have to keep calm and move when it's safe. If Sara wasn't here with the kids, then she must have gone back to her cave with Peter. I take a deep breath. It's all right; I'll find her there. When I am finally calm again, I depart, making sure there are no other witnesses as I make my way to the city gates.

CHAPTER FORTY-ONE

What Is a Monster?

It was long past nightfall by the time I made it to Sarafyna and Peter. Rushing had only put everything I'd done in danger, and moving slowly enough to avoid notice took even longer than waiting for nightfall. I mentally kick myself for running out the door of my family's home like I did. I may have avoided the fight at the safe house and prevented a potential loose end if I had just worn a fucking dress and walked there. I feel like I have been doing nothing but screwing up lately, and it's eating at me.

I don't have time to worry about that, however, as I need to find out what happened. Based on the overheard conversation, things may have taken a turn worse than my failure to show up. God, I hope that's not my fault. As I approach the cave mouth, Peter jumps and scrambles to his feet until he sees me. Then he relaxes, slumps, and returns to his seat on a log. He returns to drawing in the dirt with a stick. "You took so long, why even bother coming now?" he complains, and I wince.

"I know. I'm sorry. I've had a . . ." I begin before shaking my head to myself. The kid doesn't need to know why. He just needs me to acknowledge I messed up. "It was wrong of me to be so late. Are you okay?" I ask instead.

He turns his head away from me and insists, "I'm fine. It's Sara you need to worry about."

I feel panic but I push it to the back of my mind. This kid doesn't need me freaking him out more than he already is. If she were injured or dead, he probably wouldn't just be drawing pictures in the dirt. He's a child, but he does care about her. Of course, if she is missing, that could be exactly what he would do. There aren't many things he can do if both of us stop showing up someday. That is . . . more than an oversight. I mentally add it to my list of fuckups and forge on.

"Yeah?" I crouch down next to him and try to make eye contact, but he turns away from me. "Is Sara all right? Can you tell me what happened?" I ask as gently as I can, fighting off the adrenaline still flowing through my veins.

He just crosses his arms, still refusing to face me.

"You'll have to ask her." He pouts. "She won't tell me anything."

I can feel he is upset, and I want to comfort him, but I have to refrain from responding for a moment. The relief at hearing she is safe and just refusing to talk is palpable, and I will be unable to keep it from my voice if I speak right away.

After a deep breath, I finally respond. "All right. I'll talk to her if you like. Is she here?" He just nods his head once in the direction of the cave instead of answering. I have to restrain myself from leaving right away, as he is clearly distressed. "Thank you. And Pete?" I say, waiting for him to look over his shoulder a bit. "Thanks for looking after her for me. I'd love to talk to you after I check on her, if that's all right."

He just shrugs, looking even more dejected than before. "Yeah, okay," he agrees. I give him one last look of concern before turning toward the cave. He's obviously not all right, but I need to find out exactly what happened before I can talk to him. Trying not to rush and spook him, I step into the shadows. As my eyes struggle to adjust, I make a mental note to alter them for this type of environment. Now that my fangs are done, I need to deliberate over my next changes anyway.

In the meantime, I use a light spell and immediately reveal Sarafyna. She is curled up in the corner. Her dress is splattered with blood and shredded on one side. When she doesn't react to the light, I rush to her side and run my hand along her arm to check for wounds. "Sara, what happened?" I ask, my panic back in full force. Whatever happened wasn't good, and I need to help her.

Not just because she is so important to . . . well, everything. My whole plan relies on her, yeah, but I have also grown quite fond of her. After she finally healed the growths around her eyes, I've even continued to keep my mask on around her so she can't discern my physical age for . . . reasons. The fact of the matter is, I have put way too much on her. I should have gone last night, not her. Once I met her and connected with her so quickly, a million revisions to my initial plans became possible. I got excited and forgot: she is a traumatized woman struggling just to feel normal again.

I need more help, not just for my sake but for hers. She looks up at me for a moment and practically throws her arms around me. "Lily, I'm sorry! I messed up! I know I didn't meet you . . . I was just . . . I just . . ."

I squeeze her tighter.

"It's all right, Sara. I didn't make it either. I messed up too. Are you okay? Is this your blood?" She shakes her head into my shoulder at the last question and pulls away before wiping her nose on her one intact sleeve.

"I'm sorry," she says again. "It was . . . that priest. I don't know what happened, I just . . . couldn't think. And I . . . I . . ." As she trails off, I put my hand on her shoulder, which makes her wince at first but then relax.

"Start at the beginning," I instruct, "and take your time. Tell me everything."

So she takes a deep breath and does exactly that. She stumbles a lot and even apologizes for visiting her family home. I have to reassure her that she definitely did nothing wrong there. She should feel free to revisit whatever she wants. It doesn't matter how far out of the way it was. The rest of the story has its ups and downs.

I am actually relieved to hear she didn't try moving the kids on her own. That would have been more dangerous than leaving them where they are. But that's just our luck, for both of us. There is no denying that this plan went horribly wrong on both ends. When she tells me who the priest she killed was, I immediately understand what happened, but I let her finish the story anyway. I fail to hide my grimace as she describes the way she killed him. Slowly and deliberately. Fortunately, her gaze is fixed firmly on her feet, and I manage to suppress it before she sees.

When she is done with her story, I just sit next to her and think for a moment. The cave is quiet as we both stare forward, reflecting on the different ways this is our fault. It takes me some time to decide what to say, and I can practically feel Sarafyna coming to the wrong conclusion about why, so I finally speak up. "You know, a lot of people think I am a monster too. I hear rumors about things I've done and I watch the disgust and fear it inspires."

She is shaking her head in frustration before I finish.

"I have seen the result of what you do, Lily. It's just not the same thing," she says dismissively. I nod.

"No, but to children who lost their family, having a good reason and whether or not their parents deserved it isn't really at the forefront of their considerations. But that's not the point. The point is that, sometimes, I feel like maybe they are right. I get trapped in my own head and I wonder. Self-doubt is an easy pit to fall into," I offer, but she gives me a pained look.

"I chewed a man up, still living. I killed him as slowly and painfully as I could," she responds, the comparison clear enough without her actually making it. I wince, but she is right. My first approach is clearly not going to work, so I run through my head trying to change tracks. I could tell her that, technically, what she did might have been easiest on him. He had divine mana; killing him was going to be slow and painful regardless. Causing the pain up front might have incentivized him to stop fighting, making it end quicker.

But . . . that wouldn't make me feel any better in her shoes. Her intent wasn't to speed things up. I could point out that I have also killed people more slowly than I needed to in the past, but . . . that'll just hit the same roadblock as my first idea. I let a long breath out through my nose before speaking again. "Yeah. I can't tell you that what you did was right. At least, not the way you did it. But I can still say you aren't a monster."

This new tack already has a skeptical look on her face.

"I am though. I can't get his screams out of my head. Who but a monster could do that to another human being? And I left all those kids there!"

I lean back, looking toward the light at the entrance of the cave.

"That man dragged you away from your family and future. He listened to your father's desperate screams and your weeping as he pulled you away from anything resembling a life. He threw you, literally, into an unending nightmare to be tortured, for years. And what did he remember about you? The very same thing that inspired him to hurt you in the first place. His failure to control you," I say.

"So, what, that makes torturing him to death okay?" she retorts as she looks toward the light too. "Well, it's not okay with me. And it's not okay with the children I left behind."

"No," I respond, "it makes killing him okay, and it makes . . . the rest understandable. But you are missing the point. What he did to you, and likely others, was try to inflict an eternity of torture. Or at least a few decades; I haven't worked out the purpose for it yet. But he did it to an innocent girl, and he didn't even think about it. He enjoyed his position and forgot about you. You lashed out in rage at your abuser. He abandoned a child to torment for his own comfort. You are sobbing in a cave because of what you did. He was enjoying a life of wealth and power because of what he did. So, Sara, who do you think looks like a monster to me?"

She just bites her lip, but she doesn't have a retort this time. So I continue. "You are a victim of a group of monsters. Every bit of rage and fury you feel when you see them is justified. The desire to kill them isn't just okay, it's necessary. The fact that you hate how you did it is good. I'm not telling you to stop feeling guilty about it. Instead, remember how guilty you feel. Don't forget the result of doing things the way you did them, and carry it with you. And, if you can't face the other priests without doing the same? Lean on me. I am here for you, Sara," I promise.

New tears follow the same tracks down her cheeks.

"It's just . . . Lillith, that's the problem. Part of me is still glad I did it that way! Part of me wants to do it again, and I don't know how to separate that from the rest of myself!"

I drape my arm over her shoulders as she sobs, pulling her into me.

"I know. And you know what? Part of me is glad you did too. And part of me regrets ending some people too quickly. Because, at the end of the day, there is nothing more human than wanting the people who hurt you to hurt just as badly. You don't feel that way because you are a monster; you are just like the rest of us. And the kids? They are as much a victim of my fuckup as yours. I didn't show up. You never could have gotten them out. We both will have to do better for them." She leans into my shoulder. "Besides," I add in a more lighthearted tone, "I literally bit two divine priests on the way over here. I'm pretty sure it's just a gut reaction they inspire."

She actually lets out a little laugh at that, sniffles, and then laughs more. Not because it was impossibly funny, but because once she manages to get the first one out, she is desperate not to stop. So I let her laugh at the dumb joke until she calms down. After a while, she finally pulls herself away from me. "Thanks, Lily," she says. "It's not enough. I can't just brush off what happened. But it helped get me out of my head. I can't say I completely agree with you. I don't know if I ever will, but . . . it's not nothing."

I suppose that's as much as I can ask for. I can give a good speech, but it's not going to wipe guilt and trauma away. I'll take the laugh as my victory for now. Then I remember Peter, and I put together what is bothering him. "You may want to talk to Pete," I say, and she looks confused, so I elaborate. "You came back in a torn, bloody dress, clearly upset. You did this after leaving to save people he asked you to save. He is holding it in. Trying not to act scared, or guilty, but he probably feels both. As far as he knows, he got you hurt and his friends killed. He needs to know that's not true," I explain. She puts her hand over her mouth as her eyes widen.

"Oh, by the Collector, I'm an idiot. Poor Pete!" she exclaims, and I quickly pull her into another hug to stop her from panicking too much.

"It's all right. We are all struggling. He's a strong kid, he just needs to know the people he cares about are safe," I assure her.

She nods, then pulls away and rushes to the entrance. After only a few feet, she turns back to me.

"I don't suppose . . ." she begins, playing awkwardly with her thumb, "I don't suppose you'll stay with us, for the night? It's just . . . I don't want us to be alone tonight . . ."

I give her a warm smile. "I'm sorry. I would love to. But . . . well, I have to keep Autumn safe. She was—"

"We'll go get her," she interrupts. "She'll be safe with both of us." She's insistent, and I nod my head once in consent.

"Well, we can ask," I agree, and Sara rewards me with a gentle smile.

"Thank you, Lily," she whispers before going out to talk to Peter. I can tell she is still feeling sick with guilt, but there is just a little bit of joy tinting the emotion. I lean back against the cave wall and sigh as I wait for her to have her own talk. For just a few minutes, I can sit in the quiet cave and take a breath. This moment of quiet is . . . everything.

CHAPTER FORTY-TWO

Doubts, Practice, and Hell

Autumn

I wake up earlier than usual. It's not the low quality of the beds in Lillith's room; I slept fine when we were traveling. It's just . . . everything feels wrong. I don't really know what to do. I look over at Sarafyna on Lillith's bed and Lillith on the floor and raise an eyebrow. Is she seriously sleeping with that mask on? Why? Does she do that every night? I look at her for a moment before shaking my head and adding it to my mental list of oddities about her. Right next to the absolute nonsense she sometimes says as if she were telling an inside joke except she is the only one inside.

I can't figure her out. Sometimes, she seems so much older than me. She can feel smarter than anyone I have ever met, always considering every angle and planning out what she needs to do next for her grand plan for the country. I came here only worried about passing my classes. Then there are times like last night. When she showed up with Sarafyna and Peter, explaining that she didn't want to leave her alone but also wanted to protect me. They tried to drag me out to some cave so she could be there for all of us and . . . neither one of them considered bringing the pair here for the night. Where there are actually beds.

I understand that Sara is self-conscious about living in the city. I sort of understand that practicing her upsetting . . . magic isn't safe here. But Lillith surpassed my lifetime of tutoring in math in a week. She should have thought of this obvious solution. With the single-minded focus that girl has, I don't understand how she remembers to show up to class, much less learn years of arithmetic in a week. I sigh as I get dressed. At least Peter is finally in a suitable place. I don't know what she was thinking, leaving him outside the city.

That's what really confuses me. One day, it sounds like she is ready to burn the country and every noble in it. The next, she fights with everything she has and lets herself get hurt trying to save me. Then somehow, after saying more or less the same thing, what sounded like organizing an army suddenly sounds like some kind of . . . charity that makes the church angry? I was so scared, and now it feels like I was worried over nothing.

But which was the right response? The first time, I went for help and nothing happened. Then I wrote a letter to warn my parents, and some . . . assassin showed up with it, burned it in front of me, and demanded to know who else I had warned.

I thought Lord Godfrey and Lillith must be working together until she showed up and fought like a demon to keep me alive. The next day, I realized it didn't make any sense anyway. I'm not important. I don't matter. Why would a duke send an assassin after me? He could just order me to tell him what I'd done.

One thing is clear, however. Whatever Lillith is planning, whether it's dangerous or not, no one is going to help me. So I need to stay close to her and hope she is as benevolent as she claims to be. It's fairly hard to believe, but the emotion she was barely containing did feel real earlier. And I don't think she staged that fight. She could have died when that splinter stabbed her side. I bite my thumbnail as I shamble down the stairs. She is also trying to protect me now in case I am attacked again. I just don't know what to do.

In the moment, I almost told her I went to Godfrey earlier, but . . . I'm not so sure I should. What if I had it right the first time? If I can't get help and it turns out she is going to do something to hurt my parents or August . . . who will stop her if not me? And if she is helping people like she says . . . well, the duke didn't do anything to her. He is known to sympathize with commoners; maybe that's evidence she really does have good intentions. But if I do tell her I tried to stop her, what will she do? Best case, she wants to help people and she stops trusting me. Worst case, she is dangerous and she . . . Well, then there would be no one to do anything to stop her.

So I can't tell her what I did. If I want the most people to be as safe as possible . . . if I want to guarantee the fewest people get hurt . . . I just can't. I like Lillith. I really want to trust her. She clearly cares about me and doesn't want me hurt. Whatever she wants to do, it's obvious she truly believes it is necessary. It's obvious she believes it will help people, and she definitely cares. But . . . that doesn't mean she is right. I hope she is, and I hope what she wants to do isn't as . . . violent as it sounds sometimes. But I can't take that risk. It's not just about me.

As I reach the dining area, I see her brother Henry eating a bowl of grits alone. I immediately blush and start smoothing my hair down. There is perhaps another, more selfish reason I don't want this family to hate me. But . . . that doesn't change the reality. Part of me still wishes August and I had just left Satusmor earlier, but . . . I suppose I still would have met Lillith in the dorms. Still, everything is suddenly so complicated and I just don't know what to do. So I sit down and greet Henry. At the moment, it's all I can do.

Lillith

Once Autumn leaves, I stop pretending to be asleep and sit up. If the last couple of days have taught me anything, it's that I really need to figure out this radar spell. It has been on my to-do list for actual years now, and I have always postponed figuring it out in favor of more important tasks. So, when there was an attacker in Autumn's room or priests watching me enter a safe house, I had no idea. It's time to stop delaying and figure it out.

It shouldn't have been this difficult to do if I had focused on it from the beginning. This becomes apparent barely an hour into practice. Using an idea I had toyed with before but hadn't quite sorted, I get halfway there. Well, sort of. I can send the radio waves out and create a light barrier directly in front of my eyes that intercepts them as they return. This barrier then creates visible lightwaves corresponding to any received radio waves. This allows me to see people through walls easily enough. Well, sort of. I can see if there is someone on the other side, anyway.

This method has mostly failed in the past due to the amount of control required. I need to cast a light spell at a specific frequency that emits light but doesn't travel with it. My mana isn't always invisible and I don't need a beacon advertising my location. It's the same reason illusions can be obvious to other mages and I mostly use them against mundane guards. In hindsight, it's probably how I got caught at the temple safe house. Simultaneously, I need to cast a spell that intercepts the exact same frequency and copies its direction perfectly in another visible frequency.

I have been practicing this bit a lot over the years, and it isn't long before I'm back to my peak proficiency with it. Interestingly, mana and light stop at the same places, but blocking one doesn't block the other. In other words, mana will bounce off a wall just like light and you can't see it through solid objects. But in a room where I block off all light, I can see mana. Similarly, mana that creates light that passes through physical objects won't be visible on the other side. So if I emit the radio waves from within my dress or armor, no one will know I am casting the spell.

If I had been using it habitually over the years, this combination would have helped at least with Autumn. But it is distracting when used this way and takes a lot of focus, so I haven't been keeping it up. As such, when I do practice, it takes time just to get back to my ability the last time I did it. It'll be annoying, but I'll have to keep it up this time. While I do, I need to figure out a way to give myself three-hundred-sixty-degree sight.

I also have to tweak my chosen frequency a bit. I need one that passes through physical objects but not people. I basically need it to bounce off salt water but not wood, which isn't too difficult but takes a bit of trial and error, since I am basically forcing a mental image of the frequency I want. It won't be perfect. Metal will still trip it up. But in a medieval world, I'll still be able to see through most structures. All this to say, it takes a lot of work, but I can't keep putting it off. I need to figure it out now.

So I keep practicing and experimenting until Sarafyna sits up and looks at me blearily.

"Good morning," I say, trying to maintain my spells while talking.

Still half awake, she tilts her head at me. "Do you ever take that off?" she asks, sounding genuinely concerned. I look down at my nightgown.

"Excuse me?" I ask, looking down at my nightgown and raising an eyebrow at her. That's an . . . odd question to ask me first thing in the morning.

"Your mask, did you sleep in it?" she clarifies. My hand goes up to my face. Oh, right, that was a super weird thing to do.

"Uh, this is my face," I quip, trying to sound as insulted as I can, "and I am extremely offended by the question."

She lets out a polite laugh through her nose before looking around to get her bearings.

"How are you feeling?" I ask.

"I don't know," she answers quietly. "It was nice, sleeping in a place like this again. But . . . part of me still feels like I am back there. In hell. And part of me still wonders if I belong there," she adds after a moment.

"Give it time, Sara," I respond with a sympathetic nod. "I can't promise that feeling will ever go away, but I can promise you that you are helping people. There are already dozens of people whose lives would be their own hell without your help. Someday, you'll be living in a new world you helped create. And that's not nothing."

She gives me a half-hearted smile at this but doesn't respond. I can't blame her. A chat, a hug, and a comfortable bed are all healing things, but they aren't magic. Not that magic will help her either. I suppose that metaphor doesn't transfer well between realities. Or dimensions, or planets, I guess. I don't really know how the world I am in relates to Earth. That thought causes a little itch in my brain, and I put my hand over my mouth and chin to consider why.

I have wondered about this before, but there is literally no way to investigate it I could ever think of. But for some reason, it feels like I am missing a clue about it this time. "Hey, Sara," I ask after a moment, "did you say you felt like you were back in *hell*?"

She looks up from her own contemplations. She definitely used the English word.

"Um, yes?" she responds, concern passing through her eyes.

"Did you hear that from me?" I ask.

Confusion paints her face and she speaks slowly at first when she responds, "I'm sorry, I thought you heard it from me. That's what . . . it called itself. The Radiant Woods. It told me I was in hell. Why, where did you hear it?"

CHAPTER FORTY-THREE

What the Hell?

Are you sure that's what it said?" I ask again. "It said *hell*?"

Sara contorts her face in confusion and answers, "Yes, I couldn't forget it if I wanted to. I don't understand, what does it mean?"

I bite my thumb, trying to figure that out myself. Not what the word means—I've worked retail and am fairly familiar—but what it means that the Radiant Woods used it.

"Just, sort of . . . like the third plane but . . . hotter, I guess? If Dante is to be believed, it's like the third plane with nine planes of its own. So hot and layered, like a torment lasagna." I chuckle awkwardly and she just . . . stares at me. "Sorry, this is what I'm like when I get comfortable around someone. Just get used to the gibberish, it's . . . probably not going to stop," I explain, and she gives me a sort of amused furrowed brow.

"So it's just another word for the third plane, one I haven't heard?" she asks.

"No." I shake my head. "Well, maybe, actually. I guess the two could be the same place, but it just doesn't . . . feel that way. That's not what matters though. What matters is where it comes from. It's a word from an entirely different language," I ramble, and her confusion only grows.

"I've heard that some people use other languages, but I've never heard one. Is it from some isolated city?" she guesses as I start chewing on my thumbnail while thinking through it.

"Well, sort of. But . . . nowhere that should be involved in, well, anything here. No one but me should know it," I absent-mindedly explain. My first thought was the forest was related to someone else like me. I wasn't hit by a truck or summoned in a circle to fight the demon king. I also didn't replace a dead person. I was born here. I didn't retain my past memories; something awakened them when I was seven.

That being said, I was always me. I have no doubt in my mind that the Lillith who existed without Annie's memories was me. That means it's entirely possible everyone in this world had a past life on Earth. Or even a past life in some other world, and I am just lucky enough to remember mine. It wouldn't be that strange for another person to have the same experience. How they got from there to a hell forest is an entirely different question, but it's possible.

This does lead me to other theories, however. I am proof positive that reincarnation exists. Which supports my first theory, but also suggests . . . a lot about the universe. I'm not sure if the Collector is an actual god or just a prick with too much power, but either my mind somehow persists across realities, or planets, or wherever I am in relation to the Earth, or the soul is an actual, existing concept. If I can't dismiss the idea of the soul, I can't dismiss the idea of a deity existing. I don't know about a creator or whatever, but a powerful entity that is aware of multiple realities or worlds isn't impossible.

In other words, the Collector might actually be a god. In which case, it wouldn't be strange for him to know about Earth.

These aren't my only theories. I don't know for sure that I am in a new world. My history and religion classes here have largely been propaganda with little useful education, but one thing did stick with me from them. The history of Potestia and the history of the Collector's church start at the same time. Before them? There is no history. So an entire organized country and religion popped up out of nowhere. It's not a well-organized country, but I am growing more convinced that is by design.

In other words, this could be Earth in the far future for all I know. The constellations I know are missing, but given enough time, they would be. I think I read that in an article once, anyway. I have only seen maps of the country, and they don't even reach the oceans, assuming there are any. This would imply reincarnation is just on one planet. The advent of magic would be . . . an interesting development, but for all I know, it always existed and we just didn't know how to use it.

Basically, this doesn't actually confirm anything for me. It does, however, give me a lead to track down. And, if it turns out the Collector is a fucking god? Well, I already have more than a few impossible tasks on my list. What difference does it make if I tack deicide on at the end?

"Lily, can you hear me?" Sara interrupts, and I realize I have been lost in thought for too long.

"Sorry." I shake myself out of it. "I went down a bit of a rabbit hole there. What were you saying?"

"Why would you be the only one who knew a word from another language?" she repeats. I answer by suddenly standing and clapping my hands together.

"I'm not so sure about that myself," I announce matter-of-factly. "Let me think about it, and I'll tell you what I can tonight. First, we have work to do, which might just give us a little more context."

"W-what?" she asks, startled by my sudden energy.

"I have been led to believe that there are people who need our help underneath the temple. We both fucked up, but that doesn't mean we can't help them now, right?" I ask.

"Y-you want me to go back to the temple . . . n-now?" she splutters, her face pale. I hold my hand out to her.

"Don't worry, I'm not going to ask you to go inside again. I don't need to. You already learned more or less where they are, right? We just need to start at the safe house and dig our way in. With my earth mana, it'll be a breeze. Well, not literally. The air will probably be pretty stale, actually. But what do you say? Want to make things right?" I offer.

"B-but are you sure it's safe? Don't you think you should go without me?" she asks nervously.

"I have a feeling you're going to feel like shit if you aren't involved. You know as well as I do that things will be faster with your help. Besides, you gotta point me in the right direction," I retort. She looks at my hand, still extended to her, for a moment. Her eyes are wide and nervous, but she finally takes it and I pull her up off the bed. I can see her steel herself and I smile reassuringly.

I allow her to get dressed and we head down the stairs together. I raise my eyebrow as I see Autumn and Henry eating together. I take a moment to ask Henry to pass on a message to Mom and Pete when they wake up, which he accepts before returning his attention to the pretty girl I brought home. I roll my eyes but smile and head down to the basement with Sara. If all goes well, I should be in and out of the temple with little effort. I reprimand the little part of my brain that laughs at the idea of things going well before we set out.

It isn't long before we find ourselves in the safe house. "Can you feel them?" I ask, and Sara nervously looks around before closing her eyes. Marred face or not, the way she wrinkles her nose while focusing is pretty charming, and I just watch in silence as she tries to find them. A little while later her eyes snap open. She catches me looking at her and startles, but shakes it off.

"It's hard to tell. It's not as clear as when I was in the building. But there are two large collections of divine magic. They are both in that direction," she explains while pointing at one wall.

I shrug. "Well, if we get closer, will you be able to tell which one is the kids?"

"I . . . think so?" she offers, and bites her nail.

I give her a blank look. Well, worst-case scenario we can retreat if she can't.

"I've done more with less," I eventually say, and we get to work. I have a lot of mana to spare at the moment, and digging a tunnel toward the temple isn't difficult work. Sara is clearly agitated behind me, but she keeps pushing herself. I really do need her though. I don't know if bringing her here is a good idea—I am certainly not a qualified therapist—but I believe if she doesn't help now, she'll hate herself more. Especially if something does go wrong.

"Wait," she says, after we have moved in the direction she indicated for a while. "It's that way. There are a lot more priests this time; they are probably on alert after my last visit. But the group in that direction is disorganized, and a lot of them feel . . . weaker . . . more scared," she describes, and I nod. That way it is.

I follow her directions, and we are soon mere inches from the group she is describing. I can even hear muffled voices on the other side of the dense dirt. With my half-finished radar spell, I can make out a large number of people as well. It's hard to see how many, as there are a lot of obstructions in the room the radio waves won't pass through. "Can you tell if they are alone?" I whisper, and she responds with silence for a few moments.

"I . . . can't. Sorry. There are two of them that feel stronger but . . . I'm not sure," she finally replies. I bite my lip in thought.

"Well, nothing for it. We'll just have to expect to be attacked. Step back a little bit, I'll go in first," I say before waiting for her to retreat a bit. I think we both understand that I should be the one to handle potential combatants.

Then I take a deep breath and push the last bit of the wall down. There is an actual brick wall before I make it into the room, but clay is earth and it doesn't hold me back for long.

As I emerge into the dimly lit room, I am met with an unpleasant scene. There are rows of bunk beds packed far too closely together. They have metal frames, which explains the difficulty seeing with my spell. A couple dozen older children gape at me, while all the kids younger than Peter share his former milky, blind eyes. There is exactly one adult priest in the room, sitting on one of the beds and eating a sandwich.

We stare at each other for a moment, and he forces a large bite of bread and meat down his throat before he can say anything. "W-what are you doing here? H-how did you . . . ?" he splutters, awkwardly scrambling to his feet.

"Would you believe I am lost?" I ask, a hopeful tone coloring my voice, and his mouth opens a little. "Yeah, I was worried you might not. Truth is, I'm out for a walk. Do you think any of your friends here might want to join me?"

At that, I feel the sickly feeling of divine mana trying to wrestle control of my body away from me, and I groan. I fucking hate that feeling. As quickly as I can, I surround him with heat mana, then block all the light in the room. All but the radar, that is. No need for trick eggs this time. I've already verified my mana is faint here. Not quite invisible but not fully visible either. With his own mana in the room, he'll have a hell of a time spotting me.

"D-demon!" he shrieks, but it's too late. I pepper him with stone bullets, being careful not to hit any of the scrambling children. They tear through him easily, but he heals quickly. Fucking priests. I run through the room in an arc without casting any spells, and just as I see him trying to conjure a light spell, I pounce on him, sinking my fangs deep into his neck. It's game over from there. With his healing out of commission, I make short work of him. If only every fight could be this easy. Priests rely on their healing too much.

I then collapse my spell to only cover his body while I wipe his blood from my lips. Now I have to handle a much greater challenge, as dozens of kids try to decide how to react to me and I try to decide what to say to them.

CHAPTER FORTY-FOUR

I'm Not Alone

U h, hi," I awkwardly announce to the scared kids. "I'm here to help!" The ones who can see gape at me and my stupidly raised hand while many of them whisper to each other. I mentally kick myself for charging in here without rehearsing this first. Classic Lillith, charging in ready for a fight but with no idea what to do afterward. I was a teacher in another life, but . . . those were college students. Business majors aside, I am ill-equipped to comfort children.

I like them, I do, but they don't always feel the same way about me. I managed fine with the street kids but . . . this is a bit different. These children aren't distrusting of everyone because they have been abandoned and ignored. They are likely distrusting of me and other outsiders because they *haven't* been abandoned. Their abusers are the ones taking care of them and feeding them. The kids who already have divine magic also had their eyes healed by the people I'm here to rescue them from.

Of course, they lost their sight in the first place because of the same people, but . . . it's strange how this sort of thing can work.

Most of them are too frightened to speak to me at all, like Peter was when we met. One of the oldest boys, maybe thirteen or so, has the courage to do so on behalf of the rest, however. "Help?" he parrots. "Help how? What just happened?"

I wince as I realize I have no good answer for that. *I killed your last guardian* probably isn't going to fly, nor will *Pay no attention to the man behind the conspicuous curtain of darkness, he's not feeling well.*

I try to give them a reassuring smile, but the boy's furrowed brow and widened eyes indicate I am doing a poor job. Fortunately, another voice saves me and I sigh in relief.

"We are friends of Peter," Sarafyna announces as she emerges from the dark tunnel. "He asked us to come here."

That's right, this was Sara's job originally. She probably actually did consider what to say to them before coming here. I'm very good at raining death down on creeps, but this kind of laser focus is exactly why I struggle to organize on my own.

A few of the children look suspicious, while the younger ones start excitedly whispering to each other. "Peter? He's alive?" the same boy as earlier asks, disbelief clear in his voice.

"He is. He's alive and well. He wanted me to tell you he is happy. He can see, on his own terms. He asked me to tell you he's not alone anymore," she answers. It makes sense that Peter sent a message, but the last line doesn't make much sense. He wouldn't have been alone before; it looks like all of them are kept together. When she says it, however, there is a palpable change in the atmosphere and the suspicion vanishes from all their faces. I don't understand it, but . . . Sara seems to expect it.

"H-help us, please!" a young boy, one of the blind, cries out after a moment of silence, and the floodgates break. Sarafyna is swarmed by hopeful children in moments, and I am mostly able to melt into the background. Except the older children, the ones with divine magic, keep their eyes on me.

"Did you kill him?" the skeptical boy asks. This time, with the awkwardness and suspicion dissipated, I soften myself. I'm not going to get any real loyalty by lying to him, so, after a brief pause, I nod. "Is he behind . . . that?" he asks, and I nod again. He immediately spits into the darkness, then bows to me. "I'm Alfric. A pleasure to meet you. Do you have a way to get us out of here?"

I grin at him. "I most certainly do, and you are not going to believe it when you see it," I promise. Somehow, I know in a moment I can trust them. They haven't made it to the real programming yet, and they want out of here as much as Peter did.

"Lead the way," Alfric responds.

It takes some time for Sara to calm down the younger kids, but they all seem excited to see Peter again, in more ways than one. None of them seem to notice Sara's marred flesh, or if they do, they don't seem to care. I appreciate this, and I can tell Sara does too. With this many children, it takes nearly half an hour to get everyone in the tunnel, and another half hour to rebuild the brick wall in a way the priests won't notice . . . immediately. It won't be a huge deal when they do, as the earth behind it will be perfectly sealed. Nevertheless, I don't want to make our route too obvious. Our retreat is slow too. I also have to fill the tunnel behind me, which is more effort than emptying it. I briefly consider leaving part of it intact, but if anyone follows it back to what I have hidden in the safe house, everything could go wrong. So I move slowly. As we make our way back, I decide to clarify my confusion from earlier. "That thing about not being alone anymore—what did Peter mean by that?" I call up toward Sarafyna, but Alfric is the one who answers.

"Their . . . influence changes once they give us divine magic," he explains. "They can't control us anymore . . . at least not the same way. Not with divine magic. So just directly controlling our actions until they give us the magic doesn't work. They use that very flaw to manipulate us. When they bring us here, they get inside our heads. They twist everything and make it all feel wrong. They make us lonely, no matter how many people we are with. They make us hungry no matter what we eat, and tired no matter how much we sleep. But the loneliness is the worst of it," he explains. Things start to come together. Priests can't control other priests with divine magic, but they do need them compliant. This must be one of the ways they ensure that.

"But they keep you together, so the younger ones can be used to control you," I guess. He nods.

"They keep us together. They won't feed the younger ones unless we do what we are told, so we don't run. But they do let us talk to them. They let us tell them that we have our sight back and the loneliness is gone. They hold them as a stick to punish us with, and they use us as a carrot to tempt them with. If they behave and do as the priests tell them . . . they will go to the Radiant Woods. They will get their sight back, and they will be allowed to feel . . . normal again. They let us stay with them so they can see the carrot is real and so they will work harder to please the priests. A while back, Peter was taken to the woods, but . . ."

"But he never came back," I finish for him. he nods.

"He never came back"—he nods—"and neither did the priests who took him. That wasn't so weird, since priests fail to return all the time . . . but they have always returned when they had one of us with them." I give Sara a meaningful look. "Anyway, when you gave us his message . . . when he said he wasn't alone . . . it was like . . . he was telling us he found a way to get the carrot without the priests' help. He was telling the kids they could feel okay again. And he was telling us all in a way only we would understand." It makes sense why that one line suddenly changed everything. But . . . "The priests would know. What if we were with them?" I ask, then immediately regret giving them a reason to doubt us.

He doesn't respond for a breath, but he looks up at me and I see the rage in his eyes. Rage a kid his age should never have to feel. "We all hate them, you know. We despise them. We would do anything to get away from them. But we also know we are valuable to them. So . . . if this is a trap . . . it's just . . . worth it. But I don't think it is. They have no reason to pretend to rescue us. They already own us and . . . it sounded like something Pete would say," he explains.

After that, I allow silence to return for a while.

When we reach the escape route, the older kids' eyes grow wide, then Alfric gives me a wide grin as understanding dawns. Not long after that, we have gotten them all to safety in the safe house basement. We left Peter at the tavern with my mom, and many of the kids are disappointed he is not at our temporary destination. They are soon distracted, however, as Sara and I organize the younger kids to be healed. It's slow, but Sarafyna has gotten good at it. We don't manage to completely heal anyone's sight, but many of them clearly feel better once we are done with them. This is honestly a great time to be suspended, as this task is likely to take the full two weeks.

That evening, an exhausted Sara sits next to me on a log near the cave she's been living in. We finally enjoy a moment of quiet. "Thanks," she says after a few minutes of silence, "you were right. I needed to be there."

"No joke." I laugh. "I'd still be there trying to convince them I wasn't a demon if it weren't for you. All I thought of was how to get in and get them out. Like a moron, I completely forgot about convincing them that was a good idea."

She laughs a little at that, but it's true. That was another fuckup on my part and definite evidence of how valuable just one person with a different skill set is to me.

"Yeah, that was an odd thing to do, but that's not what I meant," she replies after a while. I think for a moment that is all she has to say. Just as I am going to answer her, she finally speaks again. "I do feel better. What we did today . . . it was good. I know I have helped you with this sort of thing before, but . . . going myself was different. And going to help the people I failed before . . . I just mean you were right. I needed it. Just as much as you needed me," she explains, and I understand.

"I'm glad. I know it doesn't make everything better. But every time you see any of these kids . . . you'll know what you are. It's certainly not a monster," I respond.

She doesn't respond to that. I can tell she doesn't agree with me, and . . . to be honest, I understand. What she did to that other priest would haunt anyone. It *should* haunt anyone, anyway. I have my own haunting moments, like that damn Captain Horrus. But Sarafyna is still a good person.

After maybe ten minutes of quiet, something seems to occur to her and she looks at me with her head tilted. "So, you said something about only you understanding some language . . . You said you would explain it later?" she pokes.

I take a deep breath through my nose. I did tell her that, didn't I?

I deliberate for a few minutes. Is it a good idea to tell her this? Then I realize there is no reason at all not to. With what she has been through, I doubt she wouldn't believe me. She won't think I'm insane or lying or anything. And it's not like I can't trust her. She already knows all my most dangerous secrets. She also might have some insight, once she has all the information.

"Well," I finally respond, "I'm not the only one who knows it. But I thought I was the only one in this world." She looks at me in confusion.

She looks at me in confusion. "This . . . world?"

I grin at her.

"Oh, did I not mention? I'm not from around these parts."

CHAPTER FORTY-FIVE

A Woman of Many Hats

Leo

I hunch over behind the bushes and vomit. Again. Lily has only been gone for a day and I thought it would be fine to go to the regular spot for breakfast. I was wrong. Of course I was wrong, but I hadn't realized how much I had grown to depend on her. I didn't think it would be so dangerous just to get food without a friend. But the people here . . . they despise me. They want me dead. I don't mean that metaphorically; I mean if they could get away with it, they would kill me and go on about their days, hearts feeling lighter than ever.

If my sponsor wasn't so prominent, they probably would have by now. I retch again, splattering the bush with bile. What was so wrong about trying to eat some eggs in a public place? I know I'm not welcome there. The only reason I got away with it before is because Lily's backer is somehow even more important than mine. But I got comfortable. I trusted the promised safety of routine and familiarity. As a result, I'm here, on my knees and puking into the dirt.

I don't know what they put in my food, or when they did it, but the message is clear. I am not to come back. At least not without Lily to back me up. Of course, none of them would ever admit to it. It was still too dangerous to do something like this openly. Even that fucking headmistress can't attack me . . . if she leaves any evidence. For a while that made me feel safe. And Lily made me feel welcome. I was able to walk proudly through campus without keeping my head down and hiding my background. Because I had important friends.

Every time I start to feel safe, however, something like this happens. Something foul is left in my food, my dorm room, or my bags. They always find a way to remind me that I am unwanted. So I have to keep looking over my shoulder. Checking my fucking breakfast and waiting until classes start before moving among them.

"Oh no, are you all right?" a polite but unwelcome voice asks, and I look up to see Iris staring over the bush at me. Her tone indicates she wants to help, but I can see the laughter in her eyes and her disgust in the wrinkle of her nose. "We do have a nurse on campus, even a priest who can heal you. I can take you to him if you want?" she offers. I keel over and vomit again. She knows damn well the priest won't help me. I don't know if she did this, or if she is just happy to find me like this, but she can go to the third plane either way.

I want to scream at her. Tell her exactly where she can shove her supposed help. "I—I'm okay, thank you, Lady Iris," I reply instead. As long as she is playing nice, I have to do the same, at least on the surface. It's the only way to survive until I graduate.

"Well, if you're sure." She smiles. "Just be careful, I wouldn't want you to stain your clothes in the dirt. It would just be dreadfully embarrassing if they started drawing too much attention to you."

I scowl internally but smile back.

"Thank you, Lady Iris, I will be," I respond before the need to puke forces me back into the bush.

Lillith

Sara stares at me, completely baffled. "When you were . . . seven?" she asks, clearly trying to wrap her head around what I just told her. I don't blame her. It's a lot to take in. For someone who hadn't spent who knows how long wandering around a magic hell forest, it would sound too fantastic to be real. Sara, on the other hand, believes me right away. Nevertheless, it's still a lot.

"Yep, when I was seven," I answer.

She looks at me with wide eyes.

"Why do you think . . . I mean, that must have been so strange. Are you sure you are the same person?"

"Completely. I didn't just remember my childhood here. I felt it. I still feel it. They aren't just facts, I feel the nostalgia, the heartache, and the joy that comes with them. I have always been Lillith. I am just Annie too."

"Annie," she says, trying the name out. "It's kind of a cute name, actually. Do you ever miss it?"

"Sometimes." I shrug. "But I think I just miss the people who used it. I like my name now just as well. Like I said, I identify with both. They both feel right, and both fit me like a—"

"Hat?" she interrupts, and I look at her, a smile tugging at the corner of my mouth.

"Sure, like a hat." I chuckle, but she is still examining me, completely serious. "A-anyway. Things were different there, mostly. Some things not as much, but even the similar parts were better. But I spoke a language called English. That's the language the word *hell* probably comes from."

She looks contemplative for a moment. "What do you mean probably?"

I shrug.

"Language is tricky. Sometimes words in different languages can sound similar but be unrelated. We had a holiday called Easter and an old god called Ishtar, and a lot of people assumed they were related because of their similar themes and names, but they weren't even from the same language. Hell is kind of the same, actually, and it throws the timeline off," I explain, getting a little lost in thought.

"What do you mean?" I rub the back of my neck.

"Well, the Collector, or at least the church, has been around for thousands of years, or so they claim. The more I learn about Potestia and the church, the murkier things get. But supposedly, both showed up at the same time, thousands of years ago. The word *hell* wouldn't have existed on Earth at the time," I think out loud.

Sara tilts her head. "So . . . you don't think the Collector is . . . uh . . . like you?" she inquires, and I can only shrug again.

"Or the force behind the Radiant Woods isn't actually the Collector, or time doesn't flow at the same rate between realities, or he can just see into all of them at once. I honestly don't know. But it does feel strange. Using the word at all implies some kind of connection to more recent English speakers, especially in that context. It's . . . a lot to consider," I answer.

We sit there in quiet for a little longer at that. Then, she finally speaks up. "I'm sorry, I just . . . I've never heard anything like this before. Forgive me if I ask too much. But . . . what was it like?"

I lean back. "It was . . . good. And bad. Better than here for sure, at least where I lived. But it was far from perfect. There were comforts people in this world would never dream of, but there were more than a few battles left to fight. Things to fight for, and to fight against. I had a fairly comfortable life though. Movies, games, and comfy little coffee shops with cute baristas. I was mostly happy, and I didn't need a fucking guardian to be that way," I answer. She looks down.

"I didn't understand a lot of that, but . . . it sounds nice. So how did you end up so . . . ready to fight?"

"Well, part of it is because I have seen a better world. It makes me feel sick to my stomach to go backward rather than forward. But even back there, I was killed fighting for something better. I just have even more to fight here. And fewer people to fight alongside. Also, no toilet paper, which would make anyone cranky," I joke.

She looks confused for a second, but then something dawns on her.

"That's why you are always saying things that make no sense!" she exclaims. "You are talking about stuff only you understand! I mean, I guess I knew that, but they are real things! It was always the most confusing thing about you, how you would make a joke or respond to something in a way that sounded like gibberish . . ." She suddenly turns a little pink. "Sorry, I didn't mean to be rude, it never bothered me! I was just excited to understand."

I laugh. "No offense taken! I know I do that. I can't help myself. I am still who I have always been. These little references to the things I once loved but can never see again . . . they keep me grounded. They tie me back to my home and make sure I don't forget it. Some of them are silly, like a goofy song I used to listen to or a video game I played when I was depressed. Some of my past experiences are important, however. They are how I know this world is . . . wrong."

"You mean like the Radiant Woods and the temple?" she asks, and I nod.

"That, yes, but everything else too. The way history doesn't seem to exist before the church and the country. The way no one seems to know about any other countries. There is no trade between Potestia and other powers—there's barely any even between cities. So-called merchants collect readily available materials and recipes from the immediate area, lash out at anyone who discovers their processes, and sell basic goods as luxury items. All to justify existing and growing wealthy when they don't even travel.

"It's like each city is an outpost in a strategy game. Started in one of many places that conveniently has a gold mine, lumber, water, and other resources lined up next to each other. And they are all the same. The same spices, the same livestock, same flora. None of it varies at all. No one has heard about anything that isn't available everywhere, so everyone sells what is easily available at a premium. It just makes no sense. That corn in the forest? That was all over the place on Earth, but I'd never even heard whispers of it before entering the woods," I rant. Sara looks at me with wide eyes.

"So . . . back on . . . your world, things were different somehow? Merchants traveled more for some reason?"

"Yeah, they did." I rub my neck again, trying to think of a quick way to explain. "Most goods were regional in some way or another. They took them from one place and sold them in another. Well, by my time there weren't really merchants anymore, and a lot more people were involved, but the point is the same. People traded goods. Yeah, things were still artificially expensive but . . . it wasn't the same. The way things work here . . . it has to be by design, I just can't figure out why. Maybe the existence of magic here changed the landscape over time, but—"

"Wait, you didn't have magic there? Not even the nobles? But things were more comfortable?" she suddenly asks.

"OH, uh, no. At least I don't think so. If we did, it was a secret. No, we sort of . . . electrocuted rocks in patterns and created our own magic with that. It wasn't really magic, but it might look like it. Then again, maybe magic here is the same way," I muse, and Sara actually rubs her temples trying to understand what I'm saying.

"You're talking about things that make no sense again," she complains.

"Sorry." I chuckle. "It'll take time, but I'll explain it all to you. Basically, we were really good at math and science, and we figured out new ways to do things. If we had magic, I like to think we would have advanced more than Potestia has. But, again, the state of things here feels like it was designed, so perhaps not," I answer.

She nods along with me, then gives me a serious look. "All right, I have one more important question for you," she begins, and I tilt my head in curiosity. "What kinds of hats did you have there?" I begin to laugh.

"Oh, we had all kinds. Top hats, bowler hats, fedoras. I was partial to a baseball cap myself, but there were dozens of styles. Maybe hundreds," I answer, and if I had a heartbeat, it would stop short as I finish that sentence. She has stars in her eyes. This is easily the most eager I have ever seen her.

"Do you think you could make them?" she begs, and I chuckle.

"I have no idea how to make a hat. I can sew a dress, but I have no confidence I could emulate a design from memory just with—"

"If I teach you, can you make them?" she cuts in.

I laugh openly for a moment . . . until I see the dead serious look she is giving me.

"Oh. Uh, I'm not a terrible artist, exactly. I can probably draw them, will that work?" I offer.

Her mouth opens a little and her eyes light up. At this moment, I can see just a little bit of the girl Sarafyna described herself as in the past. It's more than a little cute, and I start blushing a bit myself.

"I'll, uh, I'll draw some on breaks for the next couple weeks," I promise, and she pulls me into a hug without even thinking about it.

"Thank you, Lily, that would mean the world to me!" she exclaims, and I smile. Only Sarafyna could hear that I had a past life in an entirely different world . . . and be most affected by the thought of new kinds of hats. I'm just glad I can make her happy, and that I get a little bit of a break for a couple of weeks.

CHAPTER FORTY-SIX

Prodigal Brother

Godfrey

Yrow had the right of it when you were hiding away in your bookshop," Don laughs, not bothering to finish chewing first.

Yet again I have to wonder if my brother was involved in silencing me. I have met priests before, and it simply doesn't make sense that Baldwin managed to get his claws in me like he did. I had been garnering support before he showed up, however, and my time in Satusmor had been a great boon to King Donatello. Until recently, his reign went unchallenged while I was out of the picture.

I haven't found any evidence of his involvement, outside of a clear motive, but he is still my primary suspect. He certainly has the power to do it. He also has the power to simply kill me, but a fight between us would have done far too much damage. His mother may have had more mana than mine. And he may have spent more time in his circle than I. His mana exceeds mine just enough to win him the crown. But not enough to easily defeat me. If he wanted me gone, using Baldwin would have been safer. The man is a fool but not an imbecile. Proving he is involved wouldn't change anything really, but knowing for sure would protect me. If he isn't the one responsible, I have to guard myself against whoever is. I have no illusions that Baldwin managed it on his own.

When I don't respond to the taunt, Don changes his approach. The bookshop jab has been used far too liberally to maintain any sting, so he goes with a more recent perceived failing of mine. "My son tells me the girl you sponsored for the academy has already been suspended. For violence, of all things! A girl! Really, Godfrey, I've no idea what you were thinking, bringing a mongrel like that here. Were you worried the shame of hiding would fade too quickly without a fresh embarrassment to follow you around?" He smirks.

This insult fails to find any footing as well, and I smile in response. The man is as blind as he ever was. Already there are grumblings about him among the upper nobility as slaves are growing harder to find. He has no idea what the state of Satusmor is, and he hasn't noticed even his staunchest supporters growing uneasy. He will eventually, but I doubt he'll take it seriously before it's too late. All thanks to the "mongrel" I brought here.

"Who knows," I answer, "I suppose I just liked her taste in pastries."

Don just laughs at me, assuming I am trying to brush off the insult and not noticing my own smirk. "Oh, I see," he sneers, "she's more of a . . . hobby for you. You know, I'd begun to think you lost all interest after your wife died, but I suppose you simply like them young. Or do you prefer them unwashed? Not a fetish I understand, but it makes sense you would pick them from the common rabble."

This man has no idea what is coming. Neither did I, at first. When I met her, Lillith presented as a genius. Her circle is capable of changing magic forever and granting Dominic's children, should he ever sire any, with power far surpassing any of Kallon's. I'll admit I even considered her as a possible mother for them. But with her brilliance she also brings madness. The girl is an idealist like I've never seen before, which would be admirable if she weren't also mad. But with a tempering hand, I can give her the better world she wants. A version of it, anyway. And every fight benefits from a few soldiers with a touch of madness, so long as you rein them in at the right time.

I feel sorry for her. I understand why she feels the way she does, and her reaction to this corrupt country is years beyond her age. But she doesn't know what she is doing. She won't help anyone this way . . . not intentionally, anyway. But, like a controlled burn, she can handle the rot. I just hope I can save her from herself before the fire gets out of control.

"So you do pay attention to the academy," I answer, changing the subject. "I thought noble students being attacked would be beneath you." It was strange that Lillith and the other girl had been in a fight at all. I hadn't been able to find anything on their attacker myself, but Don had more direct access.

"Oh, just children squabbling, you know that. You brought one of them here." He waves me off and I groan internally. It is possible he is just distracting me, but knowing him, he genuinely doesn't think there is any more to it. As if Lady Cateline would have bothered reporting a fight between children. Although I suppose he might just have her reporting on my apprentice regardless of importance. If that's the case, he would truly have to be a fool to dismiss the event. And that, as always, is the question. How much is foolishness, and how much is calculated?

Lillith

"What if someone innocent gets too close or too curious?" Sara asks, and I understand her concern. I've worried about that myself, but I shake my head. My plan is risky. But our method traveling around the city, helping slaves escape, and sneaking Sara in is already risky on its own. This plan simply . . . scales it up. Besides, this time the problem should solve itself.

"It will be too dangerous—they'll have to set up a perimeter around it themselves or leave a massive vulnerability for us to exploit. We can use their own defenses for our gain. Yes, we'll still have to keep an eye out and be careful, but they'll do most of the work for us," I reassure.

Sara puts her finger to her lips in thought, but we are interrupted by a knock at my door. I bite my lip. I do trust my family, but I'd rather not share my entire plan with them just yet. For their own safety. Fortunately, I haven't mentioned anything specific enough to be easily understood in several minutes. We have returned home for today and are hammering out details we have considered since making our initial plan. I lower the sound barrier around us and climb to my feet to answer while Sara considers my response. "I understand your worries, I've had them myself, but this is the best shot we have," I say before opening the door to find . . . Edward.

I'm a little taken aback as he hasn't actively sought me out since our last argument in Satusmor. Behind him is the blonde I have seen him with recently. He is looking down and to the left until she puts a hand on his back and shoves him into the room. He stumbles forward a little and I raise an eyebrow.

"I'm sorry," he says under his breath, not making eye contact. I look at the woman and she leans forward, putting one hand on his shoulder.

"Come on, Ed," she urges, and he clenches his fists. Then, he pauses and looks up at me. His face is red, but he speaks louder.

"I'm sorry, Lily. Over the years . . . I have been . . . cruel. I lashed out at you for a few reasons. I told myself it was both our faults, but I've been talking to Mariah more and . . . I don't know, some things don't look the same in hindsight."

I look at him with a blank expression for a minute.

Then I give them a friendly smile and stand aside, holding my arm out to indicate they should join us. "Come on in, take a seat," I offer, and after an awkward moment, both enter and sit on Autumn's bed. I sit opposite them, and after a moment, Sara suddenly stands up.

"I, uh, have to . . . go," she awkwardly excuses herself, and I give her an amused half smile. I would have been happy to have her here, but it's kind of her to give us the room. Then I take off my mask and look at my brother.

"Why do you wear that around her, anyway?" Ed asks. I blush a little. This fact doesn't escape Mariah, whose mouth opens a bit in surprise for a second, then she chimes in.

"It's a girl thing, don't worry about it. Just say what you need to say," she instructs before giving me a wink. This makes me blush a bit more, but Ed doesn't seem to notice as he plows on.

"Right. Um, the thing is, ever since you . . . well, when you got that scar, I started thinking about things differently. Then all this happened with Baldwin and the women here, and Mariah told me about what he did to her and . . . I don't know, everything before seemed so small. So I'm sorry. When you got sick, and changed, it scared me. You used to light up when I showed up, and the smallest trick was like magic to you. Then you got sick and . . . I don't know. You tried to respond the same way, but your eyes weren't the same. The light was gone," he says.

"Right." I nod. "I'm sorry about that, I am. But—"

He cuts me off.

"No, it doesn't matter why things weren't the same. I used to think it did. At first, I blamed you for everything changing. Then when you got hurt, I thought it was both of us. I knew the way I focused on our family becoming nobles and ignored what might happen to you with Baldwin was wrong. I never should have listened to Dad. But I still thought . . . if we didn't get along, it was both our faults," he laments.

"I mean, yeah, it—" I start, but he cuts me off again.

"I'm sorry, and I know, it's not helping that I keep interrupting, but please, just let me say this," he begs, and I hold my hands open to my sides, then tilt my head forward in assent. "Sorry. I'm struggling to get this out, and I rehearsed, and . . . anyway . . . I thought it was both our faults. But I talked over everything with Mariah. Everything I remember, anyway. As we were talking, I realized something. You never sought me out. You never insulted me first. The thing that made me more and more resentful over the years was that . . . you ignored me. Not at first, but the more I . . . well, you didn't rise to what I said.

"I felt like I had lost my sister, and I wanted to win your attention back. When the same little miracles didn't get the same reaction, I tried something else. I tried teasing you, but you weren't bothered. Then I tried insulting you, and all I got was an occasional quip. But no real reaction, other than avoiding me more. Then things escalated. You got better at things than me. Before long, I was looking up at you in awe instead of the other way around, and I hated it. I felt so fucking small. So I lied to myself. I convinced myself you were doing something that—" He stops, giving Mariah a furtive glance.

"Something that still wouldn't have made you less than me," he says.

I give Mariah a glance myself and put a couple of pieces together. It's just a guess, but it's entirely possible her profession is the very same one Edward thought I had.

"Anyway, things got bad, and before I knew it, I was next to Dad, gloating that you were being forced into a marriage you obviously didn't want. And he . . ." He trails off, looking at my scar.

"The point is, it wasn't your fault, it was mine. This didn't really click until Mariah said . . . what was it you said?" Mariah smiles affectionately at him.

"When you treat someone poorly, it is never their responsibility to make you feel better about it. When you abuse someone, it isn't their job to fix you," she answers. I like this lady. Ed is lucky to know her. There is an argument to be made that I am an adult, in my mind, and he was a child, but . . . I really don't know what I could have done better than warn him of his pride and ignore his taunts.

"Right," Ed continues. "It wasn't your job to make our relationship better when it was my insecurity that was hurting it. I didn't even realize that's what I was blaming you for, but I was. Anyway, I'm sorry," he apologizes, looking down.

I look at him for a moment, my own heart aching at the thought. For a while, I didn't know if I would ever have a chance at a relationship with Edward, but here he is. This woman is a miracle worker.

"For what it's worth, I'm sorry too. Mariah is right, it wasn't my job to fix the way you treated me. But still. When we were young, I knew something was off with you. But I didn't know how to give you what you wanted. You were still my brother, but things weren't the same, and I couldn't be the little sister you knew. When things started getting worse . . . I didn't know what to do about it. I figured you were young, and if I didn't rise to your taunts *too* often, you would get bored with them. But I couldn't be who I was, so I didn't know how to fix things," I answer, trying to stumble around the issue.

The problem was, I was an adult and I had shit to do. Surpassing him is what hurt his pride, and I couldn't hold myself back to soothe it. Nothing I said or did would have made him feel better, and warnings about being controlled by pride, when they came from me, only made the problem worse. Even if I tried to teach him what I knew, it would hurt his pride that his little sister was teaching him. I had to let him work through it himself. Still, I feel guilty about how it went down. If he knew I was an adult, things might have been different. Maybe. Then I realize what it is I need to say now.

"Ed, it's all right. I forgive you. And if you are up for it, I'd like to give it another shot. Being siblings, I mean," I offer, and Edward starts crying. Gently at first, but I hear the sudden gasps for breath as Mariah rubs his back.

"It's all right, my love," Mariah encourages him. "I told you it would be all right. And you can ask her."

I am standing, moving to give my brother a hug for the first time in . . . I don't know how long, but I pause so he can ask whatever it is. It takes a moment, but after a few sniffles, he looks up at me with red eyes.

"Lily, I want to help. With everything. I want you to teach me magic," he declares with a serious expression.

"Oh," I respond, a little taken aback. "Well . . . all right."

CHAPTER FORTY-SEVEN

Back to School

Ansel

So, you failed, did you? To dispose of a little girl?" my master derides me. I wince as I kneel. It's true I failed to kill the Forrester girl initially, but I did achieve the desired result. I have decided our interests are best served if I don't make another attempt. Now I just need to convince the man on the dirty throne in front of me.

"Yes, Your Highness," I respond, shame keeping my voice low and my head down. He allows silence to reign for a few moments and my skin itches with anxiety. I hear him lean forward and his disgust poisons the air around me. Sweat drips from my head as I am dissected by his calculating gaze. He is wondering if it would be worth it to kill me. This is the curse of being a bard. I can actually feel his murderous intent like a wire wrapped around my neck and idly tightened. I don't have to guess; I know he's a breath away from pulling that wire and ensuring my final moments are on my knees.

Lifetimes pass before he speaks.

"And why, Ansel, do I need an assassin who can't kill an untrained child from a minor family?" he inquires. His voice is calm, but the weight of his displeasure presses my head down like an anvil. I have to take a deep breath and steady my heart before I can manage a response.

I don't apologize. This man has no patience for such things. Instead, I launch right into my prepared response. "The asset fought hard to keep her alive, Your Highness. When we fought, I would have needed to kill the asset just to reach the target. When the target was available again, she chose to stay with the asset. After observing the two, I determined the target was no longer a threat. I believe the scare of being attacked at all has successfully silenced her. Furthermore, after reevaluating the asset's connection to her, I determined a second attempt could derail her and harm future recruitment attempts," I explain.

I feel a flash of rage but it dissipates as quickly as it comes, like liquor on fire. Then my master returns to his regular calculating self. I hold back my sigh of relief. If I've made it this far, I am out of the woods, provided I don't reveal I am actively reading his emotions. He must know I can, but it could be fatal to remind him of the fact. He does not look kindly on the idea of anyone being inside his head.

Finally, once he has calmed himself, he responds. "Very well, Ansel. I will trust your judgment . . . for now. I assume you are prepared to pay the price if you are wrong?"

"Yes, Your Highness," I agree, trying not to sound too eager. I don't know if this is the right call, but the asset is volatile. Whether my master says it or not, I would be in just as much danger if following his instructions led to explosive results. This gamble is my best chance at survival. At the same time, I'd like to delay her recruitment as long as possible. We only need her because of my connection to His Majesty, which means once we have her . . . he will have no need for me.

"As you say," he concedes. "I have another task for you anyway." I take this as a signal that it is finally safe to meet his eyes. As I do, I see him holding out a paper. I stand and approach slowly, then accept it and scan the list of names written on it.

"Are these the targets?" I ask.

"That's right," he confirms with a hollow grin. "See to it they are given priority in labor requisitions. You are dismissed."

I fold the paper and tuck it into my coat pocket. This, at least, will be far easier to accomplish.

Lillith

Between healing the apprentice priests, drawing for Sara, and teaching Ed about magic, my suspension is over in no time at all. I leave the dorm ahead of Autumn so I can work on my radar spell while I walk across campus. It's taken work, but I have grown fairly efficient with it. Currently, I am using a gradient to indicate the direction light is coming from. I translate radar waves into visual light just as they hit light mana directly in front of my eyes. Depending on the angle it comes from, a different color will appear.

This isn't perfect, but it does help me know when someone is approaching from the side. It takes a lot of precise work and the mana flowing through my body practically vibrates as I send it in different directions. I feel like one of those one-man bands, waving my mana around like their frantic limbs as they try to play six different instruments. I don't know if it will ever be effective in a fight, but it'll give me an early warning for ambushes. In order to practice, I am essentially filtering out all other visual cues and trying to only react to the radar lights.

I ignore the beautiful gardens and magic fountains as I walk through campus, barely avoiding colliding with one of the other students on the path. The different conversations I pass are more distracting than I expect, so I tune them out as well. I am growing fairly skilled, and I decide to up the challenge in the best way I can. I unwrap an apple turnover I bought when I got on campus so I can enjoy the snack before I make it to class. I sink my teeth into it, barely avoiding another student as the pastry distracts me. My face immediately pales as I come to a horrifying realization.

This isn't apple. This was made with fucking *pear*. Who makes a pear turnover?? I immediately spit the abomination out and gag, holding my tongue out. I probably get strange looks, but they are all just lights to me. The student nearest me seems to have decidedly unimpressed body language.

"Sorry, that was just . . ." I shudder. "Absolutely vile. I have never been so disgusted in my life." I have to remember not to go back to the baker who made this. He has forgotten the face of his father.

As I see a crowd outside the building I'm headed toward, I realize I have arrived at my aspecting class. It's not uncommon for Lady Kyra to be late and leave the door locked, so this is a familiar scene. I release all the magic of my radar spell at once and breathe a sigh of relief. Practice is important, but there is no chance I can pay attention to class at the same time. As soon as I do this, I feel the pressure of a thousand eyes on me. I look between the astonished faces of my classmates and shrug it off. I'd expected this to an extent.

Once I was suspended for violence, I gave up on blending in on campus. The ship of respectability has sailed, so to speak, and I gave myself something of a makeover during my break. As I join the waiting crowd, Hugh is the first to speak. "What in the third plane happened to you? I suppose Lord Godfrey decided if you were going to act like a common brute, you should look like one?" he scoffs, his eyes glued to the newly shaved side of my head.

I'm a little annoyed to see him here since he's not actually in my aspecting class, but I remember something the headmistress said before suspending me. That's right, the first years are measuring their mana capacity today. I suppose different sections of Lady Kyra's class are combining to get it out of the way. In that case, Autumn should be here soon as well.

"What's wrong, no clever quip?" Hugh adds after I fail to respond.

"Huh?" I respond. "Sorry, I forgot you said anything. What were you whining about?"

His face cycles through the various shades a tomato might have, but before he can lash out, another girl speaks up.

"Did you pierce the top of your ears? Why? That looks dreadful," she exclaims, horrified by the unfamiliar style.

"I kind of like it, actually," another girl chimes in. "It has a daring look to it."

"It's not the weirdest thing on campus," a guy in the back dismisses while flipping idly through a book. "I heard people have seen a cross-dresser." Several people murmur about this, some gasping and others confirming they've heard the rumor as well. Well, there is no mystery who they are talking about there.

"A cross-dresser, what's that?" I ask, eliciting a strange look from a few people.

"A man who wears a woman's clothes, or vice versa, obviously. I see math isn't your only intellectual failing," Hugh mocks.

"Huh, sounds like something made up by assholes. I guess I will have to admit that's a topic you surpass me in, Hugh," I retort.

"I guess we know who the pervert is," Hugh sneers. "You know you will never find a husband like this."

I roll my eyes at this.

"Oh nooooooo, you don't think I'm pretty anymore?" I retort, holding a hand over my heart in feigned panic. Hugh still looks self-satisfied and is clearly going to respond until the professor shows up. She is dragging a cart with what looks like a massive tuning fork on it.

"All right, class, everyone stand aside. You, help me with this," she orders, and the student she gestured at immediately grabs one side of her cart to help her pull it into the classroom. She does give me an odd look but declines to comment on the new style, electing to blow a curl out of her face and roll her eyes instead. I smile at Autumn as she quietly joins the crowd, and we all follow the professor inside. She passes our usual classroom and leads us to the nearby auditorium. I suppose the original classroom would have struggled to contain all of us.

As we settle into the larger space, she claps. "All right, I know many of you have been looking forward to this, and others have been dreading it. I'm here to tell you, this isn't as important a matter as you believe. You will likely land roughly where you expect. Unless you have a position in the royal court, your mana capacity will not have a significant impact on the course of your life. Those with more mana are already on a more prestigious path. This is just for our records, and so your family can track your relative progress," she lectures to little effect.

She can say whatever she wants—we test this in front of everyone for a reason, and the confident grins on the higher-ranking students' faces are enough to explain why. Yes, we all know our relative ranking and that's unlikely to change much, barring a newly designed circle. But this demonstration of it is a reminder from the powerful to the weak. The families who have been amassing power for centuries can safely display how far above the rest of us they are.

It's definitely more than routine, in any case. All that aside, I am a bit curious. I should probably hold back, but I would like to know where I stand as compared to the other nobles. Even hundreds of years of amassing power only amounts to maybe a month inside a circle per generation. My circle is a bit slower, but I have been using it for years. I should have amassed a respectable level of mana.

"I will call you up in order of family name or affiliation," Professor Kyra announces. "When I do, simply touch the mana attunement device and pour your mana into it. It will generate a sound, which will be measured by the dial in my hand. I will not be announcing your actual score, so you'll have to judge by the volume created until I hand out numbers at the end of class. Does everyone understand?" A few people respond in the affirmative, and the silence from the rest of the class signals that she can move forward.

"All right, to begin, it looks like . . . Hugh, please come to the front of the class," she instructs, and murmurs ripple through everyone at his lack of surname. He blushes as he makes his way to the front and touches the device. I see him grimace and the fork begins to vibrate, creating a low, quiet tone. There are various snickers, and Kyra has to order people to quiet down before she can call the next name.

Every noble called after Hugh creates a far more impressive sound, and his face grows redder and redder with each fresh humiliation. It doesn't change until she finally calls for Lillith of Endings. At this point, confidence finally returns to his face. His father must have never had the chance to explain that my mana surpassed his, because as I make my way up to the front, his look of humiliation has transformed into a full-on shit-eating grin. He is looking forward to having someone to look down on.

I give him the sweetest, most innocent smile I can muster as I pass him, but his confidence doesn't waver. Finally, I make it to my destination, grin so my teeth are showing, and put my hand on the fork. I've been trying to convince myself to hold back as much as I can, but as I barely touch the device with my mana, I realize why Hugh grimaced. It pulls. I feel like my blood is being sucked from my body with a straw, but it's mana. I do everything I can to hold it back, but it's too late.

The sound created by the device drowns out all the chattering in the room, far surpassing all the students who went before me. Hugh's face drains of color, and I have a feeling mine isn't much different.

Ralf

This academy is growing boring. I have managed to charm my way into enough beds that the thrill is gone. All the women here are exactly the same. At this point, I'm not even sure I can tell which of them I have already been through. My brothers all boasted about their conquests here, but they made it sound like it never got boring. I just want, I don't know, a unique experience.

Just as I am sighing and deciding to return to one of the women who gave me more of a challenge, I see her. A woman is walking through the crowd like she is the only one there. She somehow avoids colliding with anyone even while looking down. She has ears pierced in three, no, four places. She is using some kind of spell around her crimson eyes. Combined with her matching red dress, this makes her glow. There is a scar over her left eye that is somehow fetching on her. Most astonishingly, the left side of her head is . . . bald. Or mostly bald. There is hair, but it is shorn far closer to her scalp than I have ever seen on a woman.

If this had been described to me, I would have been disgusted, but in person . . . it's actually quite exciting. I smile to myself. This is exactly what I am looking for. I push through the less interesting students around me and make my way to her. It's not long before I am caught up and wearing my most winning smile. "Hello, beautiful," I greet her, but she doesn't even look over at me. It's no matter, she wouldn't be the first to ignore me . . . until she hears my name. "I am Ralf Trouvère, it is truly a pleasure to make your acquaintance!"

Nothing. It's like she doesn't even see me. The Trouvère family is a prominent one; there is no way she hasn't heard of me. Growing irritated, I step into her path, and . . . she dodges me. She has the audacity to step around me. Even worse, she actually pulls out some kind of pastry and begins unwrapping it. I clench my fists and suppress my irritation. As she takes a bite of the apparently oh-so-important dessert, I press on. "I have been watching you for some time, I'm embarrassed to admit. It's just . . . you are radiant. I would be honored if you would allow me to treat you to a meal this eve—" I begin and . . . she spits at my feet and gags.

I stiffen. She actually dared to spit at my invitation? "Sorry, that was just . . ." she says, a look of horror contorting her previously pretty face, "absolutely vile. I have never been so disgusted in my life."

I am frozen in fury. People are snickering around me, trying not to laugh openly. For the first time I can remember, I feel completely humiliated.

"You will regret this. I will find your family name and crush you. You and everyone related to you. I am a fucking Trouvère. You will be far more humiliated than I was today," I whisper to her before turning on my heel and marching off. I don't need to see the look of fear on her face right now. I can savor that later. For now, I have to ask around and find out everything I can about her.

CHAPTER FORTY-EIGHT

Challenges

I gasp as I wrestle with the device. Mana bleeds from me like heat to ice. The resonating sound isn't deafening, but it is shocking how far it exceeds the response of the students before me. My hand doesn't want to separate from the device and it refuses my commands. In my mind's eye, I've jerked my hand away like I've just touched a hot stove, but reality refuses to comply. I begin to panic as I feel my reserves drain, and the pitch and volume it creates increase.

I am still unsure what will happen if I manage to use all my available mana, but I am all but certain it will be one of two things. It's possible I will be able to use as a reserve the mana I am still gathering indefinitely. But I consider it more likely that my body, now dependent on mana, will simply die as my blood fails to flow. In this case, the two may be one and the same since the device is devouring mana faster than I am gathering it. This stupid fucking test is more dangerous than it has any right to be, but possibly only for me. As I feel my mana reserves drain, I realize it's not going to stop until I have nothing.

In a moment of desperation, I choose to lean in the other direction. So, you won't let me pull my hand away? Fine. I bend my fingers in an attempt to grip the device, and this time my hand obeys. The base I am touching is too small for my hand, and my attempts to make a fist push it away from me, just barely. As my hand closes, I manage to break contact for the split second I need to pull myself away. My head throbs, and I realize the edges of my vision are growing darker.

I am drenched in sweat and I begin to see the aura that used to tell Annie a migraine was on its way. I find this odd, as I left those behind with my bad vision and deviated septum. In a past life. I suppose I have triggered something that causes them again, which is almost as unpleasant a surprise as a mouth full of pear. Nevertheless, my presiding emotion at the moment is relief. That was too close. I hold my hand and give it a frustrated look in response to its betrayal. *You and I are going to have words about this later, young lady.*

Then, finally, I realize the room is completely silent. As I look up, I am met by thirsty eyes drinking me in from every angle. Even Professor Kyra appraises me with a perplexed stare. Hugh looks like I just forced sewage down his throat with a funnel. At this point, I figure there is nothing for it, so I give him the same sweet smile I did before being tested. Then I work my way back to my seat as the students before me had. The room is dead quiet, and I begin to grow self-conscious about my heavy breathing and my . . . drenched dress. Several eyes have tracked me back to my place, and the tension is palpable when the professor finally speaks.

"Right, then," she says dismissively. "Autumn of Forrester, please come to the front."

Oh, it's Autumn's turn. That makes sense. Actually, August should be here too, now that I think about it. I look around for him, but he is absent. I suppose he must be attending this test with another group, like Leo. The sound created by Autumn's test is more prominent than Hugh's but exists on the lower end of the spectrum so far. Her face is pepper red as she makes her way back to her seat and I feel a bit guilty. She actually did better than I would have thought, but my performance was hard to follow. I didn't mean to do it, but that doesn't change the effect it has on her.

After that, the rest of the tests go by fairly uneventfully. I am not the strongest student in class, being beaten out by two students from centuries-old families, but I am the only one getting looks and murmurs throughout the rest of the class. It doesn't matter that Lionel and Jocelyn of whatever near-royal houses have more mana than me. That was expected. What matters is, I am centuries ahead of the power a brand-new house should have. I didn't want this to be public knowledge, but I suspect Godfrey did. Today alone may erase any perceived shame or mockery from his time in Satusmor. His apprentice, who people will assume used a circle of his design, has surpassed the currently known limits of magic. Noble houses will migrate to him as if the king were winter.

At this point, it doesn't matter if I fail out of classes, at least not to Godfrey. It would obviously be better if I displayed talent, but the point has been made. People will think Godfrey's line is destined to be king as long as his circle is the most powerful. Class ends without a lecture, and I sigh. I like Godfrey, I do. That's why I really don't want to help him consolidate power. The closer he gets to the crown, the harder it will be to convince him that no one should have it.

This is why, as I fail to sneak out of the auditorium without being swarmed by students, I curse internally.

"How did you cheat?" Hugh demands, pushing his way to the front and glaring at me. "Your family is even newer than mine! As the second in my family's line of mages, I have to have more mana than you!"

I give him that squinty-eyed look people always reserve for morons. Hugh is evidence of a theory I have held across multiple lives. Pride and stupidity are the same thing. Or at least, they have a clear cause-and-effect relationship. The concept of IQ is long defunct. If you really want to measure someone's level of idiocy, listen to how self-impressed they are.

"Your father bought your barony after you were born, Hugh," I intone. "Which means you didn't inherit his mana level. We are both first-generation mages, dipshit." There is a bit of a gasp in the crowd and I immediately realize my mistake. Not everyone here knew I was common born and Godfrey's apprentice. Those who did might not have realized I was the first mage in my family. I just sped up the rumors about me, just to mock Hugh. Well done, Lillith. Congratulate yourself on not being a prideful idiot. No way that thought process results in immediate karmic justice.

"You're a first-generation mage??" A girl gasps, and I immediately recognize her as Jocelyn, the most powerful mage in the class. She must be from Autumn's class, as I don't recognize her from mine. "How is that possible? You showed off almost as much mana as my father in there!"

Yep, I definitely didn't do myself any favors. I don't have any choice. They aren't going to just drop this. I have to give them an explanation they'll accept, and that means bolstering Godfrey's position. Fucking mana fork.

"Well," I start, rubbing the back of my neck, "it's Lord Godfrey. I'm his apprentice, so . . ." And just like that, understanding and awe decorate my classmates' faces. They are all now under the exact impression Godfrey has probably been aiming for. He knows me, and he knows I'd try to hide my magic at this measuring contest. He also would know I wouldn't be able to. I've been outplayed. That thought sits like sour milk in my stomach. On the other hand, as the wave of questions from the crowd washes over me, something else occurs to me.

How did he know I wouldn't be able to? I mean, he must have experienced this type of mana measurement before, but how did the fork stop me from pulling away?

My thoughts are interrupted by Hugh, the thorn that just won't leave my side. "So, you surpassed me while lying on your back, is that it?" he accuses.

"No," I answer, rolling my eyes, "but if I had, that would still just mean I did more to earn it than you did. Would that really make you feel better?" He huffs before responding.

"Whatever you say, whore. All that mana is useless in your hands anyway. A woman and an ignorant fool. Midterms are coming up—I'll put you in your place with those."

Again, I squint my eyes at him.

"Like, you'll show me to my seat?" I joke.

He tsks.

"I mean I want to make a bet. You are so full of yourself. So proud of Lord Godfrey's accomplishments. Surely you aren't afraid of a simple bet? Whichever of us has the higher scores in, say, mathematics wins, and the loser has to fulfill one request for them." He tries to act casual at the suggestion of math as our makeshift duel, but his intent is transparent. He still believes I know nothing of the subject since I couldn't read the notation. It may as well be an arm wrestle or a biology test.

The crowd murmurs at the challenge, and I can actually see his pants begin to bulge as he suggests the "one request." Fucking creep. I try to remember he is just a kid, but that doesn't make him less of a little pervert. So much for my hair driving men away.

I snap and give him a finger gun before answering with a single word. "Nah," I dismiss before turning around and walking away from the group.

"Coward!" he calls after me. "You know you can't win, huh? Too afraid to compete with something that wasn't handed to you?"

I just laugh and flip him off as I walk away. I have absolutely zero reason to make a bet with him, even if I have such a huge advantage. He continues raging after me, desperate to heal his wounded pride, but my mind has already moved on.

The mana device controlled my body. It was like . . . confession. I only beat it with malicious compliance. This makes me wonder: if objects can be enchanted with regular mana . . . can they be enchanted with divine magic as well?

Father Medici

"We have found no sign of them. They were there one moment, and gone the next," Brother Wynter explains. He is one of my most powerful priests, and he rarely fails an assignment. Yet his report today is the same as it has been for two weeks. No sign of the two priests who disappeared the day after the demon attack. No sign of the killer in the basement or the apprentices their victim was watching.

"What of the demon?" I ask, already knowing what answer I will receive.

"No leads, Father, I'm sorry," he replies, and I nod. That was expected. The events are obviously related. I still find it hard to grasp that a demon managed to make it into our sanctuary, chew a powerful brother to death, and disappear without leaving so much as a blood trail. Then to come back, while we are on high alert, and steal our apprentices out from under us? Whoever this is, they are more dangerous than any of my priests know.

"I am reassigning all divine priests to this task. We must find this demon at all costs," I order.

"But, Father," Wynter protests with a look of concern, "if there is no one to conduct confessions or make deliveries to our Lord . . ." I shake my head.

"You don't seem to understand, Brother Wynter," I respond. "This is no simple incident. This isn't just the loss of priests and apprentices. If need be, they can be replaced with the same method we have been using since the first disappearances. This is about so much more than that. Do you know why we are the true rulers of Potestia?" I ask. He looks confused.

"Because the Collector declared it so," he answers, and I shake my head. This is the problem with power and position through piety. Sometimes your subordinates believe the nonsense you sell them.

"No, Brother Wynter," I say. "It is because of the Collector, but not because of his declaration. It's because of the power he gives us. The power of authority over his creations and the power to choose who joins the Great Collection. We are the true rulers of Potestia because even the king must fear us. We control his people. We protect him from his people. And do you know why we exempt nobles from confession?" I ask.

He opens his mouth to answer, but I wave him off; I know he will just quote scripture. "It's because we don't need to. Nobles are sure of their power and supremacy, especially the king. They would never believe they needed to be confessed. But does that mean we can't control them? No. Because not only do we control his people here, we control the monsters of the Collector. The beasts of the forest. The two armies that could tear him from his throne in a day, mana or no mana. We are the true rulers because we have everything he fears."

"But the monsters can't leave the Radiant Woods," he protests. "They will die without the Collector's magic!"

He's right . . . in a way. The Collector holds these monsters together after changing them in ways no human could survive. "Exactly," I answer. "Without the Collector's magic. Our magic. They are an army only we can lead from the forest. That is how it is, and that is how it has always been. So, let me ask. What will the nobility do if, say, a monster shows up that we don't have control over? What will they think of us? What happens to the fear we control them with? What happens when they realize a monster is hunting us, and we can't even find it?" I ask.

His eyes widen and he whispers,

"I understand, Father."

"Very good. Then take all the divine mages and track this demon down before it causes more trouble for all of us," I order.

He pauses before turning.

"I understand, Father," he repeats, "but . . . we still need to make deliveries to the Collector. You know he won't accept any excuse if we don't, so . . . I want to propose we plant a closer section of the woods."

I clench my fists.

"No, you damn fool. That would be even worse than letting the demon go! Do you think it's an accident all our cities are so far from the Radiant Woods?" I understand his thought process. Every priest has this idea at first. When he realizes the Radiant Woods are only one place from the inside. When we see a map that reveals its entrances peppered all over the country, we all wonder if we couldn't have one in the city. No more weeks-long trips to drop off mementos. Just quick, routine deliveries. But we don't do that for a reason.

"No, Father, but if only we could deliver them more quickly, we wouldn't need to choose between—" I wave him off.

"The answer is no. It is the Collector's will that we leave the woods where they are. It's far too dangerous to keep them closer."

He looks frustrated, but he bows.

"As you wish, Father," he says before turning and leaving.

He would understand if I could explain, but that would be just as dangerous. There is a reason only fathers are told the true nature of divine magic.

CHAPTER FORTY-NINE

Friends and Siblings

As I leave my aspecting class, Autumn catches up to me. "Hey, Lily, you all right?" she asks, clear concern on her face. Most people in that classroom saw, or heard rather, the unprecedented amount of mana I have. Autumn seems to have noticed the panic and sweat instead. Of course, she saw me in the Radiant Woods, so she was likely expecting a big showing from me. Still, it's nice to have someone ask about my apparent distress.

"I'm all right," I answer. "That damn thing just . . . demanded everything I had. And I really didn't want to give it all, to say the least."

She nods at this. "Yeah, that makes sense. It really drains you, doesn't it? Did you pull away early somehow? That would explain how low your output was," she muses.

"Well, sort of. My endoaspect wasn't at its peak in there either. But I'll be all right. I think I'm going to skip class this afternoon and rest at home. With my history classes, I learn more from what they leave out than what they say anyway."

"Are you sure, with midterms coming up?" she questions with a concerned look.

I shrug. "After today, I doubt Godfrey would let them give me a failing grade. Even if he does, I'm not that concerned about passing every class. It's more about what I learn in the classes than some certification," I say dismissively, and she looks skeptical but shrugs it off. "Besides, my government professor has been in a foul mood for months. I don't have the energy for that today."

"If you say so. But I wouldn't miss a class after two weeks of suspension. We are already behind," she warns. I shrug again and we walk in silence for a while.

"Actually, there is something—" we both say in unison before looking at each other and pausing for a moment.

"Sorry, go ahead." I chuckle, and she nervously scratches behind her ear.

"Um, right. Well, it's about our room at your brother's place," she begins. I decide not to correct her. It is technically Gilbert's home legally but no one in my family sees it that way. But that doesn't matter at the moment. "Well, I know I'm allowed back at the dorm, but . . . well, you and Eleonor are always gone, so it feels like I just live there with Iris. It's been a lot more fun staying with your family and . . . well, I don't feel safe in the dorm anymore . . ."

"Well, that's convenient," I answer, "since that's the same thing I wanted to talk to you about. I don't think it's safe for you there either. But . . . I don't actually stay with my family. I stay at a . . . seedy inn closer to campus. But you are safer at my home. I have a way out for them in case things go south; you can use it as well. Will that work?" I can see her grow tense, then relaxed as I progress through the sentence. "Besides," I add, a wicked grin painting my face, "I'm sure Henry would be happy to have you for longer."

Her face burns with her blush and she rapidly looks away from me. "No, I—it's not that I just . . . It's because I . . ." she sputters, and I laugh, patting her on the back.

"It's all right, I think he likes you too. It's quite the trek though, so you'll spend a lot of time moving between classes and home. I hope that's all right," I warn, but she doesn't hear the end of my sentence. Her head is steaming as the embarrassment mixes with happiness at my first comment. I shrug. She knows how far it is. "Anyway, I'm supposed to meet Leo for lunch. I'll see you later, yeah?" I ask.

She just nods, avoiding eye contact. I chuckle before parting ways with her.

I wind my way through campus, practicing my radar spell a bit more. It's getting easier to use, but not easy enough. Finally, I arrive at the restaurant where Leo waits.

"Leo!" I call as I spot his distinctive figure crouched over near the entrance. I'm excited to see him as we haven't had much chance to interact over the past couple of weeks. "It's good to see you, lunch is on me to—" He turns and I'm stopped short.

I am a tundra, the ice emanating from me enough to freeze the air. I fail to suppress the cold fury twisting my face as I look at my friend. His lip is split open and his face is badly discolored with bruises. His clothes are clean and his wounds are at least a few days old, based on the color and scabs. He has been badly beaten, but he still ekes out a creaking smile that cracks his lip. "Hey, Lily. Good to see you."

"Who did this?" I dig, ready to raise hell for my friend.

"No, Lily. Please, just leave it. It doesn't matter, I'm okay," he pleads.

I give him a cold stare. My knuckles ache as I clench my fist and my jaw sets. But I can't force him to tell me. If I ever find out who it was, however . . . they had better hope the Collector is real and watching out for them. As Leo tries to stand and stumbles, I realize he is hurt in more places than one. I rush to his side and offer him my shoulder to prop him up, which he accepts.

"Leo, you're hurt badly. I'm so sorry, I should have been here," I apologize, and he waves me off.

"There is nothing you could have done. I'm just glad it was only me," he responds.

I grimace. "Well, there is something I can do now. You could have a broken rib—let me take you to my friend, she can help you," I beg.

He looks like he is going to protest, but as he stumbles and I see sharp pain grip his face, he changes his mind.

"The same friend you mentioned before?" he asks, and I nod.

"All right. I wanted to meet her anyway. But seriously, Lily, this is all I need, I promise," he entreats me.

I nod in assent. I want to protest. I want to find whoever did this and choke the life out of them. Captain Horrus's face flashes through my mind and I take a deep breath. This isn't the time for justice; it's a time for healing. Justice can come later. So I help him to the front gate and hire a carriage to take us to my home. We get more than a few strange looks, but we always do.

In the carriage I have Leo lie on one seat and raise his legs. I can't tell, but he could have minor internal bleeding with wounds of this severity. That probably would have caused more issues much sooner—he has survived for days—but I don't want to take the risk.

After a grueling ride, each bump in the road inciting a pained scowl on Leo's face, we arrive home and I help him in.

"Lily, you are home ear— Oh, by the Collector, what happened?" Mom demands when she spots Leo.

"I don't know," I respond. "Is Sara around? When did she last check in?"

My mom rushes to my side and we both help Leo to a room downstairs. We lay him on the bed and I put pillows under his legs.

"She's not, but she should be here soon," Mom replies. I put my hand against Leo's forehead. He has no fever, which is a good sign. It's likely he just has a few broken bones, but I want him treated as soon as possible.

"All right, good. Can you send her here as soon as she arrives? He's been ignoring his injuries for too long already, I want to treat him as soon as possible," I say. Although she does give me a perplexed look, my mom nods, then asks, "Should I get you some tea, maybe a little bread?"

"Not yet," I say. "No food until we know if he is bleeding or not."

Mom agrees and goes to wait for Sara. I'm extremely glad I have asked her to check in regularly, or I would have to waste more time retrieving her. I focus my attention on Leo again. "Why didn't you go to a clinic or something? You could die from injuries like this. You're lucky you didn't!" I lecture him, but he looks away. He has a stubborn set to his jaw, and I realize I am not getting anywhere with him right now. Maybe once he isn't in pain anymore. "Leo, let me help you. Please," I beg, but as I expected, I don't get a response.

After an eternity, Sara rushes into the room, immediately interrogating me. "What's wrong, who is hurt?"

I gesture at the bed. She runs to his side and puts her hand on him. I do the same, and with no need to discuss the next steps, we both exercise our respective powers. Leo has already agreed to this treatment, so I don't have to fight his will, and my mana permeates him. With Sara's divine magic and my mana directing it, it is quick work finding every injury.

He hasn't been bleeding internally, even from a minor vessel, which is good. Still, he did have two broken ribs and a hairline fracture to his cheekbone. Aside from that, the injuries were more minor than I feared. They were definitely too severe to ignore for days, however.

I have to work with Sara for hours to properly heal everything, and it looks like

Leo will have a scar on his cheek. Part of me wonders why we can put bone back together but can't heal scars, but I don't have time to examine it right now. Leo is passed out from the strain on his body, and Sara and I are exhausted. But he is healed. I'll talk to him about what happened when he wakes up, or at least why he didn't go to a clinic. For now, we need a break.

"I'm going to go check on Ed," I say. "Thanks so much for your help. I don't know what I would have done without you."

Sara just waves off the gratitude.

"You know you don't even have to ask. It feels good to heal. If there is one thing I actually like about this . . . magic, it's that. You go ahead, I'll keep an eye on your friend," she promises. I feel a mountain of anxiety ease off my shoulders as I turn to leave. I need to distract myself from thinking about what happened, and I am in the perfect place to do it. If there is anyone who can get me out of my head and direct my focus to more mundane things, it's my brothers. As I walk out, I'm not disappointed as Henry greets me.

"Oh, Lily, you are home! Why didn't you say anything, Mom?" he asks.

"I didn't want to worry you, sweetheart. It looks like your sister has gotten herself in trouble again," she laments, giving me a worried look.

"It had nothing to do with me this time, hand to God!" I swear, holding one hand up and the other over my heart. "I still don't know what happened, and Leo is asleep so he can't tell me how he got hurt. But I am perfectly all right, everyone is fine," I promise. My mom and brother relax a little, but Henry starts to search around the room.

"Is Autumn here?" he asks, and I give him a blank stare.

"Well, hello, my beloved brother," I mock. "It is lovely to see you too. I am truly taken aback by your concern for my well-being."

"Oh, shush, you just insisted everyone was fine, so where is she?" he asks, persistent. I might have thought he was being callous if I couldn't see his eyes. But I know Henry. He heard everyone was all right, but he saw the concern on my face. He's trying to calm me down by acting normal and by trying to make me laugh. I actually appreciate it, and it works. I laugh and give him the finger.

"Sorry, she's on a date, I'm afraid," I joke, then laugh harder as horror briefly contorts his features before he realizes I'm not serious. He sticks his tongue out at me like a much younger kid, because that is what siblings are for. My mom returns from the kitchen with two bowls of stew and offers them to me.

"Can you bring these to Ed and Mariah, please?" she asks.

"Any chance you can bring Sara one too?" I respond, taking the warm ceramic bowls.

"Of course, dear. She has been working so hard for us, I wouldn't dream of leaving her hungry."

"Thanks, Mom," I say. "I'll probably be up there for a while, I imagine Ed and Mariah could use some company. Please let me know if Leo wakes up?"

"I'll keep an eye out," Henry interjects, and I smile.

"Thanks, man. And for what it's worth, Autumn asked about you too. She's actually gonna keep staying here for a while, and without me, so . . . you know, don't do anything I wouldn't do," I say.

His face turns bright red, and I chuckle as I leave him like that to ascend the stairs and approach Ed's door. I can't knock with my hands full, so I make a knocking sound with magic. Instead of being called in as I expect, Gilbert opens the door for me.

"Ooh, stew!" he says before reaching out for a bowl. I deftly dodge him and lift the bowl over his head with force mana, gently catching it once I pass him.

"Paws off," I order. "These are for Ed and Mariah. If you're hungry, go get your own." As Gilbert grumbles about discrimination, I place the bowls just inside the magic circle I have drawn in white paint for Ed and Mariah. Both of them meet me there and sit down to eat. Ed starts in immediately, but Mariah pinches the back of his neck and he chokes.

"Thank you, Lily," Mariah says.

"Oh, uh, yeah, thanks," he adds before going back to his meal. Then I sit in the chair by his writing desk, to Gilbert's protest. As I look down, I understand why. Gilbert has been drawing again. As I look through them, I actually find a picture of me alongside portraits of the other family members. He is getting quite good.

"You need to give me some pointers," I idly comment, but his face lights up. I suspect I have just signed up for drawing lessons from my older brother. Oh well, Sara will be happy if I improve. I still don't move from his seat, however, echoing Henry by sticking my tongue out when he tries to wrestle it from me.

"So," I say, looking toward the circle, "how has it been going in there?"

CHAPTER FIFTY

Hypocrisy

Well, it's extremely boring," Ed complains, and Mariah gently backhands his shoulder.

"And here I thought my company was lovely," she jokes, feigning offense.

"Oh, you know what I mean. We've been sitting here for almost two weeks now. I want to get out and move a little. Henry said you carry your circle around with you, why can't I do that?" he asks me.

"I told you not to bother her with that," Mariah rebukes him, but I laugh it off. I pick up an empty sheet of parchment and one of my brother's quills and begin to draw before I respond.

"No, it's a fair question," I answer. "I do, in a way. I tattooed it on myself. I'll show you sometime when I'm wearing something more practical, but to answer your more relevant question, I didn't offer you the same because I don't want to kill you," I respond. Gilbert reaches for his quill and I gently smack his hand away.

"Wait," Gil cuts in while idly rubbing his hand, "are you saying your magic circle is killing you?"

I shrug. "Maybe, I sort of rushed into it. I . . . do that. But I don't think so. As far as I can tell, it only improves my health, kind of. But it does a lot of things I didn't expect. I have some worries about what happens if it keeps altering me indefinitely, but I can't afford to think about them right now. Besides, I think I can change the aspects of it that caused that. Make it a little more like a normal circle, but mobile," I explain, getting distracted a few times while thinking about possible side effects and experiments.

"So why don't you?" Ed asks.

"Well, like I said," I answer, holding up a hand to waylay his concerns, "I *think* I can avoid some of the side effects. But what if I am wrong? What if I try it on you and keep the side effects but lose whatever is making them survivable? My heart doesn't pump blood, Ed. My blood circulates with mana instead. So, let's say I remove what I think is the cause, your heart stops, and your mana doesn't take over. That means you're dead."

"All right, so don't change it, then. You aren't dead, so your circle must work," he complains.

"It kind of does. But I have a sneaking suspicion I will die if I use all my mana, even once. It's even possible I'll die if something happens to my circle, although I don't think that's likely. Hell, I'm pretty sure a normally safe test almost killed me, like, a few hours ago. But that's not all. There are other variables. First of all, I nearly died when I first made it. A magic circle rebuilds the space it is drawn around into something entirely new. In my case, that space is my body. It tore me apart and rebuilt me in an instant, and I'm lucky to have survived."

Gilbert gives me an odd look as my drawing of the Mad Hatter takes shape. I've been telling Sara stories from back home, and *Alice in Wonderland* was a recent one. She had, predictably, been particularly interested in this character. I wave him away and hold the parchment to my chest, glaring at him until he backs off. "You almost died again?" he chimes in, holding his hands up in surrender after our silent exchange.

"I'm fairly certain, yes. And that's another thing. I don't know if you'll understand the details, but I did die when I was seven. When I got sick, it killed me for a second, and I came back. There are some details about that I'm still working out, but I think that death may be the only reason I survived. Like I said, I rushed into it. It was stupid, but . . . I was adapting to some interesting changes at the time and wanted something I could control. Anyway, I think there is a good eighty percent chance it immediately kills anyone else I draw it on, and it could very well end with them dead even if they survive the initial change," I finish.

"I mean, you still could have offered, I would ha— Aaagh!" he cries as Mariah pinches the back of his neck again.

"You wouldn't actually take that risk, would you?" She balks.

Gilbert is trying to sneak up behind me to take his quill back, but I strategically dodge his swipe for it and reach out a hand to flick him.

"Yes, I could have. And I did choose to take the risk myself, so I probably look a bit like a hypocrite to you," I say, and Ed gives me a sheepish nod, "but I didn't really understand what I was risking until I felt the pain that came with it. Now that I do know, it would be beyond irresponsible to do that same thing to someone else.

"Let's say we are all starving," I add, deciding on a decent metaphor to explain my reasoning. "I find a mushroom and eat it. It poisons me and I barely survive the night, but I don't vomit. So I am less hungry than you. I then find enough safe food to survive but not be comfortable. I also find a whole field of the poisonous mushrooms. Am I a hypocrite if I don't offer you the poison? I don't think so. I only ate it because I didn't understand the danger. Once I do understand it and I offer it, well . . . that's not benevolence. If you see that I survived and decide to eat them when I offer, and you do die . . . am I guiltless in your death? Again, I don't think so."

"Easy enough to say when you are still benefitting from the risk," Ed contests, and I sigh, looking up from my drawing.

"I can see how it looks that way," I respond. "But let me tell you this. As someone benefitting, sort of, from that mistake, if I had to go back and do it over again, I wouldn't. Because I don't know if I would survive again. I wouldn't be as effective as

I am now, but I would be more effective than as a corpse. What it boils down to is: I can't explain what it was like, not really. There is something called *informed consent* that is necessary for things like this. As the only person who has been through this, I am the only person who really understands what it's like. It would be impossible for you to have the level of information necessary to really consent. So. Best-case scenario, I torture you but you are lucky to survive for now. Most likely scenario . . ." I trail off.

"Fine, fine, I get that you aren't going to use it on other people. It seems like a waste, but whatever. Still, is there any way to speed this up?" he asks.

I just chuckle. He did apologize and we are on better terms, but he's still Ed, I guess.

"I'll have you know that's a better circle than the king himself has," I say. "Well, as far as quantity and speed goes. It's going as quickly as possible. Hang in there, buddy—the longer you wait, the stronger you will be," I promise. I pull my drawing away from myself and compare it to Gilbert's. Damn. I am not a bad artist. If I were, my circle would have been much harder to draw. But he really is quite a bit better. Oh well. I look to the side and see Gilbert himself, far too close and looking at my drawing. I jump a little and he puts his hand on his chin.

"It's good. When you're older maybe you'll be better than me," he says. I know he can't know that I am actually older than him, but I narrow my eyes at him anyway. "Why such a goofy character? He doesn't seem like the kind of person you would draw."

I open my mouth to respond, but our conversation is interrupted as my mom walks in. She holds another bowl of stew, which Gilbert happily and greedily takes from her.

"Lily, your friend is awake," she whispers to me, and I hop out of the chair.

"Thanks, Mom, you're an angel," I say, giving her a kiss on the cheek before rushing down the stairs to Leo. As I burst in, I see Sara and Leo giggling together as Leo holds a bowl of stew in his lap. "What's so funny?" I inquire, and both just erupt in a new bout of laughter.

"Nothing at all, don't worry a bit," Sara assures me. I narrow my eyes at her.

"Well, I wasn't until you said that," I accuse, rubbing the back of my neck. In all my years of walking in on people talking about me, this is the most obvious it has ever been. I shrug it off. There are worse ways to be discussed than with friendly laughter, I suppose.

I sit down on the other side of the bed and hold the back of my hand to Leo's head. He hasn't had a fever, but it just feels like the thing to do. Sara is giving me an odd look, but I file that away for a later worry. "How are you feeling, bud?" I ask.

"Honestly, like new." He sits up. "I should have come here days ago." I smile in relief for a moment before giving him a serious look.

"Leo, this can't happen again. Will you tell me who hurt you?" He's already holding up a hand to stop me as the mirthful expression fades and he returns my look.

"No, Lily. This is something I have to handle. If it gets bad, I'll go to my sponsor, I promise. But please, just leave it alone," he begs. I bite my lip in frustration. There is nothing in this world that's harder than letting a friend get hurt because they don't want your help. But it's his choice to make.

"Besides, I am more worried about you," he adds, and I look at him in confusion.

"Why?" I haven't told him about most of my activities. Surely Sara didn't say anything.

"It's those noble kids you spend all your time with. You can't trust them, Lily. They hate people like us. They will always hate people like us, you know that. Every day you get closer to them, they'll just . . . You'll end up in worse shape than me," he pleads with me. I grimace. I knew he had a habit of disappearing whenever Autumn or August appeared, but I didn't realize he was so concerned for me.

"Yeah," I say. "The world they grew up in hates us, you are right. And in order to stay comfortable in that world their entire lives, they would have to hate us too, in one way or another. But . . . I don't know. They are still so bright-eyed. Uncorrupted by the sins of their families. They were born into that world; they didn't choose it. And I think they genuinely care. And if you and I ever want a better life, we are going to need friends. Some of those friends are going to be nobles." He's shaking his head before I am done.

"No, Lillith," he insists, "it is part of them, to hate us. You know what I mean. There is no world where they will ever accept us. You have had Lord Godfrey behind you this entire time, and it's been easier for you to distract from who you really are. So maybe you don't realize this, but it is not safe out there. Not for us. Not anywhere. You can't trust them."

I sit there in silence for a moment. Then I come to a decision. I have been promising him help for a long time, and he has always wanted to wait until after school. But maybe I don't need to know who hurt him if I want to protect him. Maybe I can offer him an alternative. Maybe I can help him in a different way, for now. I give Sara a look. She has been politely quiet the entire time, but I look down with my eyes, and she gives me an almost imperceptible nod. "Will you come with me, Leo? I want to show you something. We can pick this conversation up afterward."

He examines me skeptically, lets a sharp breath out of his nose, and nods. "All right. But I doubt you'll change my mind about any of this, and if you don't, promise to seriously consider my warning. You need to cut the nobles from your life. Every last one of them," he replies.

"It's a deal," I agree. He deserves to see what we can offer anyway. And maybe I can keep him safe. Besides, considering it doesn't mean I have to follow through. It's a simple promise to make.

Suddenly, I remember my drawing. "Oh, Sara," I add, and she looks up at me again. "Here, I drew the Mad Hatter for you." I hand her the drawing and she looks confused as she examines the caricature.

"Lily, this is a bit . . . insulting." She chuckles.

"Ouch," I retort as Leo gathers himself and climbs out of the bed. I reach to take the drawing back, but she pulls it away and folds it up.

"I didn't say I didn't like it. All right"—she addresses the room—"should we get going?"

I shrug and we shuffle out together. She does give me one last furrowed-brow look, but I'll ask her about it later. Right now, Leo is more important.

Sarafyna

Lily actually . . . forgot to wear her mask today. I suppose she was too worried about her friend to think of it. But she isn't ugly or horribly disfigured at all. She has a scar, but it doesn't look bad. The only surprising thing is she looks . . . really young. In retrospect, I should have expected this. She looks the same age as the kids she had with her when we met. She looks the same age as Leo, and as I was when I was left in the Radiant Woods.

She has always just . . . acted so much older than that. I always assumed she was older but . . . I guess she isn't. Still, her face doesn't look like her. It's a weird thought to have the first time you see someone but . . . it's too young for the woman I have been speaking to all this time. Something about that feels unpleasant. Disappointing in a way. Maybe I was hoping she wore the mask because she was like me? I suppose it is a bit sad we don't have that in common, but I wouldn't have expected it to bother me. In fact, I should be happy for her.

Actually, if she forgot to put it on, that must mean she doesn't wear it all the time. I glance at her again and her cheeks flush a little for some reason. Does she only wear it around me? I'm left to wonder why she would do that as we depart to show Leo everything we have been up to.

CHAPTER FIFTY-ONE

The Science of Mana

Leo

I am still having trouble processing what Lily showed me yesterday. I reach a hand to my side and rub the spot that had been causing me so much pain. I've done this countless times since her friend healed me. I can't believe how much better it is. Between that and what I saw yesterday . . . part of me wonders if she might be right. Maybe dropping out of the University and helping her . . . or letting her help me would be for the best. I had no idea she was doing so much, and the promise of everything she has done sounds . . . phenomenal. Maybe her friend really can help me and my master.

I want to believe all of that. I want to throw myself into the new world Lily offered me. But . . . they didn't heal the real damage. If she doesn't abandon her hopes of getting help from nobles, nothing will change. The bruises and the broken bones were agonizing, but it's the fear they brought with them that I need to heal. I only let my guard down for a moment. I had, like Lily, leaned on the protection of my sponsor too much. But not everyone on this campus has anything to fear from my master.

So, when I found a stray cat several days ago, I stayed on campus to take care of her. She was like me, with nowhere safe to go. Like me, she didn't trust a stranger offering help and wouldn't go with me. So I collected what I could and built a shelter for her. Somewhere warm in the bushes along a building, with a little food. For the first time in a long time, I felt pretty good about myself, but . . . by the time I was done, the gates were closed. I couldn't leave campus to find a safe inn. I had to go to my dorm. I did tense when Iris passed me on the path. I walked faster when she turned to follow.

But she isn't of high standing, and she should have been too afraid to attack me openly. So I told myself I was still safe. It was just one night; it would be okay if I got to my assigned room, closed the door, and didn't leave until my next class. Iris alone wouldn't do anything dangerous. But she wasn't alone. Just as I was approaching the dorm, another girl stepped out from behind some foliage. Jocelyn. My blood ran cold.

Jocelyn's family is important. Just as important as my master's. She couldn't publicly hurt me. It would ultimately harm both families if she did. But here, in the dark, with no witnesses? It would be her word against mine. Which means I would have to get my master involved myself. I couldn't do that. Not without risking everything she has worked for. Not against Jocelyn's family. Which meant I just had to take it. I couldn't fight back. I couldn't get help.

The two girls left me, beaten and bloodied, maybe a hundred paces from my bed. I woke up in the middle of the path, hours later, and honestly surprised to be alive. That's the damage they did. Not my broken body, but the surprise at the parts that were left. That's why I can't sign on to any future that relies on people like them. Again I rub my healed side, and again I wonder when it will next be broken, and if it will be Lily's friends who do it next time.

Lillith

I'm a bit disappointed. I had hoped, once he saw what I was doing, Leo would want to be part of it. But his wounds were too fresh. It was obviously nobles who hurt him in the first place and he's rightfully distrustful of anything that involves them. But I can't write them off either. Nobles are born nobles. It's not a choice they make, not until they are adults. Even then, the level of choice they have depends on a wide variety of factors. Women married off at fourteen or men who remain under their father's authority into adulthood don't always have the option of saying, *No, this is wrong.*

So, as I tune out the tail end of math class, I have to worry about my friend. How can I protect him and give everyone the option to do better at the same time? As I consider this dilemma, a loud thunk startles me back to the present. I notice a few things around me. Hugh is staring acid through me, but he has been doing as much since I got here and doesn't demand much attention. The cause of the noise seems to be a girl in the middle who fell asleep and right out of her seat. The most interesting observation, however, is Professor Clarrise. Rather than unamused, she seems rattled. I'm sitting closer to the front than usual, and I can perceive a slight tremor in her hands as she recovers and smooths out her dress. This merits more investigation, and as she dismisses us, I decide to approach her with a more discerning eye. I slowly make my way to the front exit, making sure I walk past her as I do. She is anxiously packing up her things, and I notice extra makeup under her eyes. She could just be exhausted; having done her job, I know how plausible that is. Nevertheless, I note her name down in my journal.

On a campus this size, I always feel my mana responding to at least one source of grief. This is true now, and I decide to approach her, when I get the chance, in isolation so I can determine if she is one of the sources. At the moment, however, I need to go to my science of mana class. That one and my aspecting class are the only ones I find truly useful. My history courses have basically taught me that, well, they don't know how this all started. Math is . . . fairly pointless at the current intro level. But my mana classes . . . they help me a lot.

It is perhaps not shocking that I couldn't learn all there is to know from Godfrey's bookshop. In retrospect, if he weren't actually a duke, it's unlikely I would have found as many resources as I did. That probably should have clued me in, actually. In any case, these are the classes that will lead me to the types of enchantments I came here to learn. Science of Mana was a bit of a disappointment at first, truth be told. It, as with math, primarily covered concepts I already understood. Based on the syllabus, however, that is supposed to change today.

I use that hurried walk unique to college students to make my way down the complex paths to the building science is in. This class has passed me by in a blur so far, but as I enter the room and pick a seat near the front, I am already paying rapt attention. It's not long before the severe Professor Judith walks in as the typical chatter dies down. As is her way, she launches right into the lecture with little fanfare.

"Mana and cognition," she begins. "Mana is, in a way, our perception made reality. A mana aspect is the form the energy of the world takes when we enforce our will on it. It is literally the reality of our minds imposed on pure mana. Please focus, students, on the word *reality*. It is not something we can picture clearly. It is not something we really want to be true. It is reality, as we see it. This is why two water mages may be capable of entirely different spells. One may be able to shoot water like a projectile while the other can only fill a bowl. Any ideas why this is?"

"Mana capacity?" ventures a student in the middle of the room.

"No." The professor shakes her head. "Well, yes and no, but mostly no. And mana can be conjured anywhere, so by constantly applying mana to a conjured element, you can propel it on its own. This is not always the most effective approach, however, and it is mana intensive. That is not the answer I am looking for. No, the reason is simple. The first mage may observe water traveling quickly through the air. Perhaps as rain or a waterfall. Perhaps from another mage's spell. But they observe it, and they believe this is how it works. When this mage aspects water mana, the mana assumes the image of water as the mage understands it, and the water will fly on its own.

"The other mage, however, knows that water needs to be propelled through the air somehow. When this mage aspects water mana, he must either keep mana flowing through it or find another way to propel it. Perhaps by utilizing another form of mana or by creating a large quantity in a small space and relying on pressure. What matters is that each mage imposes their understanding of water on mana, and that is the form the mana takes."

A dozen questions are already circulating in my head.

A boy a few seats away from me speaks up first, however. "So, we can make mana do anything if we believe hard enough?" he asks. Judith gives him an unamused stare.

"No," she says dismissively. "In theory, this may be possible, but it's not so simple as that. If I wanted mana that would make me fly through the air, for instance, I couldn't just decide to believe humans can fly. The mind is far more rigid than that.

I know people fall, so I can't aspect flight mana and fly. I'm an educated woman. I know fire needs fuel to burn, so I can't aspect fire mana that burns forever. Even if I want to believe otherwise, my belief has to be genuine."

"So why do we learn about all this stuff? If you taught us from childhood that fire burned on its own, wouldn't we be more powerful mages?" a girl asks.

I kind of understand her point. In a way, I have a major disadvantage with mana aspects. I know how things work on a far deeper and more detailed level than, well, pretty much anyone here. This means I understand limitations on aspects and therefore limit myself more than any other mage.

On the other hand, there is the professor's example of flight. I know people fall, but I also know why. I know that force can be applied in any direction, and I can therefore use it to lift myself. The concept of force isn't nonexistent in this world, of course, but it's not understood as its own concept in the same way a physics equation might represent it. They aren't exactly wrong either, but my understanding of the concept allows it to exist on its own in a unique way. And, with enough mana, I can fly.

So I do have a disadvantage, but I have an advantage as well.

"Well, no," Professor Judith responds. "Because what happens when the two mages I mentioned earlier fight? The mage who misunderstands water has the initial advantage, yes, but what if, in the middle of the fight, he observes his opponent's water magic and realizes his previous understanding is wrong? Well, he can no longer grasp his own water aspect. He loses access to his spell and has to try to aspect water again with an entirely new understanding. If his perception changes, the aspect based on it disappears. So education provides you with stability."

This makes sense from a certain angle, but it also feels wrong. What if someone knows how something really works and I can trick them into believing something false? That could be a handy trick, if hard to pull off. I guess that's what she means though. The more educated you are, the more stable your understanding of a concept and the harder it is to shake your aspect. But that's not the part that really bothers me.

"What about mana circles?" I finally chime in. "What about runes? They have aspects. Circles can also imbue someone with a specialized mana. Can a shifting understanding change aspects acquired in that way?"

"An excellent question, Lady Lillith," she says, clapping her hands. "I see your tutors were more skilled than your stylists. Lillith makes an excellent point, class. Mana circles target bone and flesh to give us mana. As she pointed out, they can give us aspects like fire or water that we can use without aspecting them ourselves. It's simply the type of mana we have in our bodies in that case. Aspects gained this way work exactly the same as any other. The same limitations and strengths. It's why we can enchant objects with reliable results. It's also why we can't enchant things or circles with endoaspects. Because runes are consistent but limited.

"The answer to why is simple. Runes were a gift from the Collector. These aren't aspects of our perception but of his. His rules and his laws. In a way, this is how we know as much as we do about the world. His perception of fire is, of course, correct. So if you emulate mana created by runes, you know you have the correct understanding of the concept and therefore an unshakeable aspect," she finishes.

My face falls.

That can't possibly be the answer. Runes and mana must be related in some other way. They are the Collector's design? That doesn't feel right at all. Even the thought makes my tattoo itch and my stomach churn. And it doesn't get me any closer to my goal. This is starting to feel like my history classes. But maybe I am just being stubborn. It's not impossible. I just . . . can't stand the Collector and don't want to believe it. But even if it's true, I need to understand how he did it. Right now, I need to understand something else first, however.

"What about communication orbs? What type of mana do they use?" I finally ask. If there is one thing I need in order to organize people more successfully, it's effective communication. I assume some sort of light and sound runes are involved, but I can't figure out how simple orbs are translating things like a phone might.

"Well, that's an interesting question. But I'm afraid I can't answer that one any differently. Those are relics of the temple. Gifts of the Collector themselves. The rest of us have no idea how to make them," she answers.

Well, fuck. That is not amazing news. But just as I am cursing to myself, I remember the mana-measuring device. The thing that reminded me of divine magic in its effect.

"What about the, uh . . . fork they use to measure our mana capacity? Is that a relic of the temple too?" I follow up.

"As a matter of fact, it is; how did you connect the two?" she inquires, eyebrows raised.

"Oh, uh, just an idle thought," I answer lamely. I try to feign interest but the implications of her answer already have me in another world, so to speak. I am focused on the possibility of communication orbs using divine magic rather than mana enchantments. Like many times before, I bless the fucking stars that I met Sarafyna.

CHAPTER FIFTY-TWO

Monsters

Um, I'm not sure. I would have to see one. I don't really know anything about that sort of thing," Sara responds absent-mindedly.

I'm excited to find out if we can start building long-distance communication now, but it doesn't surprise me that she's not really present at the moment. Tonight is the first time I am taking her with me to a noble's house. She usually waits at a safe house to help with transport and escape, but I worry I may need backup tonight.

"What's that for, by the way?" she asks, pointing at the garlic I am tucking into a pouch at my waist.

"This? Well, I'm testing out a theory of sorts. It's related to a myth from Earth," I begin, and her eyes light up. She really enjoys stories about Earth, whether they be my travels, stories, history, or even politics. "We have stories of a kind of vampire. They are, more or less, a metaphor for our version of nobility. They have fangs to drink the blood of victims and feed people their blood when they want to create a new vampire. They are afraid of the light and only come out at night, among a few other things.

"I feed my blood, or at least a toxin distilled from it, to targets. I have fangs, and I only hunt at night. On a superficial level, I have some similarities with them. That's what gave me the idea. See, priests are clearly aware of the victims of the Radiant Woods. I don't understand what function they serve yet, but based on how they were used against me, my theory is they are at least partially meant as weapons. I don't think it's their primary purpose, but ultimately it doesn't matter. If the temple has revealed their existence to royalty at any point in the last thousands of years, either as a weapon or a potential future for the defiant, we can use it against the church," I begin to rant.

"How so?" Sara inquires as she laces up her boots. I don't respond right away as I watch her. This is the first time I have convinced her to dress in something more practical, like me, and it really suits her. That familiar little flutter runs through my veins as I see the focus on her face mixing with rapt attention to my words. I have found myself going on long tirades about even small topics around her, and she never seems to get bored. It's a little strange, feeling that burst of emotion when I see someone but having no heartbeat to increase. "Lily?" she asks again. I'm glad she uses my nickname instead of *Lillith*. It just feels . . . good. "Annie?" she tries, and something about that makes me feel warm.

Then I realize why she is saying my name repeatedly and snap out of it. "Oh, sorry, I got lost in thought. What were we talking about?" I apologize.

"Using the temple's victims against them?" she reminds me.

"Right. So, let's say you are in the upper ranks of the nobility. You have some sort of complex agreement with the temple, but you both want to be in power. You support each other, but you probably don't trust each other, right?" I ask.

She nods. "All right, probably not. So . . . ?" she pushes.

"So, what happens if a supposed monster, something you believe to be in the control of the church, shows up and starts hunting your allies and stealing your assets?" I see the light turn on in Sara's eyes.

"I assume I am under attack." I snap my fingers to indicate she hit the nail on the head.

"But . . ." she continues, "what if the nobility doesn't know about the victims in the forest or their connection to the church? What if they don't assume that you're a monster at all?"

"Well, in the first case, the plan falls flat, but it provides information. If there is no reaction, or they react like anyone would at a fairy tale come to life, I now know a little more about the dynamic between the temple and the upper nobility. But if they react with hostility to the church . . . that's killing two birds with one stone," I say.

"Why would you want to do that?" she asks, horrified.

"I wouldn't!" I choke on a laugh. "It's just an expression from Earth. I don't, as a matter of habit, stone birds to death, I promise!"

She gives me the same look you might give a stranger who passes gas in an elevator.

"What a horrible expression," she laments, and I chuckle, which elicits an adorable pout.

"Anyway"—I get back on track—"as for your second question, that's partially what the garlic is for. It ties everyone I handle back to a single entity. Obviously, they will assume magic was used, but the garlic leads them to the conclusion a single person is responsible. As for the monster portion, well, I fight like a monster or demon, then let the rumors spread. I kill with only a touch—I know no other magic that can do so. But I also showcase my strength and fangs. They don't need to be certain, they just have to suspect, and it will at least plant a seed of conflict between our enemies," I finish.

She nods contemplatively as we exit the safe house, ready to head to our destination.

We travel through the quiet streets, passing from the poorly maintained and run-down homes to the extravagant and richly decorated estates of the nobility. After some quiet, Sara speaks again. "I still don't understand the choice of garlic. Why that specifically?"

"Oh, garlic is one of a vampire's supposed weaknesses. As are churches and religious iconography, actually," I respond.

With a furrowed brow, she asks, "If it's a weakness, why would you leave it behind yourself?"

"That was something of an impulse decision, but you can think of it as one of my silly references but with meaning. It's sort of a reminder for myself. Think of everything we are doing to fight these people. I want both groups to know they don't own us. They don't own anything. I emulate a monster that represents the wealthy as I tear down the building blocks of wealth. I leave garlic, a weakness of that monster, as a calling card of sorts. Because that is what we are. We are everything they are proud of turned against them. Everything they use to prop up their power, every supposed weakness they use to control us . . . I want them to grow to fear every single one. When they see garlic, they will remember why they can no longer sleep in safety and security. When they see the muzzle over our jaws, they will be reminded of the fangs underneath."

With that, we arrive at the estate we are targeting.

A nobleman, well-liked and respected by his peers. He is known for "treating his slaves well," as if believing he owns them isn't a mutually exclusive concept. Whenever someone says they treat their slaves *well*, they always mean they don't treat them *quite as poorly*, which is an entirely different concept. In either case, it won't save him. He is one of the more powerful mages I have gone after, hence my request for Sara's help. But it shouldn't be too dangerous. Before tonight, I secured an invitation to a party and watched him drink a cocktail spiked with toxins. All I need is a touch and he will end.

I flood my hood with light mana to completely conceal my face, and we creep through the estate. While I use sound and light to mask our presence, Sara begins to reshape her body. It's always fascinating, on a biological level, to watch her do this. It's like her body becomes gelatin and squirms about until it has a new shape. It's gross when taken at face value, but all things considered, it's amazing. One arm turns into three muscular tentacles, the other sprouts razor-sharp talons from her hand, and her face grows multiple eyes. "You don't have to do that, you know. You are backup in case of my failure; you can, uh, dress more comfortably until something goes wrong," I reassure her, but she shakes her head.

"You want people to see a monster? I can offer that far better than you can," she says.

I pause, my voice heavy with concern as I respond.

"You aren't a monster, Sara. You shouldn't have to pretend to be one just for my silly idea." This will actually lend a lot of extra credence to the rumors, but with Sara's insecurities about this, I don't think it's really worth it. Yes, she should use her abilities and grow comfortable with them, but intentionally showing people her abilities with the intent of being mistaken as a monster could be a bridge too far. I don't want her hurting more than she already is.

"No. I don't want to feel like a monster. I don't want to face people I care about and wonder if that's what they think of me. But these people? To them, I am happy to be a monster." Her jaw sets and I see a furious look behind her many eyes that she rarely portrays. I consider arguing further but decide this isn't the time. It is her choice to make, after all. It's also not time to be seen yet. If all goes well, I can reach the target as he sleeps and touch him before there is a fight. Then we can make a scene on our way out, after the real threat has been dispatched.

We make it to the main estate and creep through the halls. I am proficient enough with radar now that I can avoid anyone in the estate with ease, although it is hard to maintain alongside my illusions and sound barrier. I also have to pay attention, not just to the spell but to my environment. It's extremely taxing, but there aren't as many close calls as usual. We make it through the richly decorated mansion and to the largest bedchamber. I can see one person in the center of the room, and I gently push the door open and slide in. Sara waits outside to keep watch as I release the various spells making up my radar spell.

It's dangerous, but I have to see the man's face before I kill him, and the radar lights make that impossible. Silently, I walk across the room and examine him. He is sleeping peacefully in his silk sheets. I pull my glove off and reach one hand out to end him in his sleep, but just before I make contact, his eyes fly open. Mana surges around him in an instant and I feel myself flying across the room before I can react. The mana is a pale orange, and I can't quite make out what its aspect is. Whatever it is, it's powerful and radiates heat, and I collide with the half-open door and fly past Sarafyna, hitting the wall on the opposite side of the hallway.

"So it's you," the furious man growls. "The cowardly mage who has been hunting my friends. Did you really think you could just walk in here and kill me like a dog?"

I groan a bit but recover my feet quickly, forming a force spell to strike back. My mana collides with his in midair and both effects fail to form. We both pour more and more mana into overpowering the other until it becomes clear he is more powerful than me, and by a wider margin than I expected.

It's then that I realize why he woke up when he did. He has some kind of endo-aspect himself. I rarely meet mages like this, and I always maintain the advantage when I do—there tends to be plenty of grief gathered around them. But of course, this man's "kindness" to his slaves doesn't extend to thinking about them when they aren't needed, and their housing is farther from the main mansion than many others. I can sense maybe one or two in the house at this hour, likely present to attend to him at night in one way or another. But they aren't enough, and I am losing. He pushes against my mana and advances on me. Neither of us can tell what the other's aspect is, which makes it difficult to counter it naturally. We are stuck in a battle of pure power.

I feel the pressure of his aura bearing down on me as I lose the exchange, but panic fails to set in. For one, I still only need to get to him and touch him once. My other trump card makes herself known as soon as he passes through the door. Sarafyna strikes like a viper, her tentacles wrapping around him and her own mana pushing against his as well. She still can't cast spells with it, but she doesn't need to in this type of contest.

Whatever his mana is, something heat adjacent if not quite heat, it hurts her. Her flesh boils and pops as it enters his aura, but it heals just as quickly. The grimace on her mutated face only serves to strike the fear of God in him, and with both our mana combined, the scales have been tipped. Now I begin to push him back, with Sara's help. She is causing as much pain as he is, her skin coated with some kind of corrosive substance that burns and melts his bare chest as he struggles for freedom.

"W-wait, you have the wrong man, I'm a kind man, I-I'll join the rebellion! All hail the true king!" he begs as he realizes the tides have turned. I don't waste time thinking about his assumption, as both he and Sara suffer the longer this goes on. I push through our warring mana and wrap my hand around his throat. The effects are immediate. The discoloration and the bulging veins spread from his neck to the rest of his body like ink in water. He spasms in Sara's grip for a few seconds before slumping over, dead. He drank multiple glasses of the poison, hundreds of times a lethal dose. As visceral a death as it is, it ends him as quickly as any blade.

Sara lets his body drop and focuses on healing her burns as we both sag. That was far more difficult than planned, and I am glad I had her with me. As we catch our breath, I feel my mana growing more slightly powerful, and I look around. A haggard man, perhaps in his forties or fifties, stares at us. He has permanent frown lines and his hair grows in a ring around his head. He looks ill and wears a servant's uniform that fails to cover the slave mark on his neck. I stand to greet him and tell him we mean him no harm, but I stop as I see all of Sara's eyes widen and begin to water. She whispers in a tone so low it would be incomprehensible if not for the dead silence surrounding us.

"D-Dad?"

CHAPTER FIFTY-THREE

Hat in Hand

Sarafyna

This is what I wanted. Lily had promised to find him, and I knew this was part of it. But I am frozen with warring emotions. I am panic, joy, fear, shame, relief, and everything else all at once. My heart wants to tear its way from my chest. My father is here. He's alive, and I am seeing him again! I look at the corpse I just discarded with my grotesquely mutated arm. I look back at my father, at the horror and fear seizing his face. I feel sick.

"D-Dad?" I whisper, then a second later, "You're alive?" I take a step closer to him. His eyes widen and his mouth opens slightly, then he turns, and runs. I look at the tentacles I have been subconsciously reaching toward him and open my mouth again, but nothing comes out. What have I done? It's exactly like I feared when I first learned how to leave the Radiant Woods. There is no home left for me with my father. Not as I am now. All this time and . . . he ran from me. I stumble against the wall, my body reshaping into its human form as I do. I don't notice the usual discomfort, like mud flowing beneath my flesh.

I just feel agony. The look of horror on his face will be with me for the rest of my life. He was disgusted by me. I'd called him Dad and he couldn't get away from me fast enough. Why would he react any differently, after what he just witnessed? I turn, pressing my back to the wall and sliding to the floor, then hide my face in my now-human hands. I am so tired. Lily runs to my side, crouches in front of me, and puts her hand on my shoulder. She is speaking to me but I can't hear her. She can't say anything to make this better.

A howl escapes my lips, like a dying animal. All this control over my body and I can't stop the tears and snot from running down my face. It's no wonder these scars won't heal. It's not just because they aren't my body, but because they are me. I am the monster from the Radiant Woods. Not the one Lily is pretending to be. I am a creature, too far gone to face her own kindly father. I can't stop the sobbing. I don't even know if I want to. I don't want to do anything, and I don't know if I can.

Then another hand falls on my other shoulder. I don't understand, and as I fight through my gasping cries, I look up at its owner. My eyes are bleary and confused as his form takes shape, and when I can make him out, I don't believe it. It's my father. Did he . . . come . . . back? But . . . I thought he was . . . Then I look down.

He is holding something. Offering it to me with a badly shaking hand. It's wooden, a smooth dome on top of a stand. I reach out and hesitantly accept it, trying to process what's happening. The wood is old. Years old, at least. But it's been well maintained. Regularly polished and cared for.

It's a hat block. My eyes widen. It's *the* hat block. The gift I was supposed to receive after my first confession. How did he still have it? He lost everything, he was sold into slavery, and he managed to keep and care for this? His tremoring hand, now free, reaches up and glides against my cheek.

"S-Sara, I knew you were alive. I knew it, I knew it . . ." he repeats. "I'm so sorry. I don't know what happened to you. I can see so much has happened to you. It's my fault, it's all my fault. I should have kept running. I should have listened when you said you were afraid. I should have pushed harder, caught up with the wagon, and taken you home. Please, Sara, can you forgive me? Can you ever forgive me?"

I stare at him in shock. This isn't his fault, how could he believe that? Lily is staring at me, I think. It's hard to tell with the black void of her hood, but she hasn't looked at my father once.

Then the shouting starts, and she moves. "I'll take care of this, wait here" is all she says before practically flying down the hall. I can hear loud noises and clattering as she fights off the guards responding to the commotion. With this, she buys me time to look at my dad. In a moment, I push off the wall and wrap my arms around him. I don't understand why, but even with my body like it was and the half-naked corpse in my . . . tentacles, he still came back. He heard me when I called for him. He maybe even recognized me. By my hair, maybe?

"Dad, no. It's not your fault. I've never once blamed you. It's not your fault. It's not your fault, Dad. It's mine. You have been a slave for . . . I don't know how long. I could have come to find you years ago, but . . . Dad, I was afraid. I'm not who I used to be. I'm not what I used to be. So I didn't. I stayed where I was and let you hurt, Dad, I'm so sorry!" I plead. His arms tighten around me.

"Sara, please. I am your father, and I let all this happen. Let me take responsibility. I just . . . I knew you were alive. I knew it. I . . . I took care of the block. I couldn't keep the shop. I wanted to, but I couldn't do it. After what happened, I . . . But I took care of the block." He stumbles through his words but I understand what he's trying to say. My fingers tighten around the smooth wood of the finest gift I have ever received. It's probably pressing against my father's back, but neither of us can be bothered to care. I hear a loud clang and a guard flies up against the wall at the end of the hall, then slumps over.

"Dad, we need to go," I finally say, and he nods, pulling away from me. "Um . . . I have to help her. Can you . . . not watch me too closely?" I ask, looking back at the body of the man he saw me kill. The amount of grief I see behind his eyes reminds me of who I have become. It's like a vast ocean and I drown in it. But it's not what I thought. It's not fear, and it's not disgust. It's guilt, because his little girl is now me, and that's so, so much worse. Because, whatever he says, I did find my way out of the woods years ago. While he was polishing and caring for a gift for me, I was too afraid to come find him. He doesn't deserve this guilt.

But I have to face who I am now, and I have to help Lily. So I let that same feeling of wading through my own skin return, and I retake the form of the monster from the Radiant Woods, and I lead my father down the hallway. Lillith is tearing through the guards like they are wet parchment. She doesn't need my help fighting. I just need to be seen by the fleeing servants.

"Who is she?" my father asks as we see Lillith flying through the room and removing the guards that have been responsible for his captivity.

"She's . . . a friend," I answer. "She saved me. Gave me myself back. She's the reason we are here now. The reason we can see each other again."

He watches her with frowning eyes.

"I think we have a lot to talk about. Is she . . . doing all that for me?" he asks, worry decorating his voice. I shake my head.

"No." I shake my head. "She is doing that for everyone. Dad, I have so much to show you—you are going to be amazed. She and I . . . we are doing something important. You can finally rest. You should have stopped working before . . . everything. But you don't have to worry anymore!" I explain, growing excited.

He gives me a weary, baleful look.

"I will always have to worry, Sara. But thank you. I would love to see . . . whatever it is. And if you trust that woman, I will too," he replies. The skepticism in his voice hurts, a little, but I understand it. He is such a kind man; what he is looking at can't be easy. I wince as we watch Lily crush a man's head against the banister of the stairs before throwing another down them with mana. I don't know why, but part of me really worries about his opinion of her. I want him to like her. If only they could have met while she was telling one of her stories from Earth. Why couldn't it have been when she was carefree and laughing about some cute reference only she understands?

But it's too late for that now. That will have to come later, when we have brought him to safety. I don't even know why I am thinking about that right now. Of the various anxieties rushing through my head, it is a relatively small one, but it occupies an embarrassingly large degree of my attention. I don't know what to do with that, so I just push it to the back of my mind. We have other things to worry about.

"Dad, we need to go find the others. Lily isn't just here for you, but to bring everyone to safety. Then . . . we can catch up. I can tell you what I have been through, and you can do the same. You can get to know Lily when she's not . . . doing that," I say as she crushes the final guard. She then turns back and rejoins us.

"Are you two all right?" she asks, barely even out of breath. I should have helped her more, but she doesn't seem bothered by it. I nod and she moves on. It really isn't the time for an in-depth analysis of our emotional states. "All right, we need to get moving. This was a particularly loud one, so there could be other mages on their way. We need to find the worker housing," she says.

"I—I can show you where that is," my father interjects, half raising his hand like a kid.

"Lead the way," she says. "We'll keep you safe, I promise."

And so he does. After I transform into a less terrifying form, we start in another room in the mansion where a couple of young girls sleep, then head to the off-site housing for the field workers. It takes some work to convince the group to follow us, but my father smooths things along. Just like when I was growing up, he knows how to connect with people. He makes you want to trust him. To believe in him. He connects with people and holds them together. As always, he takes the emotional burden on himself so the people around him can be happy.

He has clearly been doing this for the others for a long time, and they trust him like I always did. All this time, and he is still him. He is so, completely and thoroughly, my father. The man I have always trusted more than anyone. It makes me want to cry again. It makes me feel like I am coming home. This is what was missing when I went to visit my old neighborhood. This is why it felt so foreign. Because my childhood was here, in his gentle words and kind smile.

As we finally make our way back to the safe house, I give him a look. "How long has it been, Dad?" I ask. "Where I was . . . it was hard to track the time. How long have I been gone?"

He looks at me like warm rain. "Nine years, Sara. It has been nine years."

CHAPTER FIFTY-FOUR

Midterms

I rub my temples as I walk. It is finally time for midterms, which is fine for the most part, but I have too much on my plate. I'm not in danger of failing or anything, I just . . . don't give a shit about basic math. I certainly don't care about the most incomplete history in, well, history. Sitting through testing has pretty much never been on my list of top ten hobbies, but I just don't have the energy for it this week. It's been an eventful couple of months.

Sara has been on a roller coaster since we found her father, and it's been something to see. She is overly defensive of me, which puts a gentle smile on my lips. She doesn't need to be, however. Her father is a kind man. He responded better than could reasonably be expected to his long-lost daughter going eldritch horror on a half-naked man. She is obviously concerned about the circumstances of her reunion, not just on her behalf but on mine. But her father has been nothing but kind to me. Admittedly, I haven't seen him much in the days since we got him out of the city, but still.

Then there is what happened when he handed her that hat block. I couldn't take my gaze off her. She looked into her father's eyes, and her scars were gone. Her marred flesh had healed. I don't think she even realized it; she was so absorbed in the moment. By the time I had cleared the building of threats, she was in full Lovecraft mode again, and the next time she took her human form, the scars were back. I almost doubt I saw what I did. I want to ask her about it, but . . . she seems to understand something about them that I don't already. I need to wait for her to open up first.

Nevertheless, I am fiercely curious. I think there may be some clue about the nature of divine magic there. Or maybe there is just a clue about Sara's emotional state. I have to admit, I'm not certain which possibility interests me more. I keep wondering until my curiosity turns to daydreaming while I wander the vibrant green paths of campus. Before I know it, I am standing in front of Leo's new favorite restaurant. His opinion on the old one soured while I was on suspension, and he won't tell me why, but I don't mind.

The new place is more to my taste anyway. It's smaller, more affordable, and they don't defile any of their food with the devil's fruit. I still glare at the pastry stand with the pears whenever I pass it. Leo is waiting for me outside, and I wave as I approach. "Leo, good morning!" I say, and he lights up as he sees me.

"Lily, you made it! Shall we?" he asks, and we enter the building. We haven't talked about our last, tense conversation, but we each know where the other stands. I understand why he would be particularly wary of nobles, and I certainly don't trust most of them. I can't fault him for wanting to feel safe. I'm in a better situation than he is, and I need allies more desperately. I have the luxury of trusting the twins and other nobles a bit. After I shared everything with him, he seemed to understand why I take advantage of that luxury.

So things aren't as tense as they could be. But I still hope he will take my offer, and he still hopes I will cut off the twins entirely. We sit down at a small booth in the cozy dining room and wait for the waiter to find us.

"Have you thought about what we discussed?" I poke, hoping he has come around.

He looks longingly out the window for a moment before responding.

"I want to, Lily. I really do. It's everything I have ever wanted, you know that, but . . . I owe too much to my master. I don't know where I would be without her, but it would be nowhere good. I have to finish the academy first. I promised I would. But after I do that, I do want to join you. I really do. Master will too. But I have to see this through," he answers.

I nod in understanding.

What he is saying makes sense, even if his choice to call someone *Master* scrapes my ears like a cheese grater. In his situation, at his age, I can only admire him for doing it this way. "I understand," I say. "But if you ever change your mind, I'll be here."

He smiles at me, and we have said all we need to. The conversation turns to lighter things, and we order a simple breakfast of eggs. Pancakes are a bit too heavy for a midterm day.

"So, uh, there is something I want to ask . . ." Leo trails off and I raise my eyebrow at him. He plays with his thumbs for a minute before spitting it out. "Do you like cats?" I lean back, a little surprised.

"I mean, I'm not a monster," I answer.

He leans forward in turn. "Do you want one?"

I laugh. "Why were you so nervous to ask that? I love cats, and I'd love to have one. Why?"

He blushes. "Well, a while back, I found a stray on campus. I've been taking care of her, but, well. She was pregnant, apparently. Lily, there are so many kittens. You have to help me."

I choke on laughter. "Absolutely, I will adopt one of your kittens. Why didn't you tell me you were taking care of a stray? I would have helped! I'll meet you after class. I'll help you find a home for all of them," I promise, and he sighs in relief. "Why were you so worried about asking that? It's a perfectly normal request."

He looks a bit sheepish and embarrassed. "I don't know, I got picked on a lot as a kid when I adopted strays. So I get a little anxious, it's embarrassing!" he splutters.

"It's sweet, Leo." I smile reassuringly. "Fuck whoever picked on you." The poor kid should not be getting nervous about that kind of question. I realize how long we have been sitting here, leave a few coins on the table, and stand. "Meet me here after class, all right? I have to get to my fuckin' math test. Take care, Leo."

"All right," he acknowledges. "And Lily . . . thanks." Whether he is thanking me for my earlier offer or for not making fun of him I'm not sure. But it doesn't matter.

"Think nothing of it," I answer before heading to class.

This should be my easiest midterm, so I'm not exactly stressed about it until August meets me on the way.

"Did you seriously make that bet with Hugh?" he asks, mouth agape, and I furrow my brow.

"What the fuck are you talking about?" I ask.

He closes his eyes and, under his breath, says, "Of course you didn't. That idiot."

A bad feeling creeps down my spine. "August, tell me what you are talking about," I order.

He sighs before shaking his head.

"Hugh is telling everyone you agreed to a bet with him over the midterm. He says whoever scores lower has to do everything the winner orders for a month. The rumor has spread all over class. And, well, not a lot of people have faith you'll win. There are some unsavory rumors about you already . . ." He trails off as my face darkens.

That little shit. "I told him no. I didn't even entertain the idea of a bet. Does he really think this is a good idea?" I groan.

August shrugs. "I don't know, but if enough people believe him, it's sort of the same thing, isn't it? What are you going to do?"

I sigh. "Nothing. The moron can explain himself to everyone after he loses. Or he can come up with some new lie. I don't give a shit. It's not my problem," I say dismissively.

"Are you sure? You couldn't even read the question on the first day. I know you are smart but . . . you think you'll have the higher score?" he asks, skepticism clear in his voice.

"Yes, I do. Ask Autumn when we get there. I'm not going to have any trouble scoring higher than that brat," I answer. August doesn't quite look convinced, but he doesn't look dismissive either. Instead, he simply shrugs. We arrive in the class-room together and begin to climb to the seats in the back. I blow hair out of my eye as I ignore the excited whispers from the students I pass. August looks around the room and leaves my side to find a seat by his sister.

"You may as well leave now," Hugh sneers as I pass him. "You'll never pass this test, much less win the bet."

I glare at him.

"I didn't bet anything, you stupid fuck."

"Trying to back out now, are you?" he asks with a laugh. "You should have thought of that earlier; it's too late for cold feet now. You are as good as my property now."

I rub my temple, then.

I look up at him and give him a sickly sweet smile. "Listen, kid, no one is going to believe that you made up the bet after the test. I highly advise that you admit to it now, while you can still save some face. Seriously, bail while you can," I recommend, and he replies with a full-toothed grin.

"Trying to wiggle out already, I see. Well, no matter, everyone knows the truth already. You may as well accept it and stop trying to lie."

I sigh. Before I can respond, Autumn's own laughter draws both our attention. She is looking at us as August points and I realize she just learned about the pretend bet. She is under no illusions about who will win. Hugh's expression wavers for a moment but he steadies himself.

"Suit yourself. Don't say I didn't warn you," I reply, and he makes a show of his uproarious laughter. Poor, stupid kid. This experience is not going to be gentle on his fragile pride. Before long, Professor Clarrise enters and I am struck again by how exhausted she looks. The woman needs a break as badly as I do. She hands out the tests and gives a weary speech about academic dishonesty and all that. Hugh gives me one last smirk before we all get started on our tests.

I have gotten pretty good at reading the new notation, although I do translate the problems before solving them. Maybe ten minutes later, I hand my test in to the professor, smile and wave at Hugh, and leave. The rest of my tests are uneventful, and I am able to return to my math class before meeting Leo. At the level of math we are learning, it's fairly easy to grade all our tests, and we were informed scores would be posted outside the class by the end of the day.

Other curious students are crowding the bulletin and I am jostled as I make my way within reading distance. The tone of the whispers has decidedly changed, and it's clear why. I, unsurprisingly, got a perfect score. Hugh, on the other hand . . . well, he did fine.

"I'm surprised you showed your face here, after running out of the test so quickly," Hugh laughs as he approaches behind me. "Decided to start your service early?" His taunts fail to get the response he is hoping for as several students snicker at him.

"Oh, buddy," I say in an apologetic tone. He doesn't pick up on the snark behind my faux pity until he finds my name on the board himself.

"You fucking cheater. I'll have you expelled," he snarls as his previous good mood vanishes in an instant.

CHAPTER FIFTY-FIVE

Cheating

Right this way," Leo invites me, pulling an overgrown hedge to the side. We are on a campus path I didn't even know existed. He is leading us to the back of a little-used building. I sigh as I see how extravagant even the buildings around here are, although the flowers and foliage surrounding us are far more unruly than the others I have seen on campus. I suspect the magic items supporting the life around here have been neglected for a bit too long. As I follow him, I spot a small wooden animal shelter built up against the bricks of the building. "Here we are," he says, gesturing to the little shelter.

I have to kneel to look inside, where I find one of the pillows from the dorms, upon which sits a litter of seven kittens and their mother. "Leo, they are the sweetest." I grin as I examine them. A little gray tabby is having some dinner while most of them sleep. A little tortoiseshell perks up and squeaks at me. She already has her eyes open, so I know they were born at least a few days ago. "Well, they certainly can't stay here. We'll bring them back to the dorm for tonight, and I'll bring them to my family's tavern tomorrow. I think I've already been chosen by one of them." I chuckle as I offer my finger to the tortoiseshell to smell.

"Lily, you are a lifesaver. I didn't know where to take them but I don't know if they'll survive out here. I was at my wit's end. Do you really think you'll find a home for all of them?" His tone is pleading, and I nod as I stand and rub my dirty hands on my dress.

"Oh yes, shouldn't be a problem," I assure him while I start forming a couple of magical crates for them with force, heat, and stone mana. "Let's get them back for now."

"Why the dorm, why not take them to the tavern tonight?" he asks.

"I have a feeling I'm going to be busy tonight. I have, again, offended someone by existing in the wrong way," I lament, and Leo sighs with me.

"Why can't people just leave us alone?" he groans, and I can't blame him. He has it far worse than I do. "So, what, you have to see the headmistress?"

"I'm not sure yet, but probably. You know how she is, any feeble excuse to punish us for being here in the first place. I'll be fine, I'm more worried about you," I respond as we delicately lift each cat into one of my makeshift containers. "Be careful out there; I've seen a lot of priests around town, almost like patrols. If they run into you, they may not check who your backer is before confronting you," I warn.

"Shit, seriously?" His face pales. "What a pain in the ass. Well, I suppose it's good my room is close to the school. I'll be careful," he promises.

We then make our way down the winding roads of campus, and the messy hedges slowly give way to neatly trimmed and managed gardens. We make it to the dorm and bring the mewing cats up to my room.

"Can you hang out here with them? I'll watch them tonight, but I have to deal with a couple of assholes," I say.

"Sure, no problem. Just . . . don't tell anyone else I'm here, all right?" he requests nervously.

I make the *cross my heart* motion.

"I won't. I know you'd prefer to keep a low profile while on campus," I say.

Once we have the cats settled in, I head back downstairs and open the door. As I suspected, there is a magic knight waiting for me.

"Lillith of Endings?" he inquires.

"Take me away, officer," I say, holding my hands out with my wrists together.

He examines my wrists in perplexion.

"You've been summoned to Lady Cateline's office. Follow me," he orders.

I shake my head and drop my hands to my side before following him. Hugh certainly wasted no time in reporting my cheating. Yet again I am followed by murmurs and whispers as I trail the knight to the headmistress's office. Maybe I should get some itching powder from Henry after all; Hugh more than has it coming. Or maybe I'll tell him how his father's competition with me ended. I rub the back of my head as I dismiss that idea. It might be a bit of a cruel response to a child being a child. It would only cause more problems anyway.

When we arrive at the familiar office, I'm surprised to find it empty.

"Stay here, and don't cause any trouble," the man orders.

I snap to attention and give him a sarcastic salute. "As you command, mister knight sir. I'll be the picture of innocence!" I lie, and he grumbles as he walks away. I look around the doorframe to watch him leave, then immediately cast my radar spell. Leaving me alone in this office? Yeah, "don't cause trouble," my ass. I keep an eye on the people in the building around me and immediately begin to rummage through Cateline's desk. The drawers are locked, but locks in this world are more of a polite suggestion than anything.

I fill the keyholes with force mana and easily unlock each compartment. At first, I mostly find documents. Leo and I each have our own file, which figures. I find a few interesting documents, including one labeled *Solutions to the labor shortage* that contains a list of laws she is proposing. She wants to outlaw cross-dressing, drinking on certain days of the moon cycle, and various other silly "infractions." I shrug. This is obviously an attempt to replenish the city's supply of slaves, but she's clearly forgotten why the system of law works the way it does in the first place.

Only criminals are enslaved because people are more compliant and supportive if they believe the law keeps them safe and that they can reasonably avoid its consequences. Some of the proposed laws, like enforcing the side of the road commoners may walk on, would defeat this entirely. Arrest people too freely, and that illusion shatters. It would be like making every meal and home cost millions of coins. A balance of desperation and security can control people. But that only extends so far. Once homes and food are inaccessible no matter what you do . . . well, people won't be so compliant. The same goes for trying to make people into slaves for any random violation.

She's likely not the only noble who has this idea for replenishing slaves, but if they try it, people will only be more susceptible to my ideas. Without the fucking temple, this alone would probably incite a revolution of some kind eventually. This isn't surprising information, but it is useful to know. I thought it would be another year at least before they started suggesting it. I do shake my head as she has failed to suggest, in the face of a "labor shortage," *use our magic powers instead of forced labor*, but that would, of course, require a more practical examination of society. Something tells me the nobles of this world would complain if they went to a grocery store where cashiers had stools.

I move on from that and open a lower drawer. My day brightens immediately as it slides open. A smooth, fist-sized metal sphere sits on top of a few more documents. A communication orb. I quickly tuck it into my dress pocket, then hurry to lock the desk and find a seat on the other side. This is exactly what I need, and I can't risk losing it by searching any further. I'm just in time too, as my radar reveals multiple people approaching just as I settle in.

I release the spell, and a moment later, Headmistress Cateline enters, tailed by Professor Clarrise and Hugh. "Why am I not surprised, Lady Lillith?" Cateline sighs before taking her own seat. She pauses, like she senses something is wrong, but gets distracted as she really notices me. "Do you actually have dirt on your dress? Why do you insist on besmirching the name of my academy? Never mind, don't answer that. Do you know why you are here?" she interrogates me.

I put a finger to my pursed lips as if in thought.

Hugh smirks at me, his confidence restored now that Cateline is backing him. Clarrise looks too exhausted to comment, but she gives me an apologetic half smile.

"Well, this is my place of learning. Where else would I be?" I answer, offering Cateline a sweet smile.

She rolls her eyes and Hugh scoffs.

"It's going to be like that, is it? Lady Lillith, you have been accused of cheating with credible evidence. If you confess now, I can do my best to avoid your expulsion from the academy," she offers.

"Is the credible evidence that Hugh over there reeeeaaally wants it to be true?" I ask.

"Keep a civil tongue in your mouth, I am giving you a chance here. Tell us how you cheated," she orders with a glare.

I lean forward.

"I can't tell you what you want to hear. I solved the equations provided. It was extremely easy. That's the only answer I have."

"Perfectly, and in only a few moments?" Hugh cuts in. "When you couldn't even read one at the start of class?"

"Lord Hugh, you are here as a witness. I will ask you if I need your input," Cateline reprimands him before turning her attention to me. "He is, however, correct. You were far too fast. And I'm told you didn't show your work, only including a few nonsensical scribbles followed by the answer. Isn't that right, Lady Clarrise?" she asks.

"Well, yes, but—"

"Right. So can you explain that?" Cateline asks, looking down her nose at me.

"Sure, that's my own personal notation. It helps me work quicker. As for how much time it took me, I already answered that. It was just an easy test," I respond, leaning back and examining my nails.

"Liar!" Hugh yells. "There is no way it was that easy for you, you—"

"I will not warn you again, Lord Hugh. Be silent until you are asked to speak. And you, Lady Lillith. Your flippant attitude is doing you no favors. If you insist on this lie, we will test you here and now. Lady Clarrise, how quickly can you write a new test?" Clarrise jumps.

"It shouldn't take too long. You want to test her again, here?"

"Yes," Cateline says, nodding. "If it was so easy, she should have no trouble reproducing her results. In fact, why don't you make it a little harder, since she seems to believe the one you provided was inadequate?" Cateline continues to try to get a confession out of me as Clarrise works for the next half hour or so. Before long, a new test is presented, and I am given a quill and ink to fill it out.

I smile as I look over it. It is more difficult than the last, but that's not the same thing as difficult. This time, I don't take my time with it. I solve every equation in maybe seven minutes or so and hand it over. Cateline raises her eyebrows at me, and she examines it with Clarrise. Hugh has the smuggest look I've ever seen a face burdened with, and I lean back, relaxed. Cateline's brows furrow and her mood sours as she looks over the test. "You're dismissed," she sneers after a moment. "Lord Hugh, I do not appreciate having my time wasted," she adds, redirecting her ire.

I stand and curtsy, then wink at Hugh before leaving.

That wasn't too bad. All in all, it was a good day. I hum as I make my way back to my dorm room full of kittens, communication orb safe in my pocket.

CHAPTER FIFTY-SIX

What Comes Next?

I sit in the dining area at my family's tavern and giggle to myself while Suzume, my new kitten, chases the little red dot I am moving around with light mana. "I'm sorry, Lily." Sara finally sighs, "I can feel the divine magic inside this, but I can't tell how it works. My magic has never worked exactly like the priests' does. I don't know if I can make more of these."

I purse my lips in thought and Suzume squeaks at me as the light stops moving.

"Sorry, girl," I whisper to her before looking up. "Well, I suppose we'll just have to steal the ones that are already working. It's not an ideal solution, since we can't be sure how secure they are. I'd also prefer to provide more communication between cities, and as far as I can find out, each city only has one that communicates directly with the capital. Only one that is public knowledge, in any case. We'll have to use code or something for now. Not much else to be done."

Sara's shoulders slump. "I tried, I'm sorry. I'll keep looking at it, but . . . I just don't know how any of this works," she apologizes again.

"Sarafyna, you do, well, everything. I rely on you so much I feel guilty about it. You've been looking at that orb for months, and that's just when you are here. You can take a break. I haven't figured out how the mana in it works either. I know it uses sound and light, but that's it. If you're sorry, I should be sorrier. Besides, we have time. I'll start working on an alternative in the meantime," I reassure her.

She looks disappointed, but Sam—her father—chimes in.

"She's right, Sara. You've been working yourself too hard. If it's not something you can do, it's not something you can do. I hate it when you beat yourself up like this," he says, rubbing her shoulder.

"This guy knows what he's talking about," I say, crossing my arms. It was a bit awkward around Sam at first, especially considering the violence of our first meeting, but underneath any anxiety he had was gratitude. I realized quickly I would always just be the person who brought Sara to him. Not the person who crushed a man's head in front of him. Not the person who freed him from captivity. Not even the weirdo who always puts on a mask when he visits with his daughter and blushes when she gets a little too close. Sarafyna is his entire world; bringing her back into his life could drown an ocean of sins.

I know he feels this way because that is more or less exactly how he explained it when Sara made one too many excuses for my weird habits. Since we found him, he and I have formed something of an informal Pro-Sarafyna Alliance. With both of us as a support system, she is slowly starting to grow more comfortable. She often sleeps either here or with the others now, only staying in her cave maybe a third of the time. The cave was initially a safe place to learn how to control her magic away from prying eyes, but it became a hiding place. It supported her monster narrative to hide there.

The last few months have been good for her. And me, truth be told. It's hard to say without birthdays, but I think I am between fifteen and sixteen now. A little closer to finally going on a date again. At least, going on a date comfortably. That certainly hasn't been the most fun bit of reincarnating. In a child's body, I am not attracted to anyone my age. Anyone I am attracted to... shouldn't be attracted to anyone my age. And if they were, I would likely lose interest pretty quickly. In either case, I don't have a lot of options until I look something like an adult. On the bright side, Leo hasn't been attacked, at least as visibly, in that time either. I am settling into a groove.

Sam gives me a meaningful look and I nod. Sara's scars are wavering again, replacing themselves with smooth skin. She never seems to notice when this happens, but it's growing more frequent. I have been leaving her out of combat recently as an experiment, and the scars don't appear nearly as often. This always puts a smile on my face. Not because I want her to be perfect and pretty; her scars are part of her and I'm a bit fond of them, in an odd way. But because I think she is finally taking the first little steps toward real healing.

It also suggests something interesting about divine magic, and I decide to test it. When she doesn't respond, I speak up again. "I want to try something. Here, hold these," I instruct while handing her two forks.

"Um, all right," she agrees.

I fold my fingers together.

"Okay, forget about how. Just focus on using divine magic so that when you speak into one fork, your voice comes out the other. I know you don't know how, just . . . picture it happening."

"If you say so," she agrees, reluctance in her voice. She then proceeds to . . . stare at a couple of forks for a minute. I can't sense divine magic, so that's all it looks like to me.

"What are you trying?" her dad asks.

"Let her focus," I say, holding up a finger, and we watch in awkward silence for a few more minutes. Finally, she lets out a breath and looks up.

"All right, I did my best," she says. "What now?"

I hold my hand out and she hands the forks over, although I only accept one. I then try a little sleight of magical hand and whisper into the fork, which I'm certain doesn't look silly at all. My sound mana projects my voice as though emanating from the other utensil, simulating a successful test. Sara and Sam jump a little.

"Wait, did it . . . work?" she asks.

"Here, take this back." I shrug. "Do the same thing again, but try to make it louder," I say, and she happily complies. This time she is much faster and offers me the fork again. I accept it and speak into it again, this time not faking the result. Nothing happens. "Damn," I whisper, mentally crossing that theory off the list. With the lessons I've had on mana aspecting, I had begun to hope divine magic was sort of a more flexible version. Like magic where actually believing anything makes it true. With the way her scars fluctuate, I thought I might be onto something.

Then again, I suppose if it was as simple as that, the church would be even more powerful, and the device wouldn't need regular mana as well. I sigh. "Sorry, guys, failed experiment," I say, and Sara slumps again. I'm about to explain a bit of my theory, but Ed interrupts us as he loudly descends the stairs with Mariah.

"Lily, you around? I want to work on an aspect again!" he calls.

"I'd better go help him," I apologize, and Sara waves before turning to talk to her dad. I stand and go to join Ed, then stop and look down. Suzume is lying on her back at my feet and looking up at me. "Hey, little Suzie, keep Sara company for me, okay?" I ask, and she chirps at me. As I walk away, she rolls over and defiantly follows me up the stairs.

"There you are! Come on, I am so close to an aspect I can feel it!" Ed cries as I follow him up the stairs. He gives a cursory glance at Henry's room before continuing toward the one he shares with Mariah. Ed often behaves skittish when it comes to Henry, and I suspect there is something I don't understand going on between them. But Henry never says anything about it and is perfectly friendly to Ed, so I don't bother inserting myself into whatever it is.

I spend the next few hours explaining the workings of fire to Ed, again. He's very excited to cast his first spell, but that doesn't make him a good student. Nevertheless, he starts to understand the science behind it slowly. I think he's right—he'll have fire magic any day now. I'll have to hide him from Autumn. With my improved magic circle and his stubbornness, he ended up with more mana than her and will likely have more powerful fire magic. I don't want to crush the poor girl's confidence.

As I go over aspecting with him, I mentally list my own plans in my head. I've decided to drop cold mana. I considered replacing cold and heat with thermodynamic mana, but . . . there are too many concepts in that aspect. It would take more focus than I have to impose every concept of temperature, work, energy, and everything else involved onto one aspect. So I am keeping heat. I can emulate the effects of cold with heat mana the same way I use light in place of dark mana.

I went through a similar thought process with earth mana. I wanted to replace it with matter mana, but . . . that simply contains too many possibilities. I can't include an image of every kind of matter when I aspect it, and if I leave any out, I'll understand it's an incomplete picture and the aspect won't work. Instead, I have decided to replace it with metal. This is a bit like earth but was not included in my fairly simple image of that aspect. My earth aspect is really just shale since I didn't need it to do more than, well, be a stone. Similarly, I am going to try a steel or carbon steel aspect as a replacement. It will be effective for all the same things I use stone for, and the increased mana and concentration it requires will be easier with my growing ability and experience.

Force is here to stay. It is a simple concept with endless applications. Speed had been disappointing for a couple of reasons. I can emulate its real effect with force, for one. Also, I had been thinking of experiments with light when I aspected it. As a result, it ended up closer to something like frequency. As I've grown to understand mana aspects, I've realized I don't really need it. My understanding of light and sound already includes frequency.

I decided to keep air. I don't use it much, but I think it still has utility. When I am powerful enough to fly consistently, I can avoid a good amount of ugliness just with air mana. I also think it will come in handy if I ever encounter a gaseous weapon. Lord knows Annie could have used access to clean air at all times.

This leaves me with two open slots, assuming my limit is fixed at eight aspects. My first choice is for maximum combat power and speed. I want electricity. It also has a fair amount of potential for nonmagical solutions to problems. Or it would, if I were an electrical engineer. I have no idea how to use it for anything too complex, but hey, I can make lightbulbs and fried monarchs. What more do I need?

Finally, I want to aspect water. It's a bit boring and doesn't offer nearly as much combat utility, but clean water can be a valuable resource.

If only I could use divine magic instead of any of these aspects. It seems far more versatile, and it would be easier to clear people's minds without Sara's help. That last thought gives me an idea, however. Sara can clear people's minds of brainwashing. She doesn't even have to try; if the priest who imposed it is less powerful than her, it just stops working when she goes near their victims. What if divinely enchanted items are the same? What if she can't figure out how the sphere's divine magic works because, as soon as she held it, it stopped working at all?

That makes too much sense to dismiss. After Edward begins to meditate, trying to aspect fire, I head back downstairs. Suzume trills as she sees me headed in the general direction of the kitchen and tries to kill us both by tripping me on the stairs. This kitten-inflicted danger does, of course, warm my heart. When I reach the dining area, I see Sara alone, drawing something on the table. "Hey, Sara," I call as I descend, "I had a thought about the sphere, tell me what you think!"

"All right, go ahead." As I explain my theory, she puts her finger to her lips in a remarkably adorable way.

"It's possible," she says. "But if that's the case . . . well, that will be inconvenient, considering."

I wave off her worry. "I thought of that. It means stealing them won't work, but if we can figure out how to make them, we can just enchant each one on-site. Inconvenient, but not insurmountable."

"I did always wonder why priests never had one while traveling through the Radiant Woods. I suppose that would explain it," she muses.

"Exactly. More importantly, if we can figure out why that happens, I think we can figure out how your magic works," I suggest.

She looks at me skeptically but shrugs.

"It can't hurt to investigate, I suppose. But, I'm sorry, I don't know how to do that . . ." Suzume jumps up and curls up on top of the paper where Sara was refining whatever she is drawing, and Sara scratches behind her ears before looking up at me.

"That's all right, I don't think it will be that complex. I just need to bring you divinely enchanted items, tell you what they do, and see if they look the same to you. After a while, we'll be able to make some observations. Especially with my class on enchantments next year," I say.

She tilts her head.

"A while? How many divine enchantments do you think you can find?"

"Yeah, a year or two, I suspect. We have time, Sara," I answer. I am almost done with my first year of classes now. If all goes well, I should be able to set things in motion before I graduate from the academy. That gives us plenty of time to figure out a method of communication, whether it be this or telegraphs, if I have to.

"Well, all right, I'm with you," Sara promises, and I smile. Sam walks in at the tail end of the conversation with a tray full of tea and bread. "Thanks, Dad," Sara says, lighting up.

"Yeah, thanks," I say. I'm so glad he is here. Sara is like a different person now. He looks at me with smiling eyes as he offers me tea. Then he looks at the paper Sara has been drawing on.

"Oh, is that the design for Lillith's ha—?" he starts, and she shushes him.

"Dad, not now!" she whispers. I chuckle. She gives me a side-eye and I blush a bit. Is she making me a hat? All right, Lillith. Fifteen. May the next few years pass quickly.

CHAPTER FIFTY-SEVEN

Inventions

Eustace

The monster started hunting nobles almost a year ago. At first, they said it was a serial killer. Then they said it was a rebel. The city guard says it's more than one person, and the church says it's this so-called true king. The commoners? We know better, because we are the ones it leaves alive. And it is an *it*. My sister was a maid at one of the houses hit. She saw the monster. She saw it kill not with a spell but with a single touch of its fingers. I know a man who claims to have seen it kill with fangs.

My own father swears he saw it tear a door off its hinges. I've even heard rumors of it watching with extra eyes, melting flesh with a touch, ballooning in size, or growing the razor-sharp talons of a hawk from its hands. The only rumor I've heard from a witness who called it human was one particularly drunk fool claiming it's a woman. There are dozens of rumors about it, but there is no doubt it is a monster. But we don't fear it. Whatever the guard says, and whatever the church says. Because its talons and teeth aren't the only things there are rumors about.

Sure, we feared it as much as the nobles did, at first. But, like I said, it's been almost a year. The only commoners it has killed have been the city guard. It always lets the servants leave. The maids, the stable boys. The nobles can only convince us we are all in danger for so long. Some people do think it is taking the slaves as food, but I don't. It's true they disappear without a trace. Hundreds of them have vanished by now, and no one has found them hiding anywhere. So I understand why people think it must be eating them. It just . . . doesn't make sense. Do criminals taste better than maids? No, it's doing something else with them.

For a long time, this was just a story. A fear, then a story. Some people even started to cheer it on. I was one of them; my sister was always treated poorly by the nobles she worked for. She always had to fear that twisted couple would want more than cleaning from her. So when a monster touched them and stole their lives, I cheered it on. But heroes are for the nobility. Commoners aren't allowed to have their own, and once we do, we are always punished for it.

Because the slaves are disappearing. The workers, the laborers. The people who build the mansions and create the luxury goods. There aren't enough anymore for every noble to have a staff, and they certainly aren't going to pay to hire more servants. So what do they do? Well, they get more slaves. They make more laws and they make it harder to follow the existing ones. Any one of us could find ourselves in the guard's custody. Once we become the nobles' target, we just have to hope it finds wherever the new holding cells have been set up. Or we become slaves ourselves until the monster finds us and does . . . whatever it's doing.

As I hear a pounding on my door, I know my time has come. The beast saved my sister from everything she feared, but ultimately, we are going to be slaves anyway, and her fears will likely be realized. Women like her aren't enslaved for manual labor. The door pounds again and I wince. I knew this was coming. Rent has been rising, and rising, and rising. I don't live in a nice home, but only a noble could afford these prices. They've come to evict me. Remove me, my sister, and my children from our home. And since they made homelessness illegal . . . they likely have the guards on standby to arrest us for our crime as soon as they force us to commit it. Why pretend we have somewhere else to go, after all?

I don't have the stomach to answer the door. Phoebe comes down the stairs and pales as she sees my face. She knows it's time as well. As I fail to answer the door a third time, they grow impatient. A moment later, the door flies open as the guard kicks it. A well-dressed man walks in with his nose in the air. "This is my property, Eustace," Lord Jareth sneers. "And you are delinquent on payments. I must demand that you vacate the premises so I can rent the location to a harder-working family, one who deserves it."

I lower my head and the nearest guard approaches me to put shackles on my wrists. I allow him to without a word. "You are under arrest, Mr. Eustace. By order of the king, those who cannot contribute to the city and who dirty our roads with begging are to be arrested and put to work. Be thankful you will have a place to live and meaningful work to do."

The bastards. Barely putting up a pretense, arresting me for homelessness inside my home like this. I don't bother fighting it until another guard approaches Phoebe.

I know what waits for her, I always have. But the shit-eating grin on the guard's face is a bridge too far. I'm already shackled, but I don't care. That man isn't putting a finger on my sister. "Get the fuck away from her," I growl before shoving my shoulder into the guard at my side. I throw myself at the grinning man to tackle him, but before I know it, I am being held with my face to the ground.

"It's all right, Eustace," Phoebe says. "Just . . . don't get yourself hurt."

Fuck. Useless. I'm fucking useless.

"Sir, this is the business of the city guard. I need you to move alo—"

A loud thump on the ground.

"What are you doing, you fools, kill him!" Lord Jareth screams, and the room explodes in the sound of combat. The hand holding me to the ground disappears as its owner joins the fray.

"I—It's you!" Phoebe gasps. Just as I struggle to roll over, I see it. The monster. It is shaped like a person, but . . . it is holding Lord Jareth off the ground like he's weightless. With a twitch of its fingers, there is a crack, his clawing at its arm stops, and it drops his corpse to the ground. I stare as it walks up to me. It holds a hand out, and somehow, I hear a click and the shackles loosen. I pull my hands free and Phoebe speaks again. "Eustace, it . . . it's the monster," she says.

It extends its hand again, offering to help me up. "You don't have to live in fear of men like this. If you like, I can show you a better option," it offers, and my eyes widen. Huh. It is a woman.

Lillith

It's been a year now since I grew my fangs. I've been steadily working on more physical changes since then, but it's not going well. I want to see in the dark, but that will have to wait until I no longer have to keep up a public persona. I just can't figure out a way to do it without changing how my eyes look. Instead, I have done some basic reinforcement. My skin is consistently thicker and my bones are more solid. I want to improve my hearing and sight as well, but my physical alterations simply aren't a priority, so that may take some time.

Right now, I am working on something far more valuable. Something I should have prioritized from day one. A true game changer that will instantly improve my life. Sarafyna is the one who pushed me to finally focus on it. I've wanted to for years, but I consistently chose other options to bridge the gap with powerful mages. But once she told me she had done it herself, I knew I had to do the same. Sarafyna *never* has cramps. Not once a month, not once a year, *never*. Soon, neither will I. They've already grown milder and I could not be more pleased with the decision.

Initially, I had hoped Sarafyna would be able to help me with my changes. If I could transform myself as fast as she can, I'd be a fucking terminator by now. Unfortunately, the results were not what I'd hoped. She did try, and she does a great job of healing me. But guiding her to entirely new and experimental changes just didn't work. She tried to give me the reins like when I helped bring her back to humanity, but her magic fought me and I couldn't get anywhere with it.

So I'm stuck with using direct, slow mana manipulation. Still, it's enough. The changes I have made have already made a difference in dozens of fights, and they will continue to do so. As I work on my body, I watch the sunlight traveling across my room. I am still staying in the seedy inn. I have ways around the previous barriers to staying with my family or on campus, but I can't reliably use them. Not that it would be a great idea anyway.

As the light passes a painted line I have on the floor to mark the hour, I jump up and walk across the room. On a piece of paper stapled to the floor, I have a pair of glasses I am enchanting. My class on the subject has been amazing so far. Runes are far more complex than I thought. I knew you could combine them to create new concepts. It's how I targeted my magic circle as the center of everything instead of a specific space. Even so, I had no idea how versatile it was. A skilled enchanter could use runes like a language, describing desired behavior.

On the one hand, this is a bit dangerous. I haven't actually fought any mages who were expecting combat yet, excepting the bard. A mage with a powerful enchanted weapon would be formidable, and I am definitely going to face one eventually. Thankfully, they take too long to make to distribute them to the guards. They will run out of mana eventually and just be a regular weapon if a mage isn't the one using them. Inorganic material, apparently, doesn't regenerate mana on its own like a living entity.

On the other hand, this opens up a lot of possibilities. For instance, my radar glasses. No longer must I cast a handful of exhausting spells at once. All I have to do is send out the radio waves, and, if I was successful, these glasses will respond like my previous spells did. Even better, I have learned the runes to suppress mana in the enchanted objects. In other words, the glasses won't glow like a beacon to other mages. Unless they have a thing for bookish women, I guess, but they won't know I am using magic.

The colors also only emit in one direction. So it'll be visible from some angles, but it's much less obvious.

I hesitantly pick up the glasses and take a deep breath before putting them on. I literally jump and pump my fist as I immediately see the colorful form of a woman walking down the hall outside my room. They work. I immediately dig through my things and pull out a pair of goggles I have designed. As the sun sets, I put the goggles where the glasses had been. They are made with fabric rather than rubber, but they hold fairly well. They don't need to be airtight; they just need to stay fixed to my face while I am fighting.

They also have collapsible lenses so I can lower the spell when needed. No one will be sneaking up on me for a while, and I can finally put all my focus into my other magic. As I leave the goggles to begin enchanting, I pull out another piece of paper. It's time to get back to work on designing a circle for my own communication devices. If divine magic doesn't work, well, it's a good thing I'm not quite as complacent as the kingdom's nobility.

Well, complacent may not be the word. The church seems to have a vested interest in monopolizing and limiting long-distance communication. Nevertheless, it's just one more of their advantages I intend to make them fear.

CHAPTER FIFTY-EIGHT

Insecurities

Clarrise

I look wearily at the door to my office. Work is exhausting, but it's better than home. Everywhere is better than home. It's been years since I was excited to finish grading and leave campus. It wasn't always like this. Wymond was a kind man once, or at least I thought he was. I didn't choose him as a husband, but he wasn't pushy when negotiating with my father. It was my duty to marry for the family, and I was glad to marry a man who seemed to listen to me.

The trouble didn't really start until I became a professor. Sure, I never loved him and he never loved me, but our marriage was fine. It was better than those of many of my friends, in fact. When I handled the household staff and looked pretty at parties. Then, I got less pretty, or so he tells me. I got older, anyway. I wasn't wanted at the parties anymore, but that was all right; I never liked them in the first place. He acted excited when I was hired by the academy. He said it would be good for me. I know now what he meant was it would be good for him. As soon as I was out of the house, he started requisitioning slaves, and not for labor. Women who were "still pretty."

He hid it from me for a long time. He knew it would hurt me, and more importantly, he knew how I felt about slaves. So he got me out of the house. I didn't suspect him once until we got into an argument. It was, of course, about my work. Because when he encouraged me, it wasn't because I loved math, nor was it because I loved teaching. It was because he was bored with me. It didn't occur to him that I would be good at it. It never crossed his mind that my name might become better known than his, or that I would get more invitations to more prestigious parties.

Being rid of me was, apparently, not worth feeling like he was less than me. That was what started the little comments. The "jokes" about my competence. The "friendly" jabs about how I slept my way to notoriety. The sneers I caught from the corner of my eye, replaced with sickly smiles when I turned. It hurt. It made me feel small. I tried being meek. I tried apologizing, even when I wasn't wrong. But this only made him angrier. Like I was looking down on him.

One day, he snapped. I asked him to clean a glass. He wanted to leave it for the staff. I simply said I'd prefer it be put away before then, and . . . he threw it at me. It didn't hit me, but it shattered on the cupboard over my shoulder. His eyes were cold and his aura flared. The ice in his voice hovered at my throat like a knife when he asked me if I thought he was my servant. That was when he told me about the slaves. He didn't want to avoid hurting me anymore. He hadn't for some time by then.

It's strange, how the words of someone who hates you can needle their way in. Even now his quiet words are fishhooks in my skin, pulling me down by the flesh of my frown lines. He told me about the slaves. He told me, in detail, what he did to them. He told me how much better than me they were, and how poorly he treated them anyway. He described my failures as a woman. The imperfections of my body. What a whore I was and how stupid I was to think I wasn't replaceable at the academy.

It was all bullshit, but I remember every word. I see every criticism in every reflection. I couldn't stop him from getting slaves, however much I hated it. But in the last eighteen months, the slaves have been disappearing. Wymond isn't important enough to requisition them anymore, and the ones he had were commandeered by more powerful nobles. He even tried to use my name and was still denied. That hurt his pride doubly.

I didn't realize how much they had been protecting me. They were taking his rage and insecurity on my behalf. Once they were gone . . . well, now it's all mine. I hate him. I want to scrub him from the face of the planet. If I could leave him, I would. But he's the one who earns my pay from the academy. My father wouldn't take me in. And Wymond is right; I'm replaceable. The academy won't shelter me. I have nowhere to go.

Sometimes, I wonder if I can kill him. Let the Collector judge me. It would be better than going home to that man. Better than sleeping in a guest room with a bar on the door in case he decides I actually am still pretty enough. I'll look at him and wonder if I could smother him as he sleeps. But I can't. He's a far more powerful mage than me, and I would simply be executed myself. Or perhaps, given the labor shortage, they would decide nobles make decent slaves as well.

With complete hopelessness, I rise from my desk and leave my office. I'm done with my work, and I have no excuse to delay. If I'm home late, he'll rightly accuse me of avoiding him. The campus grounds don't look beautiful to me anymore. The extravagant foliage and garden walkways mock me as I pass them. The knight at the gate lets me through, and I walk a little too slowly back to my home. I should have hired a carriage, but the quiet night is all I have left.

As I finally make it home, I wince. He's going to be furious, but . . . I need those quiet moments. Something feels off when I reach for the door. Light comes from under the crack, and as I listen, I hear my husband's voice. It's muffled, but I can tell he's angry with someone. I hesitate. Walking in on him arguing with someone could be more dangerous than being late. But . . . I don't know what to do. I have to go inside. He'd probably know I was waiting just outside. I decide there is no right answer and brace myself, then push the door open.

I am assaulted by heat as soon as I do. He is firing steam at full power at someone. He's going to boil them alive! What is happening? I have to stop him!

"Wymond, what are you doing, you'll kill them!" I plead.

He looks at me with vitriol, keeps up his spell, and shouts back, "What do you think I'm trying to do, you stupid woman? Shut up and get out of here!"

My eyes widen and I open my mouth to respond, but . . . a hand slowly appears from the steam. It has water on it, and as I focus, I realize it is surrounded with . . . heat mana? Wymond doesn't notice as he glares at me, and the fingers gently caress his cheek. That's all it takes. His skin rapidly shifts to a bluish purple, his veins bulge, and his body begins to convulse.

A few seconds later, he falls to the ground, dead.

A woman stands where the steam was. Only darkness can be seen beneath her hood. She's wearing men's clothes, but there is leather armor on top that hides her figure. I can tell anyway, just by the way she moves. It's the killer. The one hunting slave-owning nobles. I want to be terrified, but for the first time in a long time, a laugh escapes my lips, and I slap my hand over my mouth. He's dead. Killed for his secret little slaves, even after they were all gone.

I'm probably dead too. She doesn't know I didn't want the slaves. There are certainly plenty of noblewomen who happily use them to distract their husbands. She is walking toward me, further confirming my suspicion about her gender. I don't care. Wymond is dead. It's fucking worth it. I don't try to fight her. She shrugged Wymond off with ease, so I certainly don't stand a chance. At least she gave me that gift before killing me. I close my eyes, waiting for the same ugly but swift fate my husband met.

Instead, I hear a vaguely familiar voice. "Do you want to feel safe again, Clarrise?"

Father Medici

I open the door to the throne room and wave off the knight who tries to waylay me. "What do you want this time, Donatello?" I demand, and the king huffs at me.

"Do you mean *Your Majesty?*" he challenges. I spit on the ground. "I meant what I said. I am too busy for your summons and whining. Tell me what you want so I can get back to work." This fool actually thinks he rules this country. Without me, the people would have eaten him alive years ago.

"Busy? Busy undermining my rule?" he scoffs.

I have to cover my eyes with my hand to contain the exasperation. This bullshit again.

"Donatello. Don. How many times do I have to explain this to you? I am maintaining your fucking rule, you imbecile. Why would I try to undermine it?"

"Watch your tongue, priest," he growls. "I am still your king, despite your efforts. I am no fool. A monster hunting my staunchest supporters, right when a rebel faction tries to gather support? I believe you have reminded me hundreds of times that monsters belong to you, have you not?"

"You remember they belong to me, but only when you make this accusation. You seem to forget they *all* belong to me. All of them, *Your Majesty*," I sneer. "If I wanted to use them against you, your kingdom would already be gone."

"As would yours," he quips. "Don't you think I know you stand to benefit from a kingdom that still stands once you are rid of me? You are transparent. You think I don't hear the murmurs? The lesser nobles talking like I am past my prime, suggesting a new king could solve this crisis better?"

"Those whispers have been around since a fool first ascended the throne," I reply. "They are just gaining popularity. And they are right to, if you have failed to notice them grumbling about me as well. You aren't the only idiot in this city willing to believe some angry mage is a monster. Why would I undermine myself?" There is an answer to that, but it concerns me more than this idiot. I shouldn't be undermined. By the nobility maybe, but my priests have reported similar rumors from commoners.

This is dangerous. Not because they can do anything to harm me, but because they shouldn't have the capacity to question me. It suggests something far worse than some monster or mage. It suggests my control is slipping for some reason.

"Because you are a prideful fool," the king replies. "The same reason you insult your king. You are greedy, and you think you are invincible. That's why."

"I understand we have never cared for each other," I say with a flat stare, "but open your damn eyes. Someone is after both of us. Rumors of incompetence aren't the only ones I've heard, Donatello. If you want to find the person responsible, maybe you should look closer to home. Your brother stands to gain far more than I do."

"My brother?" he laughs. "The bookseller? Yes, I'm certain he is planning a coup, just as soon as he finishes his latest romance novel."

"Yes, the bookseller, you idiot. The bookseller who stopped selling books barely half a year before your 'monster' started hunting. The one who has been throwing parties with very . . . select guest lists. The one who hasn't lost a single friend this entire time. Yeah, I think he might be worth a look."

I turn on my heel and march out of the throne room. That buffoon would have ended this country long ago without my divine magic. Which is why I need to figure out, immediately, why it's failing.

CHAPTER FIFTY-NINE

Best Laid Schemes

Hugh

I grit my teeth as one of the bags and boxes I'm carrying falls to the ground; I know I'll be punished for it later.

How did it come to this? Running errands across campus for other nobles like some common beggar. Even the women look at me like I'm less than them somehow. I had actually been looking forward to coming here. But the temple rejected me. Rejected my entire family. So what if we bought our noble title? That only means we worked harder for it than anyone else!

But they refused to acknowledge us. All we needed to be respected was one simple ceremony. A christening and a house name. They denied us. We, who earned our place among the nobility. We weren't allowed even a name. So I had a target on my back the second I came here. Then that bitch showed up. The girl I fucking deigned to invite into our family, who spat in the face of my generosity. The temple acknowledged her, of course. They christened her, a girl who did nothing but work in a fucking bookshop to earn her title.

Lillith of Endings. What a stupid name for a stupid girl. I suppose that's why she spurned my kindness. She knew more about Lord Godfrey than I did, and she was . . . very welcoming of what he had to offer. It must be wonderful doing all the work you ever need to on your back. She's lucky those filthy bandits murdered my father before he could get his hands on her. I'd make her work to be here. I'd walk her like a dog around this campus, instead of being worked like one myself by even the lowest nobles. But they have names, so I can't do anything about it.

This isn't what my father paid for. But, yet again, that entitled whore only made everything worse. I almost had her, in the middle of the first year. The idiot never bothered to hire a tutor. She probably wasn't expecting professors with no interest in what was under her dress. One of the few intelligent moves this academy has made, using women like that. So she couldn't even read her numbers when she showed up. I should have won that bet. I *deserved* to win that bet. But, as always, she used the same *opening* to gain an unfair advantage and Duke Godfrey faked her scores for her.

It's fucking disgusting how unbalanced this academy is. A single word from the useless Duke of Facinley and even that ungrateful wretch can look down on her betters. If my father were alive, he'd know how to handle these insects. Someday, I'll find that Rosalind bitch and peel her skin from her bones. Because that's all I have. A single name. The bastard daughter of a noble family in Satusmor, and the one who betrayed my father. She'd killed him and all her own men, then vanished. But she can't hide forever. Once I finish with this academy, I'll find her and I'll do what my father would have done.

I flex my fingers in a failure to keep my rage contained, and just as I do, I trip, landing with one hand splattered into a bag of pastries. I groan as a foot kicks into my side. I roll over and look up at none other than Lady Iris. The lowly dog is hanging around her master, the stuck-up slut who sent me to do her chores in the first place. Lady Jocelyn.

"Oh, if it isn't nameless little Hugh?" Jocelyn sneers. "You've dropped all my things. Do you really have enough money to make such a mistake? Now you'll have to go buy new ones! Really, little Hugh, didn't your father teach you how to do your job like a man? Oh, that's right, he's not around much anymore, is he?" she taunts, and I grit my teeth. I have to add her to the list. I narrow my eyes as they focus on her still-extended foot, directly in my path. "Oh my, you're not thinking that was my fault, are you, Hugh?"

"No, my lady," I answer through gritted teeth.

"Of course you weren't. Now hurry off, I'm hungry, boy," she says.

I climb to my feet and do what I'm told, because if I don't . . . well, she has the power for now. But mana and authority only help you in direct confrontations. She won't be able to watch her back forever. I'll work up to killing her. First, I'll handle the ungrateful pig with the half-bald head, then the sycophant, then the lady herself. Then I'll feed all their bodies to Jocelyn before I kill her. It's these thoughts that keep me going as I go to buy more snacks for the bitch.

Godfrey

I rub my hand over my forehead as I look over the paper in front of me. I can't help but chuckle. My original plans for Lillith were flawed from the start. While she seems to excel in anything related to math, it's clearly through no fault of her own. I realized this from her first midterms when the rest of her scores were barely above passing. I know she's smart enough to do better than this, and it didn't take me long to realize she simply doesn't care.

That's no surprise, considering her other activities. She's driven this city into a panic, and interestingly, not just this one. I don't know how she's doing it, but she is far more effective than I ever could have dreamed. Scared nobles are malleable nobles. Where do they run to when the ground starts moving under their feet? When their peers are hunted and my fool brother feuds with the church instead of deploying the knights to catch her? Well, to the person who predicted the trouble, of course.

Many nobles laughed at me when I suggested we would have a labor shortage. They scoffed when I told them they weren't safe, and they hushed me when I said my brother would ignore their plights. I was just the crazy bookselling duke, after all. But I had carefully chosen who to share my predictions with. They may have laughed, but they didn't spread it around. They didn't tell my brother or anyone else. When my predictions started coming true, well, that was when things changed.

When their friends died around them and their luxuries became scarcer, they remembered. When the king, instead of hunting the killer, deployed his magic knights as bodyguards for his favorite nobles, they remembered who offered to protect them. When things collapse, and they *will* collapse, it's not my brother or his son who will sit on the throne to put everything back together.

It will be me.

A competent king can improve the lives of the nobility and the commoners. Even in the wake of Lillith's destruction. I can keep the pillars we really need in place while doing away with foolish tradition.

There is no reason to force slave labor. There is certainly no reason commoners can't use magic. They still won't be able to oppose us, and the work magical commoners can do will far surpass what all the slaves lost in every city could ever accomplish. We can stop relying on the church and even find a way to push past the Radiant Woods and to the sea. I will usher in a golden era for Potestia, one even Lillith can be happy in. I hope. I'd really prefer to keep her alive.

Perhaps it's a weakness of age, but I like the woman, as mad as she is. She makes me laugh. If her violent edge can be curbed, she may even be open to a marriage to Dominic. Perhaps she will calm with age. She must be roughly seventeen now. Many young mages are brash at that age. I certainly was. Besides, she has helped me in more ways than one. She exceeded my expectations when her mana was measured. I knew she would be more powerful than expected, but to amass that much mana before leaving Satusmor, her circle is truly impressive.

And even the nobles I didn't rally ahead of time think I am the one who designed it: a magic circle powerful enough to make a family that rivals a count in a fraction of the time. It's troublesome that she apparently shared it with someone in Satusmor. The noble children that arrived from Satusmor last year were, well, more powerful than they should have been. It's a good thing I was keeping an eye on it, because I was able to intercept them before anyone else.

Their growth far surpassed what their ranks would suggest. And they came from Lillith's hometown. It wasn't much of a leap of logic to presume she had given her design to them for some reason. Then again, it wasn't a circle exactly like hers. None of them would admit to gathering mana outside of a circle, and they weren't as strong as she was. Nevertheless, people assumed it was my doing. The current rumor is I went to Satusmor not to hide from responsibility, but to do magic experiments, of which Lillith was my greatest success.

The murder-happy teen has been improving my reputation on all fronts, and she's doing it with only half a head of hair! When the time comes, I'll need to apprehend her. Not for the execution her peers will demand, but to see if I can sway her. She wants what I do. A better world. But she thinks too small. Too impulsively. She has no plan for what to do after she kicks the legs out from under the people's leaders. When I explain what I can do for this country, for every country we have allowed the church to keep us from, she will see sense.

I had to laugh at the paper behind the report on Lillith's most recent grades. Cateline was complaining, again. She needs to lighten up. She wants me to force Lillith to present herself like a proper lady. To represent the academy with dignity and stop embarrassing her in front of visitors. The woman was nearly rabid. She doesn't know the half of it. To think she is worried about Lillith's hair and piercings and . . . company. I suppose she has similar complaints about both common-born students.

I respect Cateline, I do.

She fought for every ounce of respect she has, and she shouldn't have had to. She's a competent mage and a brilliant teacher. That's why she is so obsessed with appearance. The respect she has is fragile, and like with my brother's management of the kingdom, her control over her students reflects on her. She feels degraded by Lillith's very presence. But she too thinks too small. Such petty things don't matter. What matters is moving forward, and I intend to do that.

Ralf

I stand in the courtyard, my arms crossed. It's finally time to win my pride back.

Lillith of Endings. That's the name of the girl who spat in my face. I was shocked to learn, only days later, that she is sponsored by Duke Godfrey himself. I worried I would never be able to make her pay. For weeks I couldn't get it out of my head. Because of her sponsor, she thought she could humiliate me? I couldn't let it stand. I had to confront her again.

So I went to her dorm. I stood outside her room at night and used light mana to project myself up at her window. My magical specter stared inside, all night, every night. She never acted. Never tried to fight it or so much as approach her window. She was that terrified. I could see it whenever I passed her. Her head down, her eyes avoiding mine. She knew she wasn't safe.

Even when we shared a class, she was too afraid to look at me. She never made eye contact a single time. I smirked whenever she looked away, too frightened to so much as apologize or ask me to leave her alone. Of course, I dominated her in all the tests as well. It wasn't a huge victory, but I returned a small amount of the humiliation she inflicted on me. She always rushed from the class, too ashamed to risk being confronted about it.

For two years we have played this game. I keep her in her place and she bows under the pressure. Illusions at her window aren't all. I spread rumors about her.

Some were believable and likely, like her sexual relationship with Godfrey. Some were insane and only a few people repeated them. I even managed to convince one boy that she is the monster hunting nobles every night. That one was almost a prank on both of them, as he fled whenever he saw her and she watched on in panic as he did so.

Whatever the rumors, they chipped away at her. Bit by bit, until she was desperate enough to accept a duel with me. I hear she is powerful, but she's taken no combat classes, and she's a woman. So once I had beaten her spirit to a pulp over the course of years, I approached her in the middle of campus and threw a wooden shield painted with my family's crest at her feet. She paused and, just as I hoped, turned to pick it up and return it to me. The fool girl was at her wit's end, willing to try anything to end her torment. She probably thought being humiliated in one duel would be enough to satisfy me, and she could live in peace again.

She was wrong. "The first night the moon wanes, one hour past sundown, in the courtyard by the statue of the first headmistress," I announced proudly. The panicked look she gave me has nourished me ever since.

"Uh-huh," she finally agreed, too scared to even properly acknowledge the duel. Her failure to form real words was sweet like sugar. And now is that night. The night of the duel when I finally put her in her place, do it in a way above reproach, even in the eyes of Duke Godfrey. It took far longer than I would have liked, but her initial fear convinced me she would never accept if I rushed things.

Even now, she is dawdling. Dragging her feet on her way here. She's nearly an hour late, but that's all right. The slower she is, the more I'll make her regret it.

CHAPTER SIXTY

Breakthroughs

Sarafyna

I take a deep breath. It's been nearly three years since the last time I was on a mission alone. When I . . . when I tortured that man. Even now, I can't completely say I regret what happened. But I can say I wish I hadn't, and maybe that's enough. Lillith and I simply can't handle all these missions as a team anymore, and I am more equipped to fight priests. She's certainly not bad at it, but as she is fond of saying, we use their weapons against them, and I'm the one with divine magic.

Technically, I have mana as well, but even after all this time, I can't use it for much. It makes an effective counter for mages with less mana than me. I can release the aura in full force and overwhelm their spells, but I can't cast my own. A mage with as much or more mana than me will still be able to cast, and I'll be at a disadvantage. Those are few and far between, however. Every time I, well, dispose of a priest, my mana grows. Or, more accurately, their mana.

That's the real problem. The same reason my scars are only growing worse. Because they aren't me, and their mana isn't my mana. I don't have mana of my own. Of course, Dad and Lily insist my scars do go away sometimes, but they are always back by the time I see a mirror. Lily says it only happens when I am with Dad too. I have never been able to explain this to their satisfaction, but I have never really understood my abilities. I certainly can't use them like the priests do, to slither into other people's minds and take the reins.

That's what it is. Slithering. I can feel it whenever they do it around me. It always reminds me of the day I was first taken from my father. Like worms under my skin, crawling their way around. I can almost feel how they do it. The knowledge is intrinsic but vague, like a fading memory or a recurring dream. It's just so . . . wrong that I know I could never do it myself. Not just morally wrong; it *feels* wrong. It tastes like bile. But that doesn't matter. Priests are too used to having that control; they rely on it and always panic when it fails. Every single time.

Still, I am nervous. I am fighting priests on my own for the first time in a while, and I don't want to be what I was when I lived in the woods. I don't want to be a woman who tortures people. But I do have to face these priests, and I can't lean on Lillith to do it. I have everything they took from me and more. I have spent the last few years with my father. I've even been making hats again. But whenever I visit a temple, I feel so . . . powerless. Not literally; I know I am strong. But part of me is still the girl, terrified of her first confession.

Even worse, another part of me fears my own lack of self-control. Because even though I have everything back and an entirely new life . . . they still had no right to take what they did, and they still deserve to pay.

I'm not at a temple today, however. The church has grown more cautious in recent years. They take their recruits to new, hidden locations. Not beneath their temples but in different underground alcoves, not unlike Lily's safe houses.

It's pointless. They can't hide from me. My divine magic grows the same way my mana does, but I can control it. And the priests aren't the only ones with a unique use for it. None of them can see like I do, because none of them have ever needed to. Or maybe looking past their own noses is as foreign a concept to them as stealing someone's mind is to me. In either case, it has been proven time and time again that they can't see like I do. I had to live without eyes for years, surrounded by magic and mana of both varieties.

I can track divine priests across the city with ease. I can get a sense of endo-aspects as well; it's what brought Lily and me together in the first place and my range has only increased since. Priests have been visiting this old house regularly, and they go too far down into the earth for it to be a regular home. They might as well be a beacon. There are three down there right now, among a couple of dozen smaller sources of divine mana. There aren't, however, any smaller *people* with them. This gives me pause.

I came here to liberate any new recruits they've abducted, but if they have any, they haven't taken them to the Radiant Woods yet. I focus further and realize the number of smaller sources is increasing. One of the priests is channeling his magic into them and it feels like . . . well, it's not slithering like control. It's more like . . . sympathy? Or empathy, maybe? It's like an attempt to understand or . . . communicate. Then it hits me.

We've been taking their communication orbs partially to study and partially to, well, limit their communication. This isn't where they train new priests—this is where they enchant objects. I adjust my plans. Instead of forcing my way in to save captives who aren't there, I find a comfortable and dark corner to hole up in while I pour all my focus into the activity below. Because just like with their control, as I feel them use this magic, I understand it. It's like following a thread through a tapestry. As they enchant the orbs below me, I learn how to do the same.

I knew it was divine magic. I've known this for some time. I've felt the weight of that knowledge. The weight of the responsibility. Annie needs me to understand these, but I never have. Every time I have studied a sphere, I have failed to understand the trick. The secret. Whatever mechanism they use to enchant these, I have been entirely unable to discern. I get it now. I was thinking too much like Annie. Like Lillith. Trying to understand a process that doesn't exist. And that is the problem. There is no hidden technique. That's not how divine magic works. I can feel it now. It is so simple. So easy. It is an exertion of will. These don't work because they are connected the right way. They don't have a special "wavelength" as Annie describes it. They work on intent. They work because a divine mage believed that they should.

I stay there for hours. Focusing. Hiding. I stay there until the fog clears and I am certain I can manipulate my magic in the same way. It's not like with control; it's not repulsive. It's kind, in a strange way, and I can do it. It is an expression of connection. If I believe people should be able to talk to each other, they can. If I exert my magic on the world because people deserve to be connected, even from a distance, they will be able to. I can make these spheres. Because I can believe they are good, and should exist. Finally, I stand, elated at the prospect of telling Lily about this.

Leo

I look over my shoulder as I think I hear something. The roads are empty. I'm still in the wealthy quarter, not quite to my inn yet. There shouldn't be anything to fear here, not for most nobles. There's always something to fear for me, however. Every drip on the cobblestone and every shifting shadow sends pangs of panic through my heart. It's only been getting worse. It's my last year at the academy, and I'd hoped the nobles would grow bored with tormenting me, but they harass me more than ever.

I just need to make it to the end of the year. Six more months and I can do Lady Charlotte proud. I'll graduate from the academy and prove she didn't make a mistake in sponsoring me. It doesn't matter how much they hate me. I'll prove they can't keep me down, for both our sakes. Like Lillith does for Lord Godfrey, I can elevate Lady Charlotte's name with my success. They can't keep slandering her if I prove I was worth sponsoring. So I put up with the abuse, the beatings, the spoiled food, and the mockery.

It's nothing I haven't always dealt with. And at the end of it . . . at the end of it is a reward I never dreamed was possible. Lily and her friend can give me true safety for the first time in my life. Safety, security, and peace. I just have to fulfill my promise. Follow through on my obligation, and I can put this behind me. I'll never have to worry again. Never look over my shoulder and wonder, as I am doing now. Six months.

I hear a step again and I spin around. A bead of sweat runs down my head as I strain my eyes trying to make out any movement on the dark, quiet streets. It wouldn't be that strange to find another noble walking the streets, even this late at night. It's not running into someone else that scares me. It's their absence when I turn to look. It's amazing how terrifying someone can be just by . . . not being there. I hear them every time I move, but I never catch them. I could be making up the noises for all I know, but the possibility doesn't make me feel better.

I left particularly late, waiting in a tavern until sundown to travel specifically so my routine couldn't be tracked. Because once Iris told everyone she'd seen me leave campus regularly, I stopped being safe outside the gates too. I've repeatedly had to change my inn just so they don't wait for me. I grow less safe every day, and if they know where to find me, they will. I begin to walk again, then stop. Then I walk, then stop. Every time, there is another set of footsteps behind me. I'm certain now. I'm being followed.

I begin to move slowly, trying to act as normal as possible, until I pass an intersection. Just as I do, I suddenly turn and run as fast as I can. Feminine laughter and giggling trail me from at least two sources. I can't stop here. I have to get away, but I can't go back to my inn. As I hear more footsteps join the others following me, I push myself harder. I take a sharp left down an alley, then a right at the first turn. Just as I do, a stone hits the wall of the building to my right. It would have hit my back had I failed to turn when I did.

I'm not in particularly good shape and it's not long before I have a stitch in my side and I'm gasping for breath, but I can't stop. I frantically search my surroundings. The buildings around me are all quality wood and even the alley roads are well maintained. I'm still in the noble quarter and miles from help.

Then I spot it. A swinging sign for a restaurant called The King's Grace. I widen my eyes. I can't possibly be this lucky. If memory serves, there is a place to hide nearby. I just need to shake my pursuers for long enough to get there.

Just as I catch my breath, another stone hits me in the shoulder and knocks me to the ground. I try to scramble to my feet, but a mana-controlled stone slides into place just as I step. I immediately collapse again and cry out in pain to a chorus of laughter. I try to put pressure on my foot, but sharp pain surges through me as I do. My ankle is twisted, but I'm so close; I just need a distraction.

I can't fight them with spells, not with the massive difference in mana between us, but I might be able to distract them. I force myself to stand and groan with each step as I limp. There is a right-hand turn just a few paces in front of me and the discarded garbage and refuse of a restaurant against the left wall. I create a bright flash of light. This is the first mana most mages aspect, so they could be expecting it, but I maintain it for as long as I can anyway. While their vision is impaired, I duck to the left and cover myself in the filth.

They break the light spell within seconds, and I hear them catch up, then split up. One goes in the direction I've been running, and at least two go down the alley I didn't choose. It won't confuse them for long, so I have to move. I grit my teeth and use the wall to pull myself up. It takes every ounce of will I have to hold back the pained groans and wincing. As quickly as I can, I limp back the way we came. I make it a few dozen paces before I hear them giggling and running back my way.

It's too late, however, as I have found it. The abandoned restaurant is right in front of me, and I push my way through the door. I have to close it slowly to avoid making a noise, and I see two faces emerge just before the door shuts. Iris and

Jocelyn. My primary tormentors. I hold my filthy hand over my mouth to keep myself quiet. Did they see me?

The moment extends, heavy with my anxiety, but . . . they don't approach. Instead, I hear them talking in hushed tones and running in another direction. I turn and press my back to the door and slide to the ground. That was too close. I'm becoming more and more certain that if they catch me, they won't stop until I am dead. They act like it's just simple bullying, but I see the hate and disgust in their eyes. If they think they can get away with it, they will kill me. They aren't the first to look at me like that. If Lily hadn't told me where to find her safe houses, I don't know if I would have made it tonight.

I try to wipe the welling tears in my eyes on my arm but gag as I remember the filth all over my body. I can't do it anymore. I'll keep going to class for the rest of the year, but I need help. Lily . . . she won't let them kill me. I've been able to handle it until the last couple of weeks. But things have gotten so bad, I can't keep this to myself anymore. I really wanted to prove they couldn't break me. I didn't need to be saved. But who am I kidding? My pride isn't worth it. I need help. I'll stay here for now and over the next day off, but next time I see Lily, I'm telling her everything.

CHAPTER SIXTY-ONE

The Respect I Deserve

Darian

I smile to myself as I read Ansel's most recent report. Finally. At last, it is done. I am close enough to my goals that I can taste it. I can feel the gold of the throne beneath my fingertips. The weight of the crown on my head. I just need to tie up loose ends. It has been years in the making. Dearest father is going to pay for what he did to my mother. She had been the king's favorite maid. The third daughter of a minor noble house, but a beautiful one.

He'd required her services nearly every day, I'm told. That is, until her pregnancy started to show. Mana capacity is passed down from parent to child. It's why our royal family is so undefeatable; they have thousands of years of generational power. This is one reason no one has ever managed to knock them from the throne. They have nothing to fear from anyone but each other. This is why, when a powerful noble, particularly a royal, impregnates a staff member, well. They remove the threat.

They don't wait for the mother to give birth and risk the child surviving. No, they don't let it get that far. They dispose of the mother before the child can take its first breath. My mother was no exception, or she wasn't supposed to be. My dear father is the most foolish king we have had in a thousand years. He didn't behead her, hang her, or do anything that would ensure her death. No, he had her poisoned and her body abandoned outside a brothel.

He didn't have the stomach to look her in the eyes while she died. He was too much of a coward to let her know her fate before she met it. Which is why he never learned that she survived. She was rescued by the madam of the very brothel that was meant to be her grave. And with her survival came mine. It left her sickly and bedridden. I never saw my mother on her own two feet. Not a single time in my life. But I've always known who would have to pay for it. She never wanted me to risk revenge, and while she lived, I never pursued it. But ten years ago, she finally passed. The poison had finally done its work.

I had the finest magic circle I could get my hands on drawn immediately. It wasn't the circle that was my birthright, but with enough power, even the son of a sick maid can find a valuable one. I knew I could make up the difference with determination. And I have. To this day, I still sit in this room. In this circle, inside the very brothel I was raised in. I will earn the power to kill the king. Mana isn't enough, however. I have a half brother, a cousin, and my uncle on my father's side to deal with.

The only way a king can be overthrown, even by an opponent equal or greater in mana, is with allies. It takes a mage who can fight him and the support of the nobles around him. We may outclass them all in single combat, but with all the nobles on one side, there is no contest. This was my largest barrier. I was able to recruit my mother's family easily, but other nobles were hard to convince. Up until a few years ago, I only had perhaps a hundred allies total. Not nearly enough to challenge the king of the country. Especially not considering his other family members.

That's where Ansel came in. Ansel, the bard who was in love with my mother. The only man in this country who hates the king as much as I do. The bard who had become Lord Godfrey's personal assistant. Godfrey, the true threat. The lord most loved by the nobility. He has his own designs on the throne, and an excellent chance of earning it. There is nothing worse for me than a competent opponent. Ansel found, during a rare trip to a little city called Satusmor, a natural divine mage. The son of the local city lord. A mage so drunk on himself he actually thought he had his own chance of becoming king.

After stroking his ego and bringing him to the capital, Ansel drugged Godfrey's pastries and we put a leash on my dear uncle. The idiot noble believed he could control Godfrey to seize the throne. Of course, the best he could manage was keeping his pet royal docile. Everyone knows divine magic can't force someone into a fight to the death. You can't even touch a target without breaking the spell. Royal mages are beyond powerful. Godfrey would be fighting him every step of the way. The fool never stood a chance of using a royal as anything more than a pet. If he risked any more, Godfrey would have killed him. And, of course, that's exactly what happened.

That was almost the end of things. I hadn't managed to win over nearly enough allies, and Godfrey returned. His diminished reputation helped, but it wasn't enough. I knew he would eventually regain what he had lost. I had only managed to make small moves and spread the news of my existence a little. I tried minor attacks and sabotage, but my resources were limited. I hadn't even managed to dispose of Godfrey's son yet. I wasn't too worried about the prince. So long as I separate him and his father and kill them one at a time, allies will be all I need. But Godfrey's grandson is as likely to gather allies as his father. I need to eliminate my opponents' allies, have the prince removed from the city, and then kill the king.

The only chess piece I have at my disposal that would make a decent assassin is Ansel himself, and I would only do that if I was desperate. He's far too valuable in the noble court, not to mention recognizable. His build, his spells, even the way he moves in combat are distinct. A well-known bard killing high-profile nobles would be spotted immediately and executed in short order. I needed an assassin no one would expect, with abilities no one would recognize. Then, one night, one of my plans had an interesting hiccup.

I'd bribed a guard captain to turn a blind eye to my men's movements through one gate. I intended to smuggle more allies in from other cities, one of the ways I am tipping the scales in my favor, and I had one team assigned to that duty for multiple days. The captain kept other guards away and left it essentially unmonitored. But when he returned, the men had been murdered. He blamed me, and that bridge was burned. But it was worth it, once Ansel reported he had found the culprit. Godfrey had brought his own pet back from Satusmor. Some psycho bitch with a taste for blood.

The delusional child has been planning her own revolution. Ansel followed her on Godfrey's orders and discovered she had begun actually hunting nobles with slaves, and she was doing it well. For some reason, she was extremely powerful. She even managed to fight Ansel off once. Godfrey and I had the same idea. While Godfrey offered protection to powerful allies, I aimed her like a crossbow. I bribed slave handlers so large requisition requests were accepted for inconvenient nobles—inconvenient for my plans, that is. She didn't get to them right away, but she did eventually. It wasn't perfect since not all nobles use slaves, but I had my assassin.

Many of the king's staunchest supporters, all dead. Which, of course, resulted in the knights and bards being wasted as guards for those remaining. Which just soured the rest of the nobility on the king and drove allies to me. It supported Godfrey as well, but I knew something he didn't. See, there are only so many whisper spheres that can reach other cities, and their operators are quite prestigious. All of them recently found themselves in possession of quite a few slaves. Once my sweet little killer handled them, I made sure my own people earned their positions.

I may have fewer allies than either my father or my uncle, but I am the only one who will be able to call for help when I make my move. Over the last year, I have systematically faked messages to the least convenient nobles in the city, including several of Godfrey's allies and the prince himself. I had to move slowly to avoid suspicion, which I didn't entirely accomplish, but it was worth it. None of them will make it back in time to stop me. With the missing slaves, the selfish king, and the suspicion on the church from that "monster" silliness, this city is sitting on the precipice of collapse. It's been building up like a teakettle for the last few years, and I have to applaud Godfrey. He knows how to find people.

I finally look up, then ring a bell indicating I am done reading and Ansel may enter. He opens the door, crosses the room, and kneels. He is a little too slow and I narrow my eyes, then grit my teeth as he tenses. I hate when he tries to read my emotions. But I can let it go. I am having a good day because today, my little assassin finally ended the last target on my list. Before anyone inconvenient returned, as well.

"Your Highness," Ansel says.

"You've done well, Ansel." I give him a thin smile. "I have a new mission for you."

He is silent as he waits for my instructions. After she fought so hard to defend her own betrayer, I knew this Lillith girl was too unstable to approach directly—until she had done what I needed her to do. "The girl," I finally say, "I want her on my side. Do everything you can to recruit her and eliminate her if you can't. She will make a useful ally but a troublesome opponent. I have no desire to allow Godfrey to use her instead. I want to make our move on the king in three weeks."

"As you wish, Your Highness. I will handle her by tomorrow evening. Everything has been in place for some time. She will be here kneeling, or in the ground, before my next report," he says, still looking down.

"Very well. You are dismissed." Just as he stands, bows, and turns to leave, I speak again, making him pause. "And Ansel . . . don't lose again."

"I will not, Your Highness," he promises, then departs.

I can't help but smile. It is almost time to finally leave this circle. Almost time to have my revenge and this country, served up on the same platter.

Cateline

I scowl and bite the nail of my thumb. I can't stand this humiliation anymore. That useless common-born girl refuses to stop humiliating me. She is a stain on my reputation. Every noble parent who visits and sees her on campus leaves with a smirk or a sneer. I am being used as evidence that, while women should handle the children in class, a man should be headmaster.

I hear the murmurs when I enter a room. The snickers. This is the only position a woman can have in this country that commands real respect, and I am losing it. All because of some stupid child who refuses to present herself as a dignified woman. She is disrespectful, stupid, and disgusting. She wants to undo all the work I have done to force people to view women as equals. I was doing so well. I had men who were too afraid to talk down to me. But I failed to rein in one little girl with a powerful sponsor, and here I am.

When they look at me, they don't see the proud headmistress of the prestigious Facinley University. They see a woman who failed to raise even a commoner child properly. A headmistress whose professors have been resigning and disappearing for years. I can't allow it any longer. I don't care who her sponsor is. I will be rid of her. She has made enemies of more than just me. With the right incentive, I can get a few students to . . . handle the problem. No one will blame me if some other powerful noble children let things get out of hand. I just have to give her enemies a little . . . push.

CHAPTER SIXTY-TWO

Thunderclap

push myself back with force as I approach the rooftop. This has become one of my favorite ways to travel across the city over the last few years. I launch myself from a rooftop with force, then slow my fall to make a gentle landing. It's an incredibly quick mode of travel and, more importantly, makes me feel a bit like Yu Shu Lien. It initially took too much mana to keep up consistently and was far too conspicuous, but both problems have been solved.

With the changes in the city and my growing mana pool, mana limits are rarely a worry for me. I can't fight quite as well as inside the Radiant Woods, but I don't have to push myself for most spells. I've also got a fancy cloak I have enchanted to disperse light coming in my direction. It doesn't make me invisible, but at night it's pretty close. It turns my entire body into an empty void of darkness. It's extremely visible in daylight, but right now, I am as close to invisible as a moving target can be. With my gentle landings and the dark around me, I can pass unnoticed at much faster speeds.

I no longer need to call Sarafyna every time I need to rush across the city, unless I need to move especially quickly. It has, broadly speaking, been a good few years. It's been nice not caring about graduating; I haven't had to work myself into an early grave just to make sure I pass every class. That's not to say I haven't been working. The more I do, the more there is to do. The crown has been using the flimsiest of excuses to arrest its own citizens and create more slaves, who they have been keeping in more discreet locations.

I can often stop the arrests as they happen, but whether I do that or find them later, they are in much smaller groups than they used to be. They've been separating the new priest recruits as well and I haven't been able to rely on Sara's help as consistently. That's all right because, finally, we have our very own communication orbs, or whisper spheres, as Sara claims they are called by the church. It even turns out that long-distance spheres are no more difficult to manufacture than the personal ones used within the city. This is relieving and troubling in equal measure.

Long-distance communication has always been a gap I couldn't close and I worried we wouldn't be able to manage it, so I'm glad to have that worry off my chest. It also confirms, however, that the strange and artificial isolation of cities is very much by design, and I haven't figured out why. Neither the church nor the kingdom should benefit from this. In fact, it has made my job much easier. I'd like to be grateful, but it makes me uneasy.

Tensions are as high as ever between the people, the temple, and the nobility. No one trusts anyone else, and if the king pushes any harder, it will only take a spark to set this country on fire. These people are ready to fight. I can see it in their eyes as I walk through the market. I can see it in the closed windows and hushed whispers. All they need is someone to fight the pillars of power with them, the king and other mages who can hit the people back like a nuclear bomb. The king is the only one who is likely to, at least. Every other powerful mage I know about is aware that ruling people requires having people to rule.

As I fly from poor, run-down buildings to ornate mansions and wide roads, I adjust my course a bit. My radar goggles pick up a group of five priests patrolling through a nearby alley that I want to avoid. The church has been throwing everything into catching me. They've been growing more desperate as their numbers dwindle and their control fades. Fewer people have been showing up for confession to have the control reestablished as well. Commoners technically are legally required to go now, but as the king abandoned the pretense that following the law is possible, the sting of the word *criminal* began to fade.

Confession used to be more or less required by social agreement, which worked better than mandate, but with a monster running freely through the city and the previous divine suggestions gone, the appeal is not what it once was. It's now just another excuse to seize random people as slaves. All that being the case, the church has all but abandoned the practice for the time being. When they do get a confession, their control fades too quickly for it to be worthwhile. Instead, finding me is priority number one. To kill me, or I suppose to try dropping me in the Radiant Woods. But also to question me. They want their power back, and they want it bad.

Dodging them has also made things slower and more difficult. I don't have time to fight priests every time I go out, and they have been sticking closely to slave owners' homes. Fortunately, with slaves being spread out more, it's harder for them to know where to guard. I simply have to choose targets they didn't, and I always see them first. Tonight is no different. I'll simply head to the next target on my ever-shortening list. I've added names over the years, of course, but only so many people can die before a few nobles start to wonder if requisitioning new slaves is worth it.

I am endlessly grateful the church and crown seem to be uninterested in working together. I don't know if that's because of my vampire gambit, because they both want to believe they are in charge, or both. But if they both searched for me, or agreed on one spot to keep all slaves and both guarded it, this would be far more difficult. But the idiot king hasn't looked for me at all, instead focusing on shoring up his defenses. His favored nobles have certainly been well protected. Powerful mages all over their estates, and the palace, have made those targets nearly untouchable.

Little does he know I don't need to touch them. He thinks he can hide until I've been handled, and then he and his powerful friends can just emerge victorious.

But like I said. He is the only one who might nuke the people, and he will be the first royal I kill. As soon as I have gotten as many slaves as possible to safety, the time will come for just that. I simply need to draw him out. Him and Medici, the father of the temple, if I can. Once I get them in one place and within my reach, well . . . that's all she fucking wrote.

As I pass out of the entertainment district, hiding from the patrons of various upscale taverns and gambling halls, I see my destination. Not a private slave owner this time, but the manager of a cabaret. He's a particularly nasty one who uses his slaves for a fighting ring in the basement. Well, for one final night, he is. I push myself from one roof and revel as the wind blows past me. I'll never get tired of flying like this, even if it's not true flight at the moment.

As I approach the next rooftop, I extend force to slow my fall, and . . . nothing happens. My force mana disperses as soon as I aspect it. I try again, to the same effect. "Oh, fuck," I whisper just before I collide with the building at full speed. I feel myself bruise and my face smacks into the ridges of the metal roof. Still dazed, I roll down the side of the roof and slide off, landing hard on my back. My head cracks against the cobblestone and I groan in pain. I hold one hand to my face, then examine it. It's covered in blood, probably from my nose.

It's tender to the touch and I suspect it's broken. If I hadn't strengthened my muscles and bones so much over the last couple of years, my injuries would be far worse. I hit extremely hard. What the fuck happened? I've never had my mana disperse like that before. I painfully climb to my feet and strain my eyes, searching my surroundings. I didn't see any patrols in the area. Only the patrons of the various businesses. The light mana on my goggles is still working and I don't see any threats. I give my body a quick once-over. I am going to bruise everywhere, but I'm not badly hurt. Certainly not like I would have been a few years ago.

That's when I realize it. It isn't only force mana that dissipated. I can't feel any grief. None at all, from a single soul anywhere near me. Then a nearby restaurant starts to empty out. Not like it's closing—everyone inside is headed in my direction. Then another restaurant does the same, and another. There must be four dozen people circling me. The realization of what's happening dawns on me and my stomach churns. I've seen this scene before. I've caused this scene before. And it hadn't worked out too well for Baldwin. I am standing in the middle of a mana dispersal circle, designed specifically for me.

How did they know about the grief mana? I could understand force—any mage could have seen me use it, which means any aspect I have used in a fight may not work right now. But grief? Had I forgotten to extract my mana from my blood before dosing drinks or something? I wouldn't make a mistake like that, and they would need to know who I was *and* what I was doing to even think of it. When had someone gotten the chance to examine me for my aspects?

I haven't lost a tooth like Baldwin. I haven't really lost a fight since . . . oh, fuck. A phantom pain radiates from an old scar on my side. A scar I got from Autumn's old bed frame when a piece broke off and stabbed me in the side. When I fought the fucking bard. The bard who made sure to extract the large splinter before leaving. The splinter and the mana-filled blood soaking through it.

As if summoned by my realization, a familiar figure in a familiar mask rounds the corner. I take a deep breath and tense. There is nowhere to run, not yet. I am completely surrounded. I need to make a plan.

"Don't worry, Lillith of Endings, we only want to talk," the man says, holding up a placating hand to me.

What mana can I use? I have my new aspects and I haven't used them all publicly. I haven't needed to. But that doesn't mean I can use them now. If I try to check, the bard will see and he'll know what to expect. I have to wait for the right moment and hope it works. Lightning is my best bet. It's quick and a good match for whatever metal he uses. I've also never used it while hunting. If I time it right . . .

"Talk, talk about what?" I ask, scanning the emerging nobles around him. As a bard, he would be strengthened by each and every one of them. I'm stronger than I was in our last fight, but so is he.

"Oh, not going to deny your name?" he inquires, mild interest painting his voice. Why would I do that? I wasn't wearing a mask the last time I saw him. What would be the point? I have to get out of here and warn everyone to run now. These enemies could be at my house already, but . . . why had they waited all this time?

"What do you want?" I ask, instead of answering his question.

"Nothing much. I want to make you an offer. You've been . . . a great help over the years. My master would simply like to make our alliance . . . official."

I narrow my eyes. I've been helping him? I don't have time to worry about what he means by that.

"Your master?" I probe.

He holds his hands out to his side.

"Why, the rightful king of Potestia, King Darian. He's a big fan of yours, Lady Lillith. He wants your help to ascend the throne. Well, more of your help."

"The rightful king, huh?" I respond. "And what exactly does he think I can do for him?"

He laughs. "What can you do for him? All of this is thanks to you, Lillith. Don't play coy; you've practically pulled the throne from under Donatello's ass! The last thing we need to do is kill the man. With our help, you can do that. Come now, Lillith. You are no baroness. You could stand at the top of the court. Take care of your family with wealth you have never imagined. All he asks for is fealty. I think you'll find he treats you better than the current regime ever did."

For someone who seems to know so much about me, it doesn't seem like he has been paying much attention. "And if I say no?" I ask.

His face darkens.

"That would be foolish, Lillith. Look, I know you have your little crusade. You want to be a hero. A queen the people love and praise for saving them from their oppressors. But we've seen through the facade of justice. It was a good idea, pulling allies from the common people, but no one will ever accept a queen, however grateful they are. On some level, you must understand that. You want to be loved? To be seen as a hero? We can do that, and without the ridicule you'd receive if you tried to wear the crown. Come on now, come meet the true king," he offers, holding a hand out to me.

"That doesn't answer my question. What if I say no?" I repeat.

"No is, I'm afraid, not an answer we are entertaining," he replies, a distinct edge to his voice.

"So it's service or death, is that it?" I guess. He simply holds his hands out and shrugs. "I see. Well, then, Potestian, take me to your leader," I agree, and he smiles.

"I'm glad to see you are no fool," he says, then gestures to a couple of his allies. "I'm sorry about the shackles. Just a precaution, you understand. I'm afraid I misread you. I can feel it now. You don't feel greed but desperation. Which, I'm afraid, requires far more caution."

I recognize the mana-suppression shackles as two of the nobles try to reach for my wrist. Shit. I had hoped the bard himself would approach. No matter. As the first man grabs my arm, I yank as hard as I can. He screams in pain as his arm dislocates and ligaments tear. I grab his head with one hand and the head of the second man with my other.

It's hardly more difficult than crushing a couple of cantaloupes as I slam their heads together. The visceral gore draws gasps and cries from many of the lesser nobles, but the bard just scowls. I don't wait for him to respond, I jump. No force mana, just my own strength. It's still enough to reach an upper window in the building I fell from, and I crash through the glass and begin running. Once I'm out of sight, I cycle through my mana to see what I can aspect. Metal, water, light, and electricity. Well, it's not a terrible combo.

I want to run in the direction I came from, but if they finished the circle while I was already inside it, I have no guarantee where the closest edge is. I don't even know how big it is.

"You can't escape, Lillith. We know who you are. We know where you live. Where will you go?" the bard calls as he appears behind me. I try to summon a metal wall, an easy enough task usually, but it's too slow without grief mana. He, on the other hand, is empowered in a dozen ways by dozens of people, including myself. He fires his own metal projectiles at me and they tear through my flesh like bullets. My left arm is a bloody, shredded mess and my leg has a graze as well.

I grit my teeth and disappear through the nearest door. I find myself in an abandoned two-story building with a number of unfinished rooms. A future inn, perhaps.

"I don't want to kill you, Lillith. You're of more use to the rightful king alive than dead," he laments as he nonchalantly enters the room. There isn't another exit, which he must have known before we ever entered. He did his homework. The only way out is another window, far to my right. I'll never make it before he kills me, and I do believe he will this time, whether he wants to or not.

"That's the thing," I say while I prepare a light spell, which he only chuckles at, "there is no such thing as a rightful king." Then I run for the window.

He sighs and his metal shards are already flying at the window long before I make it. I don't care. I throw myself with every ounce of strength I have to the right, directly through the plaster and wood of the wall. As I am once again falling at full speed to the ground, I cast my triple-layered light spell. The world around us goes black as *Total Eclipse of the Heart*, as I like to call it, takes effect.

"That won't work, Lillith," the bard calls as I hit the cobblestone a second time, pain shooting through my arm. "Even if you don't cast another spell, I can feel your fear. Your panic. Your rage. You can't get away!"

I don't care. This spell isn't for him, it's for his friends. Because I didn't make it dark. I created a total eclipse, or the effects of one. The darkness is a distraction from the UV rays I am transmitting. UV rays that don't hurt to look at but still do damage. The darkness starts to get torn apart by various other mages and I have to dive to avoid spells of stone, wood, and fire from all directions.

I can't hold them all back, but thankfully my base mana is still enough to put up a fight. It seems the bard isn't empowered enough to directly crush my mana, even if it's a close thing. After a moment, the darkness disappears, but it's too late.

"Someone dispel the damn darkness, you morons!" the bard calls. After a moment, the darkness disappears, but it's too late. I grin, standing again, then begin pouring all my mana into a lightning spell. It takes a lot if I want to control it, but I should have enough. My total eclipse spell is far more dangerous than looking at the sun. The amount of UV light I produced at the range I produced it is far more than anyone on Earth is ever at risk of staring into. Everyone in range would have the most severe solar retinopathy in history. Well, everyone but me.

Before I can finish my spell, however, the bard flies at me at speed. I barely manage to avoid decapitation as I dodge to the side. His summoned blade still bites deep into my flesh and I have to bite back a scream. "What the fuck did you do?" he yells. "I can still feel you, you spoiled child. I can feel how relieved you are. How smug. Do you think this will stop me?"

I don't, but lightning might. Rapid blindness does more than darken the physical world. It blinds you to mana as well.

This means, while he can feel where I am with his endoaspects, he can no longer see my spells. I begin to run and he follows. He's faster than me and I narrowly avoid another hit. Thankfully, his allies panic more than he does. We both have to dodge spells flung in my general direction by the other nobles, but he can't see them. I am impressed he still manages to dodge them until I realize he is reacting to my emotions. Dodging when he feels my hope, staying the course when he feels my disappointment. The man is a fucking monster.

I turn around and stop looking. A risky move, since I won't be able to dodge his attacks, but it pays off. "Stop your spells, you damn fools, leave the bitch to me!" he shouts. The barrage of spells stops, but it's too late. The bard pausing to yell at them was the gap I needed to finish aspecting enough electricity for a bolt of lightning, which releases and strikes him faster than even he could ever dodge. The thunder cracks through the area and the blind nobles duck for cover. He stumbles and hits the ground hard, then stops moving. I want to check if he's dead, but . . .

"Th-there she is!" a man shouts, and I curse. Some of them are starting to recover a bit already. *Total Eclipse of the Heart* is a good spell, but it's inconsistent. The same effect on Earth was rare, and I could only manage blindness on everyone due to massively increased exposure. Some won't recover, but if they hadn't been looking in my direction or closed their eyes to focus or one of a dozen other variables, well . . . I have no idea how many people will be in fighting condition in a few moments, and I can't risk it. I choose to flee. I take out my whisper sphere and activate it with mana.

"Sara, I need to get out of here. Safe house thirteen, meet me there immediately!" I cry into it, and after a brief pause, I get a response.

"On my way" is all she says, clearly aware I don't have time to explain. I run through the dark streets, past the stares of onlookers, curious about the cause of the thunder. I hear cries behind me and put all my remaining will into running. Finally, I circle behind an old, abandoned butcher's shop and hurry through its alley door. Sara and Autumn are waiting for me, and both immediately grab me so I don't collapse from exhaustion.

"W-what's Autumn doing here?" I ask. It was a terrible idea to bring her. Why would she want to come?

"I—I have to warn you," Autumn stutters, "about Lady Cateline."

Shit, that doesn't sound good, but I don't have time to ask about it. "Fine, but we need to get out of here first. We need to get everyone out of here. They know who I am," I announce. Sara's and Autumn's faces pale immediately.

CHAPTER SIXTY-THREE

Eleonor

Autumn

I relax in the shared bath on campus. The last few years have been interesting. Many of my worries about Lillith simply . . . didn't happen. Yeah, things are getting tense, but the more I see the crown's response, the more it seems like she has a point. Just last week, a baker I liked was arrested and enslaved. I always went out of my way to stop at his bakery on the way from Lillith's home since he was more skilled than even the bakers on campus.

He had been accused of "operating without a license," a concept I've never heard of and have been unable to find any evidence of existing. I've always been taught slaves are repaying the kingdom for the harm they've done, but . . . the man had never done anything but make bread. No matter how I look at it, freeing slaves like him can't be framed as bad. It doesn't matter how the king responds. It doesn't matter how tense things have gotten. Her choices have always been to leave people in slavery or help them.

I don't understand all the logic behind everything. I haven't been able to keep up with what's going on but, I know that much is true. I know Lily is doing what she has to do for these people. Which is why I can't shake the guilt. I've done nothing to help, this entire time. What had Lillith said? I'm either benefitting or I'm a coward? That had felt cruel at the time, but I can't get the words out of my head. She asked me to figure out which I was. I'm a coward. I can't do what she does, but . . . I don't have the power she does. No, I'm a coward, because I got scared for my family and went to Lord Godfrey.

At the time, I was certain it was the right thing to do. It was what I had always been told to do, and it felt right. I was proud of myself, even. I found out about a threat to the kingdom and I told someone in a position to help. But . . . when Lillith promised to keep my family safe . . . I started to see her actions differently. I started to understand what she was saying. That's how I know I'm a coward. Because she sounded so dark and terrifying and wrong . . . until she stopped seeming dangerous to *me*. I don't think Godfrey believed me. Nothing ever happened. He never even investigated her for the deaths in the city.

Meanwhile, Lillith has been showing me more and more trust. I've tried to tell her, I have. But, like I said, I'm a coward. What if . . . what if she no longer wants to keep my family safe when she knows? Part of me is sure she would never punish them for that, but . . . I'm just so scared. I can't get the thought out of my head. Every time I work up the courage, I tell her I need to speak to her, and then . . . I find something else to say. I come up with anything else to say. Anything but the truth. Anything but "I stabbed you in the back, and told Godfrey everything." I don't know if I even need to. Nothing ever came of it. Three years and Godfrey hasn't even questioned her, that I know of.

She's safe, and she's keeping my family safe. That's what I keep telling myself, but part of me doesn't buy it. Part of me knows I should tell her. I shrink down into the hot water, blowing bubbles with my mouth. Maybe I'll finally get it out of my head if I tell her, but . . . what if her knowing is worse?

I'm shaken out of my thoughts as I hear other girls coming to use the bath. I groan; I specifically chose an unpopular time so I could be alone. When I hear the chatting voices and giggling in familiar voices, I curse.

Iris, Jocelyn, and the rest of their entourage are coming. I swim through the bath and hide behind a large stone in the middle. I can't stand them. They are the picture of entitled nobles. If I'm the coward, they're the ones in love with the benefits.

"Tonight?" Iris asks, and Jocelyn laughs.

"Tonight, here on campus. Lady Cateline basically said our grades would all be perfect if we handled it as soon as possible!" Jocelyn responds.

"Oh, thank the Collector, I'm about to fail at least two classes!" another girl complains.

"Well, not anymore. We do this one thing and we don't even have to go to class anymore. Plus, it'll be fun. The little pervert has been asking to be put in her place," Jocelyn says.

I quietly move up against the rock. Lady Cateline is offering them free grades for something? Why?

"D-do we have to . . . uh, you know . . ." a fourth, quieter voice tries to ask.

"Kill her?" Jocelyn finishes her sentence for her. "Yes, don't be a coward, Liora. Your dad is a magic knight, he kills people like her all the time. If it weren't for her sponsor, she'd be long dead already. Besides, don't you think she's gross? It'll be like putting a sick pet out of her misery, trust me."

I have to cover my mouth to stop a gasp from escaping. Are they seriously talking about . . . but who would they want to kill? Who would Lady Cateline want to kill?

"I—I know, but I thought we were just going to, you know, get her to drop out. Isn't killing a bit . . ." She trails off.

"Well, things change. Tell you what, Liora? You want out, fine. Leave. But I know you are struggling too. If you are happy with failing out, then do that. The rest of us are going to finish at the top of the class," Jocelyn says.

"N-no, I'll help, I will, I just wanted to ask!" Liora says.

Shit. I have to hold my breath in the quiet baths, terrified they'll hear me. They won't leave me alive if they do.

"Besides," Iris adds, "if anyone deserves it, it's her. But how are we going to corner her this time?"

"I have a plan for that, don't worry," Jocelyn replies. "Just meet me behind the mana sciences building three hours past midnight. Iris and I will get her there. And I think you should prove your dedication, Liora. Why don't you help? And we'll never have to look at that filthy commoner girl again."

I freeze. Shit, do they mean Lillith? But why does Lady Cateline want Lillith dead? Does she know about . . . But surely she would also know they don't stand a chance unless . . . unless she helps them directly. Oh no, I have to warn her. Even Lillith likes to fight on her own terms. If she's ambushed by someone like that, not to mention Lady Jocelyn, she may be in danger.

Sweat runs down my head as I listen. Their conversation moves on to milder things as though they haven't just been idly talking about murdering a woman. So secure in their right to do so that they didn't even bother checking if anyone else was here. It takes ages for them to finally leave, and even longer before I feel safe leaving myself. I get dressed as quickly as I can and call a carriage. I know Lillith isn't at the dorm, and I have no idea where to find her. If I can catch Sara, however, she can warn her in time.

The trip is agonizingly slow and I have to keep begging the driver to hurry, but this time, I am determined to do right by my friend.

Lillith

"That's when she said you were the target," Autumn finishes, and I put my hand on my chin. We've made it to campus, but Sara is still healing me from my last fight. Once she is done, we'll pick up August and Leo and run. Autumn has taken the opportunity to tell me what she overheard in the bath.

"That doesn't make sense," I respond after thinking about it. "Jocelyn made no attempt to speak to me, much less get me to go somewhere. Maybe it was before Cateline talked to her, but . . . why would she be so certain she could do it? It must be half an hour past that meeting time now. I'm definitely not there."

"I'm not sure, she just sounded so certain. I assumed Lady Cateline would try to find you or something," Autumn answers.

"But what did Iris mean 'this time'?" I wonder. "They've never bothered me before. I think Jocelyn kind of likes me, actually. It sounds more like . . ." My blood runs cold as realization dawns. "Autumn. They said I was the target, right? Are you sure?" I ask, a cold sweat breaking out. "Yes? Who else would they mean?" she asks, panic in her voice incited entirely by my own.

"Did they say my name? Did they say *Lillith*?" I ask, desperately hoping she'll say yes.

"Well, no, I guess not. They said 'that commoner girl,' I think. But there's only you and Eleonor. And, yeah, Eleonor is eccentric, but she's harmless. Why would anyone target her?"

"Sara, I need to be done now, can we go any faster?" I beg, and Sara finally speaks up, roused from her intense concentration.

"Your left arm is bad, Lily. There is still metal inside, it'll take at least another ten—"

I cut her off.

"This will have to do, I have to go now," I say, pulling my wounded arm away and stumbling to my feet as quickly as I can. I have to pause as the wound on my leg finishes closing. I can't afford to be slowed down, but it does give me time to explain what Autumn missed.

"What, what's wrong?" Sara startles, and I look at Autumn.

"You're caught up in what you know about me. To Cateline and Jocelyn, the worst thing about me is my haircut and my sharp tongue. Leo, on the other hand . . . challenges everything they believe, to their face. Him, they hate. Because he's not eccentric, and he doesn't dress strangely. He's just . . . himself. And they can't stand it," I say. "Autumn, show Sara where I'm going."

"He?" Autumn asks, but I have no time left. My leg is done, and I am out the door before she can ask for clarification.

Leo

They are after me again. I only came back to campus in hopes of finding Lily, but she wasn't here. I have to get away from campus, but Jocelyn and Iris spotted me. I don't understand why they won't just leave me alone. What did I do so wrong? It's always been like this. Everywhere I go.

I would be dead now if it weren't for Lady Charlotte. The first person I've ever known who was like me. She told me I didn't have to come here. She told me it would be dangerous. But I just . . . I wanted to help her. I wanted to prove we weren't some creeps, or monsters, or anything else they call us. I wanted to improve her reputation by doing well here and becoming a mage they could respect. I wanted to be like Lady Cateline. A woman who, through competence and sheer will, rose to a position of power and shut up everyone who ever criticized her.

If I could do that for Lady Charlotte, it would all be worth it. But when I got here, even Cateline hated me. Even she pushed me down whenever she got the chance. But I still admire her. I still want to be like her, but better. Lily gave me hope. She isn't exactly like me, but she is in a way. She made this place bearable. Gave me a shoulder to lean on when it got too hard. Promised me a future where it wasn't just my clothes that matched who I am.

But I have to survive, and they are closing in on me.

"Eleonor! Come on out!" Lady Iris calls. I duck behind a bush of large, white flowers. Jocelyn is up the other side of the path, and one of them will see me if I emerge. I don't know where to go. I wish I accepted the whisper sphere Lily offered me, but . . . I didn't want to be involved in all that. I just wanted to handle all this alone. To prove I could. Now there is nowhere to hide. I'll have to try a spell again and hope I can hide before they regain their sight.

Just when I am about to, a voice whispers behind me. "Eleonor, I can help," she whispers. Fear shoots through me and I can feel my pulse in my temples as I turn. It's another minor noble girl, crouched behind me in the foliage. One I've had a few classes with. She's never bothered me before, but I still don't trust her. "Look, I know how they've treated you. I can get you out of here, I can get you someplace safe," she offers, holding her hand out.

I search her face with wide, frantic eyes. "C-can I . . . trust you? Please, I don't . . . I don't understand why they won't leave me alone, I just want to find my friend," I beg.

She looks at me with sad eyes. "I know, but you can trust me," she promises. I search her face for signs of a lie, but she seems genuine. Nobles can't be trusted, not by people like me, but . . . I can't help but think of Lillith. Lily and Autumn, and August, and all the others who support her. I take a deep breath. All right, Lily. A leap of faith. I will try trusting one noble.

"Okay, I'll go with you. Thank you, Liora," I hesitantly agree.

"All right, wait here," she says before leaving. I hear a brief conversation and I'm frozen in fear. Is she going to betray me? Is she going to tell them? I ready a light spell, just in case but . . . she sends them away. I let out a breath I didn't realize I've been holding. Lily was right. Lily was right, and I am going to make it out, because of a noble.

She pops up a moment later and I jump. "Come on," she says, "I know a safe place you can stay, then I'll find your friend for you." She helps me up and I brush myself off.

"Thank you so much. I don't know what would have happened without you. Thank you so much," I say, my tone worshipful.

"N-no problem, Eleonor," she responds, and I follow her through the campus. Every now and then shadows pass the garden plants and my heart stops. Every sound sends a chill down my spine, but eventually, we make it to our destination.

"What are we doing here?" I ask as we circle around to the empty lot behind the science of mana building. Liora looks down and doesn't answer. I realize why in only a moment. All of Jocelyn's friends are here. Waiting. I turn to run, but Jocelyn and Iris stand in my way. Jocelyn is holding a dress up to me.

"We thought it was about time you started acting like a lady," Jocelyn sneers. I feel hot tears form in my eyes.

"Please. I'll wear the dress. I'll always wear the dress, from now on. I'll do whatever you want, but . . . please. Let me go. I-I'll wear it, I'll put on the dress, please . . ."

Lillith

I fly. I don't care if anyone sees me. I don't bother with any light spells or masks, which I left at the campus safe house. I don't care what happens. I use force mana at full power to propel myself through campus like a speeding train. The building is too far. It's too long after they were supposed to meet. When I have to land, I don't stop. I fly through the garden foliage, and the twigs and thorns leave fine cuts and slashes on my skin. I don't feel them.

I feel nothing but panic. I can't let this happen, I can't. Not to Leo. It feels like an eternity. Eons pass as I rush to save my friend. In reality, I make it in minutes, but as I arrive, I worry I was too slow. There are maybe a dozen women here, in this quiet lot. Leo is on the ground, crumpled up like a discarded receipt. He's been forced into an ill-fitting dress and the wrap he uses to bind his chest has been torn off him. It's lying a few yards away, covered in blood.

I scream, the cry of a wounded animal, and everyone stands back, even Iris and Jocelyn. They stare at me as I rush to his side and kneel down, tears already streaking down my face as I hesitantly reach my fingers to his neck, then his wrist. A pulse. I can't find a pulse.

"Well, would you look at that? Another common girl. I respect you more, Lillith, so I'll let you leave, if you want. But we have business with your friend there, and if you stand in our way, well. I suppose we'll have to put another commoner in the ground," Jocelyn threatens. I ignore her.

I can't feel anything. No. No no no no no. I can't . . . I can't do this. There is so much blood. His limbs are broken and his jaw isn't set correctly. One eye is swollen shut and bone juts out from his left leg. But Sara, Sara can fix that. He just needs to be alive. I move my fingers a little and . . . my lip quivers. Tears run down my cheeks. Because, however faint it is, I can feel a pulse. I just have to get him to Sara, who is on her way. I just have to keep him alive.

Slowly, I look up at Jocelyn's smirking face. It's time to live up to my fucking name.

CHAPTER SIXTY-FOUR

Fix Your Hearts or Die

Iris

Igrin wildly. Lillith of Endings, of all people, is the one to interrupt us. I'll admit, when a mage practically flew around the corner before we finished the little pervert off, my heart stilled. That fucking howl she made when she saw her little friend gave me gooseflesh as well. But I was just startled. By the mewling of a stray cat, no less. I couldn't be more pleased. The little bitch has far too bold a tongue for her position. With Jocelyn here, she'll have to learn to bow her head.

And if she doesn't, well . . . I lick my lips in anticipation. Every clever little quip in the world won't save her. If it weren't for her brutish strength and her luck with Lord Godfrey's circle, I'd have handled her myself years ago. But her mana has been measured and she is wanting compared to Jocelyn. I know Lillith. She won't leave quietly. Which means I get an extra show tonight. It even seems like little Ellie here rubbed off on her. She's dressed a bit like a man herself, although it looks like her outfit has been through it.

None of that matters, however. All that matters is that I, Iris of the lesser house of Bonner, am going to graduate near the top of my class and be rid of two pests at the same time.

Lillith is holding her hand to Eleonor's wrist, as if it matters whether she is still alive or not. Even if she is, she won't be for long. Neither of them is leaving here alive. Even if Lillith tries to submit, I can get a reaction out of her. Jocelyn will kill her one way or another. I'll make sure of it. I'm not like these other nameless hangers-on. Jocelyn likes me. She listens to me.

She stands and glares at us, then looks over to her right for a moment and nods. I follow her gaze but see nothing. We'll have to send someone to check over there later. It won't do to have too many witnesses, after all.

"If any of you didn't know what was happening here, or just came to see what the crowd was about, now is your chance to leave," Lillith growls.

We all stare blankly at her. What in the third plane is she talking about?

"Lillith, you are the one who should leave. And get yourself some proper clothes—you are in public, woman," Jocelyn laughs.

Lillith scans all of us with her eyes. A sudden chill passes through us. It's cold enough I would think it was a spell, if I could see or feel any mana. She starts walking toward Jocelyn.

"Oh, you really don't want to do this," Jocelyn warns, her aura flaring and putting a bit of pressure on the rest of us. It's enough that I start to sweat despite the cold.

I knew it. I fucking knew it. Oh-so-smart Lillith doesn't know when she is outmatched, even having seen Jocelyn's mana measurement for herself years ago. Of course, Lillith obviously isn't thinking clearly. She hasn't even bothered to try a spell of her own. In fact, her eyes look completely empty. They show no thought or concern for her life, just a hollow, haunting grief. For Eleonor of all people!

"This is your last warning, Lillith. I'd rather not upset Lord Godfrey, but he's hardly the king. I will kill you," Jocelyn allows one final time, and I scoff before choking back my laughter. Jocelyn is being too kind.

I can tell her patience is running out, however. Her mana is taking on the distinct orange color of her sun mana. I've seen her sear steak with this spell; Lillith won't last a single second, and Jocelyn is taking no chances. She is using more mana than I have ever seen in a spell. If it weren't for her impressive control, I'd fear for everyone here. Lillith is maybe thirty seconds from a painful death when I notice something odd. She isn't using any mana, but her ruby eyes have begun to take on a low glow. How is she doing that? I narrow my eyes and look closer. There is something coming off her face. Not mana but . . . are her tears . . . steaming?

They are. They are leaving light burn marks on her cheeks. Not bad ones; they'd heal in a few days if she lived that long. Is this an effect of Jocelyn's mana? That thought paints a grin on my face. "Bye-bye, Lily, dear," I say, holding one hand up and folding my fingers in a sarcastic wave. It's only a shame Jocelyn didn't want to play with her a bit first, like the other girl. Lillith slowly raises one hand and closes her fist, maybe a few seconds before Jocelyn kills her. Then something changes.

She still uses no mana, but Jocelyn's spell . . . crumples. Like the air and mana within were a paper that could be crushed between your fingers. Then it shatters and the spell is just gone. The air is heavy with silence for a second.

"W-what did you do?" Jocelyn demands. "How did you—"Lillith holds up her other hand and slams it into her still-closed fist. Jocelyn never gets a chance to finish her question. As Lillith's hands meet, Jocelyn's head . . . collapses. It's crushed inward, beyond recognition, like a grape between two fingers. Her corpse falls to its knees, then its torso, as blood pours from the stump of its neck.

Again the air is thick with quiet, the gentle sound of water dripping over cobblestones occupying the time alone. I don't understand what happened. Lillith didn't use a spell. No one understands. Everyone is frozen in place, unable to process our friend's sudden death. Everyone but Lillith. She points at another girl, and faster than I've ever seen an element be conjured, sharp steel erupts from the ground beneath her. It's when the two halves of her body fall to different parts of the ground that we finally react.

Two women try attacking Lillith, their ice and stone spells shattering like Jocelyn's even before Lillith jerks her head toward them. As she does, both of their necks snap and they collapse into each other. Another desperate woman actually pulls out a dagger and charges Lillith. I can see the glow of a powerful enchantment on it and hope, for a brief moment, that it will be enough to end this. But Lillith moves at the same time. She is fast. Impossibly fast. I blink and she has closed the distance and is holding the woman by her hair. Her other hand holds the woman's, keeping the dagger clenched tightly in it.

She jerks the woman's arm up and I hear a sickening snap as she doesn't bother to follow its natural movements. Then, in three quick stabs, she uses the dagger to pierce her victim's temple. The enchantment was powerful, and her head immediately begins to rot. As Lillith tosses her body aside with more force than should be possible, the woman's torso and head separate in the air. The body thumps against the wall of the building to our side, and the head . . . splatters like the rotten meat it is.

It's been maybe ten seconds since I was certain I would be watching Lillith burn. I've been gaping for ten seconds too long. I turn on my heel and run. I'm not the only one. All of us scatter. This lot is closed off a bit, which made it perfect for acting out of sight. It also makes it a death trap. Of the two exits, we all run for the one opposite Lillith, but there are too many of us. I hear choked screams all around me mixed with sobbing and begging from those who have already given up on escape.

Their pleas are all cut short, only various disgusting, squelching noises informing me of their fate. They were fools, but they slowed her down enough that I manage to clear the exit and reach the nearest path. I begin frantically looking for a place to hide. I can't outrun her, that much is obvious. There are three nearby buildings and quite a few plants decorating the walkway. Which do I run to? My heart pounds out of my chest, I can't decide which way to go, but I run out of time to think. Another of Jocelyn's sycophants is as frozen as I am, but she suddenly falls to her face.

She cries out and reaches for my ankle as something invisible drags her away by the leg. I don't see what causes her pleading to abruptly cut off as I am already running. No time to evaluate the best hiding place, I need to hide. I need to get out of here, to get help. I dive into the nearest bushes and begin to crawl. Thorns tear at my dress and skin as I crawl through them, but I can't risk moving openly. That . . . animal is focused on other victims—this is my chance.

I have to drag myself through the mud, and my face is a raw, bloody rag by the time I make it through all the rosebushes. But I make it and run to duck behind a courtyard wall of another building. I cover my mouth to hold back the sounds of the gasping. My entire body quivers. A sob is clawing its way up my throat, tugging on it and forcing my stomach to convulse, over and over again. I want to vomit. But I can't risk even the slightest sound. If I do, I'm dead.

I don't want to die, I don't want to die, I don't want to die . . . Oh, Collector, please, don't let her find me. Don't let her find me. I'll do anything. I'll go to confession, every day, please please please please . . . Another girl appears to my right. I recognize her as we make brief eye contact. It's the other girl, the one who helped us lure Eleonor in. She looks like she is about to run to join me, but just as she moves, her body rises into the air like a rag doll. A steel spike erupts from the ground, and her flying body is forcefully skewered on it.

The previously quiet night is filled with different screams and cries for help. But fewer and fewer of them. Every few moments, one stops. Sometimes alongside the slopping sounds of steaming meat. The back of my mouth grows hot and I vomit in my mouth. I hold my hand over my lips as bile and half-digested food drips through my fingers. I force myself to swallow the rest. The other sounds are disappearing and I can't afford to make any of my own. The final cry is cut short and an oppressive quiet takes over.

I hear footsteps but I can't tell if they are approaching or leaving. I choke and cry into my hand, closing my eyes. I just need to wait. I just need to wait a little longer, and it will all be all right. Just a little longer. I take a deep breath through my nose and . . . realize the footsteps are gone. I wait anyway. I wait, and I wait. Several minutes pass and my involuntary shaking grows so severe that my hand jerks from my mouth for a second and a short, strangled cry escapes my lips. But . . . nothing happens. Cautiously, I creep to the edge of the wall.

It's all right. I survived. She missed me. She missed me. I peek my head around the corner.

Oh. Her eyes are glowing. It's impossible to miss from so close.

Cateline

My hand flies to my mouth as I watch the steel bar pin Lady Iris's head to the wall. Fuck fuck fuck. This is way beyond anything I could have predicted. That Lillith is . . . she's a monster. She's *the* monster, I realize. The cold, calculating way she dispatched so many of my students with zero hesitation told the entire story. No one could kill like that without experience. The second I saw her kill Jocelyn, I knew I needed an advantage.

I ran back to my office as quickly as I could. The dispersal cloak was there. It was my only hope. It was rare, one of a kind, and there was no way Lillith could counter it. But I was too slow. Returning with my secret weapon, I was met with . . . carnage. Women's bodies, some in multiple pieces, others unrecognizable, scattered the area. The only two that were missing when I got back were Lillith's and fucking Eleonor's. I don't know where Eleonor went, but it doesn't matter.

None of that matters anymore. If I don't kill or capture Lillith now, everything is over. I begin to gather my mana. I hope I can catch her off guard, but as Iris dies, Lillith immediately looks directly at me. Sharp pain shoots through my heart as fear like I've never known wraps its icy fingers around me. She's on me in seconds and I can already feel the dispersal cloak doing its work. Mana envelops me but dissipates before it can harm me. I don't wait for her next attack to launch my own.

Lillith somehow tries to crush my mana, but I manage to maintain it. It gives me a headache and my nose and eyes bleed with the effort, but I maintain the spell. How is she so powerful? I can't even feel her aura. I launch a wave of acid at her, but her strange mana parts it in the air. It splashes on the corpses and plants around us, leaving her untouched. Small shards of steel form in a circle around her, then launch at me.

I ignore them, confident whatever mana she is using to propel them will be dispersed, but I'm mistaken. They cut deep into my flesh and I cry out. Shit, she is creating them, then propelling them somehow. The cloak only disperses active mana. As another wave assaults me, I respond with a shield of vector mana that sends them flying in random directions. Several fly into the surrounding stone, flesh, and soil. A few return to Lillith, but they bounce harmlessly off whatever shield she is using.

She tries to close the distance but I saw her before. I know she has inhuman strength. I flare my vector mana as she swings a fist, and her arm snaps at the elbow as her own strength empowers the shift in direction. She doesn't even flinch, just lets her broken arm fly uselessly to the side. Somehow, some kind of mana of hers assaults my vector mana and the direction becomes . . . neutral. Her other fist is almost to me when I manage to, just barely, summon a new wall of acid.

I hope for her to collide directly into it, but she flips unnaturally through the air, flying over me. Before she lands, she manages to summon a blade that she grabs with her good arm. She swings it at me and I dive out of the way, but its direction suddenly changes, moving completely differently than the swing of her arm suggests. I use vector mana to painfully push my body away, but I'm too slow. I cry out in agony as it cuts cleanly through my arm, leaving me with nothing from the elbow down.

I clench my teeth through the pain. I can use this. She sees and responds to every spell I cast. She figured out how to counteract vectors far too quickly. I need a trump card she can't see. Once again, I summon acid, spraying it at her in an endless wave. Using this much drains mana, but this is all or nothing. Again it splits and splashes around her, but her shield works too much like a vector spell. It's probably the same mana she uses to attack it. With this move, my desperation mana empowers me far more than it has the rest of the fight. It gives me power as it always has when I bet everything on a single gambit.

I push on her shield, and though I can't feel the shield itself, I can feel where my mana stops. I can push through. I am pouring mana into a spell I'm certain she won't see when a loud crack screams through my ears. The wave of acid erupts in dangerous sparks as some sort of . . . lightning mana tears through it. Thankfully, this attack is directed by mana, and any sparks that don't travel through the acid to the ground dissipate around my cloak.

This is my opening, and I scream as bone mana rapidly hones my ulna into a spear protruding from my still-bleeding arm. She can't see a spell that starts inside my body. No one can. As it tears from my arm, I drop the acid spell and focus all my vector mana on one point, breaking my way through her shield and allowing the bone spear to extend, all the way to her, and directly through her heart.

She slumps on the weapon, exerting pressure all the way back to my injured arm, and I cry out in pain. But it's all right. I fucking killed her. I won. Lillith of Endings is dead. I gasp and look around. Blackness is crawling from the edges of my vision. If someone doesn't stop the bleeding, I'll die too. Thankfully, this fight made too much noise. The church had refused to replace my missing whisper sphere, but my inability to request backup hasn't stopped the noise from attracting the magic knights. I am surrounded by allies. I can rest.

I am about to let the darkness take me when Lillith suddenly jerks awake, forces her own body forward, further impaling herself, and wraps her arms around me. She opens her mouth and a horrifying pair of fangs appear from behind her top row of teeth. They sink into the flesh of my cheek and the black that was flooding my vision swirls with a not entirely opaque red.

CHAPTER SIXTY-FIVE

An Audience with the King

Sarafyna

We have to go back, Sara, we have to help her!" Autumn insists. I grit my teeth.

"We can't, Autumn. If I go back and Leo dies, or you go back and die yourself . . . it will kill her. Faster than anything any noble could do. Help me get Leo out of here, we'll meet up with her later!" I insist because I know it's exactly what Lillith wants, but at the same time, part of me agrees with Autumn. I want to go back and keep her safe, but . . . Leo is dying. I can barely feel any life left in him. We need to get him back to the safe house, then far away from here.

"Can you even save her without Lily's help? We need to save Lily first, then we can keep Eleonor alive!" Autumn challenges me. In a way, she's right. My healing is usually a team effort with Lillith. But I can do enough. Enough to keep him alive until she is free.

"I'll have to. Autumn, come with me!" I beg as she hesitates, watching Lily tear through the mob that left her friend in this state.

"But . . . we need her to help Eleonor, and if she's captured . . . Sara, they'll kill her. They'll kill her, Sara, especially after this. If that happens, what do we do next?" Autumn asks, and I clench my fists.

"It's all right. She was always going to get caught. She thought it would happen long before this, in fact. It was nothing but the king's cowardice and foolishness that delayed it so long. She made me promise to get you to safety when it happened," I say.

"I can't just accept that! She's just going to let them kill her? Why?" Autumn pleads.

"No! Just . . . just trust me. I'll tell you everything once Leo is safe. Please, come with me!" I try again and she clenches her own fists, closing her eyes as tightly as she can before finally answering.

"All right. I'll trust you. But please, tell me, Lily will be okay? Tell me she's not going to die because of what I told her," she says. I nod.

"Lillith will be just fine. I promise. She *wants* to get caught, all right? It's the only way. So please, come with me." She sniffs and looks back one final time, but reluctantly gives me a slight nod of assent. As we use the commotion to make our way back to the safe house, we are spotted several times, but we are less important than the scene we are leaving.

When we finally pull Leo into the old dorm we've been using as a campus safe house, I hope I'm not a liar. Things need to go the way Lillith planned for, or she's dead. I also have to hope all that extra artwork Lily has done was enough. We put Leo on the soft sofa in the sitting room and I push my divine mana into him. I've never done such extensive work without Lillith's help before, and I can't help but sweat as I struggle to put the poor boy back together again.

Lillith

I am back in Satusmor. The filthy cobblestoned road feels like hot coals beneath my feet. The smell of fire lingers in the air and I immediately know why I am here. This isn't the first time I've revisited this night. The pillar of black smoke drawing me forward and the city around me blending like watercolor.

I always have a heartbeat again, when I have this dream. I don't know why. Every single time I can feel it, pounding in my chest like it wants to tear its way out. As always, I run through the streets. Fly through the city. Tear the world apart to reach that pillar of smoke, just a little faster. This was my worst night since waking up as Lillith. The smoke flees as it always does. The faster I run to it, the faster the distance grows.

My mind will never let me get there in time. If I cheat and use magic I didn't have that night, it cheats as well. The ugly smoke taunts me. It laughs at me, and it chokes me. My mind will never let me get there in time. Because I didn't make it the first time. The real time. I was too late. I failed.

It was the third house of penance I helped. It was nearest a popular brothel and many of its residents were sex workers, but not all. They had been so excited to become mages. So hopeful. But then Captain Horrus found them. He wanted the circle they used for himself, and they refused to show him. They fought him off. By the time he had forced his way in, the circle had been destroyed. The surviving street kids told me he had killed the nearest woman to him, right then and there.

I don't know how he figured it out. Maybe it was when they were fighting to keep him out. Maybe he had tried to order someone to come meet him. But somehow, he knew the Mages of Penance couldn't leave the house. He knew, even with an open door and a powerful reason to flee, they couldn't. So he didn't bother barring the doors or blocking the windows. When he set fire to that house of penance, he intentionally left the door open. He left it open so he could watch the panic on the faces of the people who defied him.

The street kids had tried to help. Many tried too hard. They tried to force their friends out of that open door to safety. But nothing they did could challenge the temple's mind rape. They didn't give up. Not in time. Many of them died with their friends, trapped in that fire not by mind control but by desperation and loyalty.

Very few survived by the time I made it. The building was already collapsing in on itself and anyone still inside would be killed by the smoke if not the fire.

Like every night, I use air mana to kill the fire, but like every night, no one emerges from the building. Horrus laughs. He spits on the ground and laughs after murdering them. Like every time I visit this memory, I make quick work of his soldiers. Every guard he brought with him dies and I allow none to flee. Like every night, I pin his arms and legs to the ground, although this time I use cuffs of earth instead of the spikes I used in real life.

I mount his chest and wrap my hands around his throat, just as I did in reality. When this really happened, the rage was all I was. The rage and fury and grief. I was Sara, chewing that man to death in that church. I was every victim in the ashes of the House of Penance. I was every slave this man had created from an invented crime. I choked him through his whimpers. Just as his pallor began to change, I would ease my grip. Let him breathe a little. Gave him time to gasp, and time to hope.

Then I would tighten my grip again. Close off his windpipe again. Let his vision fade, then release. I killed Captain Horrus slowly and deliberately. I don't regret this because he didn't deserve it. He did. I regret this because I didn't. I kill quickly. Without mercy when it's necessary, but quickly. I kill to remove the sickness people like Horrus and Cateline represent from the world, not to punish. Killing Horrus this way . . . left me numb. I spent a long time completely detached from the world, until I entered the Radiant Woods. Until I was used as a weapon against all those people, and until I met Sara.

Even then I wasn't back to normal for a long time. I still have this dream. I still kill Horrus slowly. But this time, I use cuffs. This time, I kill Horrus in an instant. It won't change the past, but it feels like waking up. And as he dies, I do wake up. I groan and try to pull myself up. I still have work to do. I didn't torture any of those women last night. Not physically. But I could have killed them in groups. I let each know they were going to die. I gave them time to fear and regret, and I did it to punish them.

Again, they deserved it. But I can tell, they are going to be my new dream. My new numbing agent. Because I am not supposed to kill to punish. I remove hate and danger, I don't punish . . . except when I do. I have more to work through. I lean against the hard stone wall and examine my surroundings. I am cuffed in front, with the mana-dispersal cuffs Walter once used on me. Yet again, they fail to stop my gathering mana. I can access most of my pooled mana as well.

I am in a stone room with a wall of bars separating me from a man with a powerful aura. My chest throbs, a painful itch begging for my attention. As I look down, I see my chest wrapped in bloody bandages. I am also wearing the tattered remains of my pants, which is a pleasant surprise. Considering the treatment of other prisoners, I wasn't expecting to be left any clothes.

"Those are lovely tattoos, although hardly fitting of a lady like yourself," the man in the room says as I examine myself. I hold the cuffs in front of the magic circle, although if anyone was going to notice the runes, they already have. "Did you need to get them so extensively? The doctors say you even have some on your tits," he complains, and I only respond with a closed-mouth, sarcastic smile. It's a good sign he isn't asking about my circle. Over the years I have tattooed nearly my entire torso as a way of disguising them. I even had tattoos added between each rune, depicting everything from Earth text to references I drew from pop culture.

A keen eye will likely notice the runes and may discern the circle among them, but if no one versed in the design of such things examines me, this will work in a pinch. I don't expect to be here long, in any case. Of course, it's possible he already knows about it, but I might as well obscure it until I know for sure. This man's aura bends space in the same way as Godfrey's and there is no mistaking who he is.

"Is there something I can do for you, *Your Majesty*? Aside from discussing my tits, I mean. I have heard that's one of the few topics you understand, but part of me always hoped it was an exaggeration."

The king's smile sours in an instant. "You will watch your tongue, you ungrateful whore!"

I roll my eyes, then hold up my bound wrists. "Or what, you'll have me arrested? Executed? How exactly do you plan to make the consequences of being mean to you sound scarier than those for murdering all your friends? No wonder this took so fucking long."

"You are right," he says with a smirk. "I am going to have you executed. Tomorrow afternoon, in front of the entire city. But that gives us all night. I have put many women in their place with a single night."

"You're not going to do that." I chuckle. "You're not going to do that, because you have heard the rumors. The monster who can kill with a single touch—that's me. You may not believe it. You may think it's just the commoners spreading nonsense. But . . . you also spent three years wasting your knights and guards protecting yourself and your friends instead of looking for me. Because even with all your power, all your mana and authority, you are a coward." I lean forward, not far enough to reach the bars but enough to indicate an offer. "So go ahead. Touch me. Find out if it's true. I dare you."

His smirk twists at my taunts. "I can leave you locked in here all night with a dozen knights. See how proud you are in the morning. We'll see how true those rumors are then, won't we?"

"You are welcome to leave them locked in here with me," I say, "but I hear you've had something of a high . . . turnover rate these last few years. Are you sure you can spare the manpower?"

"Where are the slaves?" he asks instead of answering my joke. "How are you moving around the city so quickly? How exactly are you killing with a touch? How did my brother make you so powerful so quickly?"

I give him a blank stare.

"You are really good at this. You should quit your day job and run interrogations instead."

"You're right. I'm not so good at this, am I? But—and maybe you missed this—I have a lot of friends. We'll get the information out of you," he answers before clapping his hands. A moment later, I hear a steel door slam shut, and a wiry man with a sack on his head appears, a belt full of unique knives and bottles around his waist. Again the king grins, and again I roll my eyes.

"Better hope your friend is quick. Pro tip. When torturing someone, don't tell them they have a public execution scheduled for the next day. Having an end in sight really ruins the effect," I advise.

His face falls.

"I'm the king, you stupid bitch. I can schedule your execution for whenever I want."

"No, you really can't. You are barely the king. Your negligence has left your entire court whispering about putting someone else in charge. You need to kill me. You need to do it publicly, and you need to do it quickly. You have to prove you are the king in front of all of them, especially since so many of the supporters you have left lost their daughters last night. But by all means, delay it. It'll make my job all that much easier," I say.

"You underestimate me. Godfrey has inflated your ego beyond sustainability. And, you idiot, you've all but admitted you did this to make Godfrey king, which means even if a day of torture isn't enough, Godfrey will have the answers your corpse fails to provide. Perhaps I'm not so bad at this after all," he says, smiling. I narrow my eyes at him, and while still feeling victorious, he stands and moves to leave. "Make sure she suffers," he orders. Just before rounding the corner the wiry man came from, he stops.

"They are calling you the Mage of Mourning, you know. The name started spreading just last night. Some say it's because of the carnage you leave in your wake, but my sources tell me you have actually aspected grief. You empower yourself by crying. How like a woman," he says before leaving.

The man he left behind opens the door to my cell and enters. He pulls a long, serrated steel blade from his belt and his raspy voice breaks the new silence. "You may want to tell me what the king wants to know," he advises. "I promise you it will be easier. You won't be killing me with a touch, I can promise you that. Where have you been hiding the slaves?" He presses the blade to my cheek, gently enough that it only draws a single drop of blood. That's all I need.

I course electricity mana through my body and it crackles through my veins like a furious river. It materializes as electricity at the point of contact and flows through the blade and into the man. His entire body tenses up as I electrocute him. I roll my eyes lazily as he fails to pull the knife away. A moment later, I release the spell and he collapses to the floor.

As the corpse of my torturer soils itself, I lean against the wall and wait for my next visitor.

CHAPTER SIXTY-SIX

We Are Not Afraid of Ruins

I hear the door swing closed again and open my eyes, raising my head to greet my newest guest. There have been a few attempts to extract knowledge from me. While the king was apparently too terrified by the death of his subordinate to send another, the temple is far more stubborn. I didn't have the opportunity to kill every divine priest who visited me, but a few got close enough to the bars that I could dispose of them without revealing my access to mana despite the shackles. The rumors about my deadly touch certainly don't hurt in that regard.

It is the bodies of my two most recent interrogators that Godfrey examines with clear bemusement before stepping over them and taking what had been the king's seat and focusing his attention on me. "So. The Mage of Mourning, huh?" he asks. "You've caused quite the trouble for me, Lillith."

"You know me," I intone, "I can get a bit persnickety."

He chuckles before pulling out a wineskin and taking a deep drink.

"Persnickety indeed. You know my brother is out for my head as much as yours? He has a rope fitted for the both of us. You made a mess like I've never seen last night, alone," he complains.

"Got any to spare?" I ask instead of responding. He scoffs, then pulls out a second wineskin and tosses it through the bars. I pick it up with my bound hands and begin inspecting it with mana, just in case. Satisfied there is no poison, I take a swig to numb the pain in my chest. "So he wants you dead because of me. Yet here you are, sitting on the other side of the bars, visiting me as a free man. You don't seem nearly as worried as your words imply," I observe.

"You are one to talk." He laughs. "A bath and a new dress and no one would know you were awaiting execution. Got something left up your sleeve?" I shrug.

"I can't help being hot. It's a curse. Really, I'm downright catatonic," I say before taking another drink.

"I can see that. Barely holding it together, even now. Nevertheless"—he leans forward—"just in case you do have some trick to get out of this, I want to warn you. Things may not go as you are hoping. Because you are right. Here I am, a free man." He spreads his arms wide. "The king can't arrest me because I have far more support than he does, thanks to you. That's a little shakier now, considering my public connection to the killer I was 'protecting' people from, but it's not gone."

I rest my good forearm on my thigh and raise an eyebrow.

"That's odd, I don't remember you doing much of anything to protect anyone from me."

"I knew who you would be after." He shrugs. "It was easy enough to create the illusion." So he's known it was me all along.

"What was it that clued you in? Baldwin? Or was it the story about being attacked on the road? I should've known. How was I supposed to know this country didn't follow any rules that make sense?" I groan.

He scoffs before taking another drink.

"It doesn't matter. What matters is, I'm as good as king. My brother intends to regain favor using you. Killing you in front of the angry rabble and tying your name to mine. But it won't be enough. He was too apathetic for too long. It won't work, but it will . . . make things a bit more difficult," he says.

"So," I respond, "what exactly do you want from me? I'm afraid I don't do political endorsements. I have an image to maintain, after all."

He laughs again. "Nothing so crass. I want to maintain the relationship we have always had. A Danish, a quip, and a deal. It's worked for us before; no reason it can't work now," he says. I take another drink and maintain eye contact, inviting him to continue. "I can get you out of here, Lillith. I don't know what you have planned, but . . . you don't stand a chance against my brother. Father Medici either. You are dead if you make it to the gallows tomorrow morning. I can get you out of here. Keep you alive. It'll even undermine the king's attempts to regain favor."

"In exchange for . . . ?" I press.

He leans forward again.

"You are right in a lot of ways. Potestia needs change. Magic needs to be shared. There is no reason to rely on slave labor when mages could move us forward like never before. We have been fools for thousands of years to ignore that fact. I can make that world happen, Lillith. As king I can build a country without slaves." I don't reply, and after a long silence, he continues. "But a country needs people, Lillith. And progress needs a lot of people. I need to know where they are. The slaves. The professors. Everyone you have squirreled away. I need their help to build a better world, and if you're dead, well, you certainly won't be doing it."

I take a deep drink of the wine before I answer. "What if they don't want to build something new with you? What if they don't want to come back?" I ask.

"Lillith." His jaw sets. "You must know that what you are doing . . . there is no future in it. You are destroying what stands, and I understand why, but you have to build something in its place, or that's all you are doing. Destroying. All you have done is crush the pillars of the country and watch it fall. That's going to make lives worse, not better. Please. Tell me where I can find them, and I can do what you are failing to. I can look forward."

I respond with a humorless laugh. "It's funny, how that always works. How people with comfortable homes and money and security respond to the threat of losing it all. You don't have a chain around your neck, Godfrey. It's all too easy to say, *You are doing more harm than good* while all you are picturing is your own comforts disappearing. But what have I been doing that threatens everything so much? Freeing slaves. Giving women a place to flee from abusive marriages. Do you see the problem? The inherent complaint hidden behind the demands for a replacement system before dismantling the old one?" His face hardens, but I don't give him a chance to answer.

"It's easy to say to me, from your seat on the other side of those bars," I continue. "But what you are saying isn't as benevolent as it sounds. I believe you believe it is. But under the thin layer of empathy is the ugly truth. You are looking in the face of the battered and bruised. The beaten-down man whose blood supports this country. You are staring them in the eye and saying, *Hang in there. Keep suffering. Keep bleeding for me. You'll be free from all this . . . as soon as I find a way to stay comfortable while I do it.* No. That's bullshit. Any plan you have that requires people to continue suffering under slavery when you could free them is no plan at all. It's just self-congratulation."

Godfrey lets a deep breath out his nose. "Pretty words. Very eloquent, Lillith. But that's all they are. The world is what it is, and you can't make changes while ignoring reality. The reality is we need something in place or people die. People suffer. And it will be your fault when that happens. Your high fucking horse isn't going to make anyone's life better. Not the slaves', not anyone's. If you want them to have a better life, tell me where they are. I can offer them real change, not a brief breath of fading freedom."

"You're wrong," I say. "I am building something new. No, that's wrong too. *We* are building something new. Something better. And no one had to keep supporting the weight of the bloated wealthy class to get there. No one needed to wait with a boot on their neck. It's not a world you could ever imagine. Sometimes it's closer, sometimes it's not. But it's better. It's just a world with no kings. Not you, not this rebel leader, and not your brother. The world you know is going to burn, Godfrey. It's going to be terrifying, and a lot of people used to the comforts of the old world will suffer, but only from withdrawal. They will suffer from losing luxuries and familiarity. This country is going to fall. But, if you don't mind a few stolen words, we are not afraid of ruins. We carry a better world in our hearts."

"Lillith. That's not happening. Tomorrow, without my help, you are going to die, and all your friends are going to lose their leader." His voice turns to a snarl. "Because you are stubborn. Because you are arrogant. Because you are so certain your fantasies can be real, you were willing to start a fire you could never douse on your own. But I can. I can give them all a better life. They won't be slaves when I find them. They will be the first commoner mages. The bedrock of a stronger kingdom than the world has ever seen. All you have to do is let go of your pride and trust me. I can offer you a world we can both be proud of!"

"Leader?" I scoff. "They have no leader. They don't need me. An organizer? Maybe. Someone to help provide direction in crisis? Perhaps. But that's not what you mean when you say *leader*. I'm not anyone's leader, not the kind with a crown on their head and threats sliding off their tongue like sugar. I'm a spear. Yeah, it'll be harder without me, but they'll be fine. Everything I know is recorded; they'll find a new spear, and they don't need a 'leader.'"

"Everyone needs a leader, Lillith," he responds. "People will always be people, and people naturally need someone to lead them. If you think the people you 'saved' don't consider you their leader, you are kidding yourself. A snake without a head is just a shuddering body. It's the way of the world. Neither of us can change that."

I roll my eyes. "Do you know what an alpha wolf is?" I ask, and his face tightens in confusion. "I didn't think you would. I haven't been able to find a single reference to the idea here. The phrase comes from . . . a place where people used to capture wolves and study their behavior. They noticed one wolf would often take a position of authority of sorts. They would have bloody fights for leadership. One wolf, the alpha, would become the natural leader of the pack through strength and teeth. The observation reached public knowledge, and everyone believed that's simply how wolves worked. Alphas were often used as a metaphor for leadership. Insecure men even started claiming the name for themselves."

Godfrey looks perplexed as he says, "That just proves my point, Lillith."

I shake my head.

"You'd think, but that's the thing. They were wrong. The wolves they studied only behaved that way in captivity. Later, when they began to observe the wolves in the wild, they didn't fight for pack leadership. The 'alpha wolf' was a myth. The packs worked more like families. It was captivity, an unnatural state for them, that created the 'alpha' as a concept. So yes. You can observe people in captivity. You can corral them and put a collar on them and say *This is natural* while forcing them to their knees. Maybe ten years later, maybe a thousand, and you can have them saying it too. *This is natural.* But it's not. It's just a false observation from keeping us captive. That's why you need me to tell you where they are. Because they don't need a leader, and that's exactly what you are afraid of," I finish.

It's Godfrey's turn to roll his eyes.

"More pretty words. More speeches that can be boiled down to *I'm right, and I won't see reason.* We aren't wolves, Lillith. We are people. We have complex minds and emotions. We all have different visions of the world, and we'll trample over each other without direction. Someone has to provide direction. The best we can hope for is a kind direction provided by someone who cares. I am asking you to give me an opportunity to provide that. You want a better world? Well, one of us is the leader who's going to bring us there, whether you admit it or not. And honestly, Lillith, a leader with no direction isn't going to cut it," he says.

"You underestimate people, Godfrey. Someday, you'll see a world without a king. A world where people are people, not dogs. But I can't tell you where they are, don't you see that? Because you believe people must have a leader. You believe it is natural. But for people to have natural authority, some people have to naturally belong in authoritative roles and others must naturally belong as their lessers. This whole theory is how we get nobles standing on the backs of commoners. Men on the throats of women.

"I've heard hundreds of versions of *some people are superior to others* and they are all shit. They all lead to the same place, even when started with good intentions. *People naturally need authority* always, always means *some people are naturally inferior*. I'm sorry, Godfrey. I like you. I like you as much as I can, for someone in your position. But I can't trust you," I say.

The air is heavy with silence as Godfrey examines me.

"So, even until the end, that's your answer? Lillith, you are mad. But it's a madness I understand. You are wrong. You are equating two things that just aren't the same. More than anything, you are a leader. And if you won't let me help them, well, I understand they need someone. That's why, even though you are so stubborn and can't see the forest through the trees, I'll still help you. I checked your home, but your family is already gone, as are your friends," he says. I feel a small spike of grief enhancing my mana. He stands and unlocks the cell, swinging the door open. "No one will stop you if you flee now. You can make it out of here and live to fight another day. In exchange . . . think about what I said. I want to heal the world, just like you do."

He walks toward the hall to leave, then pauses. "I like you too, Lillith. You were never my apprentice, I can see that now. But you have been a friend, of a sort."

I listen as he walks down the halls and the steel door fails to close behind him.

I push myself to my feet, using force mana where my broken arm and shackles prevent my arms from supporting me. I shamble over to the cell door and push it shut, allowing it to lock in place. I then return to my stone seat and take another drink of wine.

CHAPTER SIXTY-SEVEN

Lillith Must Hang

Galen

It's a cold morning. Far colder than any I would usually venture into, but I refuse to miss this. I can't miss this. I owe it to my daughter. I owe it to Liora. She was a good girl. A sweet, innocent girl. She was almost done with school. I'd arranged for a better marriage than she could have hoped for on her own and with her figure. All she needed to do was improve a few grades. But she never got the chance.

They wouldn't let most parents see the bodies. Many of my friends protested this furiously, but . . . I know better. I was one of the first knights at the scene when that . . . monster slaughtered them. I see them, all of them, every time I close my eyes. Liora was one of the . . . easiest to look at, Collector forgive me. She was impaled. Her head, hanging backward and staring in horror . . . it follows me everywhere I go. If some of the other fathers saw their girls . . . what this fucking "Mage of Mourning" did to them . . . Well, they should be glad they are being denied.

This morning's cold bites my skin and even the breeze howls, but it's only proper. Because this morning, they are executing Lillith of Endings. Duke Godfrey's little pet. The square around the gallows bursts at the seams with nobles eager to see the death of the Mage of Mourning. Not just fathers like myself either. The little bitch has been hunting us for sport for years now. Killing us in our own homes. Stealing our property and leaving our bodies to rot.

I requested the honor of pulling the lever myself. Removing the floor from beneath her feet and listening to the snap of her neck as it's broken by the rope. But I wasn't the only one to request it. It was apparently a popular fantasy, being the one to take her life. I lost out to a far more important noble. Lord Urian Cavendish. Lady Jocelyn's father. He has as much right as I do, considering the unrecognizable state Jocelyn's body was found in. They'd only identified her by the aspects in her blood and by her dress.

Still, I grit my teeth. He may have as much right as I do, but I still lament that I wasn't chosen. But it doesn't matter. What matters is, in less time than it will take me to walk home, Lillith will hang. My wife sniffles beside me, unable to face the murderer with the dignity our daughter deserves, and I scowl. I dig my nails into my palms as I wait.

King Donatello marches onto the platform first, followed by Father Medici of the temple. The old wood creaks beneath their feet and the silent anticipation of the crowd ensures it is heard.

"Lords and ladies," the king announces, his voice projected by an enchanted lapel, "for too long have you been forced to live in fear. Unable to safely sleep in your own beds and denied the labor to manage your properties. Many have said a monster stalked the streets of our beautiful city, with fangs, tentacles, and the strength of ten men. Some have, unjustly, blamed my dear friend Father Medici for the beast's continued existence. Others have doubted me and my use of the magic knights during this crisis.

"But there was no beast. No monster. There was no sick thing that escaped the Collector's control. Only a girl, elevated beyond her station by a foolish old man. Nothing to fear, not really. A commoner child and first-generation mage. What tricks she used to dispose of the powerful nobles, I'll never know. Perhaps she used tools provided by my senile brother. Perhaps he helped her all along. This is being investigated, and indeed it has been uncovered he helped her kill the lord of Satusmor before bringing her here. If he is guilty of such crimes, the Collector's judgment will find him, as it is finding his apprentice this morning." The king pauses for effect and I have to cover a scoff.

It feels like the entire world is shaking with my rage. Duke Godfrey's apprentice may be the murderer, but no one is fooled. The king hid. The knights know it better than anyone. He hoped to let this killer eliminate his detractors while he protected his allies. The man is as responsible as his brother. As I scowl, the king continues.

"Yes," he cries as if he feels wounded, "many thought of me as a fool. A coward. But I have been neither. For the foul deeds have been ended. The killer herself, Lillith of Endings, is here today!" At that, he waves his arm, directing our attention to the steps on the right of the platform. Climbing up the stairs is the woman in question. She wears filthy, bloody bandages binding her wounded chest and torn, spattered pants. A hood covers her head and she is surrounded by a half dozen knights, each holding their sword to her. She is being pulled by a chain shackled to her neck and her hands are in manacles behind her. The earth seems to tremble again as everyone recoils at the disgusting tattoos painting the killer's nearly bare torso.

"Don't worry." The king laughs at the growing disquiet. "She is thoroughly restrained with mana-dispersal chains. My doctors have also examined her pathetic endoaspect and a circle has been devised to prevent her from casting anything powerful. If that somehow fails, I will kill her myself. Lillith of Endings dies today," he cries, and for the first time, the audience explodes. The world shakes with the cries for justice.

"Lillith must hang!" I call, adding my voice to the cacophony of demands for her blood. She is marched to the center of the gallows. A hesitant knight removes the steel restraint from her neck and pulls off her hood. Greasy black hair falls over one eye and a long scar mars the other. Her ruby eyes fix on the knight as he slides the noose over her head. She bites at him, not in earnest but in an almost playful way. As the man startles and jumps back, the bitch smiles. She fucking smiles. That rumbling returns and I fix her with one of hundreds of cold stares. "Lillith must hang," I repeat through gritted teeth.

"Lillith of Endings, Mage of Mourning. You are charged with mass murder, treason, and theft of national assets. For this I, King of Potestia and chosen of the Collector, sentence you to death. If you have any final words, speak them now," the king commands. No. The bitch doesn't deserve to say her piece. Pull the fucking lever and let her swing.

"Hang her!" I protest, and dozens of voices join mine. "Lillith must hang!" The stones beneath us groan at the injustice, but we are ignored. Her words are quiet. So quiet, none of us should be able to hear them. Our own cries should drown them out, but each whisper tickles our ears, able to be parsed even among the shouts all around us. I see no mana from her, and the contradiction sends a chill through my bones.

"You leave your labor to slaves. Your grand mansions, your fields, and your meals. You use forced labor for all of it. Tending to your extravagant gardens and disposing of your shit. I wouldn't be surprised if you forced slaves to wipe your asses for you; I already know you use them to tend to your cocks. You claw your way to comfort through their efforts and rely on them so much . . . you have no idea what to do with yourselves without them. You have fucking magic, for Christ's sake. This should not be that hard. Still, you lean on forced labor instead." The words slither into my ears, and my eyes bulge.

"Please, dear Mage of Mewling, beg us all for forgiveness!" the king says, and my head snaps to him in shock. Then I realize the problem. Lillith's mouth isn't moving. She is glaring at all of us, but her lips are shut. Somehow, despite the shackles, she is speaking to us with mana. Mana we can't see. And the king can't hear it.

"You leave teaching to women, of course," she continues. "Teaching, cleaning, and even healing. Any kind of service you don't trust slaves with. All the education in your fucking kingdom is handled by women. Most of your medicine is as well. Then you take them home and tell them you own them too. You deny them their own names; you beat them. You treat them like objects to be used. Prized horses for breeding. All while saddling them with the burden of some of the most important bedrocks of your society. Because, well, they are positions of caretaking, and that's what women do." The whispers lecture while their owner's eyes cut through the crowd like knives.

"HANG HER!" I demand with the rest of the crowd. "PULL THE FUCKING LEVER!" The world continues to shake. It's not my rage, the earth is literally rumbling; it's become unmistakable.

"Now that you have fewer slaves to remind you how to breathe . . . nobody to pull your damn britches up and pick your fucking nose on your behalf . . . now that all your whipping boys have gone missing . . . you look for more. You charge your citizens more to live than you allow them to make with labor, then you arrest them when they can't pay. You walk through the common and poor parts of your cities and you pick out your new toys like candies in a glass display," she snarls in our ears while her lips remain tightly sealed.

"This is your last chance, Lillith of Endings. You are very close to exemplifying your family name. Speak now, or leave for the third plane in silence," the king orders.

I want to climb to the platform and pull the lever myself. Lillith. Must. Hang. But I stumble into the man next to me as the shaking of the earth grows more persistent.

"A boy tries to play by your rules. He goes to your school. Uses your stuck-up titles. Learns your bullshit history. But he wants to feel comfortable in his own skin. Just in a small way. So he dresses the part. He cuts his hair. Nothing serious. He just lives his life in a way that makes sense to him, all while following all your other bullshit rules. All while letting you hate him. Letting you spit on him and beat him, refusing to so much as ask for help. And what do you do? You try to kill him for his crimes. No, you send your daughters to kill him for his crimes. Then you try to hang me for stopping them," she growls, vitriol scratching at our ears.

I don't care anymore. Lillith must hang. The earth's trembling has become violent. I am pushing my way through the crowd when the king finally begins to give the order. They speak at the same time. "Well, if you have no final words, then die in peace," the king says, nodding to Lord Urian. Urian tries to pull the lever, but it won't budge. Again, there is no mana around it, but it pushes back against him. Meanwhile, the whispers continue.

"You have balanced this whole country on the backs of commoners, slaves, women. Everyone you deemed your lessers. But now they aren't yours anymore. Your whips have lost their sting. Your claws have grown dull and your cages have broken. Your priests have lost control of the people and everything you count on to stay comfortable is sliding from beneath your feet. Every weapon you use to control us will be turned against you. Every sharp word and indignity you thought gave you power will be the source of your nightmares. The leash you have led us on? We are going to strangle you with it."

At this she gives the king a toothy grin.

"Your Majesty, I'd like to speak my final words now," she says as several knights join Lord Urian and all of them start using mana to push on the unyielding lever. Father Medici cries out orders and priests start to climb onto the stage. The world is crying out that Lillith must hang! Members of the crowd are falling as the city shakes in rage. The Collector's wrath has gripped this square and it trembles beneath him; can't they feel it up there? Just manually unlatch the damn door, you fools! Lillith must hang!

The king looks at the filth and sneers. "Fine. Say your words. Then you are dying whether that lever moves or not," he orders.

Her grin widens before she speaks. "Fucking eat me, you worthless creep," she cackles, then everything changes. Her arms appear in front of her as her manacles clatter to the wood beneath her feet. My face pales and the king's mirrors it. Then the ground erupts. Earth, stone, and splinters from the gallows fly into the air and I fall. I can't make out what's happening. I have to claw my way through the struggling crowd just to regain my feet. When I do, my eyes widen even further.

A massive tree stands where the back half of the gallows once did. It splits the sky, surpassing the city walls in height. Its width cracks the stone buildings on either side of the wood platform. Had it appeared a hundred paces closer, we would all be dead but . . . its trunk stands mere inches from the killer's back. Like it was aimed. By the time I regain focus, Lillith is one of two people still standing, as if she expected it and used mana to keep her position. The gallows is in ruins and everyone else who had been standing on it is struggling to dig their way through the rubble.

My daughter's killer has one hand wrapped around the king's forearm. Another woman stands next to her, her grimacing face a battleground of burns and boils like I have never seen. Her arm is extended into . . . long ropes that wrap around Father Medici. Her other hand is clasped tightly with Lillith's, and together they touch the trunk of the tree and . . . vanish.

The killer. The monster. The king. The father. All of them are gone.

CHAPTER SIXTY-EIGHT

Rest in Piss

I stand in the Radiant Woods again, Sara's hand clasped tightly against mine. The massive tree she grew in the middle of the city stands here as well, but our surroundings have changed. I have been through this thousands of times now, traveling between hundreds of safe houses across Potestia. Typically, we don't linger for more than a breath. It's too dangerous, especially when we are moving groups of people. A blink and Sara will move us from one entrance to the other. Before the woods can sink their divine teeth into their minds.

This time is different, however. This time, we brought prey.

The king scrambles away from me while Sarafyna drops Father Medici. I wanted to kill them right away when we got here, but Sara's divine magic pulsing into me takes all my attention. She wants to heal me before we fight. A quick kill may be easier, but it's also riskier. My heart may not be pumping, but blood still runs through it. The wound is a distraction. Fortunately, with a few extra years of mana under my belt, I have even more to enhance. My mana is like a sun preparing to burst.

Sara is more powerful as well when she is here. Her control over the space around us is one thing, but the Radiant Woods also seem to respond to her like an extension of her body. Their power enforces hers. So as we work together to heal my wounds, the broken arm she is holding snaps back into place and the bones stitch together. It's a strange feeling, healing this quickly. Almost like cracking my knuckles while they are submerged in mud. The thick yet sharp feeling reverberates through my body and my chest itches as the festering wound knits itself together.

All in all, the healing process takes no longer than it did for Baldwin, and I am in fighting shape before our opponents can even process the sequence of events that led them here. Truth be told I wouldn't mind some boots or a clean pair of underwear, but I can kill a king while barefoot. I'll send this creep off in a way that would make John McClane proud. The two men carry their own tension, with the king's eyes bugging out and Medici scowling. Medici is the first to speak.

"Do you really think you can beat me here? Of all places? You brought the highest priest of the Collector to the Radiant Woods and you think you stand a chance? You are fools," he chides us. Donatello's eyes bulge when he hears where we are, and I give him a sweet, innocent smile.

"You think we brought you here?" Sara responds coldly. "You think this is a place I chose? You have a shorter memory than I do. You picked this hell for us when I was a child. A fourteen-year-old girl. You sent me here for defying you. You already tried to use it against me. Do you think I'm afraid of it now?"

Medici's eyes widen. They flick to her long auburn hair, and I see a spark of recognition. "Demon . . ." he whispers, and I scoff.

Donatello can't handle being ignored any longer at this point and finally joins the conversation.

"You arrogant little bitch," he sneers, his hands literally trembling with fury. "You think you can bring me, the Collector-damned king, here? Do you think you can actually trap me? Fight me? Snuffing the light out of your eyes will be as easy here as it would have been on the gallows."

It's finally my turn. "I don't mean to diminish your threat or anything—it was very menacing, really," I retort, "but I thought it should be mentioned, you didn't actually have that great of a go of it on the gallows."

His face turns bright red and he flares his nostrils at me.

"Your tongue won't save you here. It's high time someone showed you what gives kings the right to rule," he snaps, then releases his aura in full. It's oppressive. For a moment, I feel like Atlas with the entire world pressing down on me. The fatigue of an unbearably hot day tries to pull me down and force me to kneel in front of this man. I refuse. Instead, I simply hold two fingers up to my lips in a V and waggle my tongue through it for a moment. The obscene gesture may be lost on the king, but his expression makes it clear the inherent disrespect is not. Then I release my own aura.

Here in the Radiant Woods where thousands of years of grief saturates every blade of grass and hovers in the air like fog, my aura is a tempest. Instead of the all-encompassing pressure the king exerted, my mana lashes out in rage, crashing into him like hail and fire. He may not be able to perceive it with sight, but the impact of pure mana against his flesh has a clear and immediate effect. It envelops his aura and his threat all at once.

I feel the itch of either the woods or Medici trying to worm their way into my mind, but I have nothing to worry about. Medici never stood a chance. Even if his abilities worked on Sara and me, he would need to keep them up constantly to prevent the power of the woods from washing his control away. The king and the priest act at the exact same time.

I have to jump away from Sara as wood mana from the priest causes thick branches to erupt and bind her. At the same time, some unidentifiable mana fills the air with gas that burns my eyes and throat. The king responds in his own unique way, and one I should have expected the moment he met an opponent he couldn't overpower in an instant. He does what he has been doing in response to everything else I have done for years. He turns on his heel and runs. I roll my eyes, and Sara solves both problems for us at once. The scenery changes in an instant. The thick trees and junglelike environment give way to a field of spider lilies.

The king is still looking behind him as he runs, unable to adapt to everyone's new position, as I stand in front of him and swing my fist. I make contact easily and hear a crunch as his skull collapses from the impact. He flies through the clearing, and Sara, her tentacles again pulling Medici, intercepts his body with the priest's. I am almost shocked at how easy the fight was, until both bodies begin to rapidly heal. I had expected as much with Medici, but fucking Don? As the sky begins to storm, I realize my mistake. Just as the church keeps the king in power, the woods must want him alive. He is being healed by the environment.

Sara shifts us again to get away from the assault from the sky. We are now standing on a riverbed with two lines of trees on either side of us. Well, three of us are. Sara's clothes are in a pile near the father, who is now looking frantically around. He tries to fill the air with poison again, but it's too easy for me to filter with air mana. I don't worry about him. If Sara is missing, she is already on it. Instead, I focus on the terrified king. He is forming a powerful spell with a copper tint to the mana. I haven't seen it before but it looks familiar.

Outside the woods, it would have crushed me. Left me as a grease stain on the stones of the city. Here, as I realize what he is doing, I laugh. Pressure bears down on me like I am being pulled to the earth. That's why it's familiar; his mana is similar to my own. Gravity mana tries to grind me into the dirt like an insect, but it's easily countered. I intercept it with force mana before its pressure can increase, and while the plants in the area are flattened in a circle, I and the area around me are untouched.

Medici, however, isn't so lucky. For two men supposedly responsible for holding a country together, the two do not cooperate well. Medici's bones crack and heal repeatedly under the pressure of the king's spell, and it's not long before divine magic ends the attack on me without my having to lift a finger. I take advantage of the brief pause, however, and lightning flies from my hands. The scream of the thunder echoes through the woods as the king's flesh pops and fries at the point of contact. He is thrown from his feet, and I turn to threaten Medici with a bolt of his own.

Predicting this, he throws up a wall of wood, more as concealment than cover. I grin. Funny how easy it is to forget a missing opponent. He appears at one edge of the wall with a new spell prepped, its aspect unfamiliar to me. It fails to form and he immediately begins to scream as the ground starts to swallow him. Or rather, Sara does. She is currently closer to the form she had been in when I met her, and Medici's leg is currently dissolving in her gelatinous flesh.

I don't have time to admire the trap, as Donatello heals from my earlier attack and fire tries to devour me where I stand. I roll my eyes as I suffocate it with air mana before it can touch me. "Why is it always fire?" I ask out loud as I send lightning through the flames and strike the king a second time. I allow Sara to cover my back as I send another, and another, and another. The king screams as he heals, but he heals nonetheless. Looks like we are going to need to take a . . . French approach to this. I am forming a steel great ax with mana when howling from all directions distracts me. Looking around, I see we are surrounded by residents of the woods again.

The Radiant Woods have been keeping them away from us ever since I managed to help heal Sara, but it seems to be growing desperate. It's no matter. As I expect, I find myself in an entirely different part of the woods, this time surrounded by a curious mix of palm trees and cacti. Medici has stopped screaming, and a quick glance reveals a branch from a palm tree wrapping itself around his waist and pulling him up. His legs are bloody stumps, dripping onto the flesh that is Sarafyna. The king is trying to run again, but I still take a moment to crush the tree with force mana, forcing the father face first into the acidic skin below.

At the same time, I grab the king with my force mana and yank. He flies toward me, crying in outrage. This is one indignity too many, apparently. I see the moment when he decides fleeing won't work and directs all his prodigious mana at me at once. Compared to his previous attacks, simple distractions, this is far more dangerous. No pathetic flamethrower or gravity hammer this time. This time he uses wind, stone, and steel together. He has quite a few aspects for a resident of this world. I have to fly for the first time as a massive tornado descends on the woods. Razor-sharp stones fly through the air at breakneck speeds and I can't avoid them all, not while fighting the force of the wind coming from unpredictable directions.

As I consider the best counter for this, I briefly reflect that I'm glad Medici is a far weaker mage than the king. Then I see the mana. It's hard to spot among all the wind, but the king is trying to fly into the sky. It must be difficult with pure wind mana, but I suppose he can't be incompetent at everything.

"SHIFT!" I cry out, and a second later we are all in a new area, full of tall redwoods and pine trees. The dangerous whirlwind is missing and the king is struggling to maintain his direction as he ascends. This is how I escaped Sara in the past, so I don't want to let him get too far. I summon more lightning and it tears from the ground to the clouds above, passing through him as it does.

He falters and falls, but begins healing quickly. A massive amount of gravity mana precedes him, heading directly for Sara and Medici. It is far more powerful than the first one he used on me, enough to kill anything below it in an instant. Now that he is committed to ending the fight without escape, he isn't holding back. He has directed everything to offense. I throw force mana to protect Sara and it intercepts his attack just in time. But he is powerful. Powerful enough that, even in my boosted state, I have to struggle to hold it back. Then he shifts his attack at the last moment. I can physically feel the release of his spell as my force mana shoots up, harmlessly, into the sky.

He conjures a massive stone platform above me, plated with steel spikes on the bottom. Medici, finally free from Sara and half healed from his struggle, tries to bind me in place with his vines again. This is much slower than before as Sara has taken much of his mana for herself. As I look between him and the rapidly descending death from above, I shrug and pull him toward me with force. He screams and the stone stops in place above us. "Thanks, sport," I greet him as he makes it to my side. I think he is scowling, but he is so badly burned it's impossible to tell. In any case, I've forced the king to stop his desperate attack.

As the stone starts moving again, I realize where Sara is. She left Medici to help me. I remember how she flew from tree to tree while pursuing me, and the screaming descending from the sky tells me she has done it again. We shift again and the stone in the sky is gone. We are in an open field of thorns, and I spot Sara and the king flying directly to the ground. He had very little control while flying and her added weight in addition to the pain of her touch has sent them both downward. I don't waste any time. I force Medici to the ground and stomp on his skull, crushing it in a moment, then send force mana to catch my friend.

The king collides with the forest floor and I pin him down with steel spikes and smother him with my mana before he can heal from the impact. The world shifts again and we are back at the river bed, my victim still pinned down. The king is trying to push back and he almost succeeds, but I am far more powerful. Sara is reshaping into her human form, inside her previously discarded clothes, which is impressive. It takes nearly all my mana to keep Donatello from casting, but I have a little to spare. I begin conjuring my ax again, this time uninterrupted.

I pant as the handle forms in one hand and Donatello's eyes widen in panic. "W-wait, I can make you queen! You can rule everything, even me if you want to! I-I'll do anything, just stop!" he begs.

I take a deep breath as the ax finishes.

When I respond, I do so in English. Partially to maintain the poetry of my words, and partially as a message to the woods around me. If they understand my native language, I hope they understand this.

"Rest in piss, Your Majesty. You won't be missed."

Then I swing the completed great ax with one arm and sever his head in a single blow. There is no healing from that, and it's apparent the woods aren't going to try as his head rolls to the side and his body releases any excrement it had left in it.

"It's over, Sa—" A sharp pain stabs into my back. I look down to see I have been impaled, again. This time by what looks like a passive stinger. I turn and deflect two more from the somehow healed Medici. The pain is agonizing and I have to wonder what fucking aspect this is, but I never get the chance to ask. I hold Medici in place with force and Sara extends an arm with a slobbering, fang-filled mouth on its end.

"Rot in hell!" Sara screams, and Medici has barely a moment to regret attacking instead of fleeing before the teeth close around his neck and leave his corpse to splutter in the grip of my magic. I cough as I release the spell, then fall to my knees. For the second time in a week, blood runs down my chin as white foamy blood spurts from my chest. I feel tearing agony as Sara pulls the stinger from me, a typically terrible idea if she weren't so damn good at healing. As her magic flows through my body, it feels wrong, however, like an injection of bleach. As I look down and see the black lines extending from my wound, I realize why. Poison. Something the magic is struggling to fight.

Well, fuck that. I focus with her, and much like our first meeting, we work together to make things right. This time it's my body that needs healing. I look inward with mana and try to isolate the poison. Vaguely I am aware of the world rapidly shifting around us again. Sara must be protecting us from the woods while she saves me. I focus entirely on the poison. I can feel it, like syrup in a glass of water. It's thick and it doesn't belong. I grip it with my mana. I direct Sara's magic. Together we throttle it. Closing off veins and pushing it until it erupts, like ink, from my wound.

As soon as it is expelled, we shift focus and the blackness recedes from my vision. Again I feel my chest knitting closed and I take a deep breath of air as, both of us drenched in sweat, the wound heals completely.

"Sara," I gasp, and she looks me in the eyes. I become vaguely aware of her hands on each of my cheeks.

"Lily," she responds fondly, and I sigh.

"Get us the fuck out of here, please."

CHAPTER SIXTY-NINE

No, No, That Can't Be Right

As we emerge from the Radiant Woods, we are greeted by the setting sun on a warm beach. I am so glad she chose one of the beaches. Some of the communities we have built are in more wooded or mountainous areas, but I could really use a beach. The sunset indicates we are fairly far from Potestia, which is even better. I suspect I know where we are, but I have to ask just in case. "This is the one Clarrise lives at, yeah?"

She smiles and nods.

"Clarrise and your family, now."

I sigh in relief. I know Sara wouldn't take me to a couple of the other seaside communities while I was this exhausted, but anxiety wouldn't let me rule it out anyway. We have brought people from all over the country to different spots around the world to form communities.

The weapons of our enemies are their downfall. There is no better example of this than the Radiant Woods. The woods that allowed us to build these communities—the hell that taught Sarafyna what she is capable of. She was the first to learn how to use the woods to our advantage: creating beds of flowers to sleep on, growing radiant foliage, finding entrances, and setting up these safe houses across the country. The woods went from being absolute hell to an escape. Sara can take us anywhere in the world in an instant, anywhere the Radiant Woods grow. Potestia had no chance of finding its slaves. We only needed to get them to one of the safe houses, and then Sara could bring them somewhere safe. Somewhere like this. Isolated spots like islands and valleys have always been preferable. Each mostly consists of people from the same city, often from the same household or cellblock. As such, dozens of communities organize in dozens of different ways.

I've done my best to share my ideas with all of them as I can. Horizontal power structures, mutual aid, and the like. The nature of magic circles helps with the latter quite a bit, and it exists in some form across all the communities. But, of course, I am often less than the loudest voice. Many of these people supported each other through decades of misery. That buys more respect than ending it ever could. At least one community keeps ambushing me with arranged marriage proposals. They are trying to set up their own minimonarchy and are convinced I will marry the king of whatever new country replaces Potestia. I have explained again and again that I am no queen and never will be, but they have been struggling to picture a world different than the one they grew up in.

I can't blame them too much; at every point in history, most people thought a better way of doing things would never be found and would always be impossible. They are no different, and they haven't established any silly laws on coming and going or kneeling before their chosen leader, so they aren't a problem yet. Nevertheless, I always get a headache when I go there. Sara and I do, of course, have to go to all of the communities sometimes. They have something of a trade relationship with each other, surpassing Potestian cities by who knows how many years. Nothing predatory at the moment, but they would have a hard time doing that while relying entirely on Sara's monthly visits to manage trade. This isn't sustainable forever, but it's a start. At the very least, all of them have people willing to help me offer a similar life to everyone else in Potestia.

That and communication is far freer between these communities than Potestia's cities. Once I began recruiting different professors and tutors from around Potestia to our way of life, things really started to blow up. Give these little towns a couple of decades and the magical engineering and art they will discover will surpass thousands of years of Potestia's artificial stagnation. Which of course means the Collector or whoever wants each city isolated and in the dark so badly will come after us. But we'll be ready.

Sara has chosen one of my favorite communities. No proposals, no sad little kings, just ideas. Many of them are mine, or came from my original world, but not all. It's a good place and I could not be gladder to finally live here instead of in the fucking city.

"Fuck, I'm exhausted. How are you holding up, Sara?" I ask. "Medici was . . . Well, I know he wasn't your favorite person. Are you doing all right?"

The last time Sara confronted someone directly involved with her . . . banishment, she took a little too much joy in ending the man. It hadn't sat well with her. She still has a lot of anger. A lot of poison that's not her fault, and it very occasionally comes out, contorting the usually kind face of my friend. She looks out across the ocean and stops walking while thinking about the question.

"I'm . . . still me" is her only answer. Her tone carries a note of finality, so I decide not to press her further. She killed Medici quickly once he was pinned. I don't know if she could have killed him sooner or not, but she doesn't have the look of self-loathing I would expect if she had toyed with him. So I look out at the ocean with her in silence. It's almost hard to believe we've made it here. I reach a hand and clasp hers, which she doesn't protest. She may never feel the same way about me like I do about her, but there is clearly a fondness and familiarity we will always share. I also have a bit of a sense that my interest may not be as . . . fruitless as it would be with some other women in this world. But only time will tell.

We begin walking together in silence. I am barefoot and bloody, and my bandages are basically rags doing little more than hanging off any protruding bits, but I am in one piece. We both are. It's a good day.

It's a bit of a walk. There are two sets of woods on this island, the Radiant Woods and a more mundane forest a couple of miles away. As with other communities, we didn't start building directly outside the hell woods. The sand is cool between my toes and the breeze blows through my filthy hair as we walk together. "I don't suppose you told my family to have a bath prepared for me, did you?" I finally ask, breaking the peace. She smiles at me.

"As a matter of fact, I did. A bath and a clean bed," she answers.

"Thank god. A bath and a nap. It has been too long since both, and there is nothing in this world I want more than that," I say. I pause for a moment, then idly lament, "Well, except maybe a roll in the hay. Talk about a dry spell."

She looks at me in confusion.

"A roll in the hay? Is that one of your Earth sayings? What does it mean? Maybe I can help you with that too," she suggests, and I blush. Sarafyna, I would love nothing more than to show you exactly what that means in great detail . . . but I don't suspect you are in the right state of mind to suggest it at the moment.

"Oh, it's just a way to relieve stress. Maybe another time," I answer instead, and she shrugs it off. I've mentioned relationships that don't fit this world's norm a few times, and as with Leo, Sara has been open-minded about the idea, but she has never seemed particularly curious about who I might be interested in, so to speak. Now that we are going to live in a . . . more flexible community, I can finally test the waters a bit. I squeeze her hand at the thought. Then the simple wood homes we are looking for come into view and I let out a contented sigh.

Not long after that, a few silhouettes appear, and it's only a few minutes before my family approaches us. My mother is running, and my brothers are trailing not far behind. I pick up my pace as well and run to meet her, leaving Sara behind me. We meet in a hug and I lift my mother off the ground as we do. "Lily, sweetheart, I was so scared! I know you said you were prepared, but . . . it was so sudden, and Sara rushed us here with very little warning. No one would tell me anything and Sara buried the bit of the woods in the tavern and I forgot your dresses and . . . Lily, what are you wearing??" she finally lands on my appearance, and I laugh. As I put her down, the bandages try to go with her and she rapidly wraps a shawl around me. "My goodness, were you just going to walk into town like that?" she asks, horrified.

"No, Mom, I was gonna take the bandages off first! I don't want to look too dirty, after all."

She gives me a withering look, but as our eyes meet, it melts. It's not . . . as much of a smartass joke as she thinks, but one thing at a time.

"I'm so glad you are home, Lily. I'm so glad you made it. You are going to drive me to an early grave with all this fighting, you know . . ." She picks up a strap of torn, bloody bandage, shudders, then sets her jaw. "Well. To the bath with you," she finally announces, grabbing my hand and pulling me toward one of the nearby buildings. She has been a pretty good sport through all this, and it's not uncommon for her to focus on little things she can improve.

"Wait, Mom, let us say hello too!" Gilbert protests, and she reluctantly pauses.

"Right, well, of course. But your sister is tired, so keep it brief," she orders. Gil holds his hands up to placate her, then wraps me in a hug. He squeezes me a little too tight so I squeeze tighter and he grunts under the pressure.

"Collector be damned, Lillith, take it easy on me, I have a use for that spine!" he says. I laugh.

"You started it! And who is this?" I ask, looking at the woman next to him.

"Uh, hi, I'm Julie," she says, and I hold a hand out, which she looks at in confusion.

"Don't mind my sister, she's a bit eccentric," Gil apologizes before pushing my hand down for me. "Julie is a . . . friend," he answers, and I smirk. Gilbert isn't who he once was but he still loves women. He's had a lot of "friends" lately. The difference is that here, in this little seaside town, it's safe for women to be friends with him in that way. Any parents who try to beat celibacy into them will quickly find themselves in more trouble than their daughters. He is also far more open about it with his partners. I roll my eyes at him.

"A pleasure to meet you, Julie, really." I smile. Then I turn my attention to my other brothers. Ed and Mariah are together as usual. I have seen far less of them lately, since they moved here much earlier than the others. After a once-over of Mariah, a suspicion sparks in my mind. "Congratulations, Ed!" I say, and he hugs me, then pulls back.

"Congratulations? For what?" he asks. I look at Mariah, then at the very slight bump at her waist.

"I'll tell you later," Mariah answers before narrowing her eyes at me in a *you and I are going to have words* way. Oops, I guess she hasn't told him that yet. Well, that will be a fun surprise.

"What? But now I have to know," Ed whines. I chuckle but move on to my final brother. He is holding hands with none other than Autumn. A faint red mark on her neck indicates the two may subscribe to a similar policy as I do on stress relief. Or they have just started rounding the bases, anyway.

"You two look . . . well." I grin, and Henry blushes furiously. Autumn doesn't pick up on my meaning, instead diving headfirst into an apology.

"I'm sorry, Lillith, I didn't know. I didn't know about Leo. I would have told you sooner, I just thought . . . I don't know what I thought, but I'm sorry!" she says, and I cut her off with a hug.

"It's all right, Autumn. I'm glad you are safe. You did the best you could, and if it weren't for you, Leo would have died." At the quiet that greets me in response, I begin to panic and release Autumn from the hug. "Wait, Leo, he's—" I begin, and my mom cuts me off.

"Sh—he's alive. He's all right, he's just . . ." she says, "well. He'll be at dinner tonight. He wants to thank you, but . . . well, he'll be at dinner tonight."

I don't care for the sound of that, but he's alive. He's alive and well enough to attend a family dinner. An anxiety about him begins to nibble at my mind but I push it to the back, deciding to trust my family's judgment.

"Hey, Lil," Henry says, and I pull him into a hug as well. "I was worried about you."

"Thanks. I know it's not much, but . . . it helps me, having people who worry about me," I say.

"All right," Mom announces with a clap of her hands, "it's time to get Lily in the bath, we'll all catch up at dinner; she looks dreadful!"

"Thanks, Mom, you look pretty too," I joke, then pause and look back at Sara. Our eyes meet for a moment and we both offer a gentle smile. Then I turn to join my mother, and Sarafyna turns to greet her own visitor. A young man who has just arrived alongside an older one. Pete runs to hug her as my family did me. I let Sara, Pete, and her father catch up as I finally go to the bath.

When we make it inside and into the washroom, it could be a scene in a cartoon for how quickly my mom pulls off my filthy clothes and gets me in the water. I don't need her help, but she needs to help and I'm happy to have her. She lathers my hair with shampoo, which has thankfully become a far more popular tool since the populace was freed from mind control.

"Can you . . . stay?" Mom asks. "Before your next big plan? Just for a while?" There is a tremble in her voice.

"For a while. I need to see where all the cards land anyway. I'll be here, Mom," I promise, and she sighs in relief.

"Thank the . . . well, thank whoever," she breathes. The bath is quiet for a while and my hair is clean and drying before she speaks again. While she is scrubbing my back, she asks a much more typical question. "So . . . Henry and Autumn are a cute couple, aren't they?" I tense, the tone in her voice warning me of the direction she is going in.

"Yes . . ." I cautiously answer.

"And Mariah hasn't bled in quite a few moons, as far as I know. Ed may be starting a family soon . . ."

"Yes, I saw a bit of a bump earlier, she must be a few months along now . . ." I say, and she sighs again, this time wistfully.

"So . . . I don't suppose you've met any handsome men recently . . . someone to watch your back out there. I know, I know, you don't want to settle down, but that doesn't mean you have to be alone."

I shrug. I haven't exactly been hiding this from my mother, I just . . . My first mother hadn't responded well. I don't want to be surprised by this one doing the same. But earlier . . . earlier she corrected herself and called Leo *he*.

So I figure I might as well take the leap.

"Well, yes, there is someone I would very much like to be with," I say.

She lets out a sharp gasp but asks, feigning a milder interest than she has, "Really now? Will you tell me about him?"

I close my eyes and picture Sara's gentle smile. Her hands on my cheeks.

"Tall. Auburn hair. A soft, kind smile. Fiercely reliable and adorably passionate. Someone who truly can watch my back, and I think always will," I begin, then take a deep breath. My mom is clearly tortured at the slow response but hums along and scrubs my back. Finally, I add the final bit. "Curves you and I are both jealous of . . ."

The scrubbing pauses. There is a heavy moment, then the brush begins to move again.

When Mom responds, she is suppressing a flustered voice. "O-oh, I see," she answers. "Well. Yes. She certainly can watch your back . . ." She trails off. Then, after a moment of silence: "You . . . do mean Sarafyna, right?"

I laugh.

"I do, Mom. I really, really do."

Sarafyna

I sit with Peter and Dad in their home and eat the stew Pete has prepared. It's good to see him again, and I'm excited to live together for a bit. We have been catching up, but he looks confused at my recent musings. "Really? But, well, you are prettier than her," Peter protests, and I smile. It's kind of him to say so, but I'm not prettier than anyone. I haven't been in a long time.

"I don't know, I just . . . the first time I saw her face, she looked like . . . well, nothing special. And she always wore her mask after that. But today, I don't know. I saw her face for the first time in years and I was just, I don't know, impressed? I'm not saying I'm going to morph into her or anything, I was just remarking it's a shame she always covers it up," I say.

"That's not so strange," Dad says. "You used to say the same thing about some of our neighbors. Not about the mask, of course, but you always used to tell me you were going to look just like them when you grew up, but with a better hat." He laughs and I can't help but smile at the fond memory. "Speaking of hats, didn't you want to bring one to her?"

I jump. That's right. I have given Lily a few hats over the years, but I've put special work into this one. It isn't one from her home world, but it is perhaps the most beautiful hat I have ever made. It is also how I distracted myself while she was imprisoned.

"Oh! That's right, I do! Thanks, Dad!" I exclaim before jumping to my feet. I kiss him on the cheek and Peter on the forehead.

"What's the rush, Mom?" Peter calls as I collect the hat and run out the door. I don't answer him, in part because I don't know. I want to see her again. I don't know why I am in a hurry to do so, but I am. It's strange how much of a hurry. My dad is right; I always felt the same way about my pretty neighbors. I was probably just shocked by the contrast since the last time I saw her. But Lillith is . . . beautiful. Not in the way I always thought I wanted to be as a girl but . . . now I find myself jealous of her. Shockingly jealous. Not in a way that I resent her, but there is an odd . . . longing. One that has been there for a long time, in a way. I have often longed to be like her as a person, and this is the same, even if it's more about appearance.

It's probably just a distraction. Fighting Medici was . . . hard. I wanted to crush him. I wanted to take advantage of his healing to kill him, again and again and again. I wanted to put nine years of suffering into a single fight. But I didn't want to want that. So whenever a cruel idea occurred to me, I focused on the freshest, kindest thing in my mind. Lillith's full-mouthed smile. The way she smiles with both rows of teeth when she is truly happy. The sparkling gems of her eyes. Even with all that filth on her, I wanted to be her. It was something small, but whenever I felt my rage start to take the reins, I pictured her and calmed. It worked far better than it should have, all things considered.

I race through these thoughts as I walk across the quaint little town Lillith and I helped build, and I am still sorting through the strange jealousy when I arrive at Lillith's new home. When I walk in, I hear talking and I realize she is still in the bath. I suppose I would want a long one too, in her shoes. I decide to leave the hat on the little round table outside the washroom, then overhear Joan asking something.

"So . . . I don't suppose you've met any handsome men recently . . . someone to watch your back out there. I know, I know, you don't want to settle down, but that doesn't mean you have to be alone," she tries to ask casually. I feel a little spike of anger when she asks. That's . . . odd.

"Well, yes, there is someone I would very much like to be with," Lillith answers, and my heart sinks into my stomach. I don't know why. Maybe because, after all this, she didn't tell me? I start to feel sick and I barely catch Joan asking her daughter to describe the man who has apparently caught her interest. "Tall," Lillith says. "Auburn hair. A soft, kind smile. Fiercely reliable and adorably passionate. Someone who truly can watch my back, and I think always will." My heart starts to pound in my chest. That sounds like . . . "Curves you and I are both jealous of . . ." she adds, and I turn bright red. Wait. Wait wait wait. No, she doesn't mean . . .

"O-oh, I see," Joan responds. "Well. Yes. She certainly can watch your back . . ." I put my hands on my face. That can't be right. I mean, Lily has mentioned . . . Finally, the words I never expected to hear leave Joan's lips. "You . . . do mean Sarafyna, right?"

"I do, Mom. I really, really do," Lily sighs. My heart is going to stop working. I am a divine mage, and my heart is just going to stop working. What an embarrassing way to go.

CHAPTER SEVENTY

Give and Take

Kallon

I scowl as I look out the window at the passing countryside. Something is very wrong in this kingdom. I had been irritated, at first, when some self-impressed marquess had the gall to assign me to some minor task halfway across the country. My father hadn't even fought him on it, as far as I know. Like some baron or viscount, I was sent to check up on the local lord. It was one of many cities that failed to send the requested slaves to shore up our labor shortage, and I was supposed to ensure my father's new laws were being applied. It was busy work. These cities run themselves like little kids mimicking their father. They exist primarily to provide women and workers to their betters in Visenar. I was certain sending me away was some sort of play by some idiot who thought they could challenge my father if I, the most powerful mage in the city, was gone.

Well. Almost the most powerful. Dominic, my uncle's grandson, has a generation on me since Uncle Godfrey is so much older than his younger brother. But Dominic was given a lesser circle than me, the crown prince. As such, he technically has just slightly more mana than me. So perhaps I would be better described as the most dangerous mage in Visenar. Dominic has never practiced any combat magic. Like my father, he is complacent in his power. Anyway, his meager mana advantage is especially irrelevant as he received a similar assignment, which only supports my theory. Cities have been promising us new slaves for months, but none ever came from most. Perhaps they just wanted a particularly powerful mage to remind these lords where they stand.

That's what I had thought, anyway. When I arrived, the situation was far worse than I expected. Reports from these cities had all been positive. "Slaves are coming. Tutors are coming. We would be happy to help!" Bullshit, all of it. The city I went to was in a worse state than Visenar. A monster stalked the streets and hunted nobles in their beds. Slaves disappeared. Wives vanished. Doctors, tutors, farmers. The same exact issues that plagued my home were there but with an even poorer response. Instead of protecting his allies, the lord had tried to catch their killer. Magic knights had died by the dozens. The most important nobles in the city were dead and there was very little organization at all. Not over the commoners, anyway. The city lord I was to check on had been killed before I had even been assigned the task.

The new laws hadn't been implemented at all. As far as I could tell, the dimwit left in charge, some viscount, had entirely given up on replenishing his missing slaves. Nobles were left manually managing their own properties! Husbands were left with no mother or nurse for their children! It was a disaster, and one that hadn't been reported to the palace a single time. I had to round up random commoners and charge them with malingering just to replace the slaves the city itself had lost, much less the ones they were supposed to provide to us. An entire fifth of the city was left empty just to meet manpower needs. Even worse, the whisper sphere to communicate with the capital was missing, and the arrogant church refused to provide a new one. They claimed they had to be made in pairs to communicate long-distance, but I half believe they are responsible for all of this. It would certainly explain how we've been getting false reports all this time.

I did get it sorted, however. It turned out to be a good thing they sent me instead of some lesser noble. I am now bringing back a new sphere so we can reestablish communications with a reliable reporter. A wave of slaves will be brought as well, eventually, once they get them all sorted and categorized.

Still, something is wrong. One killer can't hunt in two cities at the same time. And this wasn't the only one that failed to provide the required slaves. It worries me that something more than a single crazed killer is at play here. This is another reason I suspect the church. There is an organized effort across cities to undermine the nobility and deplete the workforce. And the church is responsible for communication. There aren't many other explanations I would believe. In fact, there may be no other explanation I would believe.

As I work through my suspicions, the carriage lurches and slowly comes to a stop. "What in the third plane do you think you are doing?" I call before opening the wooden window between me and my coachman. The man is sitting with the reins limply in his hands, just gaping. I follow his eyeline and see that Visenar has come into view. Visenar and . . . something else. It would have been hard to make out from farther away, but I see what stopped my driver. Above the city wall is . . . a tree. It's still far off, but it is unmistakably a tree. A massive tree that exceeds the city walls in height. What the . . ." Snap out of it, you idiot, get me to the city!" I order, and the drooling driver jumps.

"Oh, uh, yes, of course. I'm sorry, Your Majesty," he says before gripping the reins and getting us moving. Idiot commoners. Dominic must be having quite a time of it with his foolish ideas. What a pathetic side of the family. They are all too soft. I grit my teeth as we approach the city gate. The tree only looks more impressive the closer we get. It would take an immensely powerful mage to grow something like that. I can't help but glance up regularly as we approach, until the walls finally obscure our view and the coachman stops at the gate. I look out again and am surprised to see not city guards but magic knights speaking with the coachman. After a moment, one of them approaches the door to the carriage and I swing it open.

"Do you have any idea who you are delaying?" I say, and he looks a bit embarrassed as he responds.

"Yes, Lord Kallon, that's why we stopped you here. The . . . king has summoned you. We've been instructed to escort you to the throne room as soon as you return," he replies. I'm thoroughly confused by this. I am at least three weeks early; why would Father have knights waiting for me at the gate already? It's like he forgot the details of the chore he sent me on. Perhaps he had simply ignored it and genuinely didn't know when I was due back.

"Well, move things along, then—escort me as you were ordered!" I snap.

"As you wish, my lord," he replies hurriedly before climbing back down. It's not long before we are back on the road and headed to the palace. Now that we have entered the city, I can again see the massive tree peeking over rooftops. I open a window to my side and call a knight over. He cautiously approaches.

"Knight, what is that tree?" I ask. "How has it grown in only a few months of my absence?"

He looks down awkwardly.

"It . . . grew this morning, my lord," he responds. "It is, apparently, an extension of the Radiant Woods."

"It's *Your Majesty*, not *my lord*, you dimwit. You are telling me that tree appeared this morning? Have you injured your head, man?" I ridicule him. This morning indeed.

"W-well, yes, my lord," he responds. "It was . . . Well, the king wishes to speak to you about it himself. I'm sorry, Lord Kallon."

There it was again, *my lord*. Has he forgotten who I am? I'll have him beaten once I speak to my father. I decide against further interrogating the useless man and wait for the carriage to arrive at the castle. The Radiant Woods, he said? There is another indicator the temple is responsible. Those priests have always thought of themselves as the true kings; perhaps they decided to try to prove it.

It's quite some time before we reach the palace. The city seems to have deteriorated quite a bit in my absence. There is no one on the streets. No commoners in the common district and no nobles in the wealthy district. Doors are closed and windows are drawn. A cloud gathers over me. Something is very, very wrong here. Something has happened, and it has something to do with that fucking tree. Did the church attack us? Is this why I was sent out of the city? As we make it to the palace, I swallow. I can't shake the feeling I'm not going to like what my father has to say. I walk past the marble pillars and through the carpeted hall I grew up in. Even the palace feels . . . off. The servants are missing and there are far too many magic knights.

Other nobles have gathered here, the first I have seen since getting back to the city. As I pass, they steal glances and whisper. One man even snickers. At me. I'll have him beaten as well. When the knights with me finally push open the massive doors of the throne room and take their positions outside, I understand everything.

Dozens of the more powerful nobles in the city are inside talking with each other. An air of panicked excitement prevails and I can see why. Sitting on the throne is not my father, but my Uncle Godfrey. He wears a new crown, simpler than my father's.

I spit on the ground immediately. "Godfrey, get out of my father's seat," I order coldly. How dare he? In front of me? He's not my match, but . . . as I speak, auras begin to release all around the room. I can't take all of them and I put the pieces together. It's a coup. Godfrey managed to gather enough nobles to fight and imprison my father. He has seized my throne and summoned me to look at him dirtying it. I'll kill him. I swear to the Collector, I'll kill him.

"Calm yourself, Kallon," he says. "A lot has happened since you left. This morning, your father was . . . abducted. He and Father Medici together were brought into the Radiant Woods."

"Then get him back, you old fool! No, get off my throne and follow my orders so we can get him back!" I snarl, and Godfrey shakes his head.

"I'm sorry, Kallon. I can't do that. No, that's not true; I won't do that. The nobility has spoken and I am to be the interim king until we recover your father. If you'll work with me, we can rebuild everything that has been lost, and we can get Donatello back," he says.

I spit again.

"We aren't rebuilding everything by sucking commoners' cocks or whatever other spineless plans you have, you senile old fuck. Now, get. Off. My. Throne," I command again.

Godfrey sighs.

"I don't want to lower the nobility, Kallon. I just want to practice a little more . . . give and take. With the commoners and with you. I think you have a lot to offer this kingdom, and as king, I can offer you help in finding your father. Then we can work forward from there. Come on, Kallon, work with me," he offers, holding one hand out to me.

Work with him? No. I scan the room, making sure I remember every face of every traitor stopping me from killing this . . . usurper here and now.

"Sure. Give and take. You took advantage of my absence and my father's apathy. And I'll give you what you deserve in return. Watch your back, Uncle. You won't always have so many protectors to hide behind," I retort. I turn on my heel to march out of the room.

"Kallon, wait. Please, look toward the future! If we turn on each other now instead of working together, we could lose everything. This entire kingdom could come to ruin. Work with me!" he begs, but I scoff.

"With you on that throne, this kingdom is already in ruin," I reply, then leave before he debases my crown any further.

There are more than a few powerful nobles who weren't in that room. We'll see how confident he is when I have more support.

CHAPTER SEVENTY-ONE

Simply Annie

I finish getting dressed and applying my makeup. God, it feels good to be clean. I have been dreaming of a clean pair of underwear for two days. I've gotten used to this medieval makeup now and apply it with far more skill than almost anyone else in town. It only recently stopped being a luxury good for most of the residents here, which makes it look a bit silly at times. Interestingly, like with soap, previous conceptions about it have disappeared and I even see men using it all the time in several communities. I am in a remarkably good mood as I finish covering my faint scar. Today I escaped an execution, scrubbed the world of two evil men, and moved to a new house. I'm on cloud nine. I also get to see Leo today. I have been constantly worrying about him since finding him that night. I know he is alive, at least. I am so excited to start working with Sara to help him like we had always promised. We will of course need to go and retrieve his sponsor as well.

I tilt my head in the mirror in a few directions to make sure I haven't missed anything. I do catch that one little hair that insists on growing out of my chin and pluck it. It's funny how I can mess with my cycle and hormones, but that little black chin hair persists no matter what I do. Finally satisfied, I stand from the vanity. Before I leave my new room, I stop to give my attention to the most important woman in my life. My most darling friend and steadfast ally. "How are you doing, little Sousaphone?" I ask as I scratch Suzume's chin. She purrs and rolls onto her back, tempting me to stay too long. But my family awaits, so I leave a treat for her and head out. My family is waiting in one of the community's public dining facilities. Our own home is too small for everyone attending tonight.

My mom provided the clothes I am wearing now. I am pleased to say she's sewn quite a few outfits consisting of blouses and pants, which she would have refused to do a few years ago. I am very excited to wear them openly . . . starting tomorrow. Tonight is . . . well, it's the first night Sarafyna is going to see my face. Well, she saw it earlier, but I'm certain I didn't exactly look like a sex goddess at the time. Tonight she'll see me without mud and blood caked to everything. I want to make a good impression, so I've chosen a lacy crop top with half sleeves and a billowy maxi skirt.

It's a bit hippy in design, and my mom stared at me for a good five minutes in silence when I described the top, but I have to say . . . I look good. If I am lucky and Sarafyna is as receptive to my lifestyle as I hope, this outfit will go a long way toward helping her realize that. Well, maybe. It's possible I am projecting since a similar outfit on another woman may have been involved in some personal revelations in my teenage years. But hey, if it worked on me . . .

"There you are, come on, everyone is waiting!" Henry calls as I round a corner. He waves me over and I follow. "You clean up nice, kid," he jokes, and I chuckle.

"Wish I could say the same, but . . . it's all right. Autumn is the charitable sort," I quip, and he holds his hands to his chest to ease the pain of a mimed arrow to the heart. He does actually look great, especially compared to his time in Baldwin's basement. Practicing alchemy in a safe environment has been good for him.

As we enter the large room with four round tables, cheers erupt and I begin to blush. All around the room, familiar faces applaud me. Autumn waves over to Henry, who hurries to join her. Next to her is August, who is clearly baffled, having been less privy to my plans than his twin. He seems to be having a good time, in any case. There are a couple of empty seats at their table that I assume belong to their parents. I don't know how they are responding to all this, but I did hear they agreed to come.

Another table houses Edward and Mariah, along with a few other women from Baldwin's . . . torture harem. My mom is sitting with Gilbert and Julie and . . . another couple. They seem about Gilbert's age and the unfamiliar woman has a hand on both my brother and the other man. Fair enough, Gilbert, fair enough. The final table houses Sam, Peter, and of course Sara. She has changed into a green sundress and a wide-brimmed hat. Her face matches her auburn hair as she, well, drinks me in. I don't know if she is awakening anything, but she is certainly looking. I have high hopes this outfit is two for two. I'm hardly one to talk, however, as I stopped scanning the room immediately when I found the curvy redhead in a sundress. She quickly finds something incredibly interesting in her meal and looks down. Well, I can work with that.

Once the applause of my loved ones dies down, I begin to make the rounds.

When I reach their table, August says, "I'm still unclear on what we are applauding for, but I'm very excited."

"Sorry, we brought him here in a hurry, haven't gotten him up to speed yet," Autumn says, and I laugh.

"Oh, don't worry about it, August is cool. I committed some light regicide. The pretty girl in the green dress helped me," I say. A strangled squeak escapes Sara's table, but it's quickly drowned out by August's coughing.

"I'm sorry, did you say regicide?" he finally asks.

Henry gives him a sympathetic glance.

"We all have our hobbies," Henry says before hurriedly changing the subject. "It's good to have you here for good, Lil. How were things looking in the city when you left?"

August gapes at me, but when his sister continues eating her steak, he just shakes his head and mumbles into his own plate. Autumn is quieter than usual but not surprised like he is.

"You know, it's hard to say. I don't think the last people I saw liked me much though. But who knows, maybe they did. Is *hang her* a friendly saying any of you have heard? You know, like *how's it hanging*?" I joke.

"I can't say I've heard it used that way before, no." Henry laughs, shaking his head.

"Guess they hated me, then. Are your parents not coming?" I change the subject and Autumn shrugs.

"They aren't . . . impressed with their accommodations, let's leave it at that," she answers. The rest of the conversation is friendly, although the twins seem to struggle to be quite as ecstatic about everything as my brother. I pick up a drink from the center of the table and excuse myself to join Sara's.

"Hello, how are you holding up?" I ask.

"You know." Sara shrugs. "Big day. Justice. Fighting. You're uh, not wearing your mask." Yet she still fails to make eye contact.

"Hmm, oh yeah, I'm hanging up the cape. Gonna be more of an open nuisance from now on," I say.

"It's good to have you back." Sam smiles at me. "Sara has been absolutely frantic with worry."

I smile back and Sara finds new shades of red to turn. Peter looks at me curiously while chewing a large bit of meat.

"I've been worried about her too. Thanks for keeping her grounded," I reply.

Sara tries to take a drink to hide her blush and I do the same. Then Pete swallows his food. He looks me dead in the eyes and says, absolutely devoid of context, "Mom says you're pretty." Sara and I both choke and spill on ourselves before sharing an awkward look.

"I . . . made you a hat," Sara says, rapidly changing the subject and giving Peter a quick, lightly murderous glance.

"O-oh, thanks, what kind is it this time?" I ask. So she said I'm pretty *before* tonight. Meaning when I was covered in filth and elbow deep in monarch corpse. That is either very encouraging or very disturbing. The rest of this conversation is fairly awkward and Sara seems to be distracted the whole time. I can't blame her, however. She likely isn't quite as desensitized as me to . . . everything. I stand to move to the last table, and she stops me by grabbing my hand.

"Wait, Lily," she says, and I pause. "After dinner can you meet me on the beach? There is something I want to talk about, if that's all right." She looks nervous.

"Sure, I'd love to," I answer. It's not surprising she wants to talk alone. I hope she isn't beating herself up again. She did a good thing today. But if she needs me to convince her of that, I am happy to help. Finally, I sit at the last table with any room for me, where Gilbert, blessedly, starts putting food on a plate for me.

"Hey, Lilith, finally made it to the reject table, huh?" he asks, and I scoff.

"Hey, that's my mother you're talking about. I'll hear none of that," I respond. "I see you brought more . . . friends. Are you going to introduce them?"

He laughs in return.

"Oh, only Julie and Mali here are my, uh, friends. Jack over there is one of Mali's, uh, friends."

Mom buries her face in her hands, completely baffled by her children.

"Good for you and all your friends, Gil. I'm glad to see the new world agrees with you. Who knows, maybe Jack can be your friend too someday," I say. Gil looks less than interested, but Mali grins at the idea. Mali and Jack whisper to each other, something about how his name isn't Jack, but I focus on my mom. She is embarrassed but has a gentle smile, like when you reach the end of a good book.

"You look happy, Mom," I say, and she meets my eyes.

"It's good to have everyone together like this," she says. "It's just . . . good." I raise a glass to that and drink before I greedily begin devouring the steak Gilbert offered me. "You seemed to enjoy your time at Sarafyna's table. Are you, uh, sure about . . . ? Well, she is a bit . . ." she whispers.

"Feminine?" I guess, and she shakes her head.

"No, the Collector knows that's not the most surprising thing I've learned about you. I mean, uh, old. She must be a decade older than you. Are you sure?"

I laugh out loud at that.

"Don't most people get married around here with a twenty- to thirty-year age gap? Of the two, I'm surprised that's the one you are having trouble with."

"Most people get married without a choice, Lily," she replies. "And it usually doesn't end happily."

I smile at her reassuringly.

"Don't worry, Mom. I know what I'm doing, I promise." I reach out a hand to cover hers for a moment.

Gilbert looks between us in confusion.

"What are you two talking about?" he asks. He never gets an answer, however, as the room suddenly quiets.

"Leo is here," Mom whispers. Finally, I was wondering where he was. I turn with an excited grin painting my face but freeze when I see him. I understand why the room quieted. My good mood vanishes and my blood runs cold. My dinner feels like razors in my gut. He's . . . healthy. More so than I expected since Sara had to heal him without my help. His mangled limbs are smooth and there are no longer broken bones jutting out. He doesn't even appear to have serious scars, which is surprising considering my failure to heal mine.

He looks . . . gorgeous. Beautiful, even. The dress he has chosen is simple but elegant. It fits his curves well. It would really suit him if it, well, suited him. His face is a fallen star. It carries the haunting beauty of quiet anguish. I feel like an idiot. His body is healed, yes. But I found him completely broken. Not just his bones. I clench my fork in my fist and it bends. His eyes meet mine and he bows his head, then moves to sit at Sara's table. The dinner guests try to recover from his arrival and quiet conversation picks up, but I've lost my appetite. I hang around for a while, but . . . I can't stay here. I don't know why, but I got a clear message from

Leo. He doesn't want to talk to me right now. I excuse myself and leave everyone else to enjoy their meals.

The town is fairly quiet. It's new, and small, so although not everyone is indoors, it still feels empty. I walk toward the beach. I am an idiot. The night air is cold and lashes against my skin. I should have worn something warmer. I leave the town behind and leave footprints down the empty beach. Once I am far enough, I sit down and hug my knees to my chest. I've been having such a good day, but Leo wasn't. Even here, he doesn't feel safe anymore. Even in the same room as me. I've failed him. I have done a lot of good, but failing someone like that . . . it doesn't matter how much good I have done. Not in this moment, anyway. Tears run down my cheeks. Some fucking applause.

It's maybe twenty minutes before Sara shows up. She doesn't say anything at first, just sits next to me. We look up at the stars together and listen to the sounds of the shore. Eventually, I release my knees and lower my legs. Seeing me growing comfortable, she finally speaks.

"You saved me, Lily. You pulled me from misery, and hate, and self-loathing in more ways than one. You found me as a monster in the forest. You burned yourself to reach out to me. You poured yourself into a stranger, and you helped me find myself again. You did the same thing for Peter. For a lot of people," she says.

I don't answer, and she is quiet for another moment.

"I can't pretend to understand what Leo is going through. Not exactly. And I'm sorry we didn't tell you ahead of time. I couldn't find the right moment, and it was . . . hard to say. But you found me and helped me remember who I was. What I went through wasn't the same, but it wasn't completely different either. As far as I understand it, anyway. You are a good person to know, for someone going through something like that, is all I'm saying," Sara finishes.

I sniff and wipe the tears off my cheeks. "I'm glad I helped you, Sara. You have no idea how glad I am. But I'm still just . . . me. You are still in pain from what you went through. Still wounded. I can see it sometimes. Leo is . . . he was hurt, badly. Because I wasn't there. Because I wasn't paying enough attention. I knew better, but I still didn't pay enough attention. I can't heal that kind of damage, and it's my fault, Sara," I say, fighting more tears.

Sara reaches out and puts one hand on my cheek, catching a drop with her thumb. "You don't have to carry the weight of the world on your shoulders like that, Annie. You don't. You killed the women responsible for what happened to Leo," she whispers. She runs her other hand along my midriff, tracing one of my tattoos with her fingers. The hairs all over my body stand at her touch. "What did you tell me this said? *I will suffer no gods*? Then why are you acting like you are one?

"What Leo is going through . . . what he is facing . . . it's not about you. It's not about what you did right or wrong. His life isn't a measure of your failures and successes. Feeling responsible to help him? That I understand. But that's not what this is. Leo is hurt and he needs to work through that hurt. He needs to find a way to feel safe again. Not just in the environment. But with himself. That much I do understand. But Annie. It's not about you. It's not. It's about Leo. You may be able to embody the grief of the people around you, but you don't own their trauma. Let Leo have some space. Let him work through what has happened to him. Let it be about Leo." You can't save everyone from every bad thing. You need to forgive yourself for the state of the world you are, frankly, saving. I am not the only person who has a life because of you. Thousands of people have a life because of you. And it's because of you I have the confidence to do what I am about to do."

Sarafyna is acting more confident than usual. She is usually mild and sweet. Very excitable about small things. Never speaking over anyone else. But she does have a fire in her blood. One that gives her confidence you wouldn't expect. A fire that burns exclusively when she is feeling particularly passionate about something.

"And what is that?" I ask.

Instead of answering, her hand moves to the back of my neck, and she pulls me to her. Her lips meet mine in a gentle kiss and my entire body tenses. Did she just . . . before I even had the chance? Her lips separate from mine, the skin of our mouths sticking together for a brief moment, then she kisses me again, her teeth gently gripping my bottom lip and pulling. I melt. No longer am I Lillith of Endings. No longer am I the Mage of Mourning, hunting slavers and liberating the masses. I'm not the woman who beheaded a despot.

As I finally wrap my arms around Sarafyna's waist and kiss her back, I am just Lillith, a girl in love. I am, for the first time in years, simply Annie.

Acknowledgments

As a child, the first job I ever wanted was to be a *writer*. There were a thousand obstacles in the way of this aspiration, and I eventually moved on from it entirely. Chief among these obstacles was a lack of support and community. I'm not a man who can easily push himself to complete a project on my own. It is thanks to those outside of myself that I was able to write this series and more.

First and foremost, I want to thank my wife, Melody. Her unflappable support and encouragement keeps me going back to writing, day after day, week after week. When I am as happy as I have ever been and when I am in a depressive episode, she is always there—making the future look brighter and my goals look more achievable.

I also want to thank my numerous sisters, whose perspectives help greatly in my writing endeavors. I am who I am today because I had so many amazing women in my life to admire. Growing up with them made me a better person and helped inform my depictions of women in my stories.

As for community, I want to thank those who push me to write with their own creative endeavors. Specifically BlueTomoshibi and StrawberryRain. I met these two on Royal Road where I first published this story, and without them I'd have only half the drive to write. Interacting with them and their stories turned a private labor into a joyful collaboration. I have written guest chapters for Pruned Trees Re-Sprout and borrowed characters from Harmony, Both authors have helped me organize, outline, and choreograph scenes in Otherworldly Anarchist. These two have completely changed my approach to writing and increased my motivation to do so.

Of course, the final version of the story is thanks to the production team at Podium Entertainment. There are too many of them to list here, but they took my rough draft on Royal Road and made it into a complete work of art. They have been kind, understanding, and helpful. Above all else, they took me from an amateur to a published author, making a childhood dream come true.

And finally, the primary way I read is through audiobooks. There are a number of reasons for this, but listening to my own book was something I never imagined, even when I had the motivation to write it. So I'd also like to thank Rachel Leblang, who's performance brought my characters to life in the way I always imagined when writing them. Her skilled and talented performance feels so surreal to listen to, and I look forward to hearing the rest of her work on the series.

About the Author

Dreamer's Riot is the author of the Otherworldly Anarchist series as well as a computer scientist and indie video game developer. Based on his experiences in the US Air Force and later as a student, his stories aim to tackle themes of power and autonomy.

JOIN THE FELLOWSHIP

follow us on our socials

 podiumentertainment.com

 @podiumentertainment

 /podiumentertainment

 @podium_ent

 @podiumentertainment